AVENUE AT SPASSKOE, TURGENEV'S
ESTATE

THE HARVARD CLASSICS
SHELF OF FICTION
SELECTED BY CHARLES W ELIOT LL D

A HOUSE OF GENTLEFOLK

AND

FATHERS AND CHILDREN

BY

IVAN TURGENEV

TRANSLATED BY CONSTANCE GARNETT

EDITED WITH NOTES AND INTRODUCTIONS
BY WILLIAM ALLAN NEILSON Ph D

P F COLLIER & SON COMPANY
NEW YORK

CONTENTS

	PAGE
THE NOVEL IN RUSSIA	iii

A HOUSE OF GENTLEFOLK

BIOGRAPHICAL NOTE	xi
CRITICISMS AND INTERPRETATIONS:	
I. BY EMILE MELCHIOR, VICOMTE DE VOGÜE . . .	xiii
II. BY WILLIAM DEAN HOWELLS	xiv
III. BY K. WALISZEWSKI	xvi
IV. RICHARD H. P. CURLE	xvii
V. BY MAURICE BARING	xix
LIST OF CHARACTERS	xxiii
CHAPTER I	1
CHAPTER II	5
CHAPTER III	9
CHAPTER IV	10
CHAPTER V	15
CHAPTER VI	18
CHAPTER VII	22
CHAPTER VIII	27
CHAPTER IX	35
CHAPTER X	39
CHAPTER XI	41
CHAPTER XII	46
CHAPTER XIII	49
CHAPTER XIV	51
CHAPTER XV	53
CHAPTER XVI	58
CHAPTER XVII	62
CHAPTER XVIII	67
CHAPTER XIX	70
CHAPTER XX	74
CHAPTER XXI	76
CHAPTER XXII	81

i

CONTENTS

	PAGE
Chapter XXIII	83
Chapter XXIV	85
Chapter XXV	88
Chapter XXVI	95
Chapter XXVII	100
Chapter XXVIII	103
Chapter XXIX	107
Chapter XXX	112
Chapter XXXI	116
Chapter XXXII	118
Chapter XXXIII	122
Chapter XXXIV	125
Chapter XXXV	131
Chapter XXXVI	137
Chapter XXXVII	141
Chapter XXXVIII	145
Chapter XXXIX	149
Chapter XL	156
Chapter XLI	163
Chapter XLII	165
Chapter XLIII	171
Chapter XLIV	176
Chapter XLV	180
Epilogue	185

THE NOVEL IN RUSSIA

PROSE fiction has a more prominent position in the literature of Russia than in that of any other great country. Turgenev, Dostoevsky, and Tolstoy occupy in their own land not only the place of Dickens, Thackeray, and George Eliot in England, but also to some degree that of Carlyle, Matthew Arnold, or Ruskin.

Their works are regarded as not merely diverting tales over which to spend pleasantly an idle hour, but as books full of suggestive and inspiring teaching on moral and social questions. "Fathers and Children" and "Crime and Punishment" are discussed and read not merely for their artistic merit, as reflections of Russian life, but as trenchant criticisms of that life. The difference is of course one of degree not of kind: Dickens and George Eliot have a definite attitude towards social questions, and in Russian literature there are writers who may be compared to Carlyle and Matthew Arnold. The fact remains, however, that while Turgenev and Dostoevsky find readers by their power as artists, discussion of them is less apt to turn on their purely æsthetic qualities than on the ethical and social point of view which, in part unconsciously, they show in their work.

This serious character of Russian fiction is due in some degree to the development of Russian literature under a despotism that forbade or at least hampered open discussion of public questions. Russians could not discuss with any freedom, either on the debating platform or in the periodical press, such questions as the emancipation of the serfs or the relations of church and state. But in a novel a writer could at least indicate his point of view; he could show the callousness and inhumanity bred by serfdom, as Turgenev did in "A Sportsman's Sketches"; he could give a sympathetic portrait of the radical young *nihilists* (who in the beginning were not terrorists, but materialistic skeptics, with a passion for natural science), as he did in "Fathers and Children"; or, on the other hand, he could show the havoc wrought in the minds of such young radicals by alienation from the national religion and the national traditions, as Dostoevsky did in "Crime and Punishment." Thus the censorship, while it compelled public discussion to turn on sympathy and sentiment rather than on accurate study of social facts, really deepened the content of Russian fiction.

Governmental repression merely strengthened the innate tendency of the Russians to vague, half-philosophic half-sentimental discussion of national problems. "When ten Englishmen meet," Turgenev tells us in "Smoke," "they immediately start talking about the submarine telegraph, the tax on paper, or methods of tanning rat skins; that is, of something positive and definite. But when ten Russians meet, the question immediately arises of the significance, the future, of Russia, and in the most general terms, without proof or result. They chew and chew on that unfortunate question, like children on a piece of rubber, without juice or sense." Lavretsky, debates with Mihalevitch and Panshin. Raskolnikov's meditations in justification of the crimes of gifted men, Levin's arguments with Serge Koznyshev, are all examples of this tendency. For such discussion fiction offered a free field.

Thus Russian novels are apt to have a political background. In "Fathers and Children" (1862) Turgenev draws a picture of a representative of the younger generation who boldly casts aside all political, social, and religious traditions, and, a skeptic to the core, devotes himself to science as the key to all truth. Though he does not identify himself with Bazarov, though he pitilessly portrays his crudity and intolerance, he nevertheless even against his will, arouses sympathy for the movements that he represents. Dostoevsky, when he exalts the infinite humility and submissiveness of Sonya in contrast to the moral arrogance of Raskolnikov, makes an attack on that same movement.

Yet Russian novels rarely present their social message in so direct and uncompromising a form as "Uncle Tom's

Cabin" or Sinclair's "Jungle"; such plain speaking would be impossible in Russia. They are rather of the type of "David Copperfield" or Mr. Herrick's "A Life for a Life," presenting the ills of the social order without any very definite suggestions for its betterment. Hence the novelists have often been misunderstood and misinterpreted. Gogol, the founder of Russian realism, became the idol of the Liberal party through his satiric portraits of venal officials; he later showed his true character by an ardent defense of the autocracy and the state church and by an attack on all attempts at popular education. Tolstoy, because of his fervent support of the sanctity of marriage in "Anna Karenin," was hastily denounced as a reactionary; the young radicals had rejected marriage as an outworn institution along with the autocracy and the state church, and were ready to distrust any man who might speak in its defense.

Thus a foreign reader may safely neglect the social implications of Russian fiction over which Russian critics wrangle so fiercely. He will be more impressed by the moral earnestness of this literature. For Turgenev, Dostoevsky, and Tolstoy regard the men and women whom they create with such marvelous skill, not as animals, actuated merely by greed and lust and restrained from crime merely by fear of punishment, but as responsible moral beings, whose whole existence is affected by moral impulses, for whom conduct is the central part of life. This does not warp their judgment or make them untrue to the facts of life; their characters are not the puppets of the Sunday-school book, created to enforce a moral lesson, but stumbling, aspiring individuals, half clay and half something finer that animates it. They present moral forces because without them no true picture of men and women can be drawn.

The ethical point of view of Russian writers is, however, far different from that familiar to men of Anglo-Saxon stock. With the word *good* we associate instinctively the idea of self-command, self-mastery, control over one's animal nature. Along with our admiration for self-command we have an equally instinctive respect for practical success: a man must be virtuous, but he must so shape his virtue as to win the regard of his fellow men; if he be a reformer, he must be guided by common sense as well as by moral fervor. The brave and thoughtless heroes of Scott's novels are only an exaggeration of the English ideal; David Copperfield is a type of it. Colonel Newcome is overtaken by misfortune in his old age, but he too is of English stock; in his earlier years he commanded respect by his energy and capacity as well as by the fine essence of a gentleman's character.

The heroes of the Russian novels, on the other hand, win our hearts by geniality and kindliness, without any Puritanic sternness, and they are usually failures in practical life. Lavretsky in "A House of Gentlefolk" is a truly Russian type; gentle and sweet of disposition, he possesses small vital force, and he sinks into oblivion without gaining any outward triumph. In "Fathers and Children" Nikolay Petrovich and his brother Pavel are likewise types of the ineffective Russian nobility, who gain our affections either by a timid gentleness or by a chivalric refinement of nature. Turgenev, speaking of his own book, remarks characteristically (in a letter of April 14, 1862) that æsthetic feeling made him choose *good* representatives of the nobility as a class, that it would have been coarse and untrue to select "officials, generals, plunderers, and the like." And when Turgenev tried to create in Bazarov a character marked by crude energy, he was not wholly successful. Bazarov's energy is in aspiration rather than performance; like the Antony of tradition, he allows his passion for a woman to wreck his life, and his creator kills him at the close of the book rather than let him continue an ineffective, blighted existence.

In Dostoevsky the case is still stronger. Raskolnikov, the hero of "Crime and Punishment," is a weak and vacillating murderer, whose native sympathy and generosity make the reader find him a higher type of humanity than the callous business man Luzhin. Absolute humility and self-sacrifice make the prostitute Sonya the most ideal figure in the volume.

The Russian adulation of kindliness rather than energy, of aspiration rather than performance, is at first sight not so prominent in the works of Tolstoy. For Tolstoy was

himself a man of fiery passions and of strong will. In "War
and Peace" he created in Prince Andrey Bolkonsky, a hero
of somewhat the English type. Yet the hero of "Anna
Karenin" is not the vigorous officer Vronsky, nor the cold
politician Karenin, both of whom know how to win success
among men of the great world, but the clumsy farmer Levin,
who attracts us by his kindly nature, and by his obstinate
search for a moral ideal that shall guide him through life.
His story at first reading may seem mawkish and commonplace, but as we review the novel, perhaps after the
lapse of years has added to our own experience, it acquires
an enduring charm. Levin loves his farm and his family;
he is happy in the respect paid him by his neighbors and
still happier in that of his peasant laborers—but his real
triumph is in his own heart; he knows that, no matter how
blundering and imperfect his conduct may be, his moral
ideals, the ethical philosophy by which he guides his life,
are constantly becoming broader and deeper.

It is characteristic of his infinitely broad range of sympathies that Tolstoy, who of all the great Russian novelists
seems in "War and Peace" (1865-69) closest to our point of
view, developed in his later years an ethical system founded
on the principle of nonresistance to evil. This is illustrated
by his parable "Ivan the Fool" (1885), in which the submissive hero wins by his humility the triumph denied to
his vigorous elder brothers.

No moral or social enthusiasm could have won the three
classic Russian novelists their enduring fame were not each
of them in his own way a great artist. No finer master
of literary form in prose fiction ever wrote than Turgenev,
no greater master of psychological analysis than Dostoevsky;
and no man has ever possessed so perfect a command of
realistic portraiture of human life in its most varied aspects
as Tolstoy.

"A House of Gentlefolk" and "Fathers and Children" are
each short novels, yet what a wealth of emotion, of poetic
insight into the finer and more tender sides of human
character they contain! Turgenev builds each of his books
around a love story; the events of his plot cover but a
few weeks and deal with but few people. His method

is that of French classic tragedy, of Corneille and Racine.
By portraying a man and a woman at the moment when
their whole being is concentrated on one great passion he
lets us see the inmost springs of their characters. He tells
of the ancestry of Lavretsky, describing briefly those crude
squires, his great-grandfather and grandfather, and pictur-
ing at greater length his doctrinaire father, who brings up
his son in an atmosphere of bookish dreams, and his
gentle peasant mother, who passes to her son the sincerity
and simple kindliness of the Russian common people. The
boy grows up unworldly but emotionally sound. His life
is ruined by the marriage into which his inexperience leads
him, then happiness seems to open before him in the love
of the sweet, pure Lisa; at last disaster overtakes the lovers
and they bow their heads before it in resignation: for
them the moral law is more potent than the supreme passion of their lives. Bazarov, in "Fathers and Children,"
spurning emotion as foolish sentimentalism, dedicates himself to the study of science. But nature is stronger than
intellect, and he yields to a passion for a woman whose
selfish force will not submit to even his strength of personality; his tragedy, with its anguish of thwarted powers,
is more profound than that of the gentle Lavretsky. Each
of these plots is developed in the Russian countryside,
with poetic pictures of quiet natural beauty, amid types of
Russian gentlefolk, each drawn with a few fine strokes.[1]

Like Turgenev, Dostoevsky bases each of his novels on the
events of a few weeks, in order to give an atmosphere of
tense, concentrated emotion. But in all else he is in direct
contrast to his rival. His novels deal with city life and
with actual physical misery and suffering. Each of his most
important works of fiction centers about a murder. Reading "Crime and Punishment," one becomes weary of the
long analysis of Raskolnikov's agonies and determines to
skip a few paragraphs, only to find some fifty pages later,
that he has missed some essential point in the close-knit
narrative. An awful, uncanny power pervades this story
of a diseased mind. Here the most obscure windings of

[1] The most distinguished contemporary English novelist, Mr. Galsworthy, treats
English life in a style strikingly similar to that of Turgenev.

self-concentrated reflection, on the downward path toward insanity, are laid bare. We may reject the author's quiescent point of view, his prescription of suffering as a panacea for the ills of humanity, but we are spellbound by the skill with which he portrays the special cases that interest him.

Far different from either of these writers is the healthy, energetic Leo Tolstoy, the man of loftiest individuality among Russian authors. No supreme author was ever so independent of literary conventions and traditions and in such close touch with the varied life around him. His early works, such as "Childhood, Boyhood, and Youth" and "Sevastopol," are almost formless, bits of reminiscence modified so as not to become literal autobiography. His method is to select with unerring instinct concrete details of everyday life that throw light on character. He deals with small emotions, exposing the thoughts and feelings of which each of us has been conscious, but which each of us has fancied unknown to anyone but himself. His masterpiece, "War and Peace," is at the other pole from the dainty work of Turgenev; it is a vast chronicle of the fortunes of five families during seven years, from 1805 to 1812; it delights us by the bewildering variety of men and women with whom it makes us acquainted as with brothers and sisters, and by the surpassing interest of each individual incident.

Even "Anna Karenin," Tolstoy's most widely read novel, is far more than the story of the heroine's love for the handsome officer Vronsky. Any one of the dozen French novelists could have told that story in one-third the number of pages that Tolstoy uses, and in one sense more effectively. Tolstoy aims not merely to tell that story, but to draw a picture of a whole world of conflicting interests, cares, and ambitions. Dolly's anxieties over her children's clothes in preparation for the communion service are as close to his heart as Anna's struggles between her love for her son and her passion for Vronsky.

Diffuse as he is when considered from the point of view of the conventional story-teller, Tolstoy has the power of concentrated suggestion more than any other novelist. One incident will illustrate this. For more than eight years Anna has lived constantly with her husband in peace and content if not in blissful happiness. She makes a visit in Moscow, meets Vronsky, and, without fully admitting the fact to herself, becomes infatuated with him. She returns home:

> In St. Petersburg, as soon as the train stopped and she got out, the first face that attracted her attention was that of her husband. "Good heavens, where did he ever get such ears?" she thought to herself, looking at his cold, dignified figure, and especially at the cartilages of his ears that had now so startled her, supporting the brim of his round hat.

During eight years she had not noticed her husband's ears, any more than any of us observe petty physical defects in those of our own family; now those ears—and Karenin's crackling fingers—will haunt her throughout the novel. Such use of small detail is attained only by the greatest poets and artists.

Tolstoy is a Puritan moralist, but at the same time the most truthful and clear-sighted observer of human life. In the meeting with Vronsky by his wife's bedside the leather-minded Karenin is for once stirred to the very depths of his being; he rises to lofty moral dignity and proffers sincere forgiveness; the scene has no superior in all fiction. The novelist might here have closed the book with Anna's death and a lasting reconciliation between the two men, joined in a common grief. But no: Anna recovers, Karenin's ears stick out once more, and his fingers crackle; the moment of moral exaltation is over, and the vicious atmosphere of worldly life drags down Karenin, Anna, and Vronsky. Tolstoy's art is broader than his morality; only in parables such as "Ivan the Fool" do they go hand in hand.

Such is Russian fiction, serious in its outlook on life, broad in its sympathies, marvelously skillful in its artistic methods. American readers must turn to it not for mere amusement, but for a criticism of life—a criticism based on the point of view of a great people whose history and whose moral outlook are widely different from our own.

G. R. N.

BIOGRAPHICAL NOTE

IVAN SERGYEVITCH TURGENEV came of an old
stock of the Russian nobility. He was born in Orel,
in the province of Orel, which lies more than a hundred miles south of Moscow, on October 28, 1818. His
education was begun by tutors at home in the great family
mansion in the town of Spask, and he studied later at the
universities of Moscow, St. Petersburg, and Berlin. The
influence of the last, and of the compatriots with whom he
associated there, was very great; and when he returned to
Moscow in 1841, he was ambitious to teach Hegel to the
students there. Before this could be arranged, however, he
entered the Ministry of the Interior at St. Petersburg.
While there his interests turned more and more toward
literature. He wrote verses and comedies, read George
Sand, and made the acquaintance of Dostoevsky and the
critic Bielinski. His mother, a tyrannical woman with an
ungovernable temper, was eager that he should make a brilliant official career; so, when he resigned from the Ministry
in 1845, she showed her disapproval by cutting down his
allowance and thus forcing him to support himself by the
profession he had chosen.

Turgenev was an enthusiastic hunter; and it was his
experiences in the woods of his native province that supplied the material for "A Sportsman's Sketches," the book
that first brought him reputation. The first of these papers
appeared in 1847, and in the same year he left Russia in
the train of Pauline Viardot, a singer and actress, to whom
he had been devoted for three or four years and with
whom he maintained relations for the rest of his life. For
a year or two he lived chiefly in Paris or at a country
house at Courtavenel in Brie, which belonged to Madame
Viardot; but in 1850 he returned to Russia. His experiences
were not such as to induce him to repatriate himself perma-

nently. He found Dostoevsky banished to Siberia and
Bielinski dead; and himself under suspicion by the government on account of the popularity of "A Sportsman's
Sketches." For praising Gogol, who had just died, he was
arrested and imprisoned for a short time, and for the next
two years kept under police surveillance. Meantime he
continued to write, and by the time that the close of the
Crimean War made it possible for him again to go to western
Europe, he was recognized as standing at the head of living
Russian authors. His mother was now dead, the estates
were settled, and with an income of about $5,000 a year
he became a wanderer. He had, or imagined he had, very
bad health, and the eminent specialists he consulted sent
him from one resort to another, to Rome, the Isle of
Wight, Soden, and the like. When Madame Viardot left
the stage in 1864 and took up her residence at Baden-Baden,
he followed her and built there a small house for himself.
They returned to France after the Franco-Prussian War,
and bought a villa at Bougival, near Paris, and this was his
home for the rest of his life. Here, on September 3, 1883,
he died after a long delirium due to his suffering from
cancer of the spinal cord. His body was taken to St.
Petersburg and was buried with national honors.

The two works by Turgenev contained in the present
volume are characteristic in their concern with social and
political questions, and in the prominence in both of them
of heroes who fail in action. Turgenev preaches no doctrine
in his novels, has no remedy for the universe; but he sees
clearly certain weaknesses of the Russian character and
exposes these with absolute candor yet without unkindness.
Much as he lived abroad, his books are intensely Russian;
yet of the great Russian novelists he alone rivals the masters
of western Europe in the matter of form. In economy of
means, condensation, felicity of language, and excellence
of structure he surpasses all his countrymen; and "Fathers
and Children" and "A House of Gentlefolk" represent his
great and delicate art at its best.

W. A. N.

always unrest, and without the hope of peace. If the end did not appear, the fact that it must be miserable always appeared. Life showed itself to me in different colors after I had once read Turgenev; it became more serious, more awful, and with mystical responsibilities I had not known before. My gay American horizons were bathed in the vast melancholy of the Slav, patient, agnostic, trustful. At the same time nature revealed herself to me through him with an intimacy she had not hitherto shown me. There are passages in this wonderful writer alive with a truth that seems drawn from the reader's own knowledge: who else but Turgenev and one's own most secret self ever felt all the rich, sad meaning of the night air drawing in at the open window, of the fires burning in the darkness on the distant fields? I try in vain to give some notion of the subtle sympathy with nature which scarcely put itself into words with him. As for the people of his fiction, though they were of orders and civilizations so remote from my experience, they were of the eternal human types whose origin and potentialities every one may find in his own heart, and I felt their verity in every touch.

I cannot describe the satisfaction his work gave me; I can only impart some sense of it, perhaps, by saying that it was like a happiness I had been waiting for all my life, and now that it had come, I was richly content forever. I do not mean to say that the art of Turgenev surpasses the art of Björnson; I think Björnson is quite as fine and true. But the Norwegian deals with simple and primitive circumstances for the most part, and always with a small world; and the Russian has to do with human nature inside of its conventional shells, and his scene is often as large as Europe. Even when it is as remote as Norway, it is still related to the great capitals by the history if not the actuality of the characters. Most of Turgenev's books I have read many times over, all of them I have read more than twice. For a number of years I read them again and again without much caring for other fiction. It was only the other day that I read "Smoke" through once more, with no diminished sense of its truth, but with somewhat less than my first satisfaction in its art. Perhaps this was because I had reached the point through my acquaintance with Tolstoy where I was impatient even of the artifice that hid itself. In "Smoke" I was now aware of an artifice that kept out of sight, but was still always present somewhere, invisibly operating the story.—From "My Literary Passions" (1895).

III

By K. Waliszewski

THE second novel of the series, "Fathers and Children," stirred up a storm the suddenness and violence of which it is not easy, nowadays, to understand. The figure of Bazarov, the first "Nihilist"—thus baptized by an inversion of epithet which was to win extraordinary success—is merely intended to reveal a mental condition which, though the fact had been insufficiently recognized, had already existed for some years. The epithet itself had been in constant use since 1829, when Nadiéjdine applied it to Pushkin, Polevoï, and some other subverters of the classic tradition. Turgenev only extended its meaning by a new interpretation, destined to be perpetuated by the tremendous success of "Fathers and Children." There is nothing, or hardly anything, in Bazarov, of the terrible revolutionary whom we have since learnt to look for under this title. Turgenev was not the man to call up such a figure. He was far too dreamy, too gentle, too good-natured a being. Already, in the character of Roudine, he had failed, in the strangest way, to catch the likeness of Bakounine, that fiery organiser of insurrection, whom all Europe knew, and whom he had selected as his model. Conceive Corot or Millet trying to paint some figure out of the Last Judgment after Michael Angelo! Bazarov is the Nihilist in his first phase, "in course of becoming," as the Germans would say, and he is a pupil of the German universities. When Turgenev shaped the character, he certainly drew on his own memories of his stay at Berlin, at a time when Bruno Bauer was laying it down as a dogma that no educated man ought to have opinions on any subject, and when Max

Stirner was convincing the young Hegelians that ideas were mere smoke and dust, seeing that the only reality in existence was the individual *Ego*. These teachings, eagerly received by the Russian youth, were destined to produce a state of moral decomposition, the earliest symptoms of which were admirably analysed by Turgenev.

Bazarov is a very clever man, but clever in thought, and especially in word, only. He scorns art, women, and family life. He does not know what the point of honour means. He is a cynic in his love affairs, and indifferent in his friendships. He has no respect even for paternal tenderness, but he is full of contradictions, even to the extent of fighting a duel about nothing at all, and sacrificing his life for the first peasant he meets. And in this the resemblance is true, much more general, indeed, than the model selected would lead one to imagine; so general, in fact, that, apart from the question of art, Turgenev—he has admitted it himself—felt as if he were drawing his own portrait; and therefore it is, no doubt, that he has made his hero so sympathetic.—From "A History of Russian Literature" (1900).

IV

By Richard H. P. Curle

BUT for the best expression of the bewilderment of life we have to turn to the portrait of a man, to the famous Bazarov of "Fathers and Children." Turgenev raises through him the eternal problem—Has personality any hold, has life any meaning at all? The reality of this figure, his contempt for nature, his egoism, his strength, his mothlike weakness are so convincing that before his philosophy all other philosophies seem to pale. He is the one who sees the life-illusion, and yet, knowing that it is the mask of night, grasps at it, loathing himself. You can hate Bazarov, you cannot have contempt for him. He is a man of genius, rid of sentiment and hope, believing in nothing but himself, to whom come, as from the darkness, all the violent questions of life and death. "Fathers and

Children" is simply an exposure of our power to mould our own lives. Bazarov is a man of astonishing intellect— he is the pawn of an emotion he despises; he is a man of gigantic will—he can do nothing but destroy his own beliefs; he is a man of intense life—he cannot avoid the first, brainless touch of death. It is the hopeless fight of mind against instinct, of determination against fate, of personality against impersonality. Bazarov disdaining everyone, sick of all smallness, is roused to fury by the obvious irritations of Pavel Petrovitch. Savagely announcing the creed of nihilism and the end of romance, he has only to feel the calm, aristocratic smile of Madame Odinstov fixed on him and he suffers all the agony of first love. Determining to live and create, he has only to play with death for a moment, and he is caught. But though he is the most positive of all Turgenev's male portraits, there are others linking up the chain of delusion. There is Rudin, typical of the unrest of the idealist; there is Nezhdanov ("Virgin Soil"), typical of the self-torture of the anarchist. There is Shubin ("On the Eve"), hiding his misery in laughter, and Lavretsky ("A House of Gentlefolk"), hiding his misery in silence. It is not necessary to search for further examples. Turgenev put his hand upon the dark things. He perceived character, struggling in the "clutch of circumstances," the tragic moments, the horrible conflicts of personality. His figures have that capability of suffering which (as someone has said) is the true sign of life. They seem like real people, dazed and uncertain. No action of theirs ever surprises you, because in each of them he has made you hear an inward soliloquy.—From "Turgenev and the Life-Illusion," in "The Fortnightly Review" (April, 1910).

V

By Maurice Baring

TURGENEV did for Russian literature what Byron did for English literature; he led the genius of Russia on a pilgrimage throughout all Europe. And in Europe his work reaped a glorious harvest of praise. Flaubert was astounded by him, George Sand looked up to him as to a master, Taine spoke of his work as being the finest artistic production since Sophocles. In Turgenev's work, Europe not only discovered Turgenev, but it discovered Russia, the simplicity and the naturalness of the Russian character; and this came as a revelation. For the first time Europe came across the Russian woman whom Pushkin was the first to paint; for the first time Europe came into contact with the Russian soul; and it was the sharpness of this revelation which accounts for the fact of Turgenev having received in the west an even greater meed of praise than he was perhaps entitled to.

In Russia Turgenev attained almost instant popularity. His "Sportsman's Sketches" and his "Nest of Gentlefolk" made him not only famous but universally popular. In 1862 the publication of his masterpiece "Fathers and Children" dealt his reputation a blow. The revolutionary elements in Russia regarded his hero, Bazarov, as a calumny and a libel; whereas the reactionary elements in Russia looked upon "Fathers and Children" as a glorification of Nihilism. Thus he satisfied nobody. He fell between two stools. This, perhaps, could only happen in Russia to this extent; and for that same reason as that which made Russian criticism didactic. The conflicting elements of Russian society were so terribly in earnest in fighting their cause, that anyone whom they did not regard as definitely for them was at once considered an enemy, and an impartial delineation of any character concerned in the political struggle was bound to displease both parties. If a novelist drew a Nihilist, he must be one or the other, a hero or a scoundrel, if either the revolutionaries or the reactionaries were to be pleased. If in England the militant suffragists suddenly had a huge mass of educated opinion behind them and a still larger mass of educated public opinion against them, and some one were to draw in a novel an impartial picture of a suffragette, the same thing would happen. On a small scale, as far as the suffragettes are concerned, it has happened in the case of Mr. Wells. But if Turgenev's popularity suffered a shock in Russia from which it with difficulty recovered, in western Europe it went on increasing. Especially in England, Turgenev became the idol of all that was eclectic, and admiration for Turgenev a hallmark of good taste. . . .

"Fathers and Children" is as beautifully constructed as a drama of Sophocles; the events move inevitably to a tragic close. There is not a touch of banality from beginning to end, and not an unnecessary word; the portraits of the old father and mother, the young Kirsanov, and all the minor characters are perfect; and amidst the trivial crowd Bazarov stands out like Lucifer, the strongest—the only strong character—that Turgenev created, the first Nihilist—for if Turgenev was not the first to invent the word, he was the first to apply it in this sense.

Bazarov is the incarnation of the Lucifer type that recurs again and again in Russian history and fiction, in sharp contrast to the meek, humble type of Ivan Durak. Lermontov's Pechorin was in some respects an anticipation of Bazarov; so were the many Russian rebels. He is the man who denies, to whom art is a silly toy, who detests abstractions, knowledge, and the love of Nature; he believes in nothing; he bows to nothing; he can break, but he cannot bend; he does break, and that is the tragedy, but, breaking, he retains his invincible pride, and

"not cowardly puts off his helmet,"

and he dies "valiantly vanquished."

In the pages which describe his death Turgenev reaches the high-water mark of his art, his moving quality, his power, his reserve. For manly pathos they rank among the greatest scenes in literature, stronger than the death of Colonel Newcome and the best of Thackeray. Among

English novelists it is, perhaps, only Meredith who has struck such strong, piercing chords, nobler than anything in Daudet or Maupassant, more reserved than anything in Victor Hugo, and worthy of the great poets, of the tragic pathos of Goethe and Dante. The character of Bazarov, as has been said, created a sensation and endless controversy. The revolutionaries thought him a caricature and a libel, the reactionaries a scandalous glorification of the Devil; and impartial men such as Dostoevsky, who knew the revolutionaries at first hand, thought the type unreal. It is impossible that Bazarov was not like the Nihilists of the sixties; but in any case as a figure in fiction, whatever the fact may be, he lives and will continue to live. . . . —From "An Outline of Russian Literature" (1914).

LIST OF CHARACTERS

MARYA DMITRIEVNA KALITIN, a widow.

MARFA TIMOFYEVNA PESTOV, her aunt.

SERGEI PETROVITCH GEDEONOVSKY, a state councillor.

FEDOR (*pr. Fyódor*) IVANITCH LAVRETSKY, kinsman of Marya.

ELISAVETA MIHALOVNA (LISA),
LENOTCHKA, } daughters of Marya.

SHUROTCHKA, an orphan girl, ward of Marfa.

NASTASYA KARPOVNA OGARKOFF, dependant of Marfa.

VLADIMIR NIKOLAITCH PANSHIN, of the Ministry of the Interior.

CHRISTOPHER FEDORITCH LEMM, a German musician.

PIOTR ANDREITCH LAVRETSKY, grandfather of Fedor.

ANNA PAVLOVNA, grandmother of Fedor.

IVAN PETROVITCH, father of Fedor.

GLAFIRA PETROVNA, aunt of Fedor.

MALANYA SERGYEVNA, mother of Fedor.

MIHALEVITCH, a student friend of Fedor.

PAVEL PETROVITCH KOROBYIN, father of Varvara.

KALLIOPA KARLOVNA, mother of Varvara.

VARVARA PAVLOVNA, wife of Fedor.

ANTON,
APRAXYA, } old servants of Fedor.

AGAFYA VLASYEVNA, nurse of Lisa.

A HOUSE OF GENTLEFOLK

A NOVEL

CHAPTER I

A BRIGHT spring day was fading into evening. High overhead in the clear heavens small rosy clouds seemed hardly to move across the sky but to be sinking into its depths of blue.

In a handsome house in one of the outlying streets of the government town of O—— (it was in the year 1842) two women were sitting at an open window; one was about fifty, the other an old lady of seventy.

The name of the former was Marya Dmitrievna Kalitin. Her husband, a shrewd determined man of obstinate bilious temperament, had been dead for ten years. He had been a provincial public prosecutor, noted in his own day as a successful man of business. He had received a fair education and had been to the university; but having been born in narrow circumstances he realised early in life the necessity of pushing his own way in the world and making money. It had been a love-match on Marya Dmitrievna's side. He was not bad-looking, was clever and could be very agreeable when he chose. Marya Dmitrievna Pestov —that was her maiden name—had lost her parents in childhood. She spent some years in a boarding-school in Moscow, and after leaving school, lived on the family estate of Pokrovskoe, about forty miles from O——, with her aunt and her elder brother. This brother soon after obtained a post in Petersburg, and made them a scanty allowance. He treated his aunt and sister very shabbily till his sudden death cut short his career. Marya Dmitrievna inherited Pokrovskoe, but she did not live there long. Two years

1

after her marriage with Kalitin, who succeeded in winning her heart in a few days, Pokrovskoe was exchanged for another estate, which yielded a much larger income, but was utterly unattractive and had no house. At the same time Kalitin took a house in the town of O——, in which he and his wife took up their permanent abode. There was a large garden round the house, which on one side looked out upon the open country away from the town.

'And so,' decided Kalitin, who had a great distaste for the quiet of country life, 'there would be no need for them to be dragging themselves off into the country.' In her heart Marya Dmitrievna more than once regretted her pretty Pokrovskoe, with its babbling brook, its wide meadows, and green copses; but she never opposed her husband in anything and had the greatest veneration for his wisdom and knowledge of the world. When after fifteen years of married life he died leaving her with a son and two daughters, Marya Dmitrievna had grown so accustomed to her house and to town life that she had no inclination to leave O——.

In her youth Marya Dmitrievna had always been spoken of as a pretty blonde; and at fifty her features had not lost all charm, though they were somewhat coarser and less delicate in outline. She was more sentimental than kindhearted; and even at her mature age, she retained the manners of the boarding-school. She was self-indulgent and easily put out, even moved to tears when she was crossed in any of her habits. She was, however, very sweet and agreeable when all her wishes were carried out and none opposed her. Her house was among the pleasantest in the town. She had a considerable fortune, not so much from her own property as from her husband's savings. Her two daughters were living with her; her son was being educated in one of the best government schools in Petersburg.

The old lady sitting with Marya Dmitrievna at the window was her father's sister, the same aunt with whom she had once spent some solitary years in Pokrovskoe. Her name was Marfa Timofyevna Pestov. She had a reputation for eccentricity as she was a woman of an independent character, told every one the truth to his face, and even in the most straitened circumstances behaved just as if she had a fortune at her disposal. She could not endure Kalitin, and directly her niece married him, she removed to her little property, where for ten whole years she lived in a smoky peasants' hut. Marya Dmitrievna was a little afraid of her. A little sharp-nosed woman with black hair and keen eyes even in her old age, Marfa Timofyevna walked briskly, held herself upright and spoke quickly and clearly in a sharp ringing voice. She always wore a white cap and a white dressing-jacket.

'What's the matter with you?' she asked Marya Dmitrievna suddenly. 'What are you sighing about, pray?'

'Nothing,' answered the latter. 'What exquisite clouds!'

'You feel sorry for them, eh?'

Marya Dmitrievna made no reply.

'Why is it Gedeonovsky does not come?' observed Marfa Timofyevna, moving her knitting needles quickly. (She was knitting a large woollen scarf.) 'He would have sighed with you—or at least he'd have had some fib to tell you.'

'How hard you always are on him! Sergei Petrovitch is a worthy man.'

'Worthy!' repeated the old lady scornfully.

'And how devoted he was to my poor husband!' observed Marya Dmitrievna; 'even now he cannot speak of him without emotion.'

'And no wonder! it was he who picked him out of the gutter,' muttered Marfa Timofyevna, and her knitting needles moved faster than ever.

'He looks so meek and mild,' she began again, 'with his grey head, but he no sooner opens his mouth than out comes a lie or a slander. And to think of his having the rank of a councillor! To be sure, though, he's only a village priest's son.'

'Every one has faults, auntie; that is his weak point, no doubt. Sergei Petrovitch has had no education: of course he does not speak French, still, say what you like, he is an agreeable man.'

'Yes, he is always ready to kiss your hands. He does not speak French—that's no great loss. I am not over strong in the French lingo myself. It would be better if he could not speak at all; he would not tell lies then. But here he is—

speak of the devil,' added Marfa Timofyevna looking into
the street. 'Here comes your agreeable man striding along.
What a lanky creature he is, just like a stork!'

Marya Dmitrievna began to arrange her curls. Marfa
Timofyevna looked at her ironically.

'What's that, not a grey hair surely? You must speak
to your Palashka, what can she be thinking about?'

'Really, auntie, you are always so . . .' muttered Marya
Dmitrievna in a tone of vexation, drumming on the arm of
her chair with her finger-tips.

'Sergei Petrovitch Gedeonovsky!' was announced in a
shrill piping voice, by a rosy-cheeked little page who made
his appearance at the door.

CHAPTER II

A TALL man entered, wearing a tidy overcoat, rather short trousers, grey doeskin gloves, and two neckties—a black one outside, and a white one below it. There was an air of decorum and propriety in everything about him, from his prosperous countenance and smoothly brushed hair, to his low-heeled, noiseless boots. He bowed first to the lady of the house, then to Marfa Timofyevna, and slowly drawing off his gloves, he advanced to take Marya Dmitrievna's hand. After kissing it respectfully twice he seated himself with deliberation in an arm-chair, and rubbing the very tips of his fingers together, he observed with a smile—

'And is Elisaveta Mihalovna quite well?'

'Yes,' replied Marya Dmitrievna, 'she's in the garden.'

'And Elena Mihalovna?'

'Lenotchka's in the garden too. Is there no news?'

'There is indeed!' replied the visitor, slowly blinking his eyes and pursing up his mouth. 'Hm! . . . yes, indeed there is a piece of news, and very surprising news too. Lavretsky—Fedor Ivanitch is here.'

'Fedya!' cried Marfa Timofyevna. 'Are you sure you are not romancing, my good man?'

'No, indeed, I saw him myself.'

'Well, that does not prove it.'

'Fedor Ivanitch looked much more robust,' continued Gedeonovsky, affecting not to have heard Marfa Timofyevna's last remark. 'Fedor Ivanitch is broader and has quite a colour.'

'He looked more robust,' said Marya Dmitrievna, dwelling on each syllable. 'I should have thought he had little enough to make him look robust.'

'Yes, indeed,' observed Gedeonovsky; 'any other man in Fedor Ivanitch's position would have hesitated to appear in society.'

'Why so, pray?' interposed Marfa Timofyevna. 'What nonsense are you talking! The man's come back to his home—where would you have him go? And has he been to blame, I should like to know!'

'The husband is always to blame, madam, I venture to assure you, when a wife misconducts herself.'

'You say that, my good sir, because you have never been married yourself.' Gedeonovsky listened with a forced smile.

'If I may be so inquisitive,' he asked, after a short pause, 'for whom is that pretty scarf intended?'

Marfa Timofyevna gave him a sharp look.

'It's intended,' she replied, 'for a man who does not talk scandal, nor play the hypocrite, nor tell lies, if there's such a man to be found in the world. I know Fedya well; he was only to blame in being too good to his wife. To be sure, he married for love, and no good ever comes of those love-matches,' added the old lady, with a sidelong glance at Marya Dmitrievna, as she got up from her place. 'And now, my good sir, you may attack any one you like, even me if you choose; I'm going, I will not hinder you.' And Marfa Timofyevna walked away.

'That's always how she is,' said Marya Dmitrievna, following her aunt with her eyes.

'We must remember your aunt's age . . . there's no help for it,' replied Gedeonovsky. 'She spoke of a man not playing the hypocrite. But who is not hypocritical nowadays? It's the age we live in. One of my friends, a most worthy man, and, I assure you, a man of no mean position, used to say, that nowadays the very hens can't pick up a grain of corn without hypocrisy—they always approach it from one side. But when I look at you, dear lady—your character is so truly angelic; let me kiss your little snow-white hand!'

Marya Dmitrievna with a faint smile held out her plump hand to him with the little finger held apart from the rest. He pressed his lips to it, and she drew her chair nearer to him, and bending a little towards him, asked in an undertone—

'So you saw him? Was he really—all right—quite well and cheerful?'

'Yes, he was well and cheerful,' replied Gedeonovsky in a whisper.

'You haven't heard where his wife is now?'

'She was lately in Paris; now, they say, she has gone away to Italy.'

'It is terrible, indeed—Fedya's position; I wonder how he can bear it. Every one, of course, has trouble; but he, one may say, has been made the talk of all Europe.'

Gedeonovsky sighed.

'Yes, indeed, yes, indeed. They do say, you know that she associates with artists and musicians, and as the saying is, with strange creatures of all kinds. She has lost all sense of shame completely.'

'I am deeply, deeply grieved,' said Marya Dmitrievna. 'On account of our relationship; you know, Sergei Petrovitch, he's my cousin many times removed.'

'Of course, of course. Don't I know everything that concerns your family? I should hope so, indeed.'

'Will he come to see us—what do you think?'

'One would suppose so; though, they say, he is intending to go home to his country place.'

Marya Dmitrievna lifted her eyes to heaven.

'Ah, Sergei Petrovitch, Sergei Petrovitch, when I think how careful we women ought to be in our conduct!'

'There are women and women, Marya Dmitrievna. There are unhappily such . . . of flighty character . . . and at a certain age too, and then they are not brought up in good principles.' (Sergei Petrovitch drew a blue checked handkerchief out of his pocket and began to unfold it.) 'There are such women, no doubt.' (Sergei Petrovitch applied a corner of the handkerchief first to one and then to the other eye.) 'But speaking generally, if one takes into consideration, I mean . . . the dust in the town is really extraordinary to-day,' he wound up.

'*Maman, maman,*' cried a pretty little girl of eleven running into the room, 'Vladimir Nikolaitch is coming on horseback!'

Marya Dmitrievna got up; Sergei Petrovitch also rose and made a bow. 'Our humble respects to Elena Mihalovna,' he said, and turning aside into a corner for good manners, he began blowing his long straight nose.

'What a splendid horse he has!' continued the little girl. 'He was at the gate just now, he told Lisa and me he would dismount at the steps.'

The sound of hoofs was heard; and a graceful young man, riding a beautiful bay horse, was seen in the street, and stopped at the open window.

CHAPTER III

'How do you do, Marya Dmitrievna?' cried the young man in a pleasant, ringing voice. 'How do you like my new purchase?'

Marya Dmitrievna went up to the window.

'How do you do, *Woldemar!* Ah, what a splendid horse! Where did you buy it?'

'I bought it from the army contractor. . . . He made me pay for it too, the brigand!'

'What's its name?'

'Orlando. . . . But it's a stupid name; I want to change it . . . *Eh bien, eh bien, mon garçon.* . . . What a restless beast it is!' The horse snorted, pawed the ground, and shook the foam off the bit.

'Lenotchka, stroke him, don't be afraid.'

The little girl stretched her hand out of the window, but Orlando suddenly reared and started. The rider with perfect self-possession gave it a cut with the whip across the neck, and keeping a tight grip with his legs forced it in spite of its opposition, to stand still again at the window.

'*Prenez garde, prenez garde,*' Marya Dmitrievna kept repeating.

'Lenotchka, pat him,' said the young man, 'I won't let him be perverse.'

The little girl again stretched out her hand and timidly patted the quivering nostrils of the horse, who kept fidgeting and champing the bit.

'Bravo!' cried Marya Dmitrievna, 'but now get off and come in to us.'

The rider adroitly turned his horse, gave him a touch of the spur, and galloping down the street soon reached the courtyard. A minute later he ran into the drawing-room by the door from the hall, flourishing his whip; at the same moment there appeared in the other doorway a tall, slender dark-haired girl of nineteen, Marya Dmitrievna's eldest daughter, Lisa.

9

S—2

CHAPTER IV

THE name of the young man whom we have just introduced to the reader was Vladimir Nikolaitch Panshin. He served in Petersburg on special commissions in the department of internal affairs. He had come to the town of O—— to carry out some temporary government commissions, and was in attendance on the Governor-General Zonnenberg, to whom he happened to be distantly related. Panshin's father, a retired cavalry officer and a notorious gambler, was a man with insinuating eyes, a battered countenance, and a nervous twitch about the mouth. He spent his whole life hanging about the aristocratic world; frequented the English clubs of both capitals, and had the reputation of a smart, not very trustworthy, but jolly good-natured fellow. In spite of his smartness, he was almost always on the brink of ruin, and the property he left his son was small and heavily encumbered. To make up for that, however, he did exert himself, after his own fashion, over his son's education. Vladimir Nikolaitch spoke French very well, English well, and German badly; that is the proper thing; fashionable people would be ashamed to speak German well; but to utter an occasional —generally a humorous—phrase in German is quite correct, *c'est même très chic,* as the Parisians of Petersburg express themselves. By the time he was fifteen, Vladimir knew how to enter any drawing-room without embarrassment, how to move about in it gracefully and to leave it at the appropriate moment. Panshin's father gained many connections for his son. He never lost an opportunity, while shuffling the cards between two rubbers, or playing a successful trump, of dropping a hint about his Volodka to any personage of importance who was a devotee of cards. And Vladimir, too, during his residence at the university, which he left without a very brilliant degree, formed an acquaintance with several young men of quality, and gained an entry into the

10

best houses. He was received cordially everywhere: he was
very good-looking, easy in his manners, amusing, always in
good health, and ready for everything; respectful, when he
ought to be; insolent, when he dared to be; excellent company, *un charmant garçon.* The promised land lay before
him. Panshin quickly learnt the secret of getting on in the
world; he knew how to yield with genuine respect to its
decrees; he knew how to take up trifles with half ironical
seriousness, and to appear to regard everything serious as
trifling; he was a capital dancer; and dressed in the English
style. In a short time he gained the reputation of being
one of the smartest and most attractive young men in
Petersburg.

Panshin was indeed very smart, not less so than his
father; but he was also very talented. He did everything well; he sang charmingly, sketched with spirit,
wrote verses, and was a very fair actor. He was only
twenty-eight, and he was already a *kammer-yunker,* and had
a very good position. Panshin had complete confidence in
himself, in his own intelligence, and his own penetration;
he made his way with light-hearted assurance, everything
went smoothly with him. He was used to being liked by
every one, old and young, and imagined that he understood
people, especially women: he certainly understood their
ordinary weaknesses. As a man of artistic leanings, he was
conscious of a capacity for passion, for being carried away,
even for enthusiasm, and, consequently, he permitted himself
various irregularities; he was dissipated, associated with
persons not belonging to good society, and, in general, conducted himself in a free and easy manner; but at heart he
was cold and false, and at the moment of the most boisterous
revelry his sharp brown eye was always alert, taking everything in. This bold, independent young man could never
forget himself and be completely carried away. To his
credit it must be said, that he never boasted of his conquests. He had found his way into Marya Dmitrievna's
house immediately he arrived in O——, and was soon perfectly at home there. Marya Dmitrievna absolutely adored
him. Panshin exchanged cordial greetings with every one
in the room; he shook hands with Marya Dmitrievna and

Lisaveta Mihalovna, clapped Gedeonovsky lightly on the shoulder, and turning round on his heels, put his hand on Lenotchka's head and kissed her on the forehead.

'Aren't you afraid to ride such a vicious horse?' Marya Dmitrievna questioned him.

'I assure you he's very quiet, but I will tell you what I am afraid of: I'm afraid to play preference with Sergei Petrovitch; yesterday he cleaned me out of everything at Madame Byelenitsin's.'

Gedeonovsky gave a thin, sympathetic little laugh; he was anxious to be in favour with the brilliant young official from Petersburg—the governor's favourite. In conversation with Marya Dmitrievna, he often alluded to Panshin's remarkable abilities. Indeed, he used to argue how can one help admiring him? The young man is making his way in the highest spheres, he is an exemplary official, and not a bit of pride about him. And, in fact, even in Petersburg Panshin was reckoned a capable official; he got through a great deal of work; he spoke of it lightly as befits a man of the world who does not attach any special importance to his labours, but he never hesitated in carrying out orders. The authorities like such subordinates; he himself had no doubt, that if he chose, he could be a minister in time.

'You are pleased to say that I cleaned you out,' replied Gedeonovsky; 'but who was it won twelve roubles of me last week and more?' . . .

'You're a malicious fellow,' Panshin interrupted, with genial but somewhat contemptuous carelessness, and, paying him no further attention, he went up to Lisa.

'I cannot get the overture of Oberon here,' he began. 'Madame Byelenitsin was boasting when she said she had all the classical music: in reality she has nothing but polkas and waltzes, but I have already written to Moscow, and within a week you will have the overture. By the way,' he went on, 'I wrote a new song yesterday, the words too are mine, would you care for me to sing it? I don't know how far it is successful. Madame Byelenitsin thought it very pretty, but her words mean nothing. I should like to know what you think of it. But I think, though, that had better be later on.'

'Why later on?' interposed Marya Dmitrievna, 'why not now?'

'I obey,' replied Panshin, with a peculiar bright and sweet smile, which came and went suddenly on his face. He drew up a chair with his knee, sat down to the piano, and striking a few chords began to sing, articulating the words clearly, the following song—

> Above the earth the moon floats high
>   Amid pale clouds;
> Its magic light in that far sky
>   Yet stirs the floods.
>
> My heart has found a moon to rule
>   Its stormy sea;
> To joy and sorrow it is moved
>   Only by thee.
>
> My soul is full of love's cruel smart,
>   And longing vain;
> But thou art calm, as that cold moon,
>   That knows not pain.

The second couplet was sung by Panshin with special power and expression, the sound of waves was heard in the stormy accompaniment. After the words 'and longing vain,' he sighed softly, dropped his eyes and let his voice gradually die away, *morendo*. When he had finished, Lisa praised the motive, Marya Dmitrievna cried, 'Charming!' but Gedeonovsky went so far as to exclaim, 'Ravishing poetry, and music equally ravishing!' Lenotchka looked with childish reverence at the singer. In short, every one present was delighted with the young dilettante's composition; but at the door leading into the drawing-room from the hall stood an old man, who had only just come in, and who, to judge by the expression of his downcast face and the shrug of his shoulders, was by no means pleased with Panshin's song, pretty though it was. After waiting a moment and flicking the dust off his boots with a coarse pocket-handkerchief, this man suddenly raised his eyes, compressed his lips with a morose expression, and his stooping figure bent forward, he entered the drawing-room.

'Ah! Christopher Fedoritch, how are you?' exclaimed Panshin before any of the others could speak, and he jumped up quickly from his seat. 'I had no suspicion that you were here,—nothing would have induced me to sing my song before you. I know you are no lover of light music.'

'I did not hear it,' declared the new-comer, in very bad Russian, and exchanging greetings with every one, he stood awkwardly in the middle of the room.

'Have you come, Monsieur Lemm,' said Marya Dmitrievna, 'to give Lisa her music lesson?'

'No, not Lisaveta Mihalovna, but Elena Mihalovna.'

'Oh! very well. Lenotchka, go up-stairs with Mr. Lemm.'

The old man was about to follow the little girl, but Panshin stopped him.

'Don't go after the lesson, Christopher Fedoritch,' he said. 'Lisaveta Mihalovna and I are going to play a duet of Beethoven's sonata.'

The old man muttered some reply, and Panshin continued in German, mispronouncing the words—

'Lisaveta Mihalovna showed me the religious cantata you dedicated to her—a beautiful thing! Pray, do not suppose that I cannot appreciate serious music—quite the contrary: it is tedious sometimes, but then it is very elevating.'

The old man crimsoned to his ears, and with a sidelong look at Lisa, he hurriedly went out of the room.

Marya Dmitrievna asked Panshin to sing his song again; but he protested that he did not wish to torture the ears of the musical German, and suggested to Lisa that they should attack Beethoven's sonata. Then Marya Dmitrievna heaved a sigh, and in her turn suggested to Gedeonovsky a walk in the garden. 'I should like,' she said, 'to have a little more talk, and to consult you about our poor Fedya.' Gedeonovsky bowed with a smirk, and with two fingers picked up his hat, on the brim of which his gloves had been tidily laid, and went away with Marya Dmitrievna. Panshin and Lisa remained alone in the room; she fetched the sonata, and opened it; both seated themselves at the piano in silence. Overhead were heard the faint sounds of scales, played by the uncertain fingers of Lenotchka.

CHAPTER V

CHRISTOPHER THEODOR GOTTLIEB LEMM was born in 1786 in the town of Chemnitz in Saxony. His parents were poor musicians. His father played the French horn, his mother the harp; he himself was practising on three different instruments by the time he was five. At eight years old he was left an orphan, and from his tenth year he began to earn his bread by his art. He led a wandering life for many years, and performed everywhere in restaurants, at fairs, at peasants' weddings, and at balls. At last he got into an orchestra, and constantly rising in it, he obtained the position of director. He was rather a poor performer; but he understood music thoroughly. At twenty-eight he migrated into Russia, on the invitation of a great nobleman, who did not care for music himself, but kept an orchestra for show. Lemm lived with him seven years in the capacity of orchestra conductor, and left him empty-handed. The nobleman was ruined, he intended to give him a promissory note, but in the sequel refused him even that—in short, did not pay him a farthing. He was advised to go away; but he was unwilling to return home in poverty from Russia, that great Russia which is a mine of gold for artists; he decided to remain and try his luck. For twenty years the poor German had been trying his luck; he had lived in various gentlemen's houses, had suffered and put up with much, had faced privation, had struggled like a fish on the ice; but the idea of returning to his own country never left him among all the hardships he endured; it was this dream alone that sustained him. But fate did not see fit to grant him this last and first happiness: at fifty, broken-down in health and prematurely aged, he drifted to the town of O——, and remained there for good, having now lost once for all every hope of leaving Russia, which he detested. He gained his poor livelihood somehow by lessons. Lemm's exterior was not prepossessing.

He was short and bent, with crooked shoulders, and a contracted chest, with large flat feet, and bluish white nails on the gnarled bony fingers of his sinewy red hands. He had a wrinkled face, sunken cheeks, and compressed lips, which he was for ever twitching and biting; and this together with his habitual taciturnity, produced an impression almost sinister. His grey hair hung in tufts on his low brow; like smouldering embers, his little set eyes glowed with dull fire. He moved painfully, at every step swinging his ungainly body forward. Some of his movements recalled the clumsy actions of an owl in a cage when it feels that it is being looked at, but itself can hardly see out of its great yellow eyes timorously and drowsily blinking. Pitiless, prolonged sorrow had laid its indelible stamp on the poor musician; it had disfigured and deformed his person, by no means attractive to begin with. But any one who was able to get over the first impression would have discerned something good, and honest, and out of the common in this half-shattered creature. A devoted admirer of Bach and Handel, a master of his art, gifted with a lively imagination and that boldness of conception which is only vouchsafed to the German race, Lemm might, in time—who knows?—have taken rank with the great composers of his fatherland, had his life been different; but he was born under an unlucky star! He had written much in his life, and it had not been granted to him to see one of his compositions produced; he did not know how to set about things in the right way, to gain favour in the right place, and to make a push at the right moment. A long, long time ago, his one friend and admirer, also a German and also poor, had published two of Lemm's sonatas at his own expense—the whole edition remained on the shelves of the music-shops; they disappeared without a trace, as though they had been thrown into a river by night. At last Lemm had renounced everything; the years too did their work; his mind had grown hard and stiff, as his fingers had stiffened. He lived alone in a little cottage not far from the Kalitin's house, with an old cook he had taken out of the poorhouse (he had never married). He took long walks, and read the Bible and the Protestant version of the Psalms, and Shakes-

peare in Schlegel's translation. He had composed nothing
for a long time; but apparently, Lisa, his best pupil, had been
able to inspire him; he had written for her the cantata to
which Panshin had made allusion. The words of this
cantata he had borrowed from his collection of hymns.
He had added a few verses of his own. It was sung by
two choruses—a chorus of the happy and a chorus of
the unhappy. The two were brought into harmony at
the end, and sang together, 'Merciful God, have pity on us
sinners, and deliver us from all evil thoughts and earthly
hopes.' On the title-page was the inscription, most carefully written and even illuminated, 'Only the righteous are
justified. A religious cantata. Composed and dedicated to
Miss Elisaveta Kalitin, his dear pupil, by her teacher, C.
T. G. Lemm.' The words, 'Only the righteous are justified'
and 'Elisaveta Kalitin,' were encircled by rays. Below was
written: 'For you alone, *für Sie allein.*' This was why
Lemm had grown red, and looked reproachfully at Lisa; he
was deeply wounded when Panshin spoke of his cantata
before him.

CHAPTER VI

PANSHIN, who was playing bass, struck the first chords of the sonata loudly and decisively, but Lisa did not begin her part. He stopped and looked at her. Lisa's eyes were fixed directly on him, and expressed displeasure. There was no smile on her lips, her whole face looked stern and even mournful.

'What's the matter?' he asked.

'Why did you not keep your word?' she said. 'I showed you Christopher Fedoritch's cantata on the express condition that you said nothing about it to him?'

'I beg your pardon, Lisaveta Mihalovna, the words slipped out unawares.'

'You have hurt his feelings and mine too. Now he will not trust even me.'

'How could I help it, Lisaveta Mihalovna? Ever since I was a little boy I could never see a German without wanting to teaze him.'

'How can you say that, Vladimir Nikolaitch? This German is poor, lonely, and broken-down—have you no pity for him? Can you wish to teaze him?'

Panshin was a little taken aback.

'You are right, Lisaveta Mihalovna,' he declared. 'It's my everlasting thoughtlessness that's to blame. No, don't contradict me; I know myself. So much harm has come to me from my want of thought. It's owing to that failing that I am thought to be an egoist.'

Panshin paused. With whatever subject he began a conversation, he generally ended by talking of himself, and the subject was changed by him so easily, so smoothly and genially, that it seemed unconscious.

'In your own household, for instance,' he went on, 'your mother certainly wishes me well, she is so kind; you—well, I don't know your opinion of me; but on the other hand your aunt simply can't bear me. I must have offended her too by

18

some thoughtless, stupid speech. You know I'm not a favourite of hers, am I?'

'No,' Lisa admitted with some reluctance, 'she doesn't like
you.'

Panshin ran his fingers quickly over the keys, and a scarcely
perceptible smile glided over his lips.

'Well, and you?' he said, 'do you too think me an egoist?'

'I know you very little,' replied Lisa, 'but I don't consider
you an egoist; on the contrary, I can't help feeling grateful
to you.'

'I know, I know what you mean to say,' Panshin interrupted, and again he ran his fingers over the keys: 'for the
music and the books I bring you, for the wretched sketches
with which I adorn your album, and so forth. I might do
all that—and be an egoist all the same. I venture to
think that you don't find me a bore, and don't think me
a bad fellow, but still you suppose that I—what's the
saying?—would sacrifice friend or father for the sake of a
witticism.'

'You are careless and forgetful, like all men of the world,'
observed Lisa, 'that is all.'

Panshin frowned a little.

'Come,' he said, 'don't let us discuss me any more; let us
play our sonata. There's only one thing I must beg of you,'
he added, smoothing out the leaves of the book on the music
stand, 'think what you like of me, call me an egoist even
—so be it! but don't call me a man of the world; that name's
insufferable to me. . . . *Anch 'io sono pittore.* I too am an
artist, though a poor one—and *that*—I mean that I'm a poor
artist, I shall show directly. Let us begin.'

'Very well, let us begin,' said Lisa.

The first *adagio* went fairly successfully though Panshin
made more than one false note. His own compositions and
what he had practised thoroughly he played very nicely, but
he played at sight badly. So the second part of the sonata
—a rather quick *allegro*—broke down completely; at the
twentieth bar, Panshin, who was two bars behind, gave in,
and pushed his chair back with a laugh.

'No!' he cried, 'I can't play to-day; it's a good thing Lemm
did not hear us; he would have had a fit.'

Lisa got up, shut the piano, and turned round to Panshin.

'What are we going to do?' she asked.

'That's just like you, that question! You can never sit with your hands idle. Well, if you like let us sketch, since it's not quite dark. Perhaps the other muse, the muse of painting—what was her name? I have forgotten . . . will be more propitious to me. Where's your album? I remember, my landscape there is not finished.'

Lisa went into the other room to fetch the album, and Panshin, left alone, drew a cambric handkerchief out of his pocket, and rubbed his nails and looked as it were critically at his hands. He had beautiful white hands; on the second finger of his left hand he wore a spiral gold ring. Lisa came back; Panshin sat down at the window, and opened the album.

'Ah!' he exclaimed: 'I see that you have begun to copy my landscape—and capitally too. Excellent! only just here—give me a pencil—the shadows are not put in strongly enough. Look.'

And Panshin with a flourish added a few long strokes. He was for ever drawing the same landscape: in the foreground large dishevelled trees, a stretch of meadow in the background, and jagged mountains on the horizon. Lisa looked over his shoulders at his work.

'In drawing, just as in life generally,' observed Panshin, holding his head to right and to left, 'lightness and boldness —are the great things.'

At that instant Lemm came into the room, and with a stiff bow was about to leave it; but Panshin, throwing aside album and pencils, placed himself in his way.

'Where are you going, dear Christopher Fedoritch? Aren't you going to stay and have tea with us?'

'I go home,' answered Lemm in a surly voice; 'my head aches.'

'Oh, what nonsense!—do stop. We'll have an argument about Shakespeare.'

'My head aches,' repeated the old man.

'We set to work on the sonata of Beethoven without you,' continued Panshin, taking hold of him affectionately and smiling brightly, 'but we couldn't get on at all. Fancy, I couldn't play two notes together correctly.'

'You'd better have sung your song again,' replied Lemm, removing Panshin's hands, and he walked away.

Lisa ran after him. She overtook him on the stairs.

'Christopher Fedoritch, I want to tell you,' she said to him in German, accompanying him over the short green grass of the yard to the gate, 'I did wrong—forgive me.'

Lemm made no answer.

'I showed Vladimir Nikolaitch your cantata; I felt sure he would appreciate it,—and he did like it very much really.'

Lemm stopped.

'It's no matter,' he said in Russian, and then added in his own language, 'but he cannot understand anything; how is it you don't see that? He's a dilettante—and that's all!'

'You are unjust to him,' replied Lisa, 'he understands everything, and he can do almost everything himself.'

'Yes, everything second-rate, cheap, scamped work. That pleases, and he pleases, and he is glad it is so—and so much the better. I'm not angry; the cantata and I—we are a pair of old fools; I'm a little ashamed, but it's no matter.'

'Forgive me, Christopher Fedoritch,' Lisa said again.

'It's no matter,' he repeated in Russian, 'you're a good girl . . . but here is some one coming to see you. Goodbye. You are a very good girl.'

And Lemm moved with hastened steps towards the gate, through which had entered some gentleman unknown to him in a grey coat and a wide straw hat. Bowing politely to him (he always saluted all new faces in the town of O——; from acquaintances he always turned aside in the street— that was the rule he had laid down for himself), Lemm passed by and disappeared behind the fence. The stranger looked after him in amazement, and after gazing attentively at Lisa, went straight up to her.

CHAPTER VII

'YOU don't recognise me,' he said, taking off his hat, 'but I recognise you in spite of its being seven years since I saw you last. You were a child then. I am Lavretsky. Is your mother at home? Can I see her?'

'Mamma will be glad to see you,' replied Lisa; 'she had heard of your arrival.'

'Let me see, I think your name is Elisaveta?' said Lavretsky, as he went up the stairs.

'Yes.'

'I remember you very well; you had even then .a face one doesn't forget. I used to bring you sweets in those days.'

Lisa blushed and thought what a queer man. Lavretsky stopped for an instant in the hall. Lisa went into the drawing-room, where Panshin's voice and laugh could be heard; he had been communicating some gossip of the town to Marya Dmitrievna, and Gedeonovsky, who by this time had come in from the garden, and he was himself laughing aloud at the story he was telling. At the name of Lavretsky, Marya Dmitrievna was all in a flutter. She turned pale and went up to meet him.

'How do you do, how do you do, my dear cousin?' she cried in a plaintive and almost tearful voice, 'how glad I am to see you!'

'How are you, cousin?' replied Lavretsky, with a friendly pressure of her out-stretched hand; 'how has Providence been treating you?'

'Sit down, sit down, my dear Fedor Ivanitch. Ah, how glad I am! But let me present my daughter Lisa to you.'

'I have already introduced myself to Lisaveta Mihalovna,' interposed Lavretsky.

'Monsieur Panshin . . . Sergei Petrovitch Gedeonovsky . . . Please sit down. When I look at you, I can hardly believe my eyes. How are you?'

'As you see, I'm flourishing. And you, too, cousin—no ill-luck to you!—have grown no thinner in eight years.'

'To think how long it is since we met!' observed Marya Dmitrievna dreamily. 'Where have you come from now? Where did you leave . . . that is, I meant to say,' she put in hastily, 'I meant to say, are you going to be with us for long?'

'I have come now from Berlin,' replied Lavretsky, 'and to-morrow I shall go into the country—probably for a long time.'

'You will live at Lavriky, I suppose?'

'No, not at Lavriky; I have a little place twenty miles from here: I am going there.'

'Is that the little estate that came to you from Glafira Petrovna?'

'Yes.'

'Really, Fedor Ivanitch! You have such a magnificent house at Lavriky.'

Lavretsky knitted his brows a little.

'Yes . . . but there's a small lodge in this little property, and I need nothing more for a time. That place is the most convenient for me now.'

Marya Dmitrievna was again thrown into such a state of agitation that she became quite stiff, and her hands hung lifeless by her sides. Panshin came to her support by entering into conversation with Lavretsky. Marya Dmitrievna regained her composure, she leaned back in her arm-chair and now and then put in a word. But she looked all the while with such sympathy at her guest, sighed so significantly, and shook her head so dejectedly, that the latter at last lost patience and asked her rather sharply if she was unwell.

'Thank God, no,' replied Marya Dmitrievna; 'why do you ask?'

'Oh, I fancied you didn't seem to be quite yourself.'

Marya Dmitrievna assumed a dignified and somewhat offended air. 'If that's how the land lies,' she thought, 'it's absolutely no matter to me; I see, my good fellow, it's all like water on a duck's back for you; any other man would have wasted away with grief, but you've grown fat on it.' Marya Dmitrievna did not mince matters in her own mind; she expressed herself with more elegance aloud.

Lavretsky certainly did not look like the victim of fate. His rosy-cheeked typical Russian face, with its large white brow, rather thick nose, and wide straight lips seemed breathing with the wild health of the steppes, with vigorous primæval energy. He was splendidly well-built, and his fair curly hair stood up on his head like a boy's. It was only in his blue eyes, with their overhanging brows and somewhat fixed look, that one could trace an expression, not exactly of melancholy, nor exactly of weariness, and his voice had almost too measured a cadence.

Panshin meanwhile continued to keep up the conversation. He turned it upon the profits of sugar-boiling, on which he had lately read two French pamphlets, and with modest composure undertook to expound their contents, without mentioning, however, a single word about the source of his information.

'Good God, it is Fedya!' came through the half-opened door the voice of Marfa Timofyevna in the next room. 'Fedya himself!' and the old woman ran hurriedly into the room. Lavretsky had not time to get up from his seat before she had him in her arms. 'Let me have a look at you,' she said, holding his face off at arm's length. 'Ah! what a splendid fellow you are! You've grown older a little, but not a bit changed for the worse, upon my word! But why are you kissing my hands—kiss my face if you're not afraid of my wrinkled cheeks. You never asked after me—whether your aunt was alive—I warrant: and you were in my arms as soon as you were born, you great rascal! Well, that is nothing to you, I suppose; why should you remember me? But it was a good idea of yours to come back. And pray,' she added, turning to Marya Dmitrievna, 'have you offered him something to eat?'

'I don't want anything,' Lavretsky hastened to declare.

'Come, you must at least have some tea, my dear. Lord have mercy on us! He has come from I don't know where, and they don't even give him a cup of tea! Lisa, run and stir them up, and make haste. I remember he was dreadfully greedy when he was a little fellow, and he likes good things now, I daresay.'

'My respects, Marfa Timofyevna,' said Panshin, approaching the delighted old lady from one side with a low bow.

'Pardon me, sir,' replied Marfa Timofyevna, 'for not observing you in my delight. You have grown like your mother, the poor darling,' she went on, turning again to Lavretsky, 'but your nose was always your father's, and your father's it has remained. Well, and are you going to be with us for long?'

'I am going to-morrow, aunt.'

'Where?'

'Home to Vassilyevskoe.'

'To-morrow?'

'Yes, to-morrow.'

'Well, if to-morrow it must be. God bless you—you know best. Only mind you come and say good-bye to me.' The old woman patted his cheek. 'I did not think I should be here to see you; not that I have made up my mind to die yet a while—I shall last another ten years, I daresay: all we Pestovs live long; your late grandfather used to say we had two lives; but you see there was no telling how much longer you were going to dangle about abroad. Well, you're a fine lad, a fine lad; can you lift twenty stone with one hand as you used to do, eh? Your late papa was fantastical in some things, if I may say so; but he did well in having that Swiss to bring you up; do you remember you used to fight with your fists with him?—gymnastics, wasn't it they called it? But there, why I am gabbling away like this; I have only been hindering Mr. Panshin (she never pronounced his name Pánshin as was correct) from holding forth. Besides, we'd better go and have tea; yes, let's go on to the terrace, my boy, and drink it there; we have some real cream, not like what you get in your Londons and Parises. Come along, come along, and you, Fedusha, give me your arm. Oh! but what an arm it is! Upon my word, no fear of my stumbling with you!'

Every one got up and went out on to the terrace, except Gedeonovsky, who quietly took his departure. During the whole of Lavretsky's conversation with Marya Dmitrievna,

Panshin, and Marfa Timofyevna, he sat in a corner, blinking attentively, with an open mouth of childish curiosity; now he was in haste to spread the news of the new arrival through the town.

. . . .

At eleven o'clock on the evening of the same day, this is what was happening in Madame Kalitin's house. Downstairs, Vladimir Nikolaitch, seizing a favourable moment, was taking leave of Lisa at the drawing-room door, and saying to her, as he held her hand, 'You know who it is draws me here; you know why I am constantly coming to your house; what need of words when all is clear as it is?' Lisa did not speak, and looked on the ground, without smiling, with her brows slightly contracted, and a flush on her cheek, but she did not draw away her hands. While up-stairs, in Marfa Timofyevna's room, by the light of a little lamp hanging before the tarnished old holy images, Lavretsky was sitting in a low chair, his elbows on his knees and his face buried in his hands; the old woman, standing before him, now and then silently stroked his hair. He spent more than an hour with her, after taking leave of his hostess; he had scarcely said anything to his kind old friend, and she did not question him . . . Indeed, what need to speak, what was there to ask? Without that she understood all, and felt for everything of which his heart was full.

CHAPTER VIII

FEDOR IVANITCH LAVRETSKY—we must ask the reader's permission to break off the thread of our story for a time—came of an old noble family. The founder of the house of Lavretsky came over from Prussia in the reign of Vassili the Blind, and received a grant of two hundred *chetverts* of land in Byezhetsk. Many of his descendants filled various offices, and served under princes and persons of eminence in outlying districts, but not one of them rose above the rank of an inspector of the Imperial table nor acquired any considerable fortune. The richest and most distinguished of all the Lavretskys was Fedor Ivanitch's great-grandfather, Andrei, a man cruel and daring, cunning and able. Even to this day stories still linger of his tyranny, his savage temper, his reckless munificence, and his insatiable avarice. He was very stout and tall, swarthy of countenance and beardless, he spoke in a thick voice and seemed half asleep; but the more quietly he spoke the more those about him trembled. He had managed to get a wife who was a fit match for him. She was a gipsy by birth, goggle-eyed and hook-nosed, with a round yellow face. She was irascible and vindictive, and never gave way in anything to her husband, who almost killed her, and whose death she did not survive, though she had been for ever quarrelling with him. The son of Andrei, Piotr, Fedor's grandfather, did not take after his father; he was a typical landowner of the steppes, rather a simpleton, loud-voiced, but slow to move, coarse but not ill-natured, hospitable and very fond of coursing with dogs. He was over thirty when he inherited from his father a property of two thousand serfs in capital condition; but he had soon dissipated it, and had partly mortgaged his estate, and demoralised his servants. All sorts of people of low position, known and unknown, came crawling like cockroaches from all parts into his spacious, warm, ill-kept halls. All this mass of people ate what they could get, but always had their fill, drank till they were drunk, and carried off what they could, praising and blessing their genial host; and their host too when he was out of humour blessed his guests—for a pack of sponging toadies, but he was bored when he was without them. Piotr Andreitch's wife was a meek-spirited creature; he had taken her from a neighbouring family by his father's choice and command; her name was Anna Pavlovna. She never interfered in anything, welcomed guests cordially, and readily paid visits herself, though being powdered, she used to declare, would be the death of her. 'They put,' she used to say in her old age, 'a fox's brush on your head, comb all the hair up over it, smear it with grease, and dust it over with flour, and stick it up with iron pins,—there's no washing it off afterwards; but to pay visits without powder was quite impossible—people would be offended. Ah, it was a torture!'

She liked being driven with fast-trotting horses, and was ready to play cards from morning till evening, and would always keep the score of the pennies she had lost or won hidden under her hand when her husband came near the card-table; but all her dowry, her whole fortune, she had put absolutely at his disposal. She bore him two children, a son Ivan, the father of Fedor, and a daughter Glafira. Ivan was not brought up at home, but lived with a rich old maiden aunt, the Princess Kubensky; she had fixed on him for her heir (but for that his father would not have let him go). She dressed him up like a doll, engaged all kinds of teachers for him, and put him in charge of a tutor, a Frenchman, who had been an abbé, a pupil of Jean-Jacques Rousseau, a certain M. Courtin de Vaucelles, a subtle and wily intriguer—the very, as she expressed it, *fine fleur* of emigration—and finished at almost seventy years old by marrying this '*fine fleur*,' and making over all her property to him. Soon afterwards, covered with rouge, and redolent of perfume *à la Richelieu*, surrounded by negro boys, delicate-shaped greyhounds and shrieking parrots, she died on a crooked silken divan of the time of Louis XV., with an enamelled snuff-box of Petitot's workmanship in her hand —and died, deserted by her husband; the insinuating M. Courtin had preferred to remove to Paris with her money.

Ivan had only reached his twentieth year when this unexpected blow (we mean the princess's marriage, not her death) fell upon him; he did not care to stay in his aunt's house, where he found himself suddenly transformed from a wealthy heir to a poor relation; the society in Petersburg in which he had grown up was closed to him; he felt an aversion for entering the government service in the lower grades, with nothing but hard work and obscurity before him,—this was at the very beginning of the reign of the Emperor Alexander. He was obliged reluctantly to return to the country to his father. How squalid, poor, and wretched his parents' home seemed to him! The stagnation and sordidness of life in the country offended him at every step. He was consumed with *ennui*. Moreover, every one in the house, except his mother, looked at him with unfriendly eyes. His father did not like his town manners, his swallow-tail coats, his frilled shirt-fronts, his books, his flute, his fastidious ways, in which he detected—not incorrectly—a disgust for his surroundings; he was for ever complaining and grumbling at his son. 'Nothing here,' he used to say, 'is to his taste; at table he is all in a fret, and doesn't eat; he can't bear the heat and close smell of the room; the sight of folks drunk upsets him, one daren't beat any one before him; he doesn't want to go into the government service; he's weakly, as you see, in health; fie upon him, the milksop! And all this because he's got his head full of Voltaire.' The old man had a special dislike to Voltaire, and the 'fanatic' Diderot, though he had not read a word of their works; reading was not in his line. Piotr Andreitch was not mistaken; his son's head for that matter was indeed full of both Diderot and Voltaire, and not only of them alone, of Rousseau too, and Helvetius, and many other writers of the same kind—but they were in his head only. The retired abbé and encyclopédist who had been Ivan Petrovitch's tutor had taken pleasure in pouring all the wisdom of the eighteenth century into his pupil, and he was simply brimming over with it; it was there in him, but without mixing in his blood, nor penetrating to his soul, nor shaping itself in any firm convictions. . . . But, indeed, could one expect convictions from a young man of fifty years ago, when even at the present day we have not succeeded in attaining them? The guests, too, who frequented his father's house, were oppressed by Ivan Petrovitch's presence; he regarded them with loathing, they were afraid of him; and with his sister Glafira, who was twelve years older than he, he could not get on at all. This Glafira was a strange creature; she was ugly, crooked, and spare, with severe, wide-open eyes, and thin compressed lips. In her face, her voice, and her quick angular movements, she took after her grandmother, the gipsy, Andrei's wife. Obstinate and fond of power, she would not even hear of marriage. The return of Ivan Petrovitch did not fit in with her plans; while the Princess Kubensky kept him with her, she had hoped to receive at least half of her father's estate; in her avarice, too, she was like her grandmother. Besides, Glafira envied her brother, he was so well educated, spoke such good French with a Parisian accent, while she was scarcely able to pronounce 'bon jour' or 'comment vous portez-vous.' To be sure, her parents did not know any French, but that was no comfort to her. Ivan Petrovitch did not know what to do with himself for wretchedness and ennui; he had spent hardly a year in the country, but that year seemed to him as long as ten. The only consolation he could find was in talking to his mother, and he would sit for whole hours in her low-pitched rooms, listening to the good woman's simple-hearted prattle, and eating preserves. It so happened that among Anna Pavlovna's maids there was one very pretty girl with clear soft eyes and refined features, Malanya by name, a modest intelligent creature. She took his fancy at first sight, and he fell in love with her: he fell in love with her timid movements, her bashful answers, her gentle voice and gentle smile; every day she seemed sweeter to him. And she became devoted to Ivan Petrovitch with all the strength of her soul, as none but Russian girls can be devoted—and she gave herself to him. In the large household of a country squire nothing can long be kept a secret; soon every one knew of the love between the young master and Malanya; the gossip even reached the ears of Piotr Andreitch himself. Under other circumstances, he would probably have paid no attention to a matter of so little importance, but he had long had a grudge against his son, and was delighted at an opportunity of humiliating the town-bred wit and dandy. A storm of fuss and clamour was raised; Malanya was locked up in the pantry, Ivan Petrovitch was summoned into his father's presence. Anna Pavlovna too ran up at the hubbub. She began trying to pacify her husband, but Piotr Andreitch would hear nothing. He pounced down like a hawk on his son, reproached him with immorality, with godlessness, with hypocrisy; he took the opportunity to vent on him all the wrath against the Princess Kubensky that had been simmering within him, and lavished abusive epithets upon him. At first Ivan Petrovitch was silent and held himself in, but when his father thought fit to threaten him with a shameful punishment he could endure it no longer. 'Ah,' he thought, 'the fanatic Diderot is brought out again, then I will take the bull by the horns, I will astonish you all.' And thereupon with a calm and even voice, though quaking inwardly in every limb, Ivan Petrovitch declared to his father, that there was no need to reproach him with immorality; that though he did not intend to justify his fault he was ready to make amends for it, the more willingly as he felt himself to be superior to every kind of prejudice—and in fact—was ready to marry Malanya. In uttering these words Ivan Petrovitch did undoubtedly attain his object; he so astonished Piotr Andreitch that the latter stood open-eyed, and was struck dumb for a moment; but instantly he came to himself, and just as he was, in a dressing-gown bordered with squirrel fur and slippers on his bare feet, he flew at Ivan Petrovitch with his fists. The latter, as though by design, had that morning arranged his locks à la Titus, and put on a new English coat of a blue colour, high boots with little tassels and very tight modish buckskin breeches. Anna Pavlovna shrieked with all her might and covered her face with her hands; but her son ran over the whole house, dashed out into the courtyard, rushed into the kitchen-garden, into the pleasure-grounds, and flew across into the road, and kept running without looking round till at last he ceased to hear the heavy tramp of his father's steps behind him and his shouts, jerked out with effort, 'Stop you scoundrel!' he cried, 'stop! or I will curse you!' Ivan Petrovitch took refuge with a neighbour,

a small landowner, and Piotr Andreïtch returned home worn
out and perspiring, and without taking breath, announced
that he should deprive his son of his blessing and inheritance,
gave orders that all his foolish books should be burnt, and
that the girl Malanya should be sent to a distant village without loss of time. Some kind-hearted people found out Ivan
Petrovitch and let him know everything. Humiliated and
driven to fury, he vowed he would be revenged on his father,
and the same night lay in wait for the peasant's cart in which
Malanya was being driven away, carried her off by force,
galloped off to the nearest town with her and married her.
He was supplied with money by the neighbour, a good-
natured retired marine officer, a confirmed tippler, who took an
intense delight in every kind of—as he expressed it—romantic story.

The next day Ivan Petrovitch wrote an ironically cold
and polite letter to Piotr Andreitch, and set off to the
village where lived his second cousin, Dmitri Pestov, with
his sister, already known to the reader, Marfa Timofyevna.
He told them all, announced his intention to go to Petersburg to try to obtain a post there, and besought them, at
least for a time, to give his wife a home. At the word
'wife' he shed tears, and in spite of his city breeding and
philosophy he bowed himself in humble, supplicating Russian
fashion at his relation's feet, and even touched the ground
with his forehead. The Pestovs, kind-hearted and compas-
sionate people, readily agreed to his request. He stayed with
them for three weeks, secretly expecting a reply from his
father; but no reply came—and there was no chance of a
reply coming.

Piotr Andreitch, on hearing of his son's marriage, took
to his bed, and forbade Ivan Petrovitch's name to be
mentioned before him; but his mother, without her
husband's knowledge, borrowed from the rector, and sent
500 roubles and a little image to his wife. She was afraid
to write, but sent a message to Ivan Petrovitch by a lean
peasant, who could walk fifty miles a day, that he was not
to take it too much to heart; that, please God, all would be
arranged, and his father's wrath would be turned to kindness; that she too would have preferred a different daughter-

in-law, but that she sent Malanya Sergyevna her motherly blessing. The lean peasant received a rouble, asked permission to see the new young mistress, to whom he happened to be godfather, kissed her hand and ran off at his best speed.

And Ivan Petrovitch set off to Petersburg with a light heart. An unknown future awaited him; poverty perhaps menaced him, but he had broken away from the country life he detested, and above all, he had not been false to his teachers, he had actually put into practice the doctrines of Rousseau, Diderot, and *la Déclaration des droits de l'homme*. A sense of having done his duty, of triumph, and of pride filled his soul; and indeed the separation from his wife did not greatly afflict him; he would have been more perturbed by the necessity of being constantly with her. That deed was done, now he wanted to set about doing something fresh. In Petersburg, contrary to his own expectations, he met with success; the Princess Kubensky, whom Monsieur Courtin had by that time deserted, but who was still living, in order to make up in some way to her nephew for having wronged him, gave him introductions to all her friends, and presented him with 5000 roubles—almost all that remained of her money—and a Lepikovsky watch with his monogram encircled by Cupids.

Three months had not passed before he obtained a position in a Russian embassy to London, and in the first English vessel that sailed (steamers were not even talked of then) he crossed the sea. A few months later he received a letter from Pestov. The good-natured landowner congratulated Ivan Petrovitch on the birth of a son, who had been born into the world in the village of Pokrovskoe on the 20th of August 1807, and named Fedor, in honour of the holy martyr Fedor Stratilat. On account of her extreme weakness Malanya Sergyevna added only a few lines; but these few lines were a surprise, for Ivan Petrovitch had not known that Marfa Timofyevna had taught his wife to read and write. Ivan Petrovitch did not long abandon himself to the sweet emotion of parental feeling; he was dancing attendance on a notorious Phryne or Lais of the day (classical names were still in vogue at that date) ; the Peace of Tilsit had only just been concluded and all the world was hurrying after pleasure, in a giddy whirl of dissipation, and his head had been turned by the black eyes of a bold beauty. He had very little money, but he was lucky at cards, made many acquaintances, took part in all entertainments, in a word, he was in the swim.

CHAPTER IX

FOR a long time the old Lavretsky could not forgive his son for his marriage. If six months later Ivan Petrovitch had come to him with a penitent face and had thrown himself at his feet, he would, very likely, have pardoned him, after giving him a pretty severe scolding, and a tap with his stick by way of intimidating him, but Ivan Petrovitch went on living abroad and apparently did not care a straw. 'Be silent! I dare you to speak of it,' Piotr Andreitch said to his wife every time she ventured to try to incline him to mercy. 'The puppy, he ought to thank God for ever that I have not laid my curse upon him; my father would have killed him, the worthless scamp, with his own hands, and he would have done right too.' At such terrible speeches Anna Pavlovna could only cross herself secretly. As for Ivan Petrovitch's wife, Piotr Andreitch at first would not even hear her name, and in answer to a letter of Pestov's, in which he mentioned his daughter-in-law, he went so far as to send him word that he knew nothing of any daughter-in-law, and that it was forbidden by law to harbour run-away wenches, a fact which he thought it his duty to remind him of. But later on, he was softened by hearing of the birth of a grandson, and he gave orders secretly that inquiries should be made about the health of the mother, and sent her a little money, also as though it did not come from him. Fedya was not a year old before Anna Pavlovna fell ill with a fatal complaint. A few days before her end, when she could no longer leave her bed, with timid tears in her eyes, fast growing dim, she informed her husband in the presence of the priest that she wanted to see her daughter-in-law and bid her farewell, and to give her grandchild her blessing. The heart-broken old man soothed her, and at once sent off his own carriage for his daughter-in-law, for the first time giving her the title of Malanya Sergyevna. Malanya came with her son and Maria Timofyevna,

who would not on any consideration allow her to go alone,
and was unwilling to expose her to any indignity. Half dead
with fright, Malanya Sergyevna went into Piotr Andreitch's
room. A nurse followed, carrying Fedya. Piotr Andreitch
looked at her without speaking; she went up to kiss his hand;
her trembling lips were only just able to touch it with a
silent kiss.

'Well, my upstart lady,' he brought out at last, 'how do
you do? let us go to the mistress.'

He got up and bent over Fedya; the baby smiled and held
out his little white hands to him. This changed the old man's
mood.

'Ah,' he said, 'poor little one, you were pleading for your
father; I will not abandon you, little bird.'

Directly Malanya Sergyevna entered Anna Pavlovna's
bedroom, she fell on her knees near the door. Anna Pavlovna
beckoned her to come to her bedside, embraced her, and
blessed her son; then turning a face contorted by cruel
suffering to her husband she made an effort to speak.

'I know, I know, what you want to ask,' said Piotr Andreitch; 'don't fret yourself, she shall stay with us, and I will
forgive Vanka for her sake.'

With an effort Anna Pavlovna took her husband's hand
and pressed it to her lips. The same evening she breathed
her last.

Piotr Andreitch kept his word. He informed his son that
for the sake of his mother's dying hours, and for the sake
of the little Fedor, he sent him his blessing and was keeping
Malanya Sergyevna in his house. Two rooms on the ground
floor were devoted to her; he presented her to his most honoured guests, the one-eyed brigadier Skurehin, and his wife,
and bestowed on her two waiting-maids and a page for er-
rands. Marfa Timofyevna took leave of her; she detested
Glafira, and in the course of one day had fallen out with her
three times.

It was a painful and embarrassing position at first for poor
Malanya, but, after a while, she learnt to bear it, and grew
used to her father-in-law. He, too, grew accustomed to her,
and even fond of her, though he scarcely ever spoke to her,
and a certain involuntary contempt was perceptible even in

his signs of affection to her. Malanya Sergeyvna had most to put up with from her sister-in-law. Even during her mother's lifetime, Glafira had succeeded by degrees in getting the whole household into her hands; every one, from her father downwards, submitted to her rule; not a piece of sugar was given out without her sanction; she would rather have died than shared her authority with another mistress —and with such a mistress! Her brother's marriage had incensed her even more than Piotr Andreitch; she set herself to give the upstart a lesson, and Malanya Sergyevna from the very first hour was her slave. And, indeed, how was she to contend against the masterful, haughty Glafira, submissive, constantly bewildered, timid, and weak in health as she was? Not a day passed without Glafira reminding her of her former position, and commending her for not forgetting herself. Malanya Sergyevna could have reconciled herself readily to these reminiscences and commendations, however bitter they might be—but Fedya was taken away from her, that was what crushed her. On the pretext that she was not capable of undertaking his education, she was scarcely allowed to see him; Glafira set herself to that task; the child was put absolutely under her control. Malanya Sergyevna began, in her distress, to beseech Ivan Petrovitch, in her letters, to return home soon. Piotr Andreitch himself wanted to see his son, but Ivan Petrovitch did nothing but write. He thanked his father on his wife's account, and for the money sent him, promised to return quickly—and did not come. The year 1812 at last summoned him home from abroad. When they met again, after six years' absence, the father embraced his son, and not by a single word made allusion to their former differences; it was not a time for that now, all Russia was rising up against the enemy, and both of them felt that they had Russian blood in their veins. Piotr Andreitch equipped a whole regiment of volunteers at his own expense. But the war came to an end, the danger was over; Ivan Petrovitch began to be bored again, and again he felt drawn away to the distance, to the world in which he had grown up, and where he felt himself at home. Malanya Sergyevna could not keep him; she meant too little to him. Even her fondest hopes came to nothing; her hus-

band considered that it was much more suitable to intrust
Fedya's education to Glafira. Ivan Petrovitch's poor wife
could not bear this blow, she could not bear a second separation; in a few days, without a murmur, she quietly passed
away. All her life she had never been able to oppose anything, and she did not struggle against her illness. When
she could no longer speak, when the shadows of death were
already on her face, her features expressed, as of old, bewildered resignation and constant, uncomplaining meekness;
with the same dumb submissiveness she looked at Glafira, and
just as Anna Pavlovna kissed her husband's hand on her
deathbed, she kissed Glafira's, commending to her, to Glafira,
her only son. So ended the earthly existence of this good
and gentle creature, torn, God knows why, like an uprooted
tree from its natural soil and at once thrown down with its
roots in the air; she had faded and passed away, leaving no
trace, and no one mourned for her. Malanya Sergyevna's
maids pitied her, and so did even Piotr Andreitch. The old
man missed her silent presence. 'Forgive me . . . farewell,
my meek one!' he whispered, as he took leave of her the last
time in church. He wept as he threw a handful of earth in
the grave.

He did not survive her long, not more than five years. In
the winter of the year 1819, he died peacefully in Moscow,
where he had moved with Glafira and his grandson, and left
instructions that he should be buried beside Anna Pavlovna
and 'Malasha.' Ivan Petrovitch was then in Paris amusing
himself; he had retired from service soon after 1815. When
he heard of his father's death he decided to return to Russia.
It was necessary to make arrangements for the management
of the property. Fedya, according to Glafira's letter, had
reached his twelfth year, and the time had come to set about
his education in earnest.

CHAPTER X

IVAN PETROVITCH returned to Russia an Anglomaniac. His short-cropped hair, his starched shirt-front, his long-skirted pea-green overcoat with its multitude of capes, the sour expression of his face, something abrupt and at the same time indifferent in his behaviour, his way of speaking through his teeth, his sudden wooden laugh, the absence of smiles, his exclusively political or politico-economical conversation, his passion for roast beef and port wine—everything about him breathed, so to speak, of Great Britain. But, marvellous to relate, while he had been transformed into an Anglomaniac, Ivan Petrovitch had at the same time become a patriot, at least he called himself a patriot, though he knew Russia little, had not retained a single Russian habit, and expressed himself in Russian rather queerly; in ordinary conversation, his language was spiritless and inanimate and constantly interspersed with Gallicisms.

Ivan Petrovitch brought with him a few schemes in manuscript, relating to the administration and reform of the government; he was much displeased with everything he saw; the lack of system especially aroused his spleen. On his meeting with his sister, at the first word he announced to her that he was determined to introduce radical reforms, that henceforth everything to do with him would be on a different system. Glafira Petrovna made no reply to Ivan Petrovitch; she only ground her teeth and thought: 'Where am I to take refuge?' After she was back in the country, however, with her brother and nephew, her fears were soon set at rest. In the house, certainly, some changes were made; idlers and dependants met with summary dismissal; among them two old women were made to suffer, one blind, another broken down by paralysis; and also a decrepit major of the days of Catherine, who, on account of his really abnormal appetite, was fed on nothing but black bread and lentils. The order went forth not to admit the guests of former days; they were replaced by a distant neighbour, a certain fair-haired, scrofulous baron, a very well educated and very stupid man. New furniture was brought from Moscow; spittoons were introduced, and bells and washing-stands; and breakfast began to be served in a different way; foreign wines replaced vodka and syrups; the servants were put into new livery; a motto was added to the family arms: *in recto virtus* . . . In reality, Glafira's power suffered no diminution; the giving out and buying of stores still depended on her. The Alsatian steward, brought from abroad, tried to fight it out with her and lost his place, in spite of the master's protection. As for the management of the house, and the administration of the estate, Glafira Petrovna had undertaken these duties also; in spite of Ivan Petrovitch's intention,—more than once expressed—to breathe new life into this chaos, everything remained as before; only the rent was in some places raised, the mistress was more strict, and the peasants were forbidden to apply direct to Ivan Petrovitch. The patriot had already a great contempt for his fellow-countrymen. Ivan Petrovitch's system was applied in its full force only to Fedya; his education really underwent a 'radical reformation;' his father devoted himself exclusively to it.

CHAPTER XI

UNTIL Ivan Petrovitch's return from abroad, Fedya was, as already related, in the hands of Glafira Petrovna. He was not eight years old when his mother died; he did not see her every day, and loved her passionately; the memory of her, of her pale and gentle face, of her dejected looks and timid caresses, were imprinted on his heart for ever; but he vaguely understood her position in the house; he felt that between him and her there existed a barrier which she dared not and could not break down. He was shy of his father, and, indeed, Ivan Petrovitch on his side never caressed him; his grandfather sometimes patted him on the head and gave him his hand to kiss, but he thought him and called him a little fool. After the death of Malanya Sergyevna, his aunt finally got him under her control. Fedya was afraid of her: he was afraid of her bright sharp eyes and her harsh voice; he dared not utter a sound in her presence; often, when he only moved a little in his chair, she would hiss out at once: 'What are you doing? sit still.' On Sundays, after mass, he was allowed to play, that is to say, he was given a thick book, a mysterious book, the work of a certain Maximovitch-Ambodik, entitled 'Symbols and Emblems.' This book was a medley of about a thousand mostly very enigmatical pictures, and as many enigmatical interpretations of them in five languages. Cupid —naked and very puffy in the body—played a leading part in these illustrations. In one of them, under the heading, 'Saffron and the Rainbow,' the interpretation appended was: 'Of this, the influence is vast;' opposite another, entitled 'A heron, flying with a violet in his beak,' stood the inscription: 'To thee they are all known.' 'Cupid and the bear licking his fur' was inscribed, 'Little by little.' Fedya used to ponder over these pictures; he knew them all to the minutest details; some of them, always the same ones, used to set him dreaming, and afforded him food for meditation; he knew no other amusements. When the time came to teach him languages and music, Glafira Petrovna engaged, for next to nothing, an old maid, a Swede, with eyes like a hare's, who spoke French and German with mistakes in every alternate word, played after a fashion on the piano, and above all, salted cucumbers to perfection. In the society of this governess, his aunt, and the old servant maid, Vassilyevna, Fedya spent four whole years. Often he would sit in the corner with his 'Emblems'; he sat there endlessly; there was a scent of geranium in the low pitched room, the solitary candle burnt dim, the cricket chirped monotonously, as though it were weary, the little clock ticked away hurriedly on the wall, a mouse scratched stealthily and gnawed at the wall-paper, and the three old women, like the Fates, swiftly and silently plied their knitting-kneedles, the shadows raced after their hands and quivered strangely in the half darkness, and strange, half dark ideas swarmed in the child's brain. No one would have called Fedya an interesting child; he was rather pale, but stout, clumsily built and awkward—a thorough peasant, as Glafira Petrovna said; the pallor would soon have vanished from his cheeks, if he had been allowed oftener to be in the open air. He learnt fairly quickly, though he was often lazy; he never cried, but at times he was overtaken by a fit of savage obstinacy; then no one could soften him. Fedya loved no one among those around him. . . . Woe to the heart that has not loved in youth!

Thus Ivan Petrovitch found him, and without loss of time he set to work to apply his system to him.

'I want above all to make a man, *un homme*, of him,' he said to Glafira Petrovna, 'and not only a man, but a Spartan.' Ivan Petrovitch began carrying out his intentions by putting his son in a Scotch kilt; the twelve-year-old boy had to go about with bare knees and a plume stuck in his Scotch cap. The Swedish lady was replaced by a young Swiss tutor, who was versed in gymnastics to perfection. Music, as a pursuit unworthy of a man, was discarded. The natural sciences, international law, mathematics, carpentry, after Jean-Jacques Rousseau's precept, and heraldry, to encourage chivalrous feelings, were what the future 'man' was to be occupied with.

He was waked at four o'clock in the morning, splashed at
once with cold water and set to running round a high pole
with a cord; he had only one meal a day, consisting of a
single dish; rode on horseback; shot with a cross-bow; at
every convenient opportunity he was exercised in acquiring
after his parent's example firmness of will, and every evening
he inscribed in a special book an account of the day and his
impressions; and Ivan Petrovitch on his side wrote him
instructions in French in which he called him *mon fils,* and
addressed him as *vous.* In Russian Fedya called his father
thou, but did not dare to sit down in his presence. The
'system' dazed the boy, confused and cramped his intellect,
but his health on the other hand was benefited by the new
manner of his life; at first he fell into a fever but soon recovered and began to grow stout and strong. His father was
proud of him and called him in his strange jargon 'a child
of nature, my creation.' When Fedya had reached his six-
teenth year, Ivan Petrovitch thought it his duty in good time
to instil into him a contempt for the female sex; and the
young Spartan, with timidity in his heart and the first down
on his lip, full of sap and strength and young blood, already
tried to seem indifferent, cold, and rude.

Meanwhile time was passing. Ivan Petrovitch spent the
greater part of the year in Lavriky (that was the name of
the principal estate inherited from his ancestors). But in
the winter he used to go to Moscow alone; there he stayed
at a tavern, diligently visited the club, made speeches and
developed his plans in drawing-rooms, and in his behaviour
was more than ever Anglomaniac, grumbling and political.
But the year 1825 came and brought much sorrow. Intimate
friends and acquaintances of Ivan Petrovitch underwent
painful experiences. Ivan Petrovitch made haste to withdraw into the country and shut himself up in his house.
Another year passed by, and suddenly Ivan Petrovitch grew
feeble, and ailing; his health began to break up. He, the
free-thinker, began to go to church and have prayers put
up for him; he, the European, began to sit in steam-baths, to
dine at two o'clock, to go to bed at nine, and to doze off to
the sound of the chatter of the old steward; he, the man of
political ideas, burnt all his schemes, all his correspondence,

trembled before the governor, and was uneasy at the sight of the police-captain; he, the man of iron will, whimpered and complained, when he had a gumboil or when they gave him a plate of cold soup. Glafira Petrovna again took control of everything in the house; once more the overseers, bailiffs and simple peasants began to come to the back stairs to speak to the 'old witch,' as the servants called her. The change in Ivan Petrovitch produced a powerful impression on his son. He had now reached his nineteenth year, and had begun to reflect and to emancipate himself from the hand that pressed like a weight upon him. Even before this time he had observed a little discrepancy between his father's words and deeds, between his wide liberal theories and his harsh petty despotism; but he had not expected such a complete breakdown. His confirmed egoism was patent now in everything. Young Lavretsky was getting ready to go to Moscow, to prepare for the university, when a new unexpected calamity overtook Ivan Petrovitch; he became blind, and hopelessly blind, in one day.

Having no confidence in the skill of Russian doctors, he began to make efforts to obtain permission to go abroad. It was refused. Then he took his son with him and for three whole years was wandering about Russia, from one doctor to another, incessantly moving from one town to another, and driving his physicians, his son, and his servants to despair by his cowardice and impatience. He returned to Lavriky a perfect wreck, a tearful and capricious child. Bitter days followed, every one had much to put up with from him. Ivan Petrovitch was only quiet when he was dining; he had never been so greedy and eaten so much; all the rest of the time he gave himself and others no peace. He prayed, cursed his fate, abused himself, abused politics, his system, abused everything he had boasted of and prided himself upon, everything he had held up to his son as a model; he declared that he believed in nothing and then began to pray again; he could not put up with one instant of solitude, and expected his household to sit by his chair continually day and night, and entertain him with stories, which he constantly interrupted with exclamations, 'You are for ever lying, . . . a pack of nonsense!'

Glafira Petrovna was specially necessary to him; he absolutely could not get on without her—and to the end she always carried out every whim of the sick man, though sometimes she could not bring herself to answer at once, for fear the sound of her voice should betray her inward anger. Thus he lingered on for two years and died on the first day of May, when he had been brought out on to the balcony into the sun. 'Glasha, Glashka! soup, soup, old foo'—— his halting tongue muttered and before he had articulated the last word, it was silent for ever. Glafira Petrovna, who had only just taken the cup of soup from the hands of the steward, stopped, looked at her brother's face, slowly made a large sign of the cross and turned away in silence; and his son, who happened to be there, also said nothing; he leaned on the railing of the balcony and gazed a long while into the garden, all fragrant and green, and shining in the rays of the golden sunshine of spring. He was twenty-three years old; how terribly, how imperceptibly quickly those twenty-three years had passed by! . . . Life was opening before him.

CHAPTER XII

AFTER burying his father and intrusting to the unchanged Glafira Petrovna the management of his estate and superintendence of his bailiffs, young Lavretsky went to Moscow, whither he felt drawn by a vague but strong attraction. He recognised the defects of his education, and formed the resolution, as far as possible, to regain lost ground. In the last five years he had read much and seen something; he had many stray ideas in his head; any professor might have envied some of his acquirements, but at the same time he did not know much that every schoolboy would have learnt long ago. Lavretsky was aware of his limitations; he was secretly conscious of being eccentric. The Anglomaniac had done his son an ill turn; his whimsical education had produced its fruits. For long years he had submitted unquestioningly to his father; when at last he began to see through him, the evil was already done, his habits were deeply-rooted. He could not get on with people; at twenty-three years old, with an unquenchable thirst for love in his shy heart, he had never yet dared to look one woman in the face. With his intellect, clear and sound, but somewhat heavy, with his tendencies to obstinacy, contemplation, and indolence he ought from his earliest years to have been thrown into the stream of life, and he had been kept instead in artificial seclusion. And now the magic circle was broken, but he continued to remain within it, prisoned and pent up within himself. It was ridiculous at his age to put on a student's dress, but he was not afraid of ridicule; his Spartan education had at least the good effect of developing in him a contempt for the opinion of others, and he put on, without embarrassment, the academical uniform. He entered the section of physics and mathematics. Robust, rosy-cheeked, bearded, and taciturn, he produced a strange impression on his companions; they did not suspect that this austere man, who came so punctually to the lectures in

46

a wide village sledge with a pair of horses, was inwardly almost a child. He appeared to them to be a queer kind of pedant; they did not care for him, and made no overtures to him, and he avoided them. During the first two years he spent in the university, he only made acquaintance with one student, from whom he took lessons in Latin. This student, Mihalevitch by name, an enthusiast and a poet, who loved Lavretsky sincerely, by chance became the means of bringing about an important change in his destiny.

One day at the theatre—Motchalov was then at the height of his fame and Lavretsky did not miss a single performance —he saw in a box in the front tier a young girl, and though no woman ever came near his grim figure without setting his heart beating, it had never beaten so violently before. The young girl sat motionless, leaning with her elbows on the velvet of the box; the light of youth and life played in every feature of her dark, oval, lovely face; subtle intelligence was expressed in the splendid eyes which gazed softly and attentively from under her fine brows, in the swift smile on her expressive lips, in the very pose of her head, her hands, her neck. She was exquisitely dressed. Beside her sat a yellow and wrinkled woman of forty-five, with a low neck, in a black headdress, with a toothless smile on her intently-preoccupied and empty face, and in the inner recesses of the box was visible an elderly man in a wide frock-coat and high cravat, with an expression of dull dignity and a kind of ingratiating distrustfulness in his little eyes, with dyed moustache and whiskers, a large meaningless forehead and wrinkled cheeks, by every sign a retired general. Lavretsky did not take his eyes off the girl who had made such an impression on him; suddenly the door of the box opened and Mihalevitch went in. The appearance of this man, almost his one acquaintance in Moscow, in the society of the one girl who was absorbing his whole attention, struck him as curious and significant. Continuing to gaze into the box, he observed that all the persons in it treated Mihalevitch as an old friend. The performance on the stage ceased to interest Lavretsky, even Motchalov, though he was that evening in his 'best form,' did not produce the usual impression on him. At one very pathetic part, Lavretsky involuntarily looked at

his beauty: she was bending forward, her cheeks glowing
under the influence of his persistent gaze, her eyes, which
were fixed on the stage, slowly turned and rested on him.
All night he was haunted by those eyes. The skilfully constructed barriers were broken down at last; he was in a
shiver and a fever, and the next day he went to Mihalevitch.
From him he learnt that the name of the beauty was Varvara
Pavlovna Korobyin; that the old people sitting with her in
the box were her father and mother; and that he, Mihalevitch, had become acquainted with them a year before, while
he was staying at Count N.'s, in the position of a tutor, near
Moscow. The enthusiast spoke in rapturous praise of Varvara Pavlovna. 'My dear fellow,' he exclaimed with the
impetuous ring in his voice peculiar to him, 'that girl is a
marvellous creature, a genius, an artist in the true sense of
the word, and she is very good too.' Noticing from Lavretsky's inquiries the impression Varvara Pavlovna had made
on him, he himself proposed to introduce him to her, adding
that he was like one of the family with them; that the general was not at all proud, and the mother was so stupid she
could not say 'Bo' to a goose. Lavretsky blushed, muttered
something unintelligible, and ran away. For five whole
days he was struggling with his timidity; on the sixth day
the young Spartan got into a new uniform and placed himself at Mihalevitch's disposal. The latter being his own
valet, confined himself to combing his hair—and both betook
themselves to the Korobyins.

CHAPTER XIII

VARVARA PAVLOVNA'S father, Pavel Petrovitch
Korobyin, a retired general-major, had spent his
whole time on duty in Petersburg. He had had the
reputation in his youth of a good dancer and driller. Through
poverty, he had served as adjutant to two or three generals
of no distinction, and had married the daughter of one of
them with a dowry of twenty-five thousand roubles. He
mastered all the science of military discipline and manœuvres
to the minutest niceties, he went on in harness, till at last,
after twenty-five years' service, he received the rank of a
general and the command of a regiment. Then he might
have relaxed his efforts and have quietly secured his
pecuniary position. Indeed this was what he reckoned upon
doing, but he managed things a little incautiously. He
devised a new method of speculating with public funds—the
method seemed an excellent one in itself—but he neglected
to bribe in the right place, and was consequently informed
against, and a more than unpleasant, a disgraceful scandal
followed. The general got out of the affair somehow, but
his career was ruined; he was advised to retire from active
duty. For two years he lingered on in Petersburg, hoping to
drop into some snug berth in the civil service, but no such
snug berth came in his way. His daughter had left school,
his expenses were increasing every day. Resigning himself
to his fate, he decided to remove to Moscow for the sake
of the greater cheapness of living, and took a tiny low-
pitched house in the Old Stables Road, with a coat of arms
seven feet long on the roof, and there began the life of a
retired general at Moscow on an income of 2750 roubles a
year. Moscow is a hospitable city, ready to welcome all
stray comers, generals by preference. Pavel Petrovitch's
heavy figure, which was not quite devoid of martial dignity,
however, soon began to be seen in the best drawing-rooms
in Moscow. His bald head with its tufts of dyed hair, and

49

the soiled ribbon of the Order of St. Anne which he wore
over a cravat of the colour of a raven's wing, began to be
familiar to all the pale and listless young men who hang
morosely about the card-tables while dancing is going on.
Pavel Petrovitch knew how to gain a footing in society; he
spoke little, but, from old habit, condescendingly—though, of
course, not when he was talking to persons of a higher rank
than his own. He played cards carefully; ate moderately
at home, but consumed enough for six at parties. Of his
wife there is scarcely anything to be said. Her name was
Kalliopa Karlovna. There was always a tear in her left
eye, on the strength of which Kalliopa Karlovna (she was,
one must add, of German extraction) considered herself a
woman of great sensibility. She was always in a state of
nervous agitation, seemed as though she were ill-nourished,
and wore a tight velvet dress, a cap, and tarnished hollow
bracelets. The only daughter of Pavel Petrovitch and Kalliopa Karlovna, Varvara Pavlovna, was only just seventeen
when she left the boarding-school, in which she had been
reckoned, if not the prettiest, at least the cleverest pupil and
the best musician, and where she had taken a decoration.
She was not yet nineteen, when Lavretsky saw her for the
first time.

CHAPTER XIV

THE young Spartan's legs shook under him when Mihalevitch conducted him into the rather shabbily furnished drawing-room of the Korobyins, and presented him to them. But his overwhelming feeling of timidity soon disappeared. In the general the good-nature innate in all Russians was intensified by that special kind of geniality which is peculiar to all people who have done something disgraceful; the general's lady was as it were overlooked by every one; and as for Varvara Pavlovna, she was so self-possessed and easily cordial that every one at once felt at home in her presence; besides, about all her fascinating person, her smiling eyes, her faultlessly sloping shoulders and rosy-tinged white hands, her light and yet languid movements, the very sound of her voice, slow and sweet, there was an impalpable, subtle charm, like a faint perfume, voluptuous, tender, soft, though still modest, something which is hard to translate into words, but which moved and kindled—and timidity was not the feeling it kindled. Lavretsky turned the conversation on the theatre, on the performance of the previous day; she at once began herself to discuss Motchalov, and did not confine herself to sighs and interjections only, but uttered a few true observations full of feminine insight in regard to his acting. Mihalevitch spoke about music; she sat down without ceremony to the piano, and very correctly played some of Chopin's mazurkas, which were then just coming into fashion. Dinner-time came; Lavretsky would have gone away, but they made him stay: at dinner the general regaled him with excellent Lafitte, which the general's lackey hurried off in a street-sledge to Dupré's to fetch. Late in the evening Lavretsky returned home; for a long while he sat without undressing, covering his eyes with his hands in the stupefaction of enchantment. It seemed to him that now for the first time he understood what made life worth living; all his previous assumptions, all his plans, all that rubbish and nonsense had vanished into nothing at once; all his soul was absorbed in one feeling, in one desire—in the desire of happiness, of possession, of love, the sweet love of a woman. From that day he began to go often to the Korobyins. Six months later he spoke to Varvara Pavlovna, and offered her his hand. His offer was accepted; the general had long before, almost on the eve of Lavretsky's first visit, inquired of Mihalevitch how many serfs Lavretsky owned; and indeed Varvara Pavlovna, who through the whole time of the young man's courtship, and even at the very moment of his declaration, had preserved her customary composure and clearness of mind—Varvara Pavlovna too was very well aware that her suitor was a wealthy man; and Kalliopa Karlovna thought *'meine Tochter macht eine schöne Partie,'* and bought herself a new cap.

CHAPTER XV

AND so his offer was accepted, but on certain conditions. In the first place, Lavretsky was at once to leave the university; who would be married to a student, and what a strange idea too—how could a landowner, a rich man, at twenty-six, take lessons and be at school? Secondly, Varvara Pavlovna took upon herself the labour of ordering and purchasing her trousseau, and even choosing her present from the bridegroom. She had much practical sense, a great deal of taste, and a very great love of comfort, together with a great faculty for obtaining it for herself. Lavretsky was especially struck by this faculty when, immediately after their wedding, he travelled alone with his wife in the comfortable carriage, bought by her, to Lavriky. How carefully everything with which he was surrounded had been thought of, devised and provided beforehand by Varvara Pavlovna! What charming travelling knick-knacks appeared from various snug corners, what fascinating toilet-cases and coffee-pots, and how delightfully Varvara Pavlovna herself made the coffee in the morning! Lavretsky, however, was not at that time disposed to be observant; he was blissful, drunk with happiness; he gave himself up to it like a child. Indeed he was as innocent as a child, this young Hercules. Not in vain was the whole personality of his young wife breathing with fascination; not in vain was her promise to the senses of a mysterious luxury of untold bliss; her fulfilment was richer than her promise. When she reached Lavriky in the very height of the summer, she found the house dark and dirty, the servants absurd and old-fashioned, but she did not think it necessary even to hint at this to her husband. If she had proposed to establish herself at Lavriky, she would have changed everything in it, beginning of course with the house; but the idea of staying in that out-of-the-way corner of the steppes never entered her head for an instant; she lived as in a tent, good-temperedly putting up with all its incon-

veniences, and indulgently making merry over them. Marfa
Timofyevna came to pay a visit to her former charge; Varvara Pavlovna liked her very much, but she did not like
Varvara Pavlovna. The new mistress did not get on with
Glafira Petrovna either; she would have left her in peace, but
old Korobyin wanted to have a hand in the management of
his son-in-law's affairs; to superintend the property of such
a near relative, he said, was not beneath the dignity even of
a general. One must add that Pavel Petrovitch would not
have been above managing the property even of a total
stranger. Varvara Pavlovna conducted her attack very skilfully, without taking any step in advance, apparently completely absorbed in the bliss of the honeymoon, in the peaceful life of the country, in music and reading, she gradually
worked Glafira up to such a point that she rushed one morning, like one possessed, into Lavretsky's study, and throwing
a bunch of keys on the table, she declared that she was not
equal to undertaking the management any longer, and did
not want to stop in the place. Lavretsky, having been suit-
ably prepared beforehand, at once agreed to her departure.
This Glafira Petrovna had not anticipated. 'Very well,' she
said, and her face darkened, 'I see that I am not wanted here!
I know who is driving me out of the home of my fathers.
Only you mark my words, nephew; you will never make a
home anywhere, you will come to be a wanderer for ever.
That is my last word to you.' The same day she went away
to her own little property, and in a week General Korobyin
was there, and with a pleasant melancholy in his looks and
movements he took the superintendence of the whole property into his hands.

In the month of September, Varvara Pavlovna carried her
husband off to Petersburg. She passed two winters in
Petersburg (for the summer she went to stay at Tsarskoe
Selo), in a splendid, light, artistically-furnished flat; they
made many acquaintances among the middle and even higher
ranks of society; went out and entertained a great deal, and
gave the most charming dances and musical evenings. Varvara Pavlovna attracted guests as a fire attracts moths.
Fedor Ivanitch did not altogether like such a frivolous life.
His wife advised him to take some office under government;

but from old association with his father, and also through his own ideas, he was unwilling to enter government service, still he remained in Petersburg for Varvara Pavlovna's pleasure. He soon discovered, however, that no one hindered him from being alone; that it was not for nothing that he had the quietest and most comfortable study in all Petersburg; that his tender wife was even ready to aid him to be alone; and from that time forth all went well. He again applied himself to his own, as he considered, unfinished education; he began again to read, and even began to learn English. It was a strange sight to see his powerful, broad-shouldered figure for ever bent over his writing table, his full-bearded ruddy face half buried in the pages of a dictionary or note-book. Every morning he set to work, then had a capital dinner (Varvara Pavlovna was unrivaled as a housekeeper), and in the evenings he entered an enchanted world of light and perfume, peopled by gay young faces, and the centre of this world was also the careful housekeeper, his wife. She rejoiced his heart by the birth of a son, but the poor child did not live long; it died in the spring, and in the summer, by the advice of the doctors, Lavretsky took his wife abroad to a watering-place. Distraction was essential for her after such a trouble, and her health, too, required a warm climate. The summer and autumn they spent in Germany and Switzerland, and for the winter, as one would naturally expect, they went to Paris. In Paris, Varvara Pavlovna bloomed like a rose, and was able to make herself a little nest as quickly and cleverly as in Petersburg. She found very pretty apartments in one of the quiet but fashionable streets in Paris; she embroidered her husband such a dressing-gown as he had never worn before; engaged a coquettish waiting maid, an excellent cook, and a smart footman, procured a fascinating carriage, and an exquisite piano. Before a week had passed, she crossed the street, wore her shawl, opened her parasol, and put on her gloves in a manner equal to the most true-born Parisian. And she soon drew round herself acquaintances. At first, only Russians visited her, afterwards Frenchmen too, very agreeable, polite, and unmarried, with excellent manners and well-sounding names; they all talked a great deal and very fast,

bowed easily, grimaced agreeably; their white teeth flashed
under their rosy lips—and how they could smile! All of
them brought their friends, and *la belle Madame de Lavretsky* was soon known from Chaussée d'Antin to Rue de
Lille. In those days—it was in 1836—there had not yet
arisen the tribe of journalists and reporters who now swarm
on all sides like ants in an ant-hill; but even then there was
seen in Varvara Pavlovna's salon a certain M. Jules, a gentleman of unprepossessing exterior, with a scandalous reputation, insolent and mean, like all duellists and men who have
been beaten. Varvara Pavlovna felt a great aversion to this
M. Jules, but she received him because he wrote for various
journals, and was incessantly mentioning her, calling her at
one time *Madame de L——tski,* at another *Madame de
——, cette grande dame russe si distinguée, qui demeure
rue de P——* and telling all the world, that is, some hun-
dreds of readers who had nothing to do with Madame de L
——tski, how charming and delightful this lady was; a true
Frenchwoman in intelligence (*une vraie française par l'esprit*)
—Frenchmen have no higher praise than this—what an extraordinary musician she was, and how marvellously she
waltzed (Varvara Pavlovna did in fact waltz so that she
drew all her hearts to the hem of her light flying skirts)——
in a word, he spread her fame through the world, and, whatever one may say, that is pleasant. Mademoiselle Mars had
already left the stage, and Mademoiselle Rachel had not
yet made her appearance; nevertheless, Varvara Pavlovna
was assiduous in visiting the theatres. She went into rap-
tures over Italian music, yawned decorously at the Comédie
Française, and wept at the acting of Madame Dorval in some
ultra-romantic melodrama; and a great thing—Liszt played
twice in her salon, and was so kind, so simple—it was charming! In such agreeable sensations was spent the winter, at
the end of which Varvara Pavlovna was even presented at
court. Fedor Ivanitch, for his part, was not bored, though
his life, at times, weighed rather heavily on him—because
it was empty. He read the papers, listened to the lectures
at the Sorbonne and the Collège de France, followed the
debates in the Chambers, and set to work on a translation of
a well-known scientific treatise on irrigation. 'I am not

wasting my time,' he thought, 'it is all of use; but next winter I must, without fail, return to Russia and set to work.' It is difficult to say whether he had any clear idea of precisely what this work would consist of; and there is no telling whether he would have succeeded in going to Russia in the winter; in the meantime, he was going with his wife to Baden . . . An unexpected incident broke up all his plans.

CHAPTER XVI

HAPPENING to go one day in Varvara Pavlovna's absence into her boudoir, Lavretsky saw on the floor a carefully folded little paper. He mechanically picked it up, unfolded it, and read the following note, written in French:

'Sweet angel Betsy (I never can make up my mind to call you Barbe or Varvara), I waited in vain for you at the corner of the boulevard; come to our little room at half-past one to-morrow. Your stout good-natured husband (*ton gros bonhomme de mari*) is usually buried in his books at that time; we will sing once more the song of your poet *Pouskine* (*de votre poète Pouskine*) that you taught me: "Old husband, cruel husband!" A thousand kisses on your little hands and feet. I await you.

'ERNEST.'

Lavretsky did not at once understand what he had read; he read it a second time, and his head began to swim, the ground began to sway under his feet like the deck of a ship in a rolling sea. He began to cry out and gasp and weep all at the same instant.

He was utterly overwhelmed. He had so blindly believed in his wife; the possibility of deception, of treason, had never presented itself to his mind. This Ernest, his wife's lover, was a fair-haired pretty boy of three-and-twenty, with a little turned-up nose and refined little moustaches, almost the most insignificant of all her acquaintances. A few minutes passed, half an hour passed, Lavretsky still stood, crushing the fatal note in his hands, and gazing senselessly at the floor; across a kind of tempest of darkness pale shapes hovered about him; his heart was numb with anguish; he seemed to be falling, falling — and a bottomless abyss was opening at his feet. A familiar light rustle of a silk dress roused him from his numbness; Varvara Pavlovna in her hat and shawl was returning in haste from her walk. Lavretsky trembled all over and rushed away; he felt that at that instant he was capable of tearing her to pieces, beating her to death, as a peasant might do, strangling her with his own hands. Varvara Pavlovna in amazement tried to stop him; he could only whisper, 'Betsy,'—and ran out of the house.

Lavretsky took a cab and ordered the man to drive him out of the town. All the rest of the day and the whole night he wandered about, constantly stopping short and wringing his hands, at one moment he was mad, and the next he was ready to laugh, was even merry after a fashion. By the morning he grew calm through exhaustion, and went into a wretched tavern in the outskirts, asked for a room and sat down on a chair before the window. He was overtaken by a fit of convulsive yawning. He could scarcely stand upright, his whole body was worn out, and he did not even feel fatigue, though fatigue began to do its work; he sat and gazed and comprehended nothing; he did not understand what had happened to him, why he found himself alone, with his limbs stiff, with a taste of bitterness in his mouth, with a load on his heart, in an empty unfamiliar room; he did not understand what had impelled her, his Varya, to give herself to this Frenchman, and how, knowing herself unfaithful, she could go on being just as calm, just as affectionate, as confidential with him as before! 'I cannot understand it!' his parched lips whispered. 'Who can guarantee now that even in Petersburg' . . . And he did not finish the question, and yawned again, shivering and shaking all over. Memories —bright and gloomy—fretted him alike; suddenly it crossed his mind how some days before she had sat down to the piano and sung before him and Ernest the song, 'Old husband, cruel husband!' He recalled the expression of her face, the strange light in her eyes, and the colour on her cheeks—and he got up from his seat, he would have liked to go to them, to tell them: 'You were wrong to play your tricks on me; my great-grandfather used to hang the peasants up by their ribs, and my grandfather was himself a peasant,' and to kill them both. Then all at once it seemed to him as if all that was happening was a dream, scarcely even a dream, but some kind of foolish joke; that he need only shake himself and look round. . . . He looked round, and like a hawk clutching its captured prey, anguish gnawed deeper and deeper into his heart. To complete it all, Lavretsky had been hoping in a few months to be a father. . . . The past, the future, his whole life was poisoned. He went back at last to Paris, stopped at an hotel and sent M. Ernest's note to Varvara Pavlovna with the following letter:—

'The enclosed scrap of paper will explain everything to you. Let me tell you by the way, that I was surprised at you; you, who are always so careful, to leave such valuable papers lying about.' (Poor Lavretsky had spent hours preparing and gloating over this phrase.) 'I cannot see you again; I imagine that you, too, would hardly desire an interview with me. I am assigning you 15,000 francs a year; I cannot give more. Send your address to the office of the estate. Do what you please; live where you please. I wish you happiness. No answer is needed.'

Lavretsky wrote to his wife that he needed no answer . . . but he waited, he thirsted for a reply, for an explanation of this incredible, inconceivable thing. Varvara Pavlovna wrote him the same day a long letter in French. It put the finishing touch; his last doubts vanished,—and he began to feel ashamed that he had still had any doubt left. Varvara Pavlovna did not attempt to defend herself; her only desire was to see him, she besought him not to condemn her irrevocably. The letter was cold and constrained, though here and there traces of tears were visible. Lavretsky smiled bitterly, and sent word by the messenger that it was all right. Three days later he was no longer in Paris; but he did not go to Russia, but to Italy. He did not know himself why he fixed upon Italy; he did not really care where he went—so long as it was not home. He sent instructions to his steward on the subject of his wife's allowance, and at the same time told him to take all control of his property out of General Korobyin's hands at once, without waiting for him to draw up an account, and to make arrangements for his Excellency's departure from Lavriky; he could picture vividly the confusion, the vain airs of self-importance of the dispossessed general, and in the midst of all his sorrow, he felt a kind of spiteful satisfaction. At the same time he asked Glafira Petrovna by letter to return to Lavriky, and drew up a deed authorising her to take possession; Glafira Petrovna did not return to Lavriky, and printed in the newspapers that the deed was cancelled, which was perfectly unnecessary on her part. Lavretsky kept out of sight in a small Italian town, but for a long time he could not help following his wife's movements. From the newspapers he learned that she had gone from Paris to Baden as she had arranged; her name soon appeared in an article written by the same M. Jules. In this article there was a kind of sympathetic condolence apparent under the habitual playfulness; there was a deep sense of disgust in the soul of Fedor Ivanitch as he read this article. Afterwards he learned that a daughter had been born to him; two months later he received a notification from his steward that Varvara Pavlovna had asked for the first quarter's allowance. Then worse and worse rumours began to reach him; at last, a tragic-comic story was reported with acclamations in all the papers. His wife played an unenviable part in it. It was the finishing stroke; Varvara Pavlovna had become a 'notoriety.'

Lavretsky ceased to follow her movements; but he could not quickly gain mastery over himself. Sometimes he was overcome by such a longing for his wife that he would have given up everything, he thought, even, perhaps . . . could have forgiven her, only to hear her caressing voice again, to feel again her hand in his. Time, however, did not pass in vain. He was not born to be a victim; his healthy nature reasserted its rights. Much became clear to him; even the blow that had fallen on him no longer seemed to him to have been quite unforeseen; he understood his wife,—we can only fully understand those who are near to us, when we are separated from them. He could take up his interests, could work again, though with nothing like his former zeal; scepticism, half-formed already by the experiences of his life, and by his education, took complete possession of his heart. He became indifferent to everything. Four years passed by, and he felt himself strong enough to return to his country, to meet his own people. Without stopping at Petersburg or at Moscow he came to the town of O——, where we parted from him, and whither we will now ask the indulgent reader to return with us.

CHAPTER XVII

THE morning after the day we have described, at ten o'clock, Lavretsky was mounting the steps of the Kalitins' house. He was met by Lisa coming out in her hat and gloves.

'Where are you going?' he asked her.

'To service. It is Sunday.'

'Why do you go to church?'

Lisa looked at him in silent amazement.

'I beg your pardon,' said Lavretsky; 'I—I did not mean to say that; I have come to say good-bye to you, I am starting for my village in an hour.'

'Is it far from here?' asked Lisa.

'Twenty miles.'

Lenotchka made her appearance in the doorway, escorted by a maid.

'Mind you don't forget us,' observed Lisa, and went down the steps.

'And don't you forget me. And listen,' he added, 'you are going to church; while you are there, pray for me, too.'

Lisa stopped short and turned round to him: 'Certainly,' she said, looking him straight in the face, 'I will pray for you too. Come, Lenotchka.'

In the drawing-room Lavretsky found Marya Dmitrievna alone. She was redolent of *eau de Cologne* and mint. She had, as she said, a headache, and had passed a restless night. She received him with her usual languid graciousness and gradually fell into conversation.

'Vladimir Nikolaitch is really a delightful young man, don't you think so?' she asked him.

'What Vladimir Nikolaitch?'

'Panshin to be sure, who was here yesterday. He took a tremendous fancy to you; I will tell you a secret, *mon cher cousin,* he is simply crazy about my Lisa. Well, he is of good family, has a capital position in the service, and a clever fellow, a kammer-yunker, and if it is God's will, I for my part, as a mother, shall be well pleased. My responsibility of course is immense; the happiness of children depends, no doubt, on parents; still I may say, up till now, for better or for worse I have done everything, I alone have been everywhere with them, that is to say, I have educated my children and taught them everything myself. Now, indeed, I have written for a French governess from Madame Boluce.'

Marya Dmitrievna launched into a description of her cares and anxieties and maternal sentiments. Lavretsky listened in silence, turning his hat in his hands. His cold, weary glance embarrassed the gossiping lady.

'And do you like Lisa?' she asked.

'Lisaveta Mihalovna is an excellent girl,' replied Lavretsky, and he got up, took his leave, and went off to Marfa Timofyevna. Marya Dmitrievna looked after him in high displeasure, and thought, 'What a dolt, a regular peasant! Well, now I understand why his wife could not remain faithful to him.'

Marfa Timofyevna was sitting in her room, surrounded by her little court. It consisted of five creatures almost equally near her heart; a big-cropped, learned bullfinch, which she had taken a fancy to because he had lost his accomplishments of whistling and drawing water; a very timid and peaceable little dog, Roska; an ill-tempered cat, Matross; a dark-faced, agile little girl of nine years old, with big eyes and a sharp nose, called Shurotchka; and an elderly woman of fifty-five, in a white cap and a cinnamon-coloured abbreviated jacket, over a dark skirt, by name, Nastasya Karpovna Ogarkov. Shurotchka was an orphan of the tradesman class. Marfa Timofyevna had taken her to her heart like Roska, from compassion; she had found the little dog and the little girl too in the street; both were thin and hungry, both were being drenched by the autumn rain; no one came in search of Roska, and Shurotchka was given up to Marfa Timofyevna with positive eagerness by her uncle, a drunken shoemaker, who did not get enough to eat himself, and did not feed his niece, but beat her over the head with his last. With Nastasya Karpovna Marfa

Timofyevna had made acquaintance on a pilgrimage at a monastery; she had gone up to her at the church (Marfa Timofyevna took a fancy to her because in her own words she said her prayers so prettily) and had addressed her and invited her to a cup of tea. From that day she never parted from her.

Nastasya Karpovna was a woman of the most cheerful and gentle disposition, a widow without children, of poor noble family; she had a round grey head, soft white hands, a soft face with large mild features, and a rather absurd turned-up nose; she stood in awe of Marfa Timofyevna, and the latter was very fond of her, though she laughed at her susceptibility. She had a soft place in her heart for every young man, and could not help blushing like a girl at the most innocent joke. Her whole fortune consisted of only 1200 roubles; she lived at Marfa Timofyevna's expense, but on an equal footing with her: Marfa Timofyevna would not have put up with any servility.

'Ah! Fedya,' she began, directly she saw him, 'last night you did not see my family, you must admire them, we are all here together for tea; this is our second, holiday tea. You can make friends with them all; only Shurotchka won't let you, and the cat will scratch. Are you starting to-day?'

'Yes.' Lavretsky sat down on a low seat, 'I have just said good-bye to Marya Dmitrievna. I saw Lisaveta Mihalovna too.'

'Call her Lisa, my dear fellow. Mihalovna indeed to you! But sit still, or you will break Shurotchka's little chair.'

'She has gone to church,' continued Lavretsky. 'Is she religious?'

'Yes, Fedya, very much so. More than you and I, Fedya.'

'Aren't you religious then?' lisped Nastasya Karpovna. 'To-day, you have not been to the early service, but you are going to the late.'

'No, not at all; you will go alone; I have grown too lazy, my dear,' replied Marfa Timofyevna. 'Already I am indulging myself with tea.' She addressed Nastasya Karpovna in the singular, though she treated her as an equal. She was not a Pestov for nothing: three Pestovs had been on the death-list of Ivan the Terrible, Marfa Timofyevna was well aware of the fact.

'Tell me please,' began Lavretsky again, 'Marya Dmitrievna has just been talking to me about this—what's his name? Panshin. What sort of a man is he?'

'What a chatterbox she is, Lord save us!' muttered Marfa Timofyevna. 'She told you, I suppose, as a secret that he has turned up as a suitor. She might have whispered it to her priest's son; no, he's not enough for her, it seems. And so far there's nothing to tell, thank God, but already she's gossiping about it.'

'Why thank God?' asked Lavretsky.

'Because I don't like the fine young gentleman; and so what is there to be glad of in it?'

'You don't like him?'

'No, he can't fascinate every one. He must be satisfied with Nastasya Karpovna's being in love with him.'

The poor widow was utterly dismayed.

'How can you, Marfa Timofyevna? you've no conscience!' she cried, and a crimson flush instantly overspread her face and neck.

'And he knows, to be sure, the rogue,' Marfa Timofyevna interrupted her, 'he knows how to captivate her; he made her a present of a snuff-box. Fedya, ask her for a pinch of snuff; you will see what a splendid snuff-box it is; on the lid a hussar on horseback. You'd better not try to defend yourself, my dear.'

Nastasya Karpovna could only fling up her hands.

'Well, but Lisa,' inquired Lavretsky, 'is she indifferent to him?'

'She seems to like him, but there, God knows! The heart of another, you know, is a dark forest, and a girl's more than any. Shurotchka's heart, for instance—I defy you to understand it! What makes her hide herself and not come out ever since you came in?'

Shurotchka choked with suppressed laughter and skipped out of the room. Lavretsky rose from his place.

'Yes,' he said in an uncertain voice, 'there is no deciphering a girl's heart.'

He began to say good-bye.

'Well, shall we see you again soon?' inquired Marfa Timofyevna.

'Very likely, aunt: it's not far off, you know.'

'Yes, to be sure you are going to Vassilyevskoe. You don't care to stay at Lavriky: well, that's your own affair, only mind you go and say a prayer at our mother's grave, and our grandmother's too while you are there. Out there in foreign parts you have picked up all kinds of ideas, but who knows? Perhaps even in their graves they will feel that you have come to them. And, Fedya, don't forget to have a service sung too for Glafira Petrovna; here's a silver rouble for you. Take it, take it, I want to pay for a service for her. I had no love for her in her lifetime, but all the same there's no denying she was a girl of character. She was a clever creature; and a good friend to you. And now go and God be with you, before I weary you.'

And Marfa Timofyevna embraced her nephew.

'And Lisa's not going to marry Panshin; don't you trouble yourself; that's not the sort of husband she deserves.'

'Oh, I'm not troubling myself,' answered Lavretsky, and went away.

CHAPTER XVIII

FOUR days later, he set off for home. His coach rolled quickly along the soft cross-road. There had been no rain for a fortnight; a fine milky mist was diffused in the air and hung over the distant woods; a smell of burning came from it. A multitude of darkish clouds with blurred edges were creeping across the pale blue sky; a fairly strong breeze blew a dry and steady gale, without dispelling the heat. Leaning back with his head on the cushion and his arms crossed on his breast, Lavretsky watched the furrowed fields unfolding like a fan before him, the willow bushes as they slowly came into sight, and the dull ravens and rooks, who looked sidelong with stupid suspicion at the approaching carriage, the long ditches, overgrown with mugwort, wormwood, and mountain ash; and as he watched the fresh fertile wilderness and solitude of this steppe country, the greenness, the long slopes, and valleys with stunted oak bushes, the grey villages, and scant birchtrees,—the whole Russian landscape, so long unseen by him, stirred emotion at once pleasant, sweet and almost painful in his heart, and he felt weighed down by a kind of pleasant oppression. Slowly his thoughts wandered; their outlines were as vague and indistinct as the outlines of the clouds which seemed to be wandering at random overhead. He remembered his childhood, his mother; he remembered her death, how they had carried him in to her, and how, clasping his head to her bosom, she had begun to wail over him, then had glanced at Glafira Petrovna—and checked herself. He remembered his father, at first vigorous, discontented with everything, with strident voice; and later, blind, tearful, with unkempt grey beard; he remembered how one day after drinking a glass too much at dinner, and spilling the gravy over his napkin, he began to relate his conquests, growing red in the face, and winking with his sightless eyes; he remembered Varvara Pavlovna,—and involuntarily shuddered, as a man shudders from a sudden internal pain, and shook his head. Then his thoughts came to a stop at Lisa.

'There,' he thought, 'is a new creature, only just entering on life. A nice girl, what will become of her? She is good-looking too. A pale, fresh face, mouth and eyes so serious, and an honest innocent expression. It is a pity she seems a little enthusiastic. A good figure, and she moves so lightly, and a soft voice. I like the way she stops suddenly, listens attentively, without a smile, then grows thoughtful and shakes back her hair. I fancy, too, that Panshin is not good enough for her. What's amiss with him, though? And besides, what business have I to wonder about it? She will go along the same road as all the rest. I had better go to sleep.' And Lavretsky closed his eyes.

He could not sleep, but he sank into the drowsy numbness of a journey. Images of the past rose slowly as before, floated in his soul, mixed and tangled up with other fancies. Lavretsky, for some unknown reason, began to think about Robert Peel, . . . about French history—of how he would gain a battle, if he were a general; he fancied the shots and the cries. . . . His head slipped on one side, he opened his eyes. The same fields, the same steppe scenery; the polished shoes of the trace-horses flashed alternately through the driving dust; the coachman's shirt, yellow with red gussets, was puffed out by the wind. . . . 'A nice home-coming!' glanced through Lavretsky's brain; and he cried, 'Get on!' wrapped himself in his cloak and pressed close into the cushion. The carriage jolted; Lavretsky sat up and opened his eyes wide. On the slope before him stretched a small hamlet; a littie to the right could be seen an ancient manor-house of small size, with closed shutters and a winding flight of steps; nettles, green and thick as hemp, grew over the wide courtyard from the very gates; in it stood a storehouse built of oak, still strong. This was Vassilyevskoe.

The coachman drove to the gates and drew up; Lavretsky's groom stood up on the box and as though in preparation for jumping down, shouted, 'Hey!' There was a sleepy, muffled sound of barking, but not even a dog made its appearance; the groom again made ready for a jump, and again shouted 'Hey!' The feeble barking was repeated, and an instant after a man from some unseen quarter ran into the courtyard, dressed in a nankeen coat, his head as white as snow; he stared at the coach, shading his eyes from the sun; all at once he slapped his thighs with both hands, ran to and fro a little, then rushed to open the gates. The coach drove into the yard, crushing the nettles with the wheels and drew up at the steps. The white-headed man, who seemed very alert, was already standing on the bottom step, his legs bent and wide apart. He unfastened the apron of the carriage, holding back the strap with a jerk and aiding his master to alight; then kissed his hand.

'How do you do, how do you do, brother?' began Lavretsky. 'Your name's Anton, I think? You are still alive, then?' The old man bowed without speaking, and ran off for the keys. While he went, the coachman sat motionless, sitting sideways and staring at the closed door, but Lavretsky's groom stood as he had leaped down in a picturesque pose with one arm thrown back on the box. The old man brought the keys, and, quite needlessly, twisting about like a snake, with his elbows raised high, he opened the door, stood on one side, and again bowed to the earth.

'So here I am at home, here I am back again,' thought Lavretsky, as he walked into the diminutive passage, while one after another the shutters were being opened with much creaking and knocking, and the light of day poured into the deserted rooms.

CHAPTER XIX

THE small manor-house to which Lavretsky had come and in which two years before Glafira Petrovna had breathed her last, had been built in the preceding century of solid pine-wood; it looked ancient, but it was still strong enough to stand another fifty years or more. Lavretsky made the tour of all the rooms, and to the great discomfiture of the aged languid flies, settled under the lintels and covered with white dust, he ordered the windows to be opened everywhere; they had not been opened ever since the death of Glafira Petrovna. Everything in the house had remained as it was; the thin-legged white miniature couches in the drawing-room, covered with glossy grey stuff, threadbare and rickety, vividly suggested the days of Catherine; in the drawing-room, too, stood the mistress's favourite arm-chair, with high straight back, against which she never leaned even in her old age. On the principal wall hung a very old portrait of Fedor's great-grandfather, Andrey Lavretsky; the dark yellow face was scarcely distinguishable from the warped and blackened background; the small cruel eyes looked grimly out from beneath the eyelids, which drooped as if they were swollen; his black unpowdered hair rose bristling above his heavy indented brow. In the corner of the portrait hung a wreath of dusty immortelles. 'Glafira Petrovna herself was pleased to make it,' Anton announced. In the bedroom stood a narrow bedstead, under a canopy of old-fashioned and very good striped material; a heap of faded cushions and a thin quilted counterpane lay on the bed, and at the head hung a picture of the Presentation in the Temple of the Holy Mother of God; it was the very picture which the old maid, dying alone and forgotten by every one, had for the last time pressed to her chilling lips. A little toilet table of inlaid wood, with brass fittings and a warped looking-glass in a tarnished frame stood in the window. Next to the bedroom was the little ikon room with bare walls and a heavy case of holy images in the corner; on the floor lay a threadbare rug spotted with wax; Glafira Petrovna used to pray bowing to the ground upon it. Anton went away with Lavretsky's groom to unlock the stable and coach-house; to replace him appeared an old woman of about the same age, with a handkerchief tied round to her very eyebrows; her head shook, and her eyes were dim, but they expressed zeal, the habit of years of submissive service, and at the same time a kind of respectful commiseration. She kissed Lavretsky's hand and stood still in the doorway awaiting his orders. He positively could not recollect her name and did not even remember whether he had ever seen her. Her name, it appeared, was Apraxya; forty years before, Glafira Petrovna had put her out of the master's house and ordered that she should be poultry-woman. She said little, however; she seemed to have lost her senses from old age, and could only gaze at him obsequiously. Besides these two old creatures and three pot-bellied children in long smocks, Anton's great-grandchildren, there was also living in the manor-house a one-armed peasant, who was exempted from servitude; he muttered like a woodcock and was of no use for anything. Not much more useful was the decrepit dog who had saluted Lavretsky's return by its barking; he had been for ten years fastened up by a heavy chain, purchased at Glafira Petrovna's command, and was scarcely able to move and drag the weight of it. Having looked over the house, Lavretsky went into the garden and was very much pleased with it. It was all overgrown with high grass, and burdock, and gooseberry and raspberry bushes, but there was plenty of shade, and many old lime-trees, which were remarkable for their immense size and the peculiar growth of their branches; they had been planted too close and at some time or other—a hundred years before—they had been lopped. At the end of the garden was a small clear pool bordered with high reddish rushes. The traces of human life very quickly pass away; Glafira Petrovna's estate had not had time to become quite wild, but already it seemed plunged in that quiet slumber in which everything reposes on earth where there is not the infection of man's restlessness. Fedor Ivanitch walked also through the village; the peasant-women stared at him from the doorways of their huts, their cheeks resting on their hands; the peasants saluted him from a distance, the children ran out, and the dogs barked indifferently. At last he began to feel hungry; but he did not expect his servants and his cook till the evening; the waggons of provisions from Lavriky had not come yet, and he had to have recourse to Anton. Anton arranged matters at once; he caught, killed, and plucked an old hen; Apraxya gave it a long rubbing and cleaning, and washed it like linen before putting it into the stew-pan; when, at last, it was cooked, Anton laid the cloth and set the table, placing beside the knife and fork a three-legged salt-cellar of tarnished plate and a cut decanter with a round glass stopper and a narrow neck; then he announced to Lavretsky in a sing-song voice that the meal was ready, and took his stand behind his chair, with a napkin twisted round his right fist, and diffusing about him a peculiar strong ancient odour, like the scent of a cypress-tree. Lavretsky tried the soup, and took out the hen; its skin was all covered with large blisters; a tough tendon ran up each leg; the meat had a flavour of wood and soda. When he had finished dinner, Lavretsky said that he would drink a cup of tea, if ——'I will bring it this minute,' the old man interrupted. And he kept his word. A pinch of tea was hunted up, twisted in a screw of red paper; a small but very fiery and loudly-hissing samovar was found, and sugar too in small lumps, which looked as if they were thawing. Lavretsky drank tea out of a large cup; he remembered this cup from childhood; there were playing-cards depicted upon it, only visitors used to drink out of it—and here was he drinking out of it like a visitor. In the evening his servants came; Lavretsky did not care to sleep in his aunt's bed; he directed them to put him up a bed in the dining-room. After extinguishing his candle he stared for a long time about him and fell into cheerless reflection; he experienced that feeling which every man knows whose lot it is to pass the night in a place long uninhabited; it seemed to him that the darkness surrounding him on all sides could not be accustomed to the new inhabitant, the very walls of the

house seemed amazed. At last he sighed, drew up the
counterpane round him and fell asleep. Anton remained up
after all the rest of the household; he was whispering a
long while with Apraxya, he sighed in an undertone, and
twice he crossed himself; they had neither of them expected
that their master would settle among them at Vassilyevskoe
when he had not far off such a splendid estate with such a
capitally built house; they did not suspect that the very
house was hateful to Lavretsky; it stirred painful memories
within him. Having gossiped to his heart's content, Anton
took a stick and struck the night watchman's board, which
had hung silent for so many years, and laid down to sleep
in the courtyard with no covering on his white head. The
May night was mild and soft, and the old man slept sweetly.

S—4

CHAPTER XX

THE next day Lavretsky got up rather early, had a talk with the village bailiff, visited the threshing-floor, ordered the chain to be taken off the yard dog, who only barked a little, but did not even come out of his kennel, and, returning home, sank into a kind of peaceful torpor, which he did not shake off the whole day.

'Here I am at the very bottom of the river,' he said to himself more than once. He sat at the window without stirring, and, as it were, listened to the current of the quiet life surrounding him, to the few sounds of the country solitude. Something from behind the nettles chirps with a shrill, shrill little note; a gnat seems to answer it. Now it has ceased, but still the gnat keeps up its sharp whirr; across the pleasant, persistent, fretful buzz of the flies sounds the hum of a big bee, constantly knocking its head against the ceiling; a cock crows in the street, hoarsely prolonging the last note; there is the rattle of a cart; in the village a gate is creaking. Then the jarring voice of a peasant woman, 'What?' 'Hey, you are my little sweetheart,' cries Anton to the little two-year-old girl he is dandling in his arms. 'Fetch the kvas,' repeats the same woman's voice, and all at once there follows a deathly silence; nothing rattles, nothing is moving; the wind is not stirring a leaf; without a sound the swallows fly one after another over the earth, and sadness weighs on the heart from their noiseless flight. 'Here I am at the very bottom of the river,' thought Lavretsky again. 'And always, at all times life here is quiet, unhasting,' he thought; 'whoever comes within its circle must submit; here there is nothing to agitate, nothing to harass; one can only get on here by making one's way slowly, as the ploughman cuts the furrow with his plough. And what vigour, what health abound in this inactive place! Here under the window the sturdy burdock creeps out of the thick grass; above it the lovage trails its juicy stalks and the

Virgin's tears fling still higher their pink tendrils; and yonder further in the fields is the silky rye, and the oats are already in ear, and every leaf on every tree, every grass on its stalk is spread to its fullest width. In the love of a woman my best years have gone by,' Lavretsky went on thinking, 'let me be sobered by the sameness of life here, let me be soothed and made ready, so that I may learn to do my duty without haste.' And again he fell to listening to the silence, expecting nothing—and at the same time constantly expecting something; the silence enfolded him on all sides, the sun moved calmly in the peaceful blue sky, and the clouds sailed calmly across it; they seemed to know why and whither they were sailing. At this same time in other places on the earth there is the seething, the bustle, the clash of life; life here slipped by noiseless, as water over marshy grass; and even till evening Lavretsky could not tear himself from the contemplation of this life as it passed and glided by; sorrow for the past was melting in his soul like snow in spring, and strange to say, never had the feeling of home been so deep and strong within him.

IN the course of a fortnight, Fedor Ivanitch had brought Glafira Petrovna's little house into order and had cleared the court-yard and the garden. From Lavriky comfortable furniture was sent him; from the town, wine, books, and papers; horses made their appearance in the stable; in brief Fedor Ivanitch provided himself with everything necessary and began to live—not precisely after the manner of a country landowner, nor precisely after the manner of a hermit. His days passed monotonously; but he was not bored though he saw no one; he set diligently and attentively to work at farming his estate, rode about the neighbourhood and did some reading. He read little, however; he found it pleasanter to listen to the tales of old Anton. Lavretsky usually sat at the window with a pipe and a cup of cold tea. Anton stood at the door, his hands crossed behind him, and began upon his slow, deliberate stories of old times, of those fabulous times when oats and rye were not sold by measure, but in great sacks, at two or three farthings a sack; when there were impassable forests, virgin steppes stretching on every side, even close to the town. 'And now,' complained the old man, whose eightieth year had passed, 'there has been so much clearing, so much ploughing everywhere, there's nowhere you may drive now.' Anton used to tell many stories, too, of his mistress, Glafira Petrovna; how prudent and saving she was; how a certain gentleman, a young neighbour, had paid her court, and used to ride over to see her, and how she was even pleased to put on her best cap, with ribbons of salmon colour, and her yellow gown of *tru-tru lévantine* for him; but how, later on, she had been angry with the gentleman neighbour for his unseemly inquiry, 'What, madam, pray, might be your fortune?' and had bade them refuse him the house; and how it was then that she had given directions that, after her decease, everything to the last rag should pass to Fedor Ivanitch. And, indeed, Lavretsky found all his aunt's household goods intact, not excepting the best cap with ribbons of salmon colour, and the yellow gown of *tru-tru lévantine*. Of old papers and interesting documents, upon which Lavretsky had reckoned, there seemed no trace, except one old book, in which his grandfather, Piotr Andreitch, had inscribed in one place, 'Celebration in the city of Saint Petersburg of the peace, concluded with the Turkish empire by his Excellency Prince Alexander Alexandrovitch Prozorovsky;' in another place a recipe for a pectoral decoction with the comment, 'This recipe was given to the general's lady, Prascovya Federovna Soltikov, by the chief priest of the Church of the Life-giving Trinity, Fedor Avksentyevitch:' in another, a piece of political news of this kind: 'Somewhat less talk of the French tigers;' and next this entry: 'In the *Moscow Gazette* an announcement of the death of Mr. Senior-Major Mihal Petrovitch Kolitchev. Is not this the son of Piotr Vassilyevitch Kolitchev? Lavretsky found also some old calendars and dream-books, and the mysterious work of Ambodik; many were the memories stirred by the well-known, but long-forgotten *Symbols and Emblems.* In Glafira Petrovna's little dressing-table, Lavretsky found a small packet, tied up with black ribbon, sealed with black sealing wax, and thrust away in the very farthest corner of the drawer. In the parcel there lay face to face a portrait. in pastel, of his father in his youth, with effeminate curls straying over his brow, with almond-shaped languid eyes and parted lips, and a portrait, almost effaced, of a pale woman in a white dress with a white rose in her hand—his mother. Of herself, Glafira Petrovna had never allowed a portrait to be taken. 'I, myself, little father, Fedor Iva-nitch,' Anton used to tell Lavretsky, 'though I did not then live in the master's house, still I can remember your great-grandfather, Andrey Afanasyevitch, seeing that I had come to my eighteenth year when he died. Once I met him in the garden, and my knees were knocking with fright indeed; however, he did nothing, only asked me my name, and sent me into his room for his pocket-handkerchief. He was a gentleman—how shall I tell you—he didn't look on any one as better than himself. For your great-grandfather had, I

do assure you, a magic amulet; a monk from Mount Athos
made him a present of this amulet. And he told him, this
monk did, "It's for your kindness, Boyar, I give you this;
wear it, and you need not fear judgment." Well, but there,
little father, we know what those times were like; what the
master fancied doing, that he did. Sometimes, if even some
gentleman saw fit to cross him in anything, he would just
stare at him and say, "You swim in shallow water?" that
was his favourite saying. And he lived, your great-grandfather of blessed memory, in a small log-house; and what
goods he left behind him, what silver, and stores of all kinds!
All the storehouses were full and overflowing. He was a
manager. That very decanter, that you were pleased to
admire, was his; he used to drink brandy out of it. But
there was your grandfather, Piotr Andreitch, built himself
a palace of stone, but he never grew rich; everything with
him went badly, and he lived worse than his father by far,
and he got no pleasure from it for himself, but spent all his
money, and now there is nothing to remember him by—not
a silver spoon has come down from him, and we have
Glafira Petrovna's management to thank for all that is
saved.'

'But is it true,' Lavretsky interrupted him, 'they called her
the old witch?'

'What sort of people called her so, I should like to know!'
replied Anton with an air of displeasure.

'And, little father,' the old man one day found courage to
ask, 'what about our mistress, where is she pleased to fix
her residence?'

'I am separated from my wife,' Lavretsky answered with
an effort, 'please do not ask questions about her.'

'Yes, sir,' replied the old man mournfully.

After three weeks had passed by, Lavretsky rode into
O—— to the Kalitins, and spent an evening with them.
Lemm was there; Lavretsky took a great liking to him.
Although thanks to his father, he played no instrument, he
was passionately fond of music, real classical music. Panshin was not at the Kalitins' that evening. The governor
had sent him off to some place out of the town. Lisa
played alone and very correctly; Lemm woke up, got excited,

twisted a piece of paper into a roll, and conducted. Marya
Dmitrievna laughed at first, as she looked at him, later on
she went off to bed; in her own words, Beethoven was too
agitating for her nerves. At midnight Lavretsky accompanied Lemm to his lodging and stopped there with him till
three o'clock in the morning. Lemm talked a great deal;
his bent figure grew erect, his eyes opened wide and flashed
fire; his hair even stood up on his forehead. It was so long
since any one had shown him any sympathy, and Lavretsky
was obviously interested in him, he was plying him with
sympathetic and attentive questions. This touched the old
man; he ended by showing the visitor his music, played and
even sang in a faded voice some extracts from his works,
among others the whole of Schiller's ballad, *Fridolin*, set by
him to music. Lavretsky admired it, made him repeat some
passages, and at parting, invited him to stay a few days
with him. Lemm, as he accompanied him as far as the
street, agreed at once, and warmly pressed his hand; but,
when he was left standing alone in the fresh, damp air, in
the just dawning sunrise, he looked round him, shuddered,
shrank into himself, and crept up to his little room, with a
guilty air. '*Ich bin wohl nicht klug*' (I must be out of my
senses), he muttered, as he lay down in his hard short bed.
He tried to say that he was ill, a few days later, when
Lavretsky drove over to fetch him in an open carriage; but
Fedor Ivanitch went up into his room and managed to per-
suade him. What produced the most powerful effect upon
Lemm was the circumstance that Lavretsky had ordered a
piano from town to be sent into the country expressly for
him.

They set off together to the Kalitins' and spent the evening with them, but not so pleasantly as on the last occasion. Panshin was there, he talked a great deal about
his expedition, and very amusingly mimicked and described
the country gentry he had seen; Lavretsky laughed, but
Lemm would not come out of his corner, and sat silent,
slightly tremulous all over like a spider, looking dull and
sullen, and he only revived when Lavretsky began to take
leave. Even when he was sitting in the carriage, the old
man was still shy and constrained; but the warm soft air,

the light breeze, and the light shadows, the scent of the grass and the birch-buds, the peaceful light of the starlit, moonless night, the pleasant tramp and snort of the horses—all the witchery of the roadside, the spring and the night, sank into the poor German's soul, and he was himself the first to begin a conversation with Lavretsky.

CHAPTER XXII

HE began talking about music, about Lisa, then of music again. He seemed to enunciate his words more slowly when he spoke of Lisa. Lavretsky turned the conversation on his compositions, and half in jest, offered to write him a libretto.

'H'm, a libretto!' replied Lemm; 'no, that is not in my line; I have not now the liveliness, the play of the imagination, which is needed for an opera; I have lost too much of my power . . . But if I were still able to do something,—I should be contented with a song; of course I should like to have beautiful words . . .'

He ceased speaking, and sat a long while motionless, his eyes lifted to the heavens.

'For instance,' he said at last, 'something in this way: "Ye stars, ye pure stars!"'

Lavretsky turned his face slightly towards him and began to look at him.

'"Ye stars, pure stars,"' repeated Lemm. . . . "You look down upon the righteous and the guilty alike . . . but only the pure in heart,"—or something of that kind—"comprehend you"—that is, no—"love you." But I am not a poet. I'm not equal to it! Something of that kind, though, something lofty.'

Lemm pushed his hat on to the back of his head; in the dim twilight of the clear night his face looked paler and younger.

'"And you too,"' he continued, his voice gradually sinking, '"ye know who loves, who can love, because ye, pure ones, ye alone can comfort" . . . No, that's not it at all! I am not a poet,' he said, 'but something of that sort.'

'I am sorry I am not a poet,' observed Lavretsky.

'Vain dreams!' replied Lemm, and he buried himself in the corner of the carriage. He closed his eyes as though he were disposing himself to sleep.

A few instants passed . . . Lavretsky listened . . .
'"Stars, pure stars, love,"' muttered the old man.

'Love,' Lavretsky repeated to himself. He sank into
thought—and his heart grew heavy.

'That is beautiful music you have set to Fridolin, Christopher Fedoritch,' he said aloud, 'but what do you suppose,
did that Fridolin do, after the Count had presented him to
his wife . . . became her lover, eh?'

'You think so,' replied Lemm, 'probably because experience,'—he stopped suddenly and turned away in confusion.
Lavretsky laughed constrainedly, and also turned away and
began gazing at the road.

The stars had begun to grow paler and the sky had turned
grey when the carriage drove up to the steps of the little
house in Vassilyevskoe. Lavretsky conducted his guest to
the room prepared for him, returned to his study and sat
down before the window. In the garden a nightingale was
singing its last song before dawn. Lavretsky remembered
that a nightingale had sung in the garden at the Kalitins'; he
remembered, too, the soft stir in Lisa's eyes, as at its first
notes, they turned towards the dark window. He began to
think of her, and his heart was calm again. 'Pure maiden,'
he murmured half-aloud: 'pure stars,' he added with a smile,
and went peacefully to bed.

But Lemm sat a long while on his bed, a music-book on
his knees. He felt as though sweet, unheard melody was
haunting him; already he was all aglow and astir, already he
felt the languor and sweetness of its presence . . . but he
could not reach it.

'Neither poet nor musician!' he muttered at last . . . And
his tired head sank wearily on to the pillows.

CHAPTER XXIII

THE next morning the master of the house and his guest drank tea in the garden under an old lime-tree.

'Maestro!' said Lavretsky among other things, 'you will soon have to compose a triumphal cantata.'

'On what occasion?'

'For the nuptials of Mr. Panshin and Lisa. Did you notice what attention he paid her yesterday? It seems as though things were in a fair way with them already.'

'That will never be!' cried Lemm.

'Why?'

'Because it is impossible. Though, indeed,' he added after a short pause, 'everything is possible in this world. Especially here among you in Russia.'

'We will leave Russia out of the question for a time; but what do you find amiss in this match?'

'Everything is amiss, everything. Lisaveta Mihalovna is a girl of high principles, serious, of lofty feelings, and he . . . he is a dilettante, in a word.'

'But suppose she loves him?'

Lemm got up from the bench.

'No, she does not love him, that is to say, she is very pure in heart, and does not know herself what it means . . . love. Madame von Kalitin tells her that he is a fine young man, and she obeys Madame von Kalitin because she is still quite a child, though she is nineteen; she says her prayers in the morning and in the evening—and that is very well; but she does not love him. She can only love what is beautiful, and he is not, that is, his soul is not beautiful.'

Lemm uttered this whole speech coherently, and with fire, walking with little steps to and fro before the tea-table, and running his eyes over the ground.

'Dearest maestro!' cried Lavretsky suddenly, 'it strikes me you are in love with my cousin yourself.'

Lemm stopped short all at once.

'I beg you,' he began in an uncertain voice, 'do not make fun of me like that. I am not crazy; I look towards the dark grave, not towards a rosy future.'

Lavretsky felt sorry for the old man; he begged his pardon. After morning tea, Lemm played him his cantata, and after dinner, at Lavretsky's initiative, there was again talk of Lisa. Lavretsky listened to him with attention and curiosity.

'What do you say, Christopher Fedoritch,' he said at last, 'you see everything here seems in good order now, and the garden is in full bloom, couldn't we invite her over here for a day with her mother and my old aunt . . . eh? Would you like it?'

Lemm bent his head over his plate.

'Invite her,' he murmured, scarcely audibly.

'But Panshin isn't wanted?'

'No, he isn't wanted,' rejoined the old man with an almost child-like smile.

Two days later Fedor Ivanitch set off to the town to see the Kalitins.

CHAPTER XXIV

H E found them all at home, but he did not at once disclose his plan to them; he wanted to discuss it first with Lisa alone. Fortune favoured him; they were left alone in the drawing-room. They had some talk; she had had time by now to grow used to him—and she was not shy as a rule with any one. He listened to her, watched her, and mentally repeated Lemm's words, and agreed with them. It sometimes happens that two people who are acquainted, but not on intimate terms with one another, all of sudden grow rapidly more intimate in a few minutes, and the consciousness of this greater intimacy is at once expressed in their eyes, in their soft and affectionate smiles, and in their very gestures. This was exactly what came to pass with Lavretsky and Lisa. 'So he is like that,' was her thought, as she turned a friendly glance on him; 'so you are like that,' he too was thinking. And so he was not very much surprised when she informed him, not without a little faltering, however, that she had long wished to say something to him, but she was afraid of offending him.

'Don't be afraid; tell me,' he replied, and stood still before her.

Lisa raised her clear eyes to him.

'You are so good,' she began, and at the same time, she thought: 'Yes, I am sure he is good' . . . 'you will forgive me, I ought not to dare to speak of it to you . . . but—how could you . . . why did you separate from your wife?'

Lavretsky shuddered: he looked at Lisa, and sat down near her.

'My child,' he began, 'I beg you, do not touch upon that wound; your hands are tender, but it will hurt me all the same.'

'I know,' Lisa went on, as though she did not hear him, 'she has been to blame towards you. I don't want to defend her; but what God has joined, how can you put asunder?'

'Our convictions on that subject are too different, Lisaveta Mihalovna,' Lavretsky observed, rather sharply; 'we cannot understand one another.'

Lisa grew paler: her whole frame was trembling slightly; but she was not silenced.

'You must forgive,' she murmured softly, 'if you wish to be forgiven.'

'Forgive!' broke in Lavretsky. 'Ought you not first to know whom you are interceding for? Forgive that woman, take her back into my home, that empty, heartless creature! And who told you she wants to return to me? She is perfectly contented with her position, I can assure you . . . But what a subject to discuss here! Her name ought never to be uttered by you. You are too pure, you are not capable of understanding such a creature.'

'Why abuse her?' Lisa articulated with an effort. The trembling of her hands was perceptible now. 'You left her yourself, Fedor Ivanitch.'

'But I tell you,' retorted Lavretsky with an involuntary outburst of impatience, 'you don't know what that woman is!'

'Then why did you marry her?' whispered Lisa, and her eyes fell.

Lavretsky got up quickly from his seat.

'Why did I marry her? I was young and inexperienced; I was deceived, I was carried away by a beautiful exterior. I knew no women. I knew nothing. God grant you may make a happier marriage! but let me tell you, you can be sure of nothing.'

'I too might be unhappy,' said Lisa (her voice had begun to be unsteady), 'but then I ought to submit, I don't know how to say it; but if we do not submit'——

Lavretsky clenched his hands and stamped with his foot.

'Don't be angry, forgive me,' Lisa faltered hurriedly.

At that instant Marya Dmitrievna came in. Lisa got up and was going away.

'Stop a minute,' Lavretsky cried after her unexpectedly. 'I have a great favour to beg of your mother and you; to pay me a visit in my new abode. You know, I have had a piano sent over; Lemm is staying with me; the lilac is in flower now; you will get a breath of country air, and you can

return the same day—will you consent?' Lisa looked towards
her mother; Marya Dmitrievna was assuming an expression
of suffering; but Lavretsky did not give her time to open her
mouth; he at once kissed both her hands. Marya Dmitrievna, who was always susceptible to demonstrations of
feeling, and did not at all anticipate such effusiveness from
the 'dolt,' was melted and gave her consent. While she
was deliberating which day to fix, Lavretsky went up to
Lisa, and, still greatly moved, whispered to her aside: 'Thank
you, you are a good girl; I was to blame.' And her pale
face glowed with a bright, shy smile; her eyes smiled too—
up to that instant she had been afraid she had offended him.

'Vladimir Nikolaitch can come with us?' inquired Marya
Dmitrievna.

'Yes,' replied Lavretsky, 'but would it not be better to be
just a family party?'

'Well, you know, it seems,' began Marya Dmitrievna.

'But as you please,' she added.

It was decided to take Lenotchka and Shurotchka. Marfa
Timofyevna refused to join in the expedition.

'It is hard for me, my darling,' she said, 'to give my old
bones a shaking; and to be sure there's nowhere for me to
sleep at your place: besides, I can't sleep in a strange bed.
Let the young folks go frolicking.'

Lavretsky did not succeed in being alone again with Lisa;
but he looked at her in such a way that she felt her heart at
rest, and a little ashamed, and sorry for him. He pressed
her hand warmly at parting; left alone, she fell to musing.

CHAPTER XXV

WHEN Lavretsky reached home, he was met at the door of the drawing-room by a tall, thin man, in a thread-bare blue coat, with a wrinkled, but lively face, with dishevelled grey whiskers, a long straight nose, and small fiery eyes. This was Mihalevitch, who had been his friend at the university. Lavretsky did not at first recognise him, but embraced him warmly directly he told his name.

They had not met since their Moscow days. Torrents of exclamations and questions followed; long-buried recollections were brought to light. Hurriedly smoking pipe after pipe, tossing off tea at a gulp, and gesticulating with his long hands, Mihalevitch related his adventures to Lavretsky; there was nothing very inspiriting in them, he could not boast of success in his undertakings—but he was constantly laughing a hoarse, nervous laugh. A month previously he had received a position in the private counting-house of a spirit-tax contractor, two hundred and fifty miles from the town of O——, and hearing of Lavretsky's return from abroad he had turned out of his way so as to see his old friend. Mihalevitch talked as impetuously as in his youth; made as much noise and was as effervescent as of old. Lavretsky was about to acquaint him with his position, but Mihalevitch interrupted him, muttering hurriedly, 'I have heard, my dear fellow, I have heard—who could have anticipated it?' and at once turned the conversation upon general subjects.

'I must set off to-morrow, my dear fellow,' he observed; 'to-day if you will excuse it, we will sit up late. I want above all to know what you are like, what are your views and convictions, what you have become, what life has taught you.' (Mihalevitch still preserved the phraseology of 1830.) 'As for me, I have changed in much; the waves of life have broken over my breast—who was it said that?—though in what is important, essential I have not changed; I believe as of old in the good, the true: but I do not only believe—I have faith now, yes, I have faith, faith. Listen, you know I write verses; there is no poetry in them, but there is truth. I will read you aloud my last poem; I have expressed my truest convictions in it. Listen.' Mihalevitch fell to reading his poem: it was rather long, and ended with the following lines:

> 'I gave myself to new feelings with all my heart,
> And my soul became as a child's!
> And I have burnt all I adored,
> And now adore all that I burnt.'

As he uttered the two last lines, Mihalevitch all but shed tears; a slight spasm—the sign of deep emotion—passed over his wide mouth, his ugly face lighted up. Lavretsky listened, and listened to him—and the spirit of antagonism was aroused in him; he was irritated by the ever-ready enthusiasm of the Moscow student, perpetually at boiling-point. Before a quarter of an hour had elapsed a heated argument had broken out between them, one of these endless arguments, of which only Russians are capable. After a separation of many years spent in two different worlds, with no clear understanding of the other's ideas or even of their own, catching at words and replying only in words, they disputed about the most abstract subjects, and they disputed as though it were a matter of life and death for both: they shouted and vociferated so that every one in the house was startled, and poor Lemm, who had locked himself up in his room directly after Mihalevitch arrived, was bewildered, and began even to feel vaguely alarmed.

'What are you after all? a pessimist?' cried Mihalevitch at one o'clock in the night.

'Are pessimists usually like this?' replied Lavretsky. 'They are usually all pale and sickly—would you like me to lift you with one hand?'

'Well, if you are not a pessimist you are a *scepteec*, that's still worse.' Mihalevitch's talk had a strong flavour of his mother-country, Little Russia. 'And what right have you to be a *scepteec*? You have had ill-luck in life, let us admit; that was not your fault; you were born with a passionate loving heart, and you were unnaturally kept out of the society of women: the first woman you came across was bound to deceive you.'

'She deceived you too,' observed Lavretsky grimly.

'Granted, granted; I was the tool of destiny in it—what nonsense I talk, though—there is no such thing as destiny; it is an old habit of expressing things inexactly. But what does that prove?'

'It proves this, that they distorted me from my childhood.'

'Well, it's for you to straighten yourself! What's the good of being a man, a male animal? And however that may be, is it possible, is it permissible, to reduce a personal, so to speak, fact to a general law, to an infallible principle?'

'How a principle?' interrupted Lavretsky; 'I don't admit—'

'No, it is your principle, your principle,' Mihalevitch interrupted in his turn.

'You are an egoist, that's what it is!' he was thundering an hour later: 'you wanted personal happiness, you wanted enjoyment in life, you wanted to live only for yourself.'

'What do you mean by personal happiness?'

'And everything deceived you; everything crumbled away under your feet.'

'What do you mean by personal happiness, I ask you?'

'And it was bound to crumble away. Either you sought support where it could not be found, or you built your house on shifting sands, or——'

'Speak more plainly, *or* I can't understand you.

'Or—you may laugh if you like—or you had no faith, no warmth of heart; intellect, nothing but one farthing's worth of intellect . . . you are simply a pitiful, antiquated Voltairean, that's what you are!'

'I'm a Voltairean?'

'Yes, like your father, and you yourself do not suspect it.'

'After that,' exclaimed Lavretsky, 'I have the right to call you a fanatic.'

'Alas!' replied Mihalevitch with a contrite air, 'I have not so far deserved such an exalted title, unhappily.'

'I have found out now what to call you,' cried the same Mihalevitch, at three o'clock in the morning. 'You are not a sceptic, nor a pessimist, nor a Voltairean, you are a loafer, and you are a vicious loafer, a conscious loafer, not a simple loafer. Simple loafers lie on the stove and do nothing because they don't know how to do anything; they don't think about anything either, but you are a man of ideas—and yet you lie on the stove; you could do something—and you do nothing; you lie idle with a full stomach and look down from above and say, "It's best to lie idle like this, because whatever people do, is all rubbish, leading to nothing." '

'And from what do you infer that I lie idle?' Lavretsky protested stoutly. 'Why do you attribute such ideas to me?'

'And, besides that, you are all, all the tribe of you,' continued Mihalevitch, 'cultivated loafers. You know which leg the German limps on, you know what's amiss with the English and the French, and your pitiful culture goes to make it worse, your shameful idleness, your abominable inactivity is justified by it. Some are even proud of it: "I'm such a clever fellow," they say, "I do nothing, while these fools are in a fuss." Yes! and there are fine gentlemen among us— though I don't say this as to you—who reduce their whole life to a kind of stupor of boredom, get used to it, live in it, like—like a mushroom in white sauce,' Mihalevitch added hastily, and he laughed at his own comparison. 'Oh! this stupor of boredom is the ruin of Russians. Ours is the age for work, and the sickening loafer' . . .

'But what is all this abuse about?' Lavretsky clamoured in his turn. 'Work—doing—you'd better say what is to be done, instead of abusing me, Desmosthenes of Poltava!'

'There, what a thing to ask! I can't tell you that, brother; that, every one ought to know for himself,' retorted the Desmosthenes ironically. 'A landowner, a nobleman, and not know what to do? You have no faith, or else you would know; no faith—and no intuition.'

'Let me at least have time to breathe; you don't let me have time to look round,' Lavretsky besought him.

'Not a minute, nor a second!' retorted Mihalevitch with an imperious wave of the hand. 'Not one second: death does not delay, and life ought not to delay.'

'And what a time what a place for men to think of loafing!' he cried at four o'clock, in a voice, however, which showed signs of sleepiness; 'among us! now! in Russia where every separate individuality has a duty resting upon him, a solemn responsibility to God, to the people, to himself. We are sleeping, and the time is slipping away; we are sleeping.' . . .

'Permit me to observe,' remarked Lavretsky, 'that we are not sleeping at present, but rather preventing others from sleeping. We are straining our throats like the cocks— listen! there is one crowing for the third time.'

This sally made Mihalevitch laugh, and calmed him down. 'Good-bye till to-morrow,' he said with a smile, and thrust his pipe into his pouch.

'Till to-morrow,' repeated Lavretsky. But the friends talked for more than an hour longer. Their voices were no longer raised, however, and their talk was quiet, sad, friendly talk.

Mihalevitch set off the next day, in spite of all Lavretsky's efforts to keep him. Fedor Ivanitch did not succeed in persuading him to remain; but he talked to him to his heart's content. Mihalevitch, it appeared, had not a penny to bless himself with. Lavretsky had noticed with pain the evening before all the tokens and habits of years of poverty: his boots were shabby, a button was off on the back of his coat, his hands were unused to gloves, his hair wanted brushing; on his arrival, he had not even thought of asking to wash, and at supper he ate like a shark, tearing his meat in his fingers, and crunching the bones with his strong black teeth. It appeared, too, that he had made nothing out of his employment, that he now rested all his hopes on the contractor who was taking him solely in order to have an 'educated man' in his office.

For all that Mihalevitch was not discouraged, but as idealist or cynic, lived on a crust of bread, sincerely rejoicing or grieving over the destinies of humanity, and his own vocation, and troubling himself very little as to how to escape dying of hunger. Mihalevitch was not married: but had been in love times beyond number, and had written poems to all the objects of his adoration; he sang with especial fervour the praises of a mysterious black-tressed 'noble Polish lady.' There were rumours, it is true, that this 'noble Polish lady' was a simple Jewess, very well known to a good many cavalry officers—but, after all, what do you think—does it really make any difference?

With Lemm, Mihalevitch did not get on; his noisy talk and brusque manners scared the German, who was unused to such behaviour. One poor devil detects another by instinct at once, but in old age he rarely gets on with him, and that is hardly astonishing, he has nothing to share with him, not even hopes.

Before setting off, Mihalevitch had another long discussion with Lavretsky, foretold his ruin, if he did not see the error of his ways, exhorted him to devote himself seriously to the welfare of his peasants, and pointed to himself as an example, saying that he had been purified in the furnace of suffering; and in the same breath called himself several times a happy man, comparing himself with the fowl of the air and the lily of the field.

'A black lily, any way,' observed Lavretsky.

'Ah, brother, don't be a snob!' retorted Mihalevitch, good-naturedly, 'but thank God rather that there is pure plebeian blood in your veins too. But I see you want some pure, heavenly creature to draw you out of your apathy.'

'Thanks, brother,' remarked Lavretsky. 'I have had quite enough of those heavenly creatures.'

'Silence, ceeneec!' cried Mihalevitch.

'Cynic,' Lavretsky corrected him.

'Ceeneec, just so,' repeated Mihalevitch unabashed.

Even when he had taken his seat in the carriage, to which his flat, yellow, strangely light trunk was carried, he still talked; muffled in a kind of Spanish cloak with a collar, brown with age, and a clasp of two lion's paws; he went on developing his views on the destiny of Russia, and waving his swarthy hand in the air, as though he were sowing the seeds of her future prosperity. The horses started at last.

'Remember my three last words,' he cried, thrusting his whole body out of the carriage and balancing so, 'Religion, progress, humanity! . . . Farewell.'

His head, with a foraging cap pulled down over his eyes, disappeared. Lavretsky was left standing alone on the steps, and he gazed steadily into the distance along the road till the carriage disappeared out of sight. 'Perhaps he is right, after all,' he thought as he went back into the house; 'perhaps I am a loafer.' Many of Mihalevitch's words had sunk irresistibly into his heart, though he had disputed and disagreed with him. If a man only has a good heart, no one can resist him.

CHAPTER XXVI

TWO days later, Marya Dmitrievna visited Vassilyevskoe according to her promise, with all her young
people. The little girls ran at once into the garden,
while Marya Dmitrievna languidly walked through the rooms
and languidly admired everything. She regarded her visit
to Lavretsky as a sign of great condescension, almost as a
deed of charity. She smiled graciously when Anton and
Apraxya kissed her hand in the old-fashioned house-serv-
ants' style; and in a weak voice, speaking through her nose,
asked for some tea. To the great vexation of Anton, who
had put on knitted white gloves for the purpose, tea was not
handed to the grand lady visitor by him, but by Lavretsky's
hired valet, who in the old man's words, had not a notion
of what was proper. To make up for this, Anton resumed
his rights at dinner: he took up a firm position behind Marya
Dmitrievna's chair, and would not surrender his post to any
one. The appearance of guests after so long an interval at
Vassilyevskoe fluttered and delighted the old man; it was
a pleasure to him to see that his master was acquainted with
such fine gentlefolk. He was not, however, the only one who
was fluttered that day; Lemm, too, was in agitation. He
had put on a rather short snuff-coloured coat with a swallow-
tail, and tied his neckhandkerchief stiffly, and he kept incessantly coughing and making way for people with a cordial
and affable air. Lavretsky noticed with pleasure that his relations with Lisa were becoming more intimate; she had held
out her hand to him affectionately directly she came in.
After dinner Lemm drew out of his coat-tail pocket, into
which he had continually been fumbling, a small roll of music-
paper and compressing his lips he laid it without speaking
on the pianoforte. It was a song composed by him the evening before, to some old-fashioned German words, in which
mention was made of the stars. Lisa sat down at once to
the piano and played at sight the song. . . . Alas! the music

turned out to be complicated and painfully strained; it was
clear that the composer had striven to express something
passionate and deep, but nothing had come of it; the effort
had remained an effort. Lavretsky and Lisa both felt this,
and Lemm understood it. Without uttering a single word,
he put his song back into his pocket, and in reply to Lisa's
proposal to play it again, he only shook his head and said
significantly: 'Now—enough!' and shrinking into himself he
turned away.

Towards evening the whole party went out to fish. In
the pond behind the garden there were plenty of carp and
groundlings. Marya Dmitrievna was put in an arm-chair
near the banks, in the shade, with a rug under her feet and
the best line was given to her. Anton as an old experienced
angler offered her his services. He zealously put on the
worms, and clapped his hand on them, spat on them and even
threw in the line with a graceful forward swing of his whole
body. Marya Dmitrievna spoke the same day to
Fedor Ivanitch in the following phrase, in boarding-school
French: *'Il n'y a plus maintenant de ces gens comme ça,
comme autrefois.'* Lemm with the two little girls went off
further to the dam of the pond; Lavretsky took up his position near Lisa. The fish were continually biting, the carp
were constantly flashing in the air with golden and silvery
sides as they were drawn in; the cries of pleasure of the little
girls were incessant, even Marya Dmitrievna uttered a little
feminine shriek on two occasions. The fewest fish were
caught by Lavretsky and Lisa; probably this was because
they paid less attention than the others to the angling, and
allowed their floats to swim back right up to the bank. The
high reddish reeds rustled quietly around, the still water
shone quietly before them, and quietly too they talked together. Lisa was standing on a small raft; Lavretsky sat on
the inclined trunk of a willow; Lisa wore a white gown,
tied round the waist with a broad ribbon, also white; her
straw hat was hanging on one hand, and in the other with
some effort she held up the crooked rod. Lavretsky gazed
at her pure, somewhat severe profile, at her hair drawn back
behind her ears, at her soft cheeks, which glowed like a
little child's, and thought, 'Oh, how sweet you are, bend-

ing over my pond!' Lisa did not turn to him, but looked
at the water, half frowning, to keep the sun out of her
eyes, half smiling. The shade of the lime-tree near fell
upon both.

'Do you know,' began Lavretsky, 'I have been thinking
over our last conversation a great deal, and have come to
the conclusion that you are exceedingly good.'

'That was not at all my intention in——' Lisa was beginning to reply, and she was overcome with embarrassment.

'You are good,' repeated Lavretsky. 'I am a rough fellow,
but I feel that every one must love you. There's Lemm for
instance; he is simply in love with you.'

Lisa's brows did not exactly frown, they contracted
slightly; it always happened with her when she heard something disagreeable to her.

'I was very sorry for him to-day,' Lavretsky added, 'with
his unsuccessful song. To be young and to fail is bearable;
but to be old and not be successful is hard to bear. And
how mortifying it is to feel that one's forces are deserting
one! It is hard for an old man to bear such blows! . . .
Be careful, you have a bite. . . . They say,' added Lavretsky
after a short pause, 'that Vladimir Nikolaitch has written
a very pretty song.'

'Yes,' replied Lisa, 'it is only a trifle, but not bad.'

'And what do you think,' inquired Lavretsky; 'is he a
good musician?'

'I think he has great talent for music; but so far he has
not worked at it, as he should.'

'Ah! And is he a good sort of man?'

Lisa laughed and glanced quickly at Fedor Ivanitch.

'What a queer question!' she exclaimed, drawing up her
line and throwing it in again further off.

'Why is it queer? I ask you about him, as one who has
only lately come here, as a relation.'

'A relation?'

'Yes. I am, it seems, a sort of uncle of yours?'

'Vladimir Nikolaitch has a good heart,' said Lisa, 'and
he is clever; *maman* likes him very much.'

'And do you like him?'

'He is nice; why should I not like him?'

'Ah!' Lavretsky uttered and ceased speaking. A half-mournful, half-ironical expression passed over his face. His steadfast gaze embarrassed Lisa, but he went on smiling.— 'Well God grant them happiness!' he muttered at last, as though to himself, and turned away his head.

Lisa flushed.

'You are mistaken, Fedor Ivanitch,' she said: 'you are wrong in thinking. . . . But don't you like Vladimir Nikolaitch?' she asked suddenly.

'No, I don't.'

'Why?'

'I think he has no heart.'

The smile left Lisa's face.

'It is your habit to judge people severely,' she observed after a long silence.

'I don't think it is. What right have I to judge others severely, do you suppose, when I must ask for indulgence myself? Or have you forgotten that I am a laughing stock to everyone, who is not too indifferent even to scoff? . . . By the way,' he added, 'did you keep your promise?'

'What promise?'

'Did you pray for me?'

'Yes, I prayed for you, and I pray for you every day. But please do not speak lightly of that.'

Lavretsky began to assure Lisa that the idea of doing so had never entered his head, that he had the deepest reverence for every conviction; then he went off into a discourse upon religion, its significance in the history of mankind, the significance of Christianity.

'One must be a Christian,' observed Lisa, not without some effort, 'not so as to know the divine . . . and the . . . earthly, because every man has to die.'

Lavretsky raised his eyes in involuntary astonishment upon Lisa and met her gaze.

'What a strange saying you have just uttered!' he said.

'It is not my saying,' she replied.

'Not yours. . . . But what made you speak of death?'

'I don't know. I often think of it.'

'Often?'

'Yes.'

'One would not suppose so, looking at you now; you have such a bright, happy face, you are smiling.'

'Yes, I am very happy just now,' replied Lisa simply.

Lavretsky would have liked to seize both her hands, and press them warmly.

'Lisa, Lisa!' cried Marya Dmitrievna, 'do come here, and look what a fine carp I have caught.'

'In a minute, *maman*,' replied Lisa, and went towards her, but Lavretsky remained sitting on his willow. 'I talk to her just as if life were not over for me,' he thought. As she went away, Lisa hung her hat on a twig; with strange, almost tender emotion, Lavretsky looked at the hat, and its long rather crumpled ribbons. Lisa soon came back to him, and again took her stand on the platform.

'What makes you think Vladimir Nikolaitch has no heart?' she asked a few minutes later.

'I have told you already that I may be mistaken; time will show, however.'

Lisa grew thoughtful. Lavretsky began to tell her about his daily life at Vassilyevskoe, about Mihalevitch, and about Anton; he felt a need to talk to Lisa, to share with her everything that was passing in his heart; she listened so sweetly, so attentively; her few replies and observations seemed to him so simple and so intelligent. He even told her so.

Lisa was surprised.

'Really?' she said; 'I thought that I was like my maid, Nastya, I had no words of my own. She said one day to her sweetheart: "You must be dull with me; you always talk so finely to me, and I have no words of my own."'

'And thank God for it!' thought Lavretsky.

CHAPTER XXVII

MEANWHILE the evening had come on, Marya Dmitrievna expressed a desire to return home, and the little girls were with difficulty torn away from the pond, and made ready. Lavretsky declared that he would escort his guests half-way, and ordered his horse to be saddled. As he was handing Marya Dmitrievna into the coach, he bethought himself of Lemm; but the old man could nowhere be found. He had disappeared directly after the angling was over. Anton, with an energy remarkable for his years, slammed the doors, and called sharply, 'Go on, coachman!' The coach started. Marya Dmitrievna and Lisa were seated in the back seat; the children and their maid in the front. The evening was warm and still, and the windows were open on both sides. Lavretsky trotted near the coach on the side of Lisa, with his arm leaning on the door—he had thrown the reins on the neck of his smoothly-pacing horse—and now and then he exchanged a few words with the young girl. The glow of sunset was disappearing; night came on, but the air seemed to grow even warmer. Marya Dmitrievna was soon slumbering, the little girls and the maid fell asleep also. The coach rolled swiftly and smoothly along; Lisa was bending forward, she felt happy; the rising moon lighted up her face, the fragrant night breeze breathed on her eyes and cheeks. Her hand rested on the coach door near Lavretsky's hand. And he was happy; borne along in the still warmth of the night, never taking his eyes off the good young face, listening to the young voice that was melodious even in a whisper, as it spoke of simple, good things, he did not even notice that he had gone more than half-way. He did not want to wake Marya Dmitrievna, he lightly pressed Lisa's hand and said, 'I think we are friends now, aren't we?' She nodded, he stopped his horse, and the coach rolled away, lightly swaying and oscillating up and down; Lavretsky turned homeward at a walking pace. The witchery of the summer night enfolded him; all around him seemed suddenly so strange—and at the same time so long known, so sweetly familiar. Everywhere near and afar—and one could see into the far distance, though the eye could not make out clearly much of what was seen— all was at peace; youthful, blossoming life seemed expressed in this deep peace. Lavretsky's horse stepped out bravely, swaying evenly to right and left; its great black shadow moved along beside it. There was something strangely sweet in the tramp of its hoofs, a strange charm in the ringing cry of the quails. The stars were lost in a bright mist; the moon, not yet at the full, shone with steady brilliance; its light was shed in an azure stream over the sky, and fell in patches of smoky gold on the thin clouds as they drifted near. The freshness of the air drew a slight moisture into the eyes, sweetly folded all the limbs, and flowed freely into the lungs. Lavretsky rejoiced in it, and was glad at his own rejoicing. 'Come, we are still alive,' he thought; 'we have not been altogether destroyed by'—he did not say—by whom or by what. Then he fell to thinking of Lisa, that she could hardly love Panshin, that if he had met her under different circumstances—God knows what might have come of it; that he understood Lemm though Lisa had no words of 'her own;' but that, he thought, was not true; she had words of her own. 'Don't speak lightly of that,' came back to Lavretsky's mind. He rode a long way with his head bent in thought, then drawing himself up, he slowly repeated aloud:

> 'And I have burnt all I adored,
> And now I adore all that I burnt.'

Then he gave his horse a switch with the whip, and galloped all the way home.

Dismounting from his horse, he looked round for the last time with an involuntary smile of gratitude. Night, still, kindly night stretched over hills and valleys; from afar, out of its fragrant depths—God knows whence—whether from the heavens or the earth—rose a soft, gentle warmth. Lavretsky sent a last greeting to Lisa, and ran up the steps.

The next day passed rather dully. Rain was falling from early morning; Lemm wore a scowl, and kept more and more

tightly compressing his lips, as though he had taken an oath
never to open them again. When he went to his room,
Lavretsky took up to bed with him a whole bundle of French
newspapers, which had been lying for more than a fortnight on his table unopened. He began indifferently to tear
open the wrappings, and glanced hastily over the columns
of the newspapers—in which, however, there was nothing
new. He was just about to throw them down—and all at
once he leaped out of bed as if he had been stung. In an
article in one of the papers, M. Jules, with whom we are
already familiar, communicated to his readers a 'mournful
intelligence, that charming, fascinating Moscow lady,' he
wrote, 'one of the queens of fashion, who adorned Parisian
salons, Madame de Lavretsky, had died almost suddenly, and
this intelligence, unhappily only too well-founded, had only
just reached him, M. Jules. He was,' so he continued, 'he
might say a friend of the deceased.'

Lavretsky dressed, went out into the garden, and till morning he walked up and down the same path.

CHAPTER XXVIII

THE next morning, over their tea, Lemm asked Lavretsky to let him have the horses to return to town. 'It's time for me to set to work, that is, to my lessons,' observed the old man. 'Besides, I am only wasting time here.' Lavretsky did not reply at once; he seemed abstracted. 'Very good,' he said at last; 'I will come with you myself.' Unaided by the servants, Lemm, groaning and wrathful, packed his small box and tore up and burnt a few sheets of music-paper. The horses were harnessed. As he came out of his own room, Lavretsky put the paper he had read last night in his pocket. During the whole course of the journey both Lemm and Lavretsky spoke little to one another; each was occupied with his own thoughts, and each was glad not to be disturbed by the other; and they parted rather coolly, which is often the way, however, with friends in Russia. Lavretsky conducted the old man to his little house; the latter got out, took his trunk, and without holding out his hand to his friend (he was holding his trunk in both arms before his breast), without even looking at him, he said to him in Russian, 'good-bye!' 'Good-bye,' repeated Lavretsky, and bade the coachman drive to his lodging. He had taken rooms in the town of O—— ... After writing a few letters and hastily dining, Lavretsky went to the Kalitins'. In their drawing-room he found only Panshin, who informed him that Marya Dmitrievna would be in directly, and at once, with charming cordiality, entered into conversation with him. Until that day, Panshin had always treated Lavretsky, not exactly haughtily, but at least condescendingly; but Lisa, in describing her expedition of the previous day to Panshin, had spoken of Lavretsky as an excellent and clever man, that was enough; he felt bound to make a conquest of an 'excellent man.' Panshin began with compliments to Lavretsky, with a description of the rapture in which, according to him, the whole family of

Marya Dmitrievna spoke of Vassilyevskoe; and then, according to his custom, passing neatly to himself, began to talk about his pursuits, and his views on life, the world and government service; uttered a sentence or two upon the future of Russia, and the duty of rulers to keep a strict hand over the country; and at this point laughed lightheartedly at his own expense, and added that among other things he had been intrusted in Petersburg with the duty *de populariser l'idée du cadastre*. He spoke somewhat at length, passing over all difficulties with careless self-confidence, and playing with the weightiest administrative and political questions, as a juggler plays with balls. The expressions: 'That's what I would do if I were in the government;' 'you as a man of intelligence, will agree with me at once,' were constantly on his lips. Lavretsky listened coldly to Panshin's chatter; he did not like this handsome, clever, easily-elegant young man, with his bright smile, affable voice, and inquisitive eyes. Panshin, with the quick insight into the feelings of others, which was peculiar to him, soon guessed that he was not giving his companion any special satisfaction, and made a plausible excuse to go away, inwardly deciding that Lavretsky might be an 'excellent man,' but he was unattractive, *aigri*, and, *en somme*, rather absurd. Marya Dmitrievna made her appearance escorted by Gedeonovsky, then Marfa Timofyevna and Lisa came in; and after them the other members of the household; and then the musical amateur, Madame Byelenitsin, arrived, a little thinnish lady, with a languid, pretty, almost childish little face, wearing a rustling dress, a striped fan, and heavy gold bracelets. Her husband was with her, a fat red-faced man, with large hands and feet, white eye-lashes, and an immovable smile on his thick lips; his wife never spoke to him in company, but at home, in moments of tenderness, she used to call him her little sucking-pig. Panshin returned; the rooms were very full of people and noise. Such a crowd was not to Lavretsky's taste; and he was particularly irritated by Madame Byelenitsin, who kept staring at him through her eye-glasses. He would have gone away at once but for Lisa; he wanted to say a few words to her alone, but for a long time he could not get a favourable opportunity, and had to content himself with following her in secret delight with his eyes; never had her face seemed sweeter and more noble to him. She gained much from being near Madame Byelenitsin. The latter was for ever fidgeting in her chair, shrugging her narrow shoulders, giving little girlish giggles, and screwing up her eyes and then opening them wide; Lisa sat quietly, looked directly at every one and did not laugh at all. Madame Kalitin sat down to a game of cards with Marfa Timofyevna, Madame Byelenitsin, and Gedeonovsky, who played very slowly, and constantly made mistakes, frowning and wiping his face with his handkerchief. Panshin assumed a melancholy air, and expressed himself in brief, pregnant, and gloomy phrases, played the part, in fact, of the unappreciated genius, but in spite of the entreaties of Madame Byelenitsin, who was very coquettish with him, he would not consent to sing his song; he felt Lavretsky's presence a constraint. Fedor Ivanitch also spoke little; the peculiar expression of his face struck Lisa directly he came into the room; she felt at once that he had something to tell her, and though she could not herself have said why, she was afraid to question him. At last, as she was going into the next room to pour out tea, she involuntarily turned her head in his direction. He at once went after her.

'What is the matter?' she said, setting the teapot on the samovar.

'Why, have you noticed anything?' he asked.

'You are not the same to-day as I have always seen you before.'

Lavretsky bent over the table.

'I wanted,' he began, 'to tell you a piece of news, but now it is impossible. However, you can read what is marked with pencil in that article,' he added, handing her the paper he had brought with him. 'Let me ask you to keep it a secret; I will come to-morrow morning.'

Lisa was greatly bewildered. Panshin appeared in the doorway. She put the newspaper in her pocket.

'Have you read Obermann, Lisaveta Mihalovna?' Panshin asked her pensively.

Lisa made him a reply in passing, and went out of the room and up-stairs. Lavretsky went back to the drawing-room and drew near the card-table. Marfa Timofyevna, flinging back the ribbons of her cap and flushing with annoyance, began to complain of her partner, Gedeonovsky, who in her words, could not play a bit.

'Card-playing, you see,' she said, 'is not so easy as talking scandal.'

The latter continued to blink and wipe his face. Lisa came into the drawing-room and sat down in a corner; Lavretsky looked at her, she looked at him, and both felt the position insufferable. He read perplexity and a kind of secret reproachfulness in her face. He could not talk to her as he would have liked to do; to remain in the same room with her, a guest among other guests, was too painful; he decided to go away. As he took leave of her, he managed to repeat that he would come to-morrow, and added that he trusted in her friendship.

'Come,' she answered with the same perplexity on her face.

Panshin brightened up at Lavretsky's departure: he began to give advice to Gedeonovsky, paid ironical attentions to Madame Byelenitsin, and at last sang his song. But with Lisa he still spoke and looked as before, impressively and rather mournfully.

Again Lavretsky did not sleep all night. He was not sad, he was not agitated, he was quite calm; but he could not sleep. He did not even remember the past; he simply looked at his life; his heart beat slowly and evenly; the hours glided by; he did not even think of sleep. Only at times the thought flashed through his brain: 'But it is not true, it is all nonsense,' and he stood still, bowed his head and again began to ponder on the life before him.

CHAPTER XXIX

MARYA DMITRIEVNA did not give Lavretsky an over-cordial welcome when he made his appearance the following day. 'Upon my word, he's always in and out,' she thought. She did not much care for him, and Panshin, under whose influence she was, had been very artful and disparaging in his praises of him the evening before. And as she did not regard him as a visitor, and did not consider it necessary to entertain a relation, almost one of the family, it came to pass that in less than half-an-hour's time he found himself walking in an avenue in the grounds with Lisa. Lenotchka and Shurotchka were running about a few paces from them in the flower-garden.

Lisa was as calm as usual but more than usually pale. She took out of her pocket and held out to Lavretsky the sheet of the newspaper folded up small.

'That is terrible!' she said.

Lavretsky made no reply.

'But perhaps it is not true, though,' added Lisa.

'That is why I asked you not to speak of it to any one.'

Lisa walked on a little.

'Tell me,' she began: 'you are not grieved? not at all?'

'I do not know myself what I feel,' replied Lavretsky.

'But you loved her once?'

'Yes.'

'Very much?'

'Yes.'

'So you are not grieved at her death?'

'She was dead to me long ago.'

'It is sinful to say that. Do not be angry with me. You call me your friend: a friend may say everything. To me it is really terrible. . . . Yesterday there was an evil look in your face. . . . Do you remember not long ago how you abused her, and she, perhaps, at that very time was dead? It is terrible. It has been sent to you as a punishment.'

Lavretsky smiled bitterly.

'Do you think so? At least, I am now free.'

Lisa gave a slight shudder.

'Stop, do not talk like that. Of what use is your freedom to you? You ought not to be thinking of that now, but of forgiveness.'

'I forgave her long ago,' Lavretsky interposed with a gesture of the hand.

'No, that is not it,' replied Lisa, flushing. 'You did not understand me. You ought to be seeking to be forgiven.'

'To be forgiven by whom?'

'By whom? God. Who can forgive us, but God?'

Lavretsky seized her hand.

'Ah, Lisaveta Mihalovna, believe me,' he cried, 'I have been punished enough as it is. I have expiated everything already, believe me.'

'That you cannot know,' Lisa murmured in an undertone. 'You have forgotten—not long ago, when you were talking to me—you were not ready to forgive her.'

She walked in silence along the avenue.

'And what about your daughter?' Lisa asked, suddenly stopping short.

Lavretsky started.

'Oh, don't be uneasy! I have already sent letters in all directions. The future of my daughter, as you call—as you say—is assured. Do not be uneasy.'

Lisa smiled mournfully.

'But you are right,' continued Lavretsky, 'what can I do with my freedom? What good is it to me?'

'When did you get that paper?' said Lisa, without replying to his question.

'The day after your visit.'

'And is it possible you did not even shed tears?'

'No. I was thunderstruck; but where were tears to come from? Should I weep over the past? but it is utterly extinct for me! Her very fault did not destroy my happiness, but only showed me that it had never been at all. What is there to weep over now? Though indeed, who knows? I might, perhaps, have been more grieved if I had got this news a fortnight sooner.'

'A fortnight?' repeated Lisa. 'But what has happened then in the last fortnight?'

Lavretsky made no answer, and suddenly Lisa flushed even more than before.

'Yes, yes, you guess why,' Lavretsky cried suddenly, 'in the course of this fortnight I have come to know the value of a pure woman's heart, and my past seems further from me than ever.'

Lisa was confused, and went gently into the flower-garden towards Lenotchka and Shurotchka.

'But I am glad I showed you that newspaper,' said Lavretsky, walking after her; 'already I have grown used to hiding nothing from you, and I hope you will repay me with the same confidence.'

'Do you expect it?' said Lisa, standing still. 'In that case I ought—but no! It is impossible.'

'What is it? Tell me, tell me.'

'Really, I believe I ought not—after all, though,' added Lisa, turning to Lavretsky with a smile, 'what's the good of half confidence? Do you know I received a letter to-day?'

'From Panshin?'

'Yes. How did you know?'

'He asks for your hand?'

'Yes,' replied Lisa, looking Lavretsky straight in the face with a serious expression.

Lavretsky on his side looked seriously at Lisa.

'Well, and what answer have you given him?' he managed to say at last.

'I don't know what answer to give,' replied Lisa, letting her clasped hands fall.

'How is that? Do you love him, then?'

'Yes, I like him; he seems a nice man.'

'You said the very same thing, and in the very same words, three days ago. I want to know do you love him with that intense passionate feeling which we usually call love?'

'As you understand it—no.'

'You're not in love with him?'

'No. But is that necessary?'

'What do you mean?'

'Mamma likes him,' continued Lisa, 'he is kind; I have nothing against him.'

'You hesitate, however.'

'Yes—and perhaps—you, your words are the cause of it. Do you remember what you said three days ago? But that is weakness.'

'O my child!' cried Lavretsky suddenly, and his voice was shaking, 'don't cheat yourself with sophistries, don't call weakness the cry of your heart, which is not ready to give itself without love. Do not take on yourself such a fearful responsibility to this man, whom you don't love, though you are ready to belong to him.'

'I'm obeying, I take nothing on myself,' Lisa was murmuring.

'Obey your heart; only that will tell you the truth,' Lavretsky interrupted her. 'Experience, prudence, all that is dust and ashes! Do not deprive yourself of the best, of the sole happiness on earth.'

'Do you say that, Fedor Ivanitch? You yourself married for love, and were you happy?'

Lavretsky threw up his arms.

'Ah, don't talk about me! You can't even understand all that a young, inexperienced, badly brought-up boy may mistake for love! Indeed though, after all, why should I be unfair to myself? I told you just now that I had not had happiness. No! I was happy!'

'It seems to me, Fedor Ivanitch,' Lisa murmured in a low voice—when she did not agree with the person whom she was talking to, she always dropped her voice; and now too she was deeply moved—'happiness on earth does not depend on ourselves.'

'On ourselves, ourselves, believe me' (he seized both her hands; Lisa grew pale and almost with terror but still steadfastly looked at him): 'if only we do not ruin our lives. For some people marriage for love may be unhappiness; but not for you, with your calm temperament, and your clear soul; I beseech you, do not marry without love, from a sense of duty, self-sacrifice, or anything. . . . That is infidelity, that is mercenary, and worse still. Believe me,—I have the right to say so; I have paid dearly for the right. And if your God——.'

At that instant Lavretsky noticed that Lenotchka and Shurotchka were standing near Lisa, and staring in dumb amazement at him. He dropped Lisa's hands, saying hurriedly, 'I beg your pardon,' and turned away towards the house.

'One thing only I beg of you,' he added, returning again to Lisa: 'don't decide at once, wait a little, think of what I have said to you. Even if you don't believe me, even if you did decide on a marriage of prudence—even in that case you mustn't marry Panshin. He can't be your husband. You will promise me not to be in a hurry, won't you?'

Lisa tried to answer Lavretsky, but she did not utter a word—not because she was resolved to 'be in a hurry,' but because her heart was beating too violently and a feeling, akin to terror, stopped her breath.

CHAPTER XXX

AS he was coming away from the Kalitins, Lavretsky met Panshin; they bowed coldly to one another. Lavretsky went to his lodgings, and locked himself in. He was experiencing emotions such as he had hardly ever experienced before. How long ago was it since he had thought himself in a state of peaceful petrifaction? How long was it since he had felt as he had expressed himself at the very bottom of the river? What had changed his position? What had brought him out of his solitude? The most ordinary, inevitable, though always unexpected event, death? Yes; but he was not thinking so much of his wife's death and his own freedom, as of this question—what answer would Lisa give Panshin? He felt that in the course of the last three days, he had come to look at her with different eyes; he remembered how after returning home when he thought of her in the silence of the night, he had said to himself, 'if only!' . . . That 'if only'—in which he had referred to the past, to the impossible had come to pass, though not as he had imagined it,—but his freedom alone was little. 'She will obey her mother,' he thought, 'she will marry Panshin; but even if she refuses him, won't it be just the same as far as I am concerned?' Going up to the looking-glass he minutely scrutinised his own face and shrugged his shoulders.

The day passed quickly by in these meditations; and evening came. Lavretsky went to the Kalitins'. He walked quickly, but his pace slackened as he drew near the house. Before the steps was standing Panshin's light carriage. 'Come,' thought Lavretsky, 'I will not be an egoist'—and he went into the house. He met with no one within-doors, and there was no sound in the drawing-room; he opened the door and saw Marya Dmitrievna playing picquet with Panshin. Panshin bowed to him without speaking, but the lady of the house cried, 'Well, this is unexpected!' and slightly frowned. Lavretsky sat down near her, and began to look at her cards.

'Do you know how to play picquet?' she asked him with a kind of hidden vexation, and then declared that she had thrown away a wrong card.

Panshin counted ninety, and began calmly and urbanely taking tricks with a severe and dignified expression of face. So it befits diplomatists to play; this was no doubt how he played in Petersburg with some influential dignitary, whom he wished to impress with a favourable opinion of his solidity and maturity. 'A hundred and one, a hundred and two, hearts, a hundred and three,' sounded his voice in measured tones, and Lavretsky could not decide whether it had a ring of reproach or of self-satisfaction.

'Can I see Marfa Timofyevna?' he inquired, observing that Panshin was setting to work to shuffle the cards with still more dignity. There was not a trace of the artist to be detected in him now.

'I think you can. She is at home, up-stairs,' replied Marya Dmitrievna; 'inquire for her.'

Lavretsky went up-stairs. He found Marfa Timofyevna also at cards; she was playing old maid with Nastasya Karpovna. Roska barked at him; but both the old ladies welcomed him cordially. Marfa Timofyevna especially seemed in excellent spirits.

'Ah! Fedya!' she began, 'pray sit down, my dear. We are just finishing our game. Would you like some preserve? Shurotchka, bring him a pot of strawberry. You don't want any? Well, sit there; only you mustn't smoke; I can't bear your tobacco, and it makes Matross sneeze.'

Lavretsky made haste to assure her that he had not the least desire to smoke.

'Have you been down-stairs?' the old lady continued. 'Whom did you see there? Is Panshin still on view? Did you see Lisa? No? She was meaning to come up here. And here she is: speak of angels——'

Lisa came into the room, and she flushed when she saw Lavretsky.

'I came in for a minute, Marfa Timofyevna,' she was beginning.

'Why for a minute?' interposed the old lady. 'Why are you always in such a hurry, you young people? You see I have a visitor; talk to him a little, and entertain him.'

Lisa sat down on the edge of a chair; she raised her eyes to Lavretsky—and felt that it was impossible not to let him know how her interview with Panshin had ended. But how was she to do it? She felt both awkward and ashamed. She had not long known him, this man who rarely went to church, and took his wife's death so calmly—and here was she, confiding all her secrets to him. . . . It was true he took an interest in her; she herself trusted him and felt drawn to him; but all the same, she was ashamed, as though a stranger had been into her pure, maiden bower.

Marfa Timofyevna came to her assistance.

'Well, if you won't entertain him,' said Marfa Timofyevna, 'who will, poor fellow? I am too old for him, he is too clever for me, and for Nastasya Karpovna he's too old, it's only the quite young men she will look at.'

'How can I entertain Fedor Ivanitch?' said Lisa. 'If he likes, had I not better play him something on the piano?' she added irresolutely.

'Capital; you're my clever girl,' rejoined Marfa Timofyevna. 'Step down-stairs, my dears; when you have finished, come back: I have been made old maid, I don't like it, I want to have my revenge.'

Lisa got up. Lavretsky went after her. As she went down the staircase, Lisa stopped.

'They say truly,' she began, 'that people's hearts are full of contradictions. Your example ought to frighten me, to make me distrust marriage for love; but I——'

'You have refused him?' interrupted Lavretsky.

'No; but I have not consented either. I told him everything, everything I felt, and asked him to wait a little. Are you pleased with me?' she added with a swift smile—and with a light touch of her hand on the banister she ran down the stairs.

'What shall I play to you?' she asked, opening the piano.

'What you like,' answered Lavretsky as he sat down so that he could look at her.

Lisa began to play, and for a long while she did not lift her eyes from her fingers. She glanced at last at Lavretsky, and stopped short; his face seemed strange and beautiful to her.

'What is the matter with you?' she asked.

'Nothing,' he replied; 'I'm very happy; I'm glad of you, I'm glad to see you—go on.'

'It seems to me,' said Lisa a few moments later, 'that if he had really loved me, he would not have written that letter; he must have felt that I could not give him an answer now.'

'That is of no consequence,' observed Lavretsky, 'what is important is that you don't love him.'

'Stop, how can we talk like this? I keep thinking of your dead wife, and you frighten me.'

'Don't you think, Voldemar, that Liseta plays charmingly?' Marya Dmitrievna was saying at that moment to Panshin.

'Yes,' answered Panshin, 'very charmingly.'

Marya Dmitrievna looked tenderly at her young partner, but the latter assumed a still more important and care-worn air and called fourteen kings.

CHAPTER XXXI

LAVRETSKY was not a young man; he could not long delude himself as to the nature of the feeling inspired in him by Lisa; he was brought on that day to the final conviction that he loved her. This conviction did not give him any great pleasure. 'Have I really nothing better to do,' he thought, 'at thirty-five than to put my soul into a woman's keeping again? But Lisa is not like *her;* she would not demand degrading sacrifices from me: she would not tempt me away from my duties; she would herself incite me to hard honest work, and we would walk hand in hand towards a noble aim. Yes,' he concluded his reflections, 'that's all very fine, but the worst of it is that she does not in the least wish to walk hand in hand with me. She meant it when she said that I frightened her. But she doesn't love Panshin either—a poor consolation!'

Lavretsky went back to Vassilyevskoe, but he could not get through four days there—so dull it seemed to him. He was also in agonies of suspense; the news announced by M. Jules required confirmation, and he had received no letters of any kind. He returned to the town and spent an evening at the Kalitins'. He could easily see that Marya Dmitrievna had been set against him; but he succeeded in softening her a little, by losing fifteen roubles to her at picquet, and he spent nearly half an hour almost alone with Lisa in spite of the fact that her mother had advised her the previous evening not to be too intimate with a man *qui a un si grand ridicule.* He found a change in her; she had become, as it were, more thoughtful. She reproached him for his absence and asked him would he not go on the morrow to mass? (The next day was Sunday.)

'Do go,' she said before he had time to answer, 'we will pray together for the repose of her soul.' Then she added that she did not know how to act—she did not know whether she had the right to make Panshin wait any longer for her decision.

'Why so?' inquired Lavretsky.

'Because,' she said, 'I begin now to suspect what that decision will be.'

She declared that her head ached and went to her own room up-stairs, hesitatingly holding out the tips of her fingers to Lavretsky.

The next day Lavretsky went to mass. Lisa was already in the church when he came in. She noticed him though she did not turn round towards him. She prayed fervently, her eyes were full of a calm light, calmly she bowed her head and lifted it again. He felt that she was praying for him too, and his heart was filled with a marvellous tenderness. He was happy and a little ashamed. The people reverently standing, the homely faces, the harmonious singing, the scent of incense, the long slanting gleams of light from the windows, the very darkness of the walls and arched roofs, all went to his heart. For long he had not been to church, for long he had not turned to God: even now he uttered no words of prayer—he did not even pray without words—but, at least, for a moment in all his mind, if not in his body, he bowed down and meekly humbled himself to earth. He remembered how, in his childhood, he had always prayed in church until he had felt, as it were, a cool touch on his brow; that, he used to think then, is the guardian angel receiving me, laying on me the seal of grace. He glanced at Lisa. 'You brought me here,' he thought, 'touch me, touch my soul.' She was still praying calmly; her face seemed to him full of joy, and he was softened anew: he prayed for another soul, peace; for his own, forgiveness.

They met in the porch; she greeted him with glad and gracious seriousness. The sun brightly lighted up the young grass in the church-yard, and the striped dresses and kerchiefs of the women; the bells of the churches near were tinkling overhead; and the crows were cawing about the hedges. Lavretsky stood with uncovered head, a smile on his lips; the light breeze lifted his hair, and the ribbons of Lisa's hat. He put Lisa and Lenotchka who was with her into their carriage, divided all his money among the poor, and peacefully sauntered home.

CHAPTER XXXII

PAINFUL days followed for Fedor Ivanitch. He found himself in a continual fever. Every morning he made for the post, and tore open letters and papers in agitation, and nowhere did he find anything which could confirm or disprove the fateful rumour. Sometimes he was disgusting to himself. 'What am I about,' he thought, 'waiting, like a vulture for blood, for certain news of my wife's death?' He went to the Kalitins every day, but things had grown no easier for him there; the lady of the house was obviously sulky with him, and received him very condescendingly. Panshin treated him with exaggerated politeness; Lemm had entrenched himself in his misanthropy and hardly bowed to him, and, worst of all, Lisa seemed to avoid him. When she happened to be left alone with him, instead of her former candour there was visible embarrassment on her part, she did not know what to say to him, and he, too, felt confused. In the space of a few days Lisa had become quite different from what she was as he knew her: in her movements, her voice, her very laugh a secret tremor, an unevenness never there before was apparent. Marya Dmitrievna, like a true egoist, suspected nothing; but Marfa Timofyevna began to keep a watch over her favourite. Lavretsky more than once reproached himself for having shown Lisa the newspaper he had received; he could not but be conscious that in his spiritual condition there was something revolting to a pure nature. He imagined also that the change in Lisa was the result of her inward conflicts, her doubts as to what answer to give Panshin.

One day she brought him a book, a novel of Walter Scott's, which she had herself asked him for.

'Have you read it?' he said.

'No; I can't bring myself to read just now,' she answered, and was about to go away.

'Stop a minute, it is so long since I have been alone with you. You seem to be afraid of me.'

'Yes.'

'Why so, pray?'

'I don't know.'

Lavretsky was silent.

'Tell me,' he began, 'you haven't yet decided?'

'What do you mean?' she said, not raising her eyes.

'You understand me.'

Lisa flushed crimson all at once.

'Don't ask me about anything!' she broke out hotly. 'I know nothing; I don't know myself.' And instantly she was gone.

The following day Lavretsky arrived at the Kalitins' after dinner and found there all the preparations for an evening service. In the corner of the dining-room on a square table covered with a clean cloth were already arranged, leaning up against the wall, the small holy pictures, in gold frames, set with tarnished jewels. The old servant in a grey coat and shoes was moving noiselessly and without haste all about the room; he set two wax-candles in the slim candlesticks before the holy pictures, crossed himself, bowed, and slowly went out. The unlighted drawing-room was empty. Lavretsky went into the dining-room and asked if it was some one's name-day.

In a whisper they told him no, but that the evening service had been arranged at the desire of Lisaveta Mihalovna and Marfa Timofyevna; that it had been intended to invite a wonder-working image, but that the latter had gone thirty versts away to visit a sick man. Soon the priest arrived with the deacons; he was a man no longer young, with a large bald head; he coughed loudly in the hall: the ladies at once filed slowly out of the boudoir, and went up to receive his blessing; Lavretsky bowed to them in silence; and in silence they bowed to him. The priest stood still for a little while, coughed once again, and asked in a bass undertone—

'You wish me to begin?'

'Pray begin, father,' replied Marya Dmitrievna.

He began to put on his robes; a deacon in a surplice asked obsequiously for a hot ember; there was a scent of incense.

The maids and men-servants came out from the hall and
remained huddled close together before the door. Roska,
who never came down from up-stairs, suddenly ran into
the dining-room; they began to chase her out; she was
scared, doubled back into the room and sat down; a footman
picked her up and carried her away.

The evening service began. Lavretsky squeezed himself
into a corner; his emotions were strange, almost sad; he
could not himself make out clearly what he was feeling.
Marya Dmitrievna stood in front of all, before the chairs;
she crossed herself with languid carelessness, like a grand
lady, and first looked about her, then suddenly lifted her
eyes to the ceiling; she was bored. Marfa Timofyevna
looked worried; Nastasya Karpovna bowed down to the
ground and got up with a kind of discreet, subdued rustle;
Lisa remained standing in her place motionless; from the
concentrated expression of her face it could be seen that she
was praying steadfastly and fervently. When she bowed to
the cross at the end of the service, she also kissed the large
red hand of the priest. Marya Dmitrievna invited the latter
to have some tea; he took off his vestment, assumed a somewhat more worldly air, and passed into the drawing-room
with the ladies. Conversation—not too lively—began. The
priest drank four cups of tea, incessantly wiping his bald
head with his handkerchief; he related among other things
that the merchant Avoshnikov was subscribing seven hundred roubles to gilding the 'cumpola' of the church, and
informed them of a sure remedy against freckles. Lavretsky tried to sit near Lisa, but her manner was severe,
almost stern, and she did not once glance at him. She
appeared intentionally not to observe him; a kind of cold,
grave enthusiasm seemed to have taken possession of her.
Lavretsky for some reason or other tried to smile and to
say something amusing; but there was perplexity in his heart,
and he went away at last in secret bewilderment. . . . He
felt there was something in Lisa to which he could never
penetrate.

Another time Lavretsky was sitting in the drawing-room
listening to the sly but tedious gossip of Gedeonovsky, when
suddenly, without himself knowing why, he turned round and

caught a profound, attentive questioning look in Lisa's eyes. . . . It was bent on him, this enigmatic look. Lavretsky thought of it the whole night long. His love was not like a boy's; sighs and agonies were not in his line, and Lisa herself did not inspire a passion of that kind; but for every age love has its tortures—and he was spared none of them.

CHAPTER XXXIII

ONE day Lavretsky, according to his habit, was at the Kalitins'. After an exhaustingly hot day, such a lovely evening had set in that Marya Dmitrievna, in spite of her aversion to a draught, ordered all the windows and doors into the garden to be thrown open, and declared that she would not play cards, that it was a sin to play cards in such weather, and one ought to enjoy nature. Panshin was the only guest. He was stimulated by the beauty of the evening, and conscious of a flood of artistic sensations, but he did not care to sing before Lavretsky, so he fell to reading poetry; he read aloud well, but too self-consciously and with unnecessary refinements, a few poems of Lermontov (Pushkin had not then come into fashion again). Then suddenly, as though ashamed of his enthusiasm, began, *à propos* of the well-known poem, 'A Reverie,' to attack and fall foul of the younger generation. While doing so he did not lose the opportunity of expounding how he would change everything after his own fashion, if the power were in his hands. 'Russia,' he said, 'has fallen behind Europe; we must catch her up. It is maintained that we are young—that's nonsense. Moreover we have no inventiveness: Homakov himself admits that we have not even invented mouse-traps. Consequently, whether we will or no, we must borrow from others. We are sick, Lermontov says—I agree with him. But we are sick from having only half become Europeans, we must take a hair of the dog that bit us ('*le cadastre,*' thought Lavretsky). 'The best heads, *les meilleures têtes,*' he continued, 'among us have long been convinced of it. All peoples are essentially alike; only introduce among them good institutions, and the thing is done. Of course there may be adaptation to the existing national life; that is our affair—the affair of the official (he almost said "governing") class. But in case of need don't be uneasy. The institutions will transform the life itself.' Marya Dmitrievna most feelingly assented to all Panshin said. 'What a clever man,' she thought, 'is talking in my drawing-room!' Lisa sat in silence leaning back against the window; Lavretsky too was silent. Marfa Timofyevna, playing cards with her old friend in the corner, muttered something to herself. Panshin walked up and down the room, and spoke eloquently, but with secret exasperation. It seemed as if he were abusing not a whole generation but a few people known to him. In a great lilac-bush in the Kalitins' garden a nightingale had built its nest; its first evening notes filled the pauses of the eloquent speech; the first stars were beginning to shine in the rosy sky over the motionless tops of the limes. Lavretsky got up and began to answer Panshin; an argument sprang up. Lavretsky championed the youth and the independence of Russia; he was ready to throw over himself and his generation, but he stood up for the new men, their convictions and desires. Panshin answered sharply and irritably. He maintained that the intelligent people ought to change everything, and was at last even brought to the point of forgetting his position as a *kammer-yunker,* and his career as an official, and calling Lavretsky an antiquated conservative, even hinting—very remotely it is true—at his dubious position in society. Lavretsky did not lose his temper. He did not raise his voice (he recollected that Mihalevitch too had called him antiquated but an antiquated Voltairean), and calmly proceeded to refute Panshin at all points. He proved to him the impracticability of sudden leaps and reforms from above, founded neither on knowledge of the mother-country, nor on any genuine faith in any ideal, even a negative one. He brought forward his own education as an example, and demanded before all things a recognition of the true spirit of the people and submission to it, without which even a courageous combat against error is impossible. Finally he admitted the reproach—well-deserved as he thought—of reckless waste of time and strength.

'That is all very fine!' cried Panshin at last, getting angry. 'You now have just returned to Russia, what do you intend to do?'

'Cultivate the soil,' answered Lavretsky, 'and try to cultivate it as well as possible.'

'That is very praiseworthy, no doubt,' rejoined Panshin, 'and I have been told that you have already had great success in that line; but you must allow that not every one is fit for pursuits of that kind.'

'*Une nature poétique*,' observed Marya Dmitrievna, 'cannot, to be sure, cultivate . . . *et puis*, it is your vocation, Vladimir Nikolaitch, to do everything *en grand*.'

This was too much even for Panshin: he grew confused, and changed the conversation. He tried to turn it upon the beauty of the starlit sky, the music of Schubert; nothing was successful. He ended by proposing to Marya Dmitrievna a game of picquet. 'What! on such an evening?' she replied feebly. She ordered the cards to be brought in, however. Panshin tore open a new pack of cards with a loud crash, and Lisa and Lavretsky both got up as if by agreement, and went and placed themselves near Marfa Timofyevna. They both felt all at once so happy that they were even a little afraid of remaining alone together, and at the same time they both felt that the embarrassment they had been conscious of for the last few days had vanished, and would return no more. The old lady stealthily patted Lavretsky on the cheek, slyly screwed up her eyes, and shook her head once or twice, adding in a whisper, 'You have shut up our clever friend, many thanks.' Everything was hushed in the room; the only sound was the faint crackling of the waxcandles, and sometimes the tap of a hand on the table, and an exclamation or reckoning of points; and the rich torrent of the nightingale's song, powerful piercingly sweet, poured in at the window, together with the dewy freshness of the night.

CHAPTER XXXIV

LISA had not uttered a word in the course of the dispute between Lavretsky and Panshin, but she had followed it attentively and was completely on Lavretsky's side. Politics interested her very little; but the supercilious tone of the worldly official (he had never delivered himself in that way before) repelled her; his contempt for Russia wounded her. It had never occurred to Lisa that she was a patriot; but her heart was with the Russian people; the Russian turn of mind delighted her; she would talk for hours together without ceremony to the peasant-overseer of her mother's property when he came to the town, and she talked to him as to an equal, without any of the condescension of a superior. Lavretsky felt all this; he would not have troubled himself to answer Panshin by himself; he had spoken only for Lisa's sake. They had said nothing to one another, their eyes even had seldom met. But they both knew that they had grown closer that evening, they knew that they liked and disliked the same things. On one point only were they divided; but Lisa secretly hoped to bring him to God. They sat near Marfa Timofyevna, and appeared to be following her play; indeed, they were really following it, but meanwhile their hearts were full, and nothing was lost on them; for them the nightingale sang, and the stars shone, and the trees gently murmured, lulled to sleep by the summer warmth and softness. Lavretsky was completely carried away, and surrendered himself wholly to his passion—and rejoiced in it. But no word can express what was passing in the pure heart of the young girl. It was a mystery for herself. Let it remain a mystery for all. No one knows, no one has seen, nor will ever see, how the grain, destined to life and growth, swells and ripens in the bosom of the earth.

Ten o'clock struck. Marfa Timofyevna went off up-stairs to her own apartments with Nastasya Karpovna. Lavretsky and Lisa walked across the room, stopped at the open door into the garden, looked into the darkness in the distance and then at one another, and smiled. They could have taken each other's hands, it seemed, and talked to their hearts' content. They returned to Marya Dmitrievna and Panshin, where a game of picquet was still dragging on. The last king was called at last, and the lady of the house rose, sighing and groaning from her well-cushioned easy chair. Panshin took his hat, kissed Marya Dmitrievna's hand, remarking that nothing hindered some happy people now from sleeping, but that he had to sit up over stupid papers till morning, and departed, bowing coldly to Lisa (he had not expected that she would ask him to wait so long for an answer to his offer, and he was cross with her for it). Lavretsky followed him. They parted at the gate. Panshin waked his coachman by poking him in the neck with the end of his stick, took his seat in the carriage and rolled away. Lavretsky did not want to go home. He walked away from the town into the open country. The night was still and clear, though there was no moon. Lavretsky rambled a long time over the dewy grass. He came across a little narrow path; and went along it. It led him up to a long fence, and to a little gate; he tried, not knowing why, to push it open. With a faint creak the gate opened, as though it had been awaiting the touch of his hand. Lavretsky went into the garden. After a few paces along a walk of lime-trees he stopped short in amazement; he recognised the Kalitins' garden.

He moved at once into a black patch of shade thrown by a thick clump of hazels, and stood a long while without moving, shrugging his shoulders in astonishment.

'This cannot be for nothing,' he thought.

All was hushed around. From the direction of the house not a sound reached him. He went cautiously forward. At the bend of an avenue suddenly the whole house confronted him with its dark face; in two upstair-windows only a light was shining. In Lisa's room behind the white curtain a candle was burning, and in Marfa Timofyevna's bedroom a lamp shone with red-fire before the holy picture, and was reflected with equal brilliance on the gold frame. Below, the door on to the balcony gaped wide open. Lavretsky sat down on a wooden garden-seat, leaned on his elbow, and began to watch this door and Lisa's window. In the town it struck midnight; a little clock in the house shrilly clanged out twelve; the watchman beat it with jerky strokes upon his board. Lavretsky had no thought, no expectation; it was sweet to him to feel himself near Lisa, to sit in her garden on the seat where she herself had sat more than once.

The light in Lisa's room vanished.

'Sleep well, my sweet girl,' whispered Lavretsky, still sitting motionless, his eyes fixed on the darkened window.

Suddenly the light appeared in one of the windows of the ground-floor, then changed into another, and a third. . . . Some one was walking through the rooms with a candle. 'Can it be Lisa? It cannot be.' Lavretsky got up. . . . He caught a glimpse of a well-known face—Lisa came into the drawing-room. In a white gown, her plaits hanging loose on her shoulders, she went quietly up to the table, bent over it, put down the candle, and began looking for something. Then turning round facing the garden, she drew near the open door, and stood on the threshold, a light slender figure all in white. A shiver passed over Lavretsky.

'Lisa!' broke hardly audibly from his lips.

She started and began to gaze into the darkness.

'Lisa!' Lavretsky repeated louder, and he came out of the shadow of the avenue.

Lisa raised her head in alarm, and shrank back. She had recognised him. He called to her a third time, and stretched out his hands to her. She came away from the door and stepped into the garden.

'Is it you?' she said. 'You here?'

'I—I—listen to me,' whispered Lavretsky, and seizing her hand he led her to the seat.

She followed him without resistance, her pale face, her fixed eyes, and all her gestures expressed an unutterable bewilderment. Lavretsky made her sit down and stood before her.

'I did not mean to come here,' he began. 'Something brought me. . . . I—I love you,' he uttered in involuntary terror.

Lisa slowly looked at him. It seemed as though she only

at that instant knew where she was and what was happening. She tried to get up, she could not, and she covered her face with her hands.

'Lisa,' murmured Lavretsky. 'Lisa,' he repeated, and fell at her feet.

Her shoulders began to heave slightly; the fingers of her pale hands were pressed more closely to her face.

'What is it?' Lavretsky urged, and he heard a subdued sob. His heart stood still. . . . He knew the meaning of those tears. 'Can it be that you love me?' he whispered, and caressed her knees.

'Get up,' he heard her voice, 'get up, Fedor Ivanitch. What are we doing?'

He got up and sat beside her on the seat. She was not weeping now, and she looked at him steadfastly with her wet eyes.

'It frightens me: what are we doing?' she repeated.

'I love you,' he said again. 'I am ready to devote my whole life to you.'

She shuddered again, as though something had stung her, and lifted her eyes towards heaven.

'All that is in God's hands,' she said.

'But you love me, Lisa? We shall be happy.' She dropped her eyes; he softly drew her to him, and her head sank on to his shoulder. . . . He bent his head a little and touched her pale lips.

Half an hour later Lavretsky was standing before the little garden gate. He found it locked and was obliged to get over the fence. He returned to the town and walked along the slumbering streets. A sense of immense, unhoped-for happiness filled his soul; all his doubts had died away. 'Away, dark phantom of the past,' he thought. 'She loves me, she will be mine.' Suddenly it seemed to him that in the air over his head were floating strains of divine triumphant music. He stood still. The music resounded in still greater magnificence; a mighty flood of melody—and all his bliss seemed speaking and singing in its strains. He looked about him; the music floated down from two upper windows of a small house.

'Lemm?' cried Lavretsky as he ran to the house. 'Lemm! Lemm!' he repeated aloud.

The sounds died away and the figure of the old man in a dressing-gown, with his throat bare and his hair dishevelled, appeared at the window.

'Aha!' he said with dignity, 'is it you?'

'Christopher Fedoritch, what marvellous music! for mercy's sake, let me in.'

Without uttering a word, the old man with a majestic flourish of the arm dropped the key of the street door from the window.

Lavretsky hastened up-stairs, went into the room and was about to rush up to Lemm; but the latter imperiously motioned him to a seat, saying abruptly in Russian, 'Sit down and listen,' sat down himself to the piano, and looking proudly and severely about him, he began to play. It was long since Lavretsky had listened to anything like it. The sweet passionate melody went to his heart from the first note; it was glowing and languishing with inspiration, happiness and beauty; it swelled and melted away; it touched on all that is precious, mysterious, and holy on earth. It breathed of deathless sorrow and mounted dying away to the heavens. Lavretsky drew himself up, and rose cold and pale with ecstasy. This music seemed to clutch his very soul, so lately shaken by the rapture of love, the music was glowing with love too. 'Again!' he whispered as the last chord sounded. The old man threw him an eagle glance, struck his hand on his chest and saying deliberately in his own tongue, 'This is my work, I am a great musician,' he played again his marvellous composition. There was no candle in the room; the light of the rising moon fell aslant on the window; the soft air was vibrating with sound; the poor little room seemed a holy place, and the old man's head stood out noble and inspired in the silvery half light. Lavretsky went up to him and embraced him. At first Lemm did not respond to his embrace, and even pushed him away with his elbow. For a long while without moving in any limb he kept the same severe, almost morose expression, and only growled out twice, 'aha.' At last his face relaxed, changed, and grew calmer, and in response to Lavretsky's warm congratulations he smiled a little at first, then burst into tears, and sobbed weakly like a child.

'It is wonderful,' he said, 'that you have come just at this moment; but I know all, I know all.'

'You know all?' Lavretsky repeated in amazement.

'You have heard me,' replied Lemm, 'did you not understand that I knew all?'

Till daybreak Lavretsky could not sleep, all night he was sitting on his bed. And Lisa too did not sleep; she was praying.

CHAPTER XXXV

THE reader knows how Lavretsky grew up and developed. Let us say a few words about Lisa's education. She was in her tenth year when her father died; but he had not troubled himself much about her. Weighed down with business cares, for ever anxious for the increase of his property, bilious, sharp and impatient, he gave money unsparingly for the teachers, tutors, dress and other necessities of his children; but he could not endure, as he expressed it, 'to be dandling his squallers,' and indeed he had no time to dandle them. He worked, took no rest from business, slept little, rarely played cards, and worked again. He compared himself to a horse harnessed to a threshing-machine. 'My life has soon come to an end,' was his comment on his death-bed, with a bitter smile on his parched lips. Marya Dmitrievna did not in reality trouble herself about Lisa any more than her husband, though she had boasted to Lavretsky that she alone had educated her children. She dressed her up like a doll, stroked her on the head before visitors and called her a clever child and a darling to her face, and that was all. Any kind of continuous care was too exhausting for the indolent lady. During her father's lifetime, Lisa was in the hands of a governess, Mademoiselle Moreau from Paris, after his death she passed into the charge of Marfa Timofyevna. Marfa Timofyevna the reader knows already; Mademoiselle Moreau was a tiny wrinkled creature with little bird-like ways and a bird's intellect. In her youth she had led a very dissipated life, but in old age she had only two passions left—gluttony and cards. When she had eaten her fill, and was neither playing cards nor chattering, her face assumed an expression almost death-like. She was sitting, looking, breathing—yet it was clear that there was not an idea in her head. One could not even call her good-natured. Birds are not good-natured. Either as a result of her frivolous youth or of the air of Paris, which she had breathed from childhood, a kind of cheap universal scepticism had found its way into her, usually expressed by the words: *tout ça c'est des bêtises*. She spoke ungrammatically, but in a pure Parisian jargon, did not talk scandal and had no caprices—what more can one desire in a governess? Over Lisa she had little influence; all the stronger was the influence on her of her nurse, Agafya Vlasyevna.

This woman's story was remarkable. She came of a peasant family. She was married at sixteen to a peasant; but she was strikingly different from her peasant sisters. Her father had been twenty years starosta, and had made a good deal of money, and he spoiled her. She was exceptionally beautiful, the best-dressed girl in the whole district, clever, ready with her tongue, and daring. Her master Dmitri Pestov, Marya Dmitrievna's father, a man of modest and gentle character, saw her one day at the threshing-floor, talked to her and fell passionately in love with her. She was soon left a widow; Pestov, though he was a married man, took her into his house and dressed her like a lady. Agafya at once adapted herself to her new position, just as if she had never lived differently all her life. She grew fairer and plumper; her arms grew as 'floury white' under her muslin-sleeves as a merchant's lady's; the samovar never left her table; she would wear nothing except silk or velvet, and slept on well-stuffed feather-beds. This blissful existence lasted for five years, but Dmitri Pestov died; his widow, a kind-hearted woman, out of regard for the memory of the deceased, did not wish to treat her rival unfairly, all the more because Agafya had never forgotten herself in her presence. She married her, however, to a shepherd, and sent her a long way off. Three years passed. It happened one hot summer day that her mistress in driving past stopped at the cattle-yard. Agafya regaled her with such delicious cool cream, behaved so modestly, and was so neat, so bright, and so contented with everything that her mistress signified her forgiveness to her and allowed her to return to the house. Within six months she had become so much attached to her that she raised her to be housekeeper, and intrusted the whole household management to her. Agafya again returned to power, and again grew plump and fair; her mis-

tress put the most complete confidence in her. So passed
five years more. Misfortune again overtook Agafya. Her
husband, whom she had promoted to be a footman, began to
drink, took to vanishing from the house, and ended by steal-
ing six of the mistress' silver spoons and hiding them till a
favourable moment in his wife's box. It was opened. He
was sent to be a shepherd again, and Agafya fell into disgrace. She was not turned out of the house, but was
degraded from housekeeper to being a sewing-woman and
was ordered to wear a kerchief on her head instead of a
cap. To the astonishment of every one, Agafya accepted
with humble resignation the blow that had fallen upon her.
She was at that time about thirty, all her children were dead
and her husband did not live much longer. The time had
come for her to reflect. And she did reflect. She became
very silent and devout, never missed a single matin's service
nor a single mass, and gave away all her fine clothes. She
spent fifteen years quietly, peacefully, and soberly, never
quarrelling with any one and giving way to every one. If
any one scolded her, she only bowed to them and thanked
them for the admonition. Her mistress had long ago forgiven her, raised her out of disgrace, and had made her a
present of a cap of her own. But she was herself unwilling
to give up the kerchief and always wore a dark dress. After
her mistress' death she became still more quiet and humble.
A Russian readily feels fear, and affection; but it is hard
to gain his respect: it is not soon given, nor to every one.
For Agafya every one in the house had great respect; no
one even remembered her previous sins, as though they had
been buried with the old master.

When Kalitin became Marya Dmitrievna's husband, he
wanted to intrust the care of the house to Agafya. But
she refused 'on account of temptation;' he scolded her, but
she bowed humbly and left the room. Kalitin was clever in
understanding men; he understood Agafya and did not forget
her. When he moved to the town, he gave her, with her
consent, the place of nurse to Lisa, who was only just five
years old.

Lisa was at first frightened by the austere and serious
face of her new nurse; but she soon grew used to her and

began to love her. She was herself a serious child. Her features recalled Kalitin's decided and regular profile, only her eyes were not her father's; they were lighted up by a gentle attentiveness and goodness, rare in children. She did not care to play with dolls, never laughed loudly or for long, and behaved with great decorum. She was not often thoughtful, but when she was, it was almost always with some reason. After a short silence, she usually turned to some grown-up person with a question which showed that her brain had been at work upon some new impression. She very early got over childish lispings, and by the time she was four years old spoke perfectly plainly. She was afraid of her father; her feeling towards her mother was undefinable, she was not afraid of her, nor was she demonstrative to her; but she was not demonstrative even towards Agafya, though she was the only person she loved. Agafya never left her. It was curious to see them together. Agafya, all in black, with a dark handkerchief on her head, her face thin and transparent as wax, but still beautiful and expressive, would be sitting upright, knitting a stocking; Lisa would sit at her feet in a little arm-chair, also busied over some kind of work, and seriously raising her clear eyes, listening to what Agafya was relating to her. And Agafya did not tell her stories; but in even measured accents she would narrate the life of the Holy Virgin, the lives of hermits, saints, and holy men. She would tell Lisa how the holy men lived in deserts, how they were saved, how they suffered hunger and want, and did not fear kings, but confessed Christ; how fowls of the air brought them food and wild beasts listened to them, and flowers sprang up on the spots where their blood had been spilt. 'Wall-flowers?' asked Lisa one day, she was very fond of flowers. . . . Agafya spoke to Lisa gravely and meekly, as though she felt herself to be unworthy to utter such high and holy words. Lisa listened to her, and the image of the all-seeing, all-knowing God penetrated with a kind of sweet power into her very soul, filling it with pure and reverent awe; but Christ became for her something near, well-known, almost familiar. Agafya taught her to pray also. Sometimes she wakened Lisa early at daybreak, dressed her hurriedly, and took her in secret to matins. Lisa followed her on tiptoe, almost holding her breath. The cold and twilight of the early morning, the freshness and emptiness of the church, the very secrecy of these unexpected expeditions, the cautious return home and to her little bed, all these mingled impressions of the forbidden, strange, and holy agitated the little girl and penetrated to the very innermost depths of her nature. Agafya never censured any one, and never scolded Lisa for being naughty. When she was displeased at anything, she only kept silence. And Lisa understood this silence; with a child's quick-sightedness she knew very well, too, when Agafya was displeased with other people, Marya Dmitrievna, or Kalitin himself. For a little over three years Agafya waited on Lisa, then Mademoiselle Moreau replaced her; but the frivolous Frenchwoman, with her cold ways and exclamation, *tout ça c'est des bêtises,* could never dislodge her dear nurse from Lisa's heart; the seeds that had been dropped into it had become too deeply rooted. Besides, though Agafya no longer waited on Lisa, she was still in the house and often saw her charge, who believed in her as before.

Agafya did not, however, get on well with Marfa Timofyevna, when she came to live in the Kalitins' house. Such gravity and dignity on the part of one who had once worn the motley skirt of a peasant wench displeased the impatient and self-willed old lady. Agafya asked leave to go on a pilgrimage and she never came back. There were dark rumours that she had gone off to a retreat of sectaries. But the impression she had left in Lisa's soul was never obliterated. She went as before to the mass as to a festival, she prayed with rapture, with a kind of restrained and shamefaced transport, at which Marya Dmitrievna secretly marvelled not a little, and even Marfa Timofyevna, though she did not restrain Lisa in any way, tried to temper her zeal, and would not let her make too many prostrations to the earth in her prayers; it was not a lady-like habit, she would say. In her studies Lisa worked well, that is to say perseveringly; she was not gifted with specially brilliant abilities, or great intellect; she could not succeed in anything without labour. She played the piano well, but only Lemm knew what it had cost her. She had read little; she had not 'words of her own,' but she had her own ideas, and she went her own way. It was not only on the surface that she took after her father; he, too, had never asked other people what was to be done. So she had grown up tranquilly and restfully till she had reached the age of nineteen. She was very charming, without being aware of it herself. Her every movement was full of spontaneous, somewhat awkward gracefulness; her voice had the silvery ring of untouched youth, the least feeling of pleasure called forth an enchanting smile on her lips, and added a deep light and a kind of mystic sweetness to her kindling eyes. Penetrated through and through by a sense of duty, by the dread of hurting any one whatever, with a kind and tender heart, she had loved all men, and no one in particular; God only she had loved passionately, timidly, and tenderly. Lavretsky was the first to break in upon her peaceful inner life.

Such was Lisa.

CHAPTER XXXVI

ON the following day at twelve o'clock, Lavretsky set off to the Kalitins. On the way he met Panshin, who galloped past him on horseback, his hat pulled down to his very eyebrows. At the Kalitins', Lavretsky was not admitted for the first time since he had been acquainted with them. Marya Dmitrievna was 'resting,' so the footman informed him; her excellency had a headache. Marfa Timofyevna and Lisaveta Mihalovna were not at home. Lavretsky walked round the garden in the faint hope of meeting Lisa, but he saw no one. He came back two hours later and received the same answer, accompanied by a rather dubious look from the footman. Lavretsky thought it would be unseemly to call for a third time the same day, and he decided to drive over to Vassilyevskoe, where he had business moreover. On the road he made various plans for the future, each better than the last; but he was overtaken by a melancholy mood when he reached his aunt's little village. He fell into conversation with Anton; the old man, as if purposely, seemed full of cheerless fancies. He told Lavretsky how, at her death, Glafira Petrovna had bitten her own arm, and after a brief pause, added with a sigh: 'Every man, dear master, is destined to devour himself.' It was late when Lavretsky set off on the way back. He was haunted by the music of the day before, and Lisa's image returned to him in all its sweet distinctness; he mused with melting tenderness over the thought that she loved him, and reached his little house in the town, soothed and happy.

The first thing that struck him as he went into the entrance hall was a scent of patchouli, always distasteful to him; there were some high travelling-trunks standing there. The face of his groom, who ran out to meet him, seemed strange to him. Not stopping to analyse his impressions, he crossed the threshold of the drawing-room. . . . On his entrance there rose from the sofa a lady in a black silk dress with

flounces, who, raising a cambric handkerchief to her pale
face, made a few paces forward, bent her carefully dressed,
perfumed head, and fell at his feet. . . . Then, only, he
recognised her : this lady was his wife !

He caught his breath. . . . He leaned against the wall.

'*Théodore*, do not repulse me !' she said in French, and her
voice cut to his heart like a knife.

He looked at her senselessly, and yet he noticed involuntarily at once that she had grown both whiter and fatter.

'*Théodore !*' she went on, from time to time lifting her eyes
and discreetly wringing her marvellously-beautiful fingers
with their rosy, polished nails. '*Théodore*, I have wronged
you, deeply wronged you ; I will say more, I have sinned :
but hear me ; I am tortured by remorse, I have grown
hateful to myself, I could endure my position no longer ;
how many times have I thought of turning to you, but I
feared your anger ; I resolved to break every tie with the
past. . . . *Puis j'ai été si malade.* . . . I have been so ill,'
she added, and passed her hand over her brow and cheek.
I took advantage of the widely-spread rumour of my death,
I gave up everything ; without resting day or night I hastened hither ; I hesitated long to appear before you, my
judge. . . . *paraître devant vous, mon juge ;* but I resolved
at last, remembering your constant goodness, to come to
you ; I found your address at Moscow. Believe me,' she
went on, slowly getting up from the floor and sitting on the
very edge of an arm-chair, 'I have often thought of death,
and I should have found courage enough to take my life . . .
ah ! life is a burden unbearable for me now ! . . . but the
thought of my daughter, my little Ada, stopped me. She is
here, she is asleep in the next room, the poor child ! She
is tired—you shall see her ; she at least has done you no
wrong, and I am so unhappy, so unhappy !' cried Madame
Lavretsky, and she melted into tears.

Lavretsky came to himself at last ; he moved away from
the wall and turned towards the door.

'You are going ?' cried his wife in a voice of despair. 'Oh,
this is cruel ! Without uttering one word to me, not even
a reproach. This contempt will kill me, it is terrible !'

Lavretsky stood still.

'What do you want to hear from me?' he articulated in an expressionless voice.

'Nothing, nothing,' she rejoined quickly, 'I know I have no right to expect anything; I am not mad, believe me; I do not hope, I do not dare to hope for your forgiveness; I only venture to entreat you to command me what I am to do, where I am to live. Like a slave I will fulfil your commands whatever they may be.'

'I have no commands to give you,' replied Lavretsky in the same colourless voice; 'you know, all is over between us . . . and now more than ever; you can live where you like; and if your allowance is too little——'

'Ah, don't say such dreadful things,' Varvara Pavlovna interrupted him, 'spare me, if only . . . if only for the sake of this angel.' And as she uttered these words, Varvara Pavlovna ran impulsively into the next room, and returned at once with a small and very elegantly dressed little girl in her arms.

Thick flaxen curls fell over her pretty rosy little face, and on to her large sleepy black eyes; she smi'ed and blinked her eyes at the light and laid a chubby little hand on her mother's neck.

'*Ada, vois, c'est ton père,*' said Varvara Pavlovna, pushing the curls back from her eyes and kissing her vigorously, '*prie le avec moi.*'

'*C'est ça, papa?*' stammered the little girl lisping.

'*Oui, mon enfant, n'est-ce pas que tu l'aimes?*'

But this was more than Lavretsky could stand.

'In such a melodrama must there really be a scene like this?' he muttered, and went out of the room.

Varvara Pavlovna stood still for some time in the same place, slightly shrugged her shoulders, carried the little girl off into the next room, undressed her and put her to bed. Then she took up a book and sat down near the lamp, and after staying up for an hour she went to bed herself.

'*Eh bien, madame?*' queried her maid, a Frenchwoman whom she had brought from Paris, as she unlaced her corset.

'*Eh bien, Justine,*' she replied, 'he is a good deal older, but I fancy he is just the same good-natured fellow. Give me my gloves for the night, and get out my grey high-necked dress for to-morrow, and don't forget the mutton cutlets for Ada. . . . I daresay it will be difficult to get them here; but we must try.'

'*A la guerre comme à la guerre,*' replied Justine, as she put out the candle.

CHAPTER XXXVII

FOR more than two hours Lavretsky wandered about the streets of the town. The night he had spent in the outskirts of Paris returned to his mind. His heart was bursting and his head, dull and stunned, was filled again with the same dark senseless angry thoughts, constantly recurring. 'She is alive, she is here,' he muttered, with ever fresh amazement. He felt that he had lost Lisa. His wrath choked him; this blow had fallen too suddenly upon him. How could he so readily have believed in the nonsensical gossip of a journal, a wretched scrap of paper? 'Well, if I had not believed it,' he thought, 'what difference would it have made? I should not have known that Lisa loved me; she would not have known it herself.' He could not rid himself of the image, the voice, the eyes of his wife . . . and he cursed himself, he cursed everything in the world.

Wearied out he went towards morning to Lemm's. For a long while he could make no one hear; at last at a window the old man's head appeared in a nightcap, sour, wrinkled, and utterly unlike the inspired austere visage which twenty-four hours before had looked down imperiously upon Lavretsky in all the dignity of artistic grandeur.

'What do you want?' queried Lemm. 'I can't play to you every night, I have taken a decoction for a cold.' But Lavretsky's face, apparently, struck him as strange; the old man made a shade for his eyes with his hand, took a look at his belated visitor, and let him in.

Lavretsky went into the room and sank into a chair. The old man stood still before him, wrapping the skirts of his shabby striped dressing-gown around him, shrinking together and gnawing his lips.

'My wife is here,' Lavretsky brought out. He raised his head and suddenly broke into involuntary laughter.

Lemm's face expressed bewilderment, but he did not even smile, only wrapped himself closer in his dressing-gown.

141

'Of course, you don't know,' Lavretsky went on, 'I had imagined . . . I read in a paper that she was dead.'

'O—oh, did you read that lately?' asked Lemm.

'Yes, lately.'

'O—oh,' repeated the old man, raising his eyebrows. 'And she is here?'

'Yes. She is at my house now; and I . . . I am an unlucky fellow.'

And he laughed again.

'You are an unlucky fellow,' Lemm repeated slowly.

'Christopher Fedoritch,' began Lavretsky, 'would you undertake to carry a note for me?'

'H'm. May I know to whom?'

'Lisavet——'

'Ah . . . yes, yes, I understand. Very good. And when must the letter be received?'

'To-morrow, as early as possible.'

'H'm. I can send Katrine, my cook. No, I will go myself.'

'And you will bring me an answer?'

'Yes, I will bring an answer.'

Lemm sighed.

'Yes, my poor young friend; you are certainly an unlucky young man.'

Lavretsky wrote a few words to Lisa. He told her of his wife's arrival, begged her to appoint a meeting with him,— then he flung himself on the narrow sofa, with his face to the wall; and the old man lay down on the bed, and kept muttering a long while, coughing and drinking off his decoction by gulps.

The morning came; they both got up. With strange eyes they looked at one another. At that moment Lavretsky longed to kill himself. The cook, Katrine, brought them some villainous coffee. It struck eight. Lemm put on his hat, and saying that he was going to give a lesson at the Kalitins' at ten, but he could find a suitable pretext for going there now, he set off. Lavretsky flung himself again on the little sofa, and once more the same bitter laugh stirred in the depth of his soul. He thought of how his wife had driven him out of his house; he imagined Lisa's position, covered his eyes and clasped his hands behind his head. At last Lemm came back and brought him a scrap of paper, on which Lisa had scribbled in pencil the following words: 'We cannot meet to-day; perhaps, to-morrow evening. Good-bye.' Lavretsky thanked Lemm briefly and indifferently, and went home.

He found his wife at breakfast; Ada, in curl-papers, in a little white frock with blue ribbons, was eating her mutton cutlet. Varvara Pavlovna rose at once directly Lavretsky entered the room, and went to meet him with humility in her face. He asked her to follow him into the study, shut the door after them, and began to walk up and down; she sat down, modestly laying one hand over the other, and began to follow his movements with her eyes, which were still beautiful, though they were pencilled lightly under their lids.

For some time Lavretsky could not speak; he felt that he could not master himself, he saw clearly that Varvara Pavlovna was not in the least afraid of him, but was assuming an appearance of being ready to faint away in another instant.

'Listen, madam,' he began at last, breathing with difficulty and at moments setting his teeth: 'it is useless for us to make pretences with one another; I don't believe in your penitence; and even if it were sincere, to be with you again, to live with you, would be impossible for me.'

Varvara Pavlovna bit her lips and half-closed her eyes. 'It is aversion,' she thought; 'all is over; in his eyes I am not even a woman.'

'Impossible,' repeated Lavretsky, fastening the top buttons of his coat. 'I don't know what induced you to come here; I suppose you have come to the end of your money.'

'Ah! you hurt me!' whispered Varvara Pavlovna.

'However that may be—you are, any way, my wife, unhappily. I cannot drive you away . . . and this is the proposal I make you. You may to-day, if you like, set off to Lavriky, and live there; there is, as you know, a good house there; you will have everything you need in addition to your allowance . . . Do you agree?'—Varvara Pavlovna raised an embroidered handkerchief to her face.

'I have told you already,' she said, her lips twitching nervously, 'that I will consent to whatever you think fit to do with me; at present it only remains for me to beg of you—will you allow me at least to thank you for your magnanimity?'

'No thanks, I beg—it is better without that,' Lavretsky said hurriedly. 'So then,' he pursued, approaching the door, 'I may reckon on——'

'To-morrow I will be at Lavriky,' Varvara Pavlovna declared, rising respectfully from her place. 'But Fedor Ivanitch——' (She no longer called him *'Théodore.'*)

'What do you want?'

'I know, I have not yet gained any right to forgiveness; may I hope at least that with time——'

'Ah, Varvara Pavlovna,' Lavretsky broke in, 'you are a clever woman, but I too am not a fool; I know that you don't want forgiveness in the least. And I have forgiven you long ago; but there was always a great gulf between us.'

'I know how to submit,' rejoined Varvara Pavlovna, bowing her head. 'I have not forgotten my sin; I should not have been surprised if I had learnt that you even rejoiced at the news of my death,' she added softly, slightly pointing with her hand to the copy of the journal which was lying forgotten by Lavretsky on the table.

Fedor Ivanitch started; the paper had been marked in pencil. Varvara Pavlovna gazed at him with still greater humility. She was superb at that moment. Her grey Parisian gown clung gracefully round her supple, almost girlish figure; her slender, soft neck, encircled by a white collar, her bosom gently stirred by her even breathing, her hands innocent of bracelets and rings—her whole figure, from her shining hair to the tip of her just visible little shoe, was so artistic . . .

Lavretsky took her in with a glance of hatred; scarcely could he refrain from crying: 'Bravo!' scarcely could he refrain from felling her with a blow of his fist on her shapely head—and he turned on his heel. An hour later he had started for Vassilyevskoe, and two hours later Varvara Pavlovna had bespoken the best carriage in the town, had put on a simple straw hat with a black veil, and a modest mantle, given Ada into the charge of Justine, and set off to the Kalitins'. From the inquiries she had made among the servants, she had learnt that her husband went to see them every day.

CHAPTER XXXVIII

THE day of the arrival of Lavretsky's wife at the town of O——, a sorrowful day for him, had been also a day of misery for Lisa. She had not had time to go down-stairs and say good-morning to her mother, when the tramp of hoofs was heard under the window, and with secret dismay she saw Panshin riding into the courtyard. 'He has come so early for a final explanation,' she thought, and she was not mistaken. After a turn in the drawing-room, he suggested that she should go with him into the garden, and then asked her for the decision of his fate. Lisa summoned up all her courage and told him that she could not be his wife. He heard her to the end, standing on one side of her and pulling his hat down over his forehead; courteously, but in a changed voice, he asked her, 'Was this her last word, and had he given her any ground for such a change in her views?'—then pressed his hand to his eyes, sighed softly and abruptly, and took his hand away from his face again.

'I did not want to go along the beaten track,' he said huskily. 'I wanted to choose a wife according to the dictates of my heart; but it seems this was not to be. Farewell, fond dream!' He made Lisa a profound bow, and went back into the house.

She hoped that he would go away at once; but he went into Marya Dmitrievna's room and remained nearly an hour with her. As he came out, he said to Lisa: '*Votre mère vous appelle; adieu à jamais,*' . . . mounted his horse, and set off at full trot from the very steps. Lisa went in to Marya Dmitrievna and found her in tears; Panshin had informed her of his ill-luck.

'Do you want to be the death of me? Do you want to be the death of me?' was how the disconsolate widow began her lamentations. 'Whom do you want? Wasn't he good enough for you? A *kammer-junker!* not interesting! He

might have married any Maid of Honour he liked in Petersburg. And I—I had so hoped for it! Is it long that you
have changed towards him? How has this misfortune come
on us,—it cannot have come of itself! Is it that dolt of a
cousin's doing? A nice person you have picked up to advise
you!'

'And he, poor darling,' Marya Dmitrievna went on, 'how
respectful he is, how attentive even in his sorrow! He has
promised not to desert me. Ah, I can never bear that! Ah,
my head aches fit to split! Send me Palashka. You will be
the death of me, if you don't think better of it,—do you
hear?'

And, calling ner twice an ungrateful girl, Marya Dmitrievna dismissed her.

She went to her own room. But she had not had time to
recover from her interviews with Panshin and her mother
before another storm broke over her head, and this time
from a quarter from which she would least have expected
it. Marfa Timofyevna came into her room, and at once
slammed the door after her. The old lady's face was pale,
her cap was awry, her eyes were flashing, and her hands
and lips were trembling. Lisa was astonished; she had
never before seen her sensible and reasonable aunt in such
a condition.

'A pretty thing, miss,' Marfa Timofyevna began in a shaking and broken whisper, 'a pretty thing! Who taught you
such ways, I should like to know, miss? . . . Give me some
water; I can't speak.'

'Calm yourself, auntie, what is the matter?' said Lisa, giving her a glass of water 'Why, I thought you did not think
much of Mr Panshin yourself'

Marfa Timofyevna pushed away the glass.

'I can't drink; I shall knock my last teeth out if I try to
What's Panshin to do with it? Why bring Panshin in?
You had better tell me who has taught you to make appoint-
ments at night—eh? miss?'

Lisa turned pale.

'Now, please, don't try to deny it,' pursued Marfa Timofyevna; 'Shurotchka herself saw it all and told me. I have
had to forbid her chattering, but she is not a liar.'

'I don't deny it, auntie,' Lisa uttered scarcely audibly.

'Ah, ah! That's it, is it, miss; you made an appointment with him, that old sinner, who seems so meek?'

'No.'

'How then?'

'I went down into the drawing-room for a book; he was in the garden—and he called me.'

'And you went? A pretty thing! So you love him, eh?'

'I love him,' answered Lisa softly.

'Merciful Heavens! She loves him!' Marfa Timofyevna snatched off her cap. 'She loves a married man! Ah! she loves him.'

'He told me' .. began Lisa.

'What has he told you, the scoundrel, eh?'

'He told me that his wife was dead.'

Marfa Timofyevna crossed herself. 'Peace be with her,' she muttered; 'she was a vain hussy, God forgive her. So, then, he's a widower, I suppose. And he's losing no time, I see. He has buried one wife and now he's after another. He's a nice person: only let me tell you one thing, niece; in my day, when I was young, harm came to young girls from such goings on. Don't be angry with me, my girl, only fools are angry at the truth. I have given orders not to admit him to-day. I love him, but I shall never forgive him for this. Upon my word, a widower! Give me some water. But as for your sending Panshin about his business, I think you're a first-rate girl for that. Only don't you go sitting of nights with any animals of that sort; don't break my old heart, or else you'll see I'm not all fondness—I can bite too ... a widower!'

Marfa Timofyevna went off, and Lisa sat down in a corner and began to cry. There was bitterness in her soul. She had not deserved such humiliation. Love had proved no happiness to her: she was weeping for a second time since yesterday evening. This new unexpected feeling had only just arisen in her heart, and already what a heavy price she had paid for it, how coarsely had strange hands touched her sacred secret. She felt ashamed, and bitter, and sick; but she had no doubt and no dread—and Lavretsky was dearer to her than ever. She had hesitated while she did not understand herself; but after that meeting, after that kiss—she could hesitate no more: she knew that she loved, and now she loved honestly and seriously, she was bound firmly for all her life, and she did not fear reproaches. She felt that by no violence could they break that bond.

CHAPTER XXXIX

MARYA DMITRIEVNA was much agitated when she received the announcement of the arrival of Varvara Pavlovna Lavretsky, she did not even know whether to receive her; she was afraid of giving offence to Fedor Ivanitch. At last curiosity prevailed. 'Why,' she reflected, 'she too is a relation,' and, taking up her position in an arm-chair, she said to the footman, 'Show her in.' A few moments passed; the door opened, Varvara Pavlovna, swiftly and with scarcely audible steps, approached Marya Dmitrievna, and not allowing her to rise from her chair, bent almost on her knees before her.

'I thank you, dear aunt,' she began in a soft voice full of emotion, speaking Russian; 'I thank you; I did not hope for such condescension on your part; you are an angel of goodness.'

As she uttered these words Varvara Pavlovna quite unexpectedly took possession of one of Marya Dmitrievna's hands, and pressing it lightly in her pale lavender gloves. she raised it in a fawning way to her full rosy lips. Marya Dmitrievna quite lost her head, seeing such a handsome and charmingly dressed woman almost at her feet. She did not know where she was. And she tried to withdraw her hand, while, at the same time, she was inclined to make her sit down, and to say something affectionate to her. She ended by raising Varvara Pavlovna and kissing her on her smooth perfumed brow. Varvara Pavlovna was completely overcome by this kiss.

'How do you do, *bonjour,*' said Marya Dmitrievna. 'Of course I did not expect . . . but, of course, I am glad to see you. You understand, my dear, it's not for me to judge between man and wife' . . .

'My husband is in the right in everything,' Varvara Pavlovna interposed; 'I alone am to blame.'

'That is a very praiseworthy feeling,' rejoined Marya

Dmitrievna, 'very. Have you been here long? Have you seen him? But sit down, please.'

'I arrived yesterday,' answered Varvara Pavlovna, sitting down meekly. 'I have seen Fedor Ivanitch; I have talked with him

'Ah! Well, and how was he?'

'I was afraid my sudden arrival would provoke his anger,' continued Varvara Pavlovna, 'but he did not refuse to see me.'

'That is to say, he did not . . Yes, yes, I understand,' commented Marya Dmitrievna. 'He is only a little rough on the surface, but his heart is soft.'

'Fedor Ivanitch has not forgiven me; he would not hear me. But he was so good as to assign me Lavriky as a place of residence.'

'Ah! a splendid estate!'

'I am setting off there to-morrow in fulfilment of his wish; but I esteemed it a duty to visit you first.'

'I am very, very much obliged to you, my dear. Relations ought never to forget one another. And do you know I am surprised how well you speak Russian. *C'est étonnant.*'

Varvara Pavlovna sighed.

'I have been too long abroad, Marya Dmitrievna, I know that; but my heart has always been Russian, and I have not forgotten my country.'

'Ah, ah; that is good. Fedor Ivanitch did not, however, expect you at all. Yes; you may trust my experience, *la patrie avant tout.* Ah, show me, if you please—what a charming mantle you have.'

'Do you like it?' Varvara Pavlovna slipped it quickly off her shoulders; 'it is a very simple little thing from Madame Baudran.'

'One can see it at once. From Madame Baudran? How sweet, and what taste! I am sure you have brought a number of fascinating things with you. If I could only see them.'

'All my things are at your service, dearest auntie. If you permit, I can show some patterns to your maid. I have a woman with me from Paris—a wonderfully clever dress-maker.'

'You are very good, my dear. But, really, I am ashamed.' . . .

'Ashamed!' repeated Varvara Pavlovna reproachfully. 'If you want to make me happy, dispose of me as if I were your property.'

Marya Dmitrievna was completely melted.

'*Vous êtes charmante*,' she said. 'But why don't you take off your hat and gloves?'

'What? you will allow me?' asked Varvara Pavlovna, and slightly, as though with emotion, clasped her hands.

'Of course, you will dine with us, I hope. I—I will introduce you to my daughter.' Marya Dmitrievna was a little confused. 'Well! we are in for it! here goes!' she thought. 'She is not very well to-day.'

'*O ma tante*, how good you are!' cried Varvara Pavlovna, and she raised her handkerchief to her eyes.

A page announced the arrival of Gedeonovsky. The old gossip came in bowing and smiling. Marya Dmitrievna presented him to her visitor. He was thrown into confusion for the first moment; but Varvara Pavlovna behaved with such coquettish respectfulness to him, that his ears began to tingle, and gossip, slander, and civility dropped like honey from his lips. Varvara Pavlovna listened to him with a restrained smile and began by degrees to talk herself. She spoke modestly of Paris, of her travels, of Baden; twice she made Marya Dmitrievna laugh, and each time she sighed a little afterwards, and seemed to be inwardly reproaching herself for misplaced levity. She obtained permission to bring Ada; taking off her gloves, with her smooth hands, redolent of soap *à la guimauve*, she showed how and where flounces were worn and ruches and lace and rosettes. She promised to bring a bottle of the new English scent, Victoria Essence; and was as happy as a child when Marya Dmitrievna consented to accept it as a gift. She was moved to tears over the recollection of the emotion she experienced, when, for the first time, she heard the Russian bells. 'They went so deeply to my heart,' she explained.

At that instant Lisa came in.

Ever since the morning, from the very instant when, chill with horror, she had read Lavretsky's note, Lisa had been preparing herself for the meeting with his wife. She had a presentiment that she would see her. She resolved not to avoid her, as a punishment of her, as she called them, sinful hopes. The sudden crisis in her destiny had shaken her to the foundations. In some two hours her face seemed to have grown thin. But she did not shed a single tear. 'It's what I deserve!' she said to herself, repressing with difficulty and dismay some bitter impulses of hatred which frightened her in her soul. 'Well, I must go down!' she thought directly she heard of Madame Lavretsky's arrival, and she went down. . . . She stood a long while at the drawing-room door before she could summon up courage to open it. With the thought, 'I have done her wrong,' she crossed the threshold and forced herself to look at her, forced herself to smile. Varvara Pavlovna went to meet her directly she caught sight of her, and bowed to her slightly, but still respectfully. 'Allow me to introduce myself,' she began in an insinuating voice, 'your *maman* is so indulgent to me that I hope that you too will be . . . good to me.' The expression of Varvara Pavlovna, when she uttered these last words, cold and at the same time soft, her hypocritical smile, the action of her hands, and her shoulders, her very dress, her whole being aroused such a feeling of repulsion in Lisa that she could make no reply to her, and only held out her hand with an effort. 'This young lady disdains me,' thought Varvara Pavlovna, warmly pressing Lisa's cold fingers, and turning to Marya Dmitrievna, she observed in an undertone, *'mais elle est délicieuse!'* Lisa faintly flushed; she heard ridicule, insult in this exclamation. But she resolved not to trust her impressions, and sat down by the window at her embroidery-frame. Even here Varvara Pavlovna did not leave her in peace. She began to admire her taste, her skill. . . Lisa's heart beat violently and painfully. She could scarcely control herself, she could scarcely sit in her place. It seemed to her that Varvara Pavlovna knew all, and was mocking at her in secret triumph. To her relief, Gedeonovsky began to talk to Varvara Pavlovna, and drew off her attention. Lisa bent over her frame, and secretly watched her. 'That woman,' she thought, 'was loved by *him.*' But she at once drove away the very thought of

Lavretsky; she was afraid of losing her control over herself, she felt that her head was going round. Marya Dmitrievna began to talk of music.

'I have heard, my dear,' she began, 'that you are a wonderful performer.'

'It is long since I have played,' replied Varvara Pavlovna, seating herself without delay at the piano, and running her fingers smartly over the keys. 'Do you wish it?'

'If you will be so kind.'

Varvara Pavlovna played a brilliant and difficult *étude* by Hertz very correctly. She had great power and execution.

'*Sylphide!*' cried Gedeonovsky.

'Marvellous!' Marya Dmitrievna chimed in. 'Well, Varvara Pavlovna, I confess,' she observed, for the first time calling her by her name, 'you have astonished me; you might give concerts. We have a musician here, an old German, a queer fellow, but a very clever musician. He gives Lisa lessons. He will be simply crazy over you.'

'Lisaveta Mihalovna is also musical?' asked Varvara Pavlovna, turning her head slightly towards her.

'Yes, she plays fairly, and is fond of music; but what is that beside you? But there is one young man here too—with whom we must make you acquainted. He is an artist in soul, and composes very charmingly. He alone will be able to appreciate you fully.'

'A young man?' said Varvara Pavlovna: 'Who is he? Some poor man?'

'Oh dear no, our chief beau, and not only among us—*et à Petersbourg*. A *kammer-junker*, and received in the best society. You must have heard of him: Panshin, Vladimir Nikolaitch. He is here on a government commission . . . a future minister, I daresay!'

'And an artist?'

'An artist at heart, and so well-bred. You shall see him. He has been here very often of late: I invited him for this evening; I *hope* he will come,' added Marya Dmitrievna with a gentle sigh, and an oblique smile of bitterness.

Lisa knew the meaning of this smile, but it was nothing to her now.

'And young?' repeated Varvara Pavlovna, lightly modulating from tone to tone.

'Twenty-eight, and of the most prepossessing appearance. *Un jeune homme accompli*, indeed.'

'An exemplary young man, one may say,' observed Gedeonovsky.

Varvara Pavlovna began suddenly playing a noisy waltz of Strauss, opening with such a loud and rapid trill that Gedeonovsky was quite startled. In the very middle of the waltz she suddenly passed into a pathetic motive, and finished up with an air from 'Lucia' *Fra poco*. . . . She reflected that lively music was not in keeping with her position. The air from 'Lucia,' with emphasis on the sentimental passages, moved Marya Dmitrievna greatly.

'What soul!' she observed in an undertone to Gedeonovsky.

'A *sylphide!*' repeated Gedeonovsky, raising his eyes towards heaven.

The dinner hour arrived. Marfa Timofyevna came down from up-stairs, when the soup was already on the table. She treated Varvara Pavlovna very drily, replied in half-sentences to her civilities, and did not look at her. Varvara Pavlovna soon realised that there was nothing to be got out of this old lady, and gave up trying to talk to her. To make up for this, Marya Dmitrievna became still more cordial to her guest; her aunt's discourtesy irritated her. Marfa Timofyevna, however, did not only avoid looking at Varvara Pavlovna; she did not look at Lisa either, though her eyes seemed literally blazing. She sat as though she were of stone, yellow and pale, her lips compressed, and ate nothing. Lisa seemed calm; and in reality, her heart was more at rest; a strange apathy, the apathy of the condemned had come upon her. At dinner Varvara Pavlovna spoke little; she seemed to have grown timid again, and her countenance was overspread with an expression of modest melancholy. Gedeonovsky alone enlivened the conversation with his tales, though he constantly looked timorously towards Marfa Timofyevna and coughed—he was always overtaken by a fit of coughing when he was going to tell a lie in her presence—but she did not hinder him by any interruption.

After dinner it seemed that Varvara Pavlovna was quite
devoted to preference; at this Marya Dmitrievna was so
delighted that she felt quite overcome, and thought to herself, 'Really what a fool Fedor Ivanitch must be; not able
to appreciate a woman like this!'

She sat down to play cards together with her and Gedeonovsky, and Marfa Timofyevna led Lisa away up-stairs with
her, saying that she looked shocking, and that she must certainly have a headache.

'Yes, she has an awful headache,' observed Marya Dmitrievna, turning to Varvara Pavlovna and rolling her eyes,
'I myself have often just such sick headaches.'

'Really!' rejoined Varvara Pavlovna.

Lisa went into her aunt's room, and sank powerless into a
chair. Marfa Timofyevna gazed long at her in silence,
slowly she knelt down before her—and began still in the
same silence to kiss her hands alternately. Lisa bent forward, crimsoning—and began to weep, but she did not make
Marfa Timofyevna get up, she did not take away her hands;
she felt that she had not the right to take them away, that
she had not the right to hinder the old lady from expressing
her penitence, and her sympathy, from begging forgiveness
for what had passed the day before. And Marfa Timofyevna
could not kiss enough those poor, pale, powerless hands, and
silent tears flowed from her eyes and from Lisa's; while
the cat Matross purred in the wide arm-chair among the
knitting wool, and the long flame of the little lamp faintly
stirred and flickered before the holy picture. In the next
room, behind the door, stood Nastasya Karpovna, and she
too was furtively wiping her eyes with her check pocket-
handkerchief rolled up in a ball.

CHAPTER XL

MEANWHILE, down-stairs, preference was going on merrily in the drawing-room; Marya Dmitrievna was winning, and was in high good-humour. A servant came in and announced that Panshin was below.

Marya Dmitrievna dropped her cards and moved restlessly in her arm-chair; Varvara Pavlovna looked at her with a half-smile, then turned her eyes towards the door. Panshin made his appearance in a black frock-coat buttoned up to the throat, and a high English collar. 'It was hard for me to obey; but you see I have come,' this was what was expressed by his unsmiling, freshly shaven countenance.

'Well, *Woldemar,*' cried Marya Dmitrievna, 'you used to come in unannounced!'

Panshin only replied to Marya Dmitrievna by a single glance. He bowed courteously to her, but did not kiss her hand. She presented him to Varvara Pavlovna; he stepped back a pace, bowed to her with the same courtesy, but with still greater elegance and respect, and took a seat near the card-table. The game of preference was soon over. Panshin inquired after Lisaveta Mihalovna, learnt that she was not quite well, and expressed his regret. Then he began to talk to Varvara Pavlovna, diplomatically weighing each word and giving it its full value, and politely hearing her answers to the end. But the dignity of his diplomatic tone did not impress Varvara Pavlovna, and she did not adopt it. On the contrary, she looked him in the face with light-hearted attention and talked easily, while her delicate nostrils were quivering as though with suppressed laughter. Marya Dmitrievna began to enlarge on her talent; Panshin courteously inclined his head, so far as his collar would permit him, declared that, 'he felt sure of it beforehand,' and almost turned the conversation to the diplomatic topic of Metternich himself. Varvara Pavlovna, with an expressive look in her velvety eyes, said in a low voice, 'Why, but you too are an

156

artist, *un confrère,*' adding still lower, *'venez!*' with a nod towards the piano. The single word *venez* thrown at him, instantly, as though by magic, effected a complete transformation in Panshin's whole appearance. His care-worn air disappeared; he smiled and grew lively, unbuttoned his coat, and repeating 'a poor artist, alas! Now you, I have heard, are a real artist;' he followed Varvara Pavlovna to the piano. . . .

'Make him sing his song, "How the Moon Floats,"' cried Marya Dmitrievna.

'Do you sing?' said Varvara Pavlovna, enfolding him in a rapid radiant look. 'Sit down.'

Panshin began to cry off.

'Sit down,' she repeated insistently, tapping on a chair behind him.

He sat down, coughed, tugged at his collar, and sang his song.

'*Charmant,*' pronounced Varvara Pavlovna, 'you sing very well, *vous avez du style,* again.'

She walked round the piano and stood just opposite Panshin. He sang it again, increasing the melodramatic tremor in his voice. Varvara Pavlovna stared steadily at him, leaning her elbows on the piano and holding her white hands on a level with her lips. Panshin finished the song.

'*Charmant, charmante idée,*' she said with the calm self-confidence of a connoisseur. 'Tell me, have you composed anything for a woman's voice, for a mezzo-soprano?'

'I hardly compose at all,' replied Panshin. 'That was only thrown off in the intervals of business . . . but do you sing?'

'Yes.'

'Oh! sing us something,' urged Marya Dmitrievna.

Varvara Pavlovna pushed her hair back off her glowing cheeks and gave her head a little shake.

'Our voices ought to go well together,' she observed, turning to Panshin; 'let us sing a duet. Do you know *Son geloso,* or *La ci darem* or *Mira la bianca luna?*'

'I used to sing *Mira la bianca luna,* once,' replied Panshin, 'but long ago; I have forgotten it.'

'Never mind, we will rehearse it in a low voice. Allow me.'

Varvara Pavlovna sat down at the piano, Panshin stood by
her. They sang through the duet in an undertone, and Varvara Pavlovna corrected him several times as they did so, then
they sang it aloud, and then twice repeated the performance of
Mira la bianca lu-u-una. Varvara Pavlovna's voice had lost
its freshness, but she managed it with great skill. Panshin
at first was hesitating, and a little out of tune, then he
warmed up, and if his singing was not quite beyond criticism,
at least he shrugged his shoulders, swayed his whole person,
and lifted his hand from time to time in the most genuine
style. Varvara Pavlovna played two or three little things of
Thalberg's, and coquettishly rendered a little French ballad.
Marya Dmitrievna did not know how to express her delight;
she several times tried to send for Lisa. Gedeonovsky, too,
was at a loss for words, and could only nod his head, but all
at once he gave an unexpected yawn, and hardly had time
to cover his mouth with his hand. This yawn did not escape
Varvara Pavlovna; she at once turned her back on the piano,
observing, *'Assez de musique comme ça;* let us talk,' and she
folded her arms. *'Oui, assez de musique,'* repeated Panshin
gaily, and at once he dropped into a chat, alert, light, and in
French. 'Precisely as in the best Parisian salon,' thought
Marya Dmitrievna, as she listened to their fluent and quick-
witted sentences. Panshin had a sense of complete satisfaction; his eyes shone, and he smiled. At first he passed his
hand across his face, contracted his brows, and sighed
spasmodically whenever he chanced to encounter Marya
Dmitrievna's eyes. But later on he forgot her altogether,
and gave himself up entirely to the enjoyment of a half-
worldly, half-artistic chat. Varvara Pavlovna proved to be
a great philosopher; she had a ready answer for everything;
she never hesitated, never doubted about anything; one
could see that she had conversed much with clever men of
all kinds. All her ideas, all her feelings revolved round
Paris. Panshin turned the conversation upon literature;
it seemed that, like himself, she read only French books.
George Sand drove her to exasperation, Balzac she respected,
but he wearied her; in Sue and Scribe she saw great knowledge of human nature, Dumas and Féval she adored. In her
heart she preferred Paul de Kock to all of them, but of

course she did not even mention his name. To tell the truth, literature had no great interest for her. Varvara Pavlovna very skilfully avoided all that could even remotely recall her position; there was no reference to love in her remarks; on the contrary, they were rather expressive of austerity in regard to the allurements of passion, of disillusionment and resignation. Panshin disputed with her; she did not agree with him . . . but, strange to say! . . . at the very time when words of censure—often of severe censure—were coming from her lips, these words had a soft caressing sound, and her eyes spoke . . . precisely what those lovely eyes spoke, it was hard to say; but at least their utterances were anything but severe, and were full of undefined sweetness.

Panshin tried to interpret their secret meaning, he tried to make his own eyes speak, but he felt he was not successful; he was conscious that Varvara Pavlovna, in the character of a real lioness from abroad, stood high above him, and consequently was not completely master of himself. Varvara Pavlovna had a habit in conversation of lightly touching the sleeve of the person she was talking to; these momentary contacts had a most disquieting influence on Vladimir Nikolaitch. Varvara Pavlovna possessed the faculty of getting on easily with every one; before two hours had passed it seemed to Panshin that he had known her for an age, and Lisa, the same Lisa whom, at any-rate, he had loved, to whom he had the evening before offered his hand, had vanished as it were into a mist. Tea was brought in; the conversation became still more unconstrained. Marya Dmitrievna rang for the page and gave orders to ask Lisa to come down if her head were better. Panshin, hearing Lisa's name, fell to discussing self-sacrifice and the question which was more capable of sacrifice—man or woman. Marya Dmitrievna at once became excited, began to maintain that woman is the more ready for sacrifice, declared that she would prove it in a couple of words, got confused and finished up by a rather unfortunate comparison. Varvara Pavlovna took up a music-book and half-hiding behind it and bending towards Panshin, she observed in a whisper, as she nibbled a biscuit, with a serene smile on her lips and in

her eyes, '*Elle n'a pas inventé la poudre, la bonne dame.*'
Panshin was a little taken aback and amazed at Varvara
Pavlovna's audacity; but he did not realise how much contempt for himself was concealed in this unexpected out-
break, and forgetting Marya Dmitrievna's kindness and devotion, forgetting all the dinners she had given him, and the
money she had lent him, he replied (luckless mortal!) with
the same smile and in the same tone, '*je crois bien,*' and not
even, *je crois bien,* but *j'crois ben!*

Varvara Pavlovna flung him a friendly glance and got up.
Lisa came in: Marfa Timofyevna had tried in vain to hinder
her; she was resolved to go through with her sufferings to
the end. Varvara Pavlovna went to meet her together with
Panshin, on whose face the former diplomatic expression
had reappeared.

'How are you?' he asked Lisa.

'I am better now, thank you,' she replied.

'We have been having a little music here; it's a pity you
did not hear Varvara Pavlovna, she sings superbly, *en artiste
consommée.*'

'Come here, my dear,' sounded Marya Dmitrievna's voice.

Varvara Pavlovna went to her at once with the submissiveness of a child, and sat down on a little stool at her feet.
Marya Dmitrievna had called her so as to leave her daughter,
at least for a moment, alone with Panshin; she was still
secretly hoping that she would come round. Besides, an
idea had entered her head, to which she was anxious to give
expression at once.

'Do you know,' she whispered to Varvara Pavlovna, 'I
want to endeavour to reconcile you and your husband; I
won't answer for my success, but I will make an effort. He
has, you know, a great respect for me.'

Varvara Pavlovna slowly raised her eyes to Marya
Dmitrievna, and eloquently clasped her hands.

'You would be my saviour, *ma tante,*' she said in a mournful voice: 'I don't know how to thank you for all your kindness; but I have been too guilty towards Fedor Ivanitch; he
can not forgive me.'

'But did you—in reality——' Marya Dmitrievna was beginning inquisitively.

'Don't question me,' Varvara Pavlovna interrupted her, and she cast down her eyes. 'I was young, frivolous. But I don't want to justify myself.'

'Well, anyway, why not try? Don't despair,' rejoined Marya Dmitrievna, and she was on the point of patting her on the cheek, but after a glance at her she had not the courage. 'She is humble, very humble,' she thought, 'but still she is a lioness.'

'Are you ill?' Panshin was saying to Lisa meanwhile.

'Yes, I am not well.'

'I understand you,' he brought out after a rather protracted silence. 'Yes, I understand you.'

'What?'

'I understand you,' Panshin repeated significantly; he simply did not know what to say.

Lisa felt embarrassed, and then 'so be it!' she thought. Panshin assumed a mysterious air and kept silent, looking severely away.

'I fancy though it's struck eleven,' remarked Marya Dmitrievna.

Her guests took the hint and began to say good-bye. Varvara Pavlovna had to promise that she would come to dinner the following day and bring Ada. Gedeonovsky, who had all but fallen asleep sitting in his corner, offered to escort her home. Panshin took leave solemnly of all, but at the steps as he put Varvara Pavlovna into her carriage he pressed her hand, and cried after her, '*au revoir!*' Gedeonovsky sat beside her all the way home. She amused herself by pressing the tip of her little foot as though accidentally on his foot; he was thrown into confusion and began paying her compliments. She tittered and made eyes at him when the light of a street lamp fell into the carriage. The waltz she had played was ringing in her head, and exciting her; whatever position she might find herself in, she had only to imagine lights, a ballroom, rapid whirling to the strains of music—and her blood was on fire, her eyes glittered strangely, a smile strayed about her lips, and something of bacchanalian grace was visible over her whole frame. When she reached home Varvara Pavlovna bounded lightly out of the carriage—only real lionesses know how to bound like that—and turning round to Gedeonovsky she burst suddenly into a ringing laugh right in his face.

'An attractive person,' thought the counsellor of state as he made his way to his lodgings, where his servant was awaiting him with a glass of opodeldoc: 'It's well I'm a steady fellow—only, what was she laughing at?'

Marfa Timofyevna spent the whole night sitting beside Lisa's bed.

CHAPTER XLI

LAVRETSKY spent a day and a half at Vassilyevskoe, and employed almost all the time in wandering about the neighbourhood. He could not stop long in one place: he was devoured by anguish; he was torn unceasingly by impotent violent impulses. He remembered the feeling which had taken possession of him the day after his arrival in the country; he remembered his plans then and was intensely exasperated with himself. What had been able to tear him away from what he recognised as his duty—as the one task set before him in the future? The thirst for happiness—again the same thirst for happiness.

'It seems Mihalevitch was right,' he thought; 'you wanted a second time to taste happiness in life,' he said to himself, 'you forgot that it is a luxury, an undeserved bliss, if it even comes once to a man. It was not complete, it was not genuine, you say; but prove your right to full, genuine happiness! Look round and see who is happy, who enjoys life about you? Look at that peasant going to the mowing; is he contented with his fate? . . . What! would you care to change places with him? Remember your mother; how infinitely little she asked of life, and what a life fell to her lot. You were only bragging it seems when you said to Panshin that you had come back to Russia to cultivate the soil; you have come back to dangle after young girls in your old age. Directly the news of your freedom came, you threw up everything, forgot everything; you ran like a boy after a butterfly.' . . .

The image of Lisa continually presented itself in the midst of his broodings. He drove it away with an effort together with another importunate figure, other serenely wily, beautiful, hated features. Old Anton noticed that the master was not himself: after sighing several times outside the door and several times in the doorway, he made up his mind to go up to him, and advised him to take a hot drink of something. Lavretsky swore at him; ordered him out; afterwards he begged his pardon, but that only made Anton still more sorrowful. Lavretsky could not stay in the drawing-room; it seemed to him that his great-grandfather Andrey, was looking contemptuously from the canvas at his feeble descendant. 'Bah: you swim in shallow water,' the distorted lips seemed to be saying. 'Is it possible,' he thought, 'that I cannot master myself, that I am going to give in to this . . . nonsense?' (Those who are badly wounded in war always call their wounds 'nonsense.' If man did not deceive himself, he could not live on earth.) 'Am I really a boy? Ah, well; I saw quite close, I almost held in my hands the possibility of happiness for my whole life; yes, in the lottery too—turn the wheel a little and the beggar perhaps would be a rich man. If it does not happen, then it does not—and it's all over. I will set to work, with my teeth clenched, and make myself be quiet; it's as well, it's not the first time I have had to hold myself in. And why have I run away, why am I stopping here sticking my head in a bush, like an ostrich? A fearful thing to face trouble . . . nonsense! Anton,' he called aloud, 'order the coach to be brought round at once. Yes,' he thought again, 'I must grin and bear it, I must keep myself well in hand.'

With such reasonings Lavretsky tried to ease his pain; but it was deep and intense; and even Apraxya who had outlived all emotion as well as intelligence shook her head and followed him mournfully with her eyes, as he took his seat in the coach to drive to the town. The horses galloped away; he sat upright and motionless, and looked fixedly at the road before him.

CHAPTER XLII

LISA had written to Lavretsky the day before, to tell him to come in the evening; but he first went home to his lodgings. He found neither his wife nor his daughter at home; from the servants he learned that she had gone with the child to the Kalitins'. This information astounded and maddened him. 'Varvara Pavlovna has made up her mind not to let me live at all, it seems,' he thought with a passion of hatred in his heart. He began to walk up and down, and his hands and feet were constantly knocking up against child's toys, books and feminine belongings; he called Justine and told her to clear away all this 'litter.' *'Oui, monsieur,'* she said with a grimace, and began to set the room in order, stooping gracefully. and letting Lavretsky feel in every movement that she regarded him as an unpolished bear.

He looked with aversion at her faded, but still 'piquante,' ironical, Parisian face, at her white elbow-sleeves, her silk apron, and little light cap. He sent her away at last, and after long hesitation (as Varvara Pavlovna still did not return) he decided to go to the Kalitins'—not to see Marya Dmitrievna (he would not for anything in the world have gone into that drawing-room, the room where his wife was), but to go up to Marfa Timofyevna's. He remembered that the back staircase from the servants' entrance led straight to her apartment. He acted on this plan; fortune favoured him; he met Shurotchka in the court-yard; she conducted him up to Marfa Timofyevna's. He found her, contrary to her usual habit, alone; she was sitting without a cap in a corner, bent, and her arms crossed over her breast. The old lady was much upset on seeing Lavretsky, she got up quickly and began to move to and fro in the room as if she were looking for her cap.

'Ah, it's you,' she began, fidgeting about and avoiding meeting his eyes, 'well, how do you do? Well, well, what's to be

165

done! Where were you yesterday? Well, she has come, so there, there! Well, it must . . . one way or another.'

Lavretsky dropped into a chair.

'Well, sit down, sit down,' the old lady went on. 'Did you come straight up-stairs? Well, there, of course. So . . . you came to see me? Thanks.'

The old lady was silent for a little; Lavretsky did not know what to say to her; but she understood him.

'Lisa . . . yes, Lisa was here just now,' pursued Marfa Timofyevna, tying and untying the tassels of her reticule. 'She was not quite well. Shurotchka, where are you? Come here, my girl; why can't you sit still a little? My head aches too. It must be the effect of the singing and music.'

'What singing, auntie?'

'Why, we have been having those—upon my word, what do you call them—duets here. And all in Italian: chi-chi—and cha-cha—like magpies for all the world with their long drawn-out notes as if they'd pull your very soul out. That's Panshin, and your wife too. And how quickly everything was settled; just as though it were all among relations, without ceremony. However, one may well say, even a dog will try to find a home; and won't be lost so long as folks don't drive it out.'

'Still, I confess I did not expect this,' rejoined Lavretsky; 'there must be great effrontery to do this.'

'No, my darling, it's not effrontery, it's calculation, God forgive her! They say you are sending her off to Lavriky; is it true?'

'Yes, I am giving up that property to Varvara Pavlovna.'

'Has she asked you for money?'

'Not yet.'

'Well, that won't be long in coming. But I have only now got a look at you. Are you quite well?'

'Yes.'

'Shurotchka!' cried Marfa Timofyevna suddenly, 'run and tell Lisaveta Mihalovna,—at least, no, ask her . . . is she down-stairs?'

'Yes.'

'Well, then; ask her where she put my book? she will know.'

'Very well.'

The old lady grew fidgety again and began opening a drawer in the chest. Lavretsky sat still without stirring in his place.

All at once light footsteps were heard on the stairs—and Lisa came in.

Lavretsky stood up and bowed; Lisa remained at the door.

'Lisa, Lisa, darling,' began Marfa Timofyevna eagerly, 'where is my book? where did you put my book?'

'What book, auntie?'

'Why, goodness me, that book! But I didn't call you though . . . There, it doesn't matter. What are you doing down-stairs? Here Fedor Ivanitch has come. How is your head?'

'It's nothing.'

'You keep saying it's nothing. What have you going on down-stairs—music?'

'No—they are playing cards.'

'Well, she's ready for anything. Shurotchka, I see you want a run in the garden—run along.'

'Oh, no, Marfa Timofyevna.'

'Don't argue, if you please, run along. Nastasya Karpovna has gone out into the garden all by herself; you keep her company. You must treat the old with respect.'— Shurotchka departed—'But where is my cap? Where has it got to?'

'Let me look for it,' said Lisa.

'Sit down, sit down; I have still the use of my legs. It must be inside in my bedroom.'

And flinging a sidelong glance in Lavretsky's direction, Marfa Timofyevna went out. She left the door open; but suddenly she came back to it and shut it.

Lisa leant back against her chair and quietly covered her face with her hands; Lavretsky remained where he was.

'This is how we were to meet again!' he brought out at last.

Lisa took her hands from her face.

'Yes,' she said faintly: 'we were quickly punished.'

'Punished,' said Lavretsky. . . . 'What had you done to be punished?'

Lisa raised her eyes to him. There was neither sorrow nor disquiet expressed in them: they seemed smaller and dimmer. Her face was pale; and pale too her slightly parted lips.

Lavretsky's heart shuddered for pity and love.

'You wrote to me; all is over,' he whispered, 'yes, all is over—before it had begun.'

'We must forget all that,' Lisa brought out; 'I am glad that you have come; I wanted to write to you, but it is better so. Only we must take advantage quickly of these minutes. It is left for both of us to do our duty. You, Fedor Ivanitch, must be reconciled with your wife.'

'Lisa!'

'I beg you to do so; by that alone can we expiate . . . all that has happened. You will think about it—and will not refuse me.'

'Lisa, for God's sake,—you are asking what is impossible. I am ready to do everything you tell me; but to be reconciled to her *now!* . . . I consent to everything, I have forgotten everything; but I cannot force my heart. . . . Indeed, this is cruel!'

'I do not even ask of you, . . . what you say; do not live with her, if you cannot; but be reconciled,' replied Lisa, and again she hid her eyes in her hand.—'Remember your little girl; do it for my sake.'

'Very well,' Lavretsky muttered between his teeth: 'I will do that, I suppose in that I shall fulfil my duty. But you— what does your duty consist in?'

'That I know myself.'

Lavretsky started suddenly.

'You cannot be making up your mind to marry Panshin?' he said.

Lisa gave an almost imperceptible smile.

'Oh, no!' she said.

'Ah, Lisa, Lisa!' cried Lavretsky 'how happy you might have been!'

Lisa looked at him again.

'Now you see yourself, Fedor Ivanitch, that happiness does not depend on us, but on God.'

'Yes, because you——'

The door from the adjoining room opened quickly and Marfa Timofyevna came in with her cap in her hand.

'I have found it at last,' she said, standing between Lavretsky and Lisa; 'I had laid it down myself. That's what age does for one, alack—though youth's not much better.'

'Well, and are you going to Lavriky yourself with your wife?' she added, turning to Lavretsky.

'To Lavriky with her? I don't know,' he said, after a moment's hesitation.

'You are not going down-stairs.'

'To-day,—no, I'm not.'

'Well, well, you know best; but you, Lisa, I think, ought to go down. Ah, merciful powers, I have forgotten to feed my bullfinch. There, stop a minute, I'll soon——' And Marfa Timofyevna ran off without putting on her cap.

Lavretsky walked quickly up to Lisa.

'Lisa,' he began in a voice of entreaty, 'we are parting for ever, my heart is torn,—give me your hand at parting.'

Lisa raised her head, her wearied eyes, their light almost extinct, rested upon him. . . . 'No,' she uttered, and she drew back the hand she was holding out. 'No, Lavretsky (it was the first time she had used this name), I will not give you my hand. What is the good? Go away, I beseech you. You know I love you . . . yes, I love you,' she added with an effort; 'but no . . . no.'

She pressed her handkerchief to her lips.

'Give me, at least, that handkerchief.'

The door creaked . . . the handkerchief slid on to Lisa's lap. Lavretsky snatched it before it had time to fall to the floor, thrust it quickly into a side pocket, and turning round met Marfa Timofyevna's eyes.

'Lisa, darling, I fancy your mother is calling you,' the old lady declared.

Lisa at once got up and went away.

Marfa Timofyevna sat down again in her corner. Lavretsky began to take leave of her.

'Fedor,' she said suddenly.

'What is it?'

'Are you an honest man?'

'What?'

S—7

'I ask you, are you an honest man?'

'I hope so.'

'H'm. But give me your word of honour that you will be an honest man.'

'Certainly. But why?'

'I know why. And you too, my dear friend, if you think well, you're no fool—will understand why I ask it of you. And now, good-bye, my dear. Thanks for your visit; and remember you have given your word, Fedya, and kiss me. Oh, my dear, it's hard for you, I know; but there, it's not easy for any one. Once I used to envy the flies: I thought, it's for them it's good to be alive, but one night I heard a fly complaining in a spider's web—no, I think, they too have their troubles. There's no help, Fedya; but remember your promise all the same. Good-bye.'

Lavretsky went down the back staircase, and had reached the gates when a man-servant overtook him.

'Marya Dmitrievna told me to ask you to go in to her,' he commenced to Lavretsky.

'Tell her, my boy, that just now I can't——' Fedor Ivanitch was beginning.

'Her excellency told me to ask you very particularly,' continued the servant. 'She gave orders to say she was at home.'

'Have the visitors gone?' asked Lavretsky.

'Certainly, sir,' replied the servant with a grin.

Lavretsky shrugged his shoulders and followed him.

CHAPTER XLIII

MARYA DMITRIEVNA was sitting alone in her boudoir in any easy-chair, sniffing *eau de cologne;* a glass of orange-flower-water was standing on a little table near her. She was agitated and seemed nervous.

Lavretsky came in.

'You wanted to see me,' he said, bowing coldly.

'Yes,' replied Marya Dmitrievna, and she sipped a little water: 'I heard that you had gone straight up to my aunt; I gave orders that you should be asked to come in; I wanted to have a little talk with you. Sit down, please,' Marya Dmitrievna took breath. 'You know,' she went on, 'your wife has come.'

'I was aware of that,' remarked Lavretsky.

'Well, then, that is, I wanted to say, she came to me, and I received her; that is what I wanted to explain to you, Fedor Ivanitch. Thank God I have, I may say, gained universal respect, and for no consideration in the world would I do anything improper. Though I foresaw that it would be disagreeable to you, still I could not make up my mind to deny myself to her, Fedor Ivanitch; she is a relation of mine—through you; put yourself in my position, what right had I to shut my doors on her—you will agree with me?'

'You are exciting yourself needlessly, Marya Dmitrievna,' replied Lavretsky; 'you acted very well, I am not angry. I have not the least intention of depriving Varvara Pavlovna of the opportunity of seeing her friends; I did not come in to you to-day simply because I did not care to meet her—that was all.'

'Ah, how glad I am to hear you say that, Fedor Ivanitch,' cried Marya Dmitrievna, 'but I always expected it of your noble sentiments. And as for my being excited—that's not to be wondered at; I am a woman and a mother. And your wife . . . of course I cannot judge between you and her—as I said to her herself; but she is such a delightful woman that she can produce nothing but a pleasant impression.'

Lavretsky gave a laugh and played with his hat.

'And this is what I wanted to say to you besides, Fedor Ivanitch,' continued Marya Dmitrievna, moving slightly nearer up to him, 'if you had seen the modesty of her behaviour, how respectful she is! Really, it is quite touching. And if you had heard how she spoke of you! I have been to blame towards him, she said, altogether; I did not know how to appreciate him, she said; he is an angel, she said, and not a man. Really, that is what she said—an angel. Her penitence is such . . . Ah, upon my word, I have never seen such penitence!'

'Well, Marya Dmitrievna,' observed Lavretsky, 'if I may be inquisitive: I am told that Varvara Pavlovna has been singing in your drawing-room; did she sing during the time of her penitence, or how was it?'

'Ah, I wonder you are not ashamed to talk like that! She sang and played the piano only to do me a kindness, because I positively entreated, almost commanded her to do so. I saw that she was sad, so sad; I thought how to distract her mind—and I heard that she had such marvellous talent! I assure you, Fedor Ivanitch, she is utterly crushed, ask Sergei Petrovitch even; a heart-broken woman, *tout à fait*: what do you say?'

Lavretsky only shrugged his shoulders.

'And then what a little angel is that Adotchka of yours, what a darling! How sweet she is, what a clever little thing; how she speaks French; and understands Russian too—she called me "auntie" in Russian. And you know that as for shyness—almost all children at her age are shy—there's not a trace of it. She's so like you, Fedor Ivanitch, it's amazing. The eyes, the forehead—well, it's you over again, precisely you. I am not particularly fond of little children, I must own; but I simply lost my heart to your little girl.'

'Marya Dmitrievna,' Lavretsky blurted out suddenly, allow me to ask you what is your object in talking to me like this?'

'What object?' Marya Dmitrievna sniffed her *eau de cologne* again, and took a sip of water. 'Why, I am speaking to you, Fedor Ivanitch, because—I am a relation of yours, you know, I take the warmest interest in you—I know your heart is of the best. Listen to me, *mon cousin*. I am at any rate a woman of experience, and I shall not talk at random: forgive her, forgive your wife.' Marya Dmitrievna's eyes suddenly filled with tears. 'Only think: her youth, her inexperience . . . and who knows, perhaps, bad example; she had not a mother who could bring her up in the right way. Forgive her, Fedor Ivanitch, she has been punished enough.'

The tears were trickling down Marya Dmitrievna's cheeks: she did not wipe them away; she was fond of weeping. Lavretsky sat as if on thorns. 'Good God,' he thought, 'what torture, what a day I have had to-day!'

'You make no reply,' Marya Dmitrievna began again. 'How am I to understand you? Can you really be so cruel? No, I will not believe it. I feel that my words have influenced you, Fedor Ivanitch. God reward you for your goodness, and now receive your wife from my hands.'

Involuntarily Lavretsky jumped up from his chair; Marya Dmitrievna also rose and running quickly behind a screen, she led forth Varvara Pavlovna. Pale, almost lifeless, with downcast eyes, she seemed to have renounced all thought, all will of her own, and to have surrendered herself completely to Marya Dmitrievna.

Lavretsky stepped back a pace.

"You have been here all the time!' he cried.

'Do not blame her,' explained Marya Dmitrievna; 'she was most unwilling to stay, but I forced her to remain. I put her behind the screen. She assured me that this would only anger you more; I would not even listen to her; I know you better than she does. Take your wife back from my hands; come, Varya, do not fear, fall at your husband's feet (she gave a pull at her arm) and my blessing' . . .

'Stop a minute, Marya Dmitrievna,' said Lavretsky in a low but startlingly impressive voice. 'I dare say you are fond of affecting scenes' (Lavretsky was right, Marya Dmitrievna still retained her school-girl's passion for a little melodramatic effect), 'they amuse you; but they may be anything but pleasant for other people. But I am not going to talk to you; in *this* scene you are not the principal character. What do you want to get out of me, madam?' he added, turning to his wife. 'Haven't I done all I could for you? Don't tell me you did not contrive this interview; I shall not believe you—and you know that I cannot possibly believe you. What is it you want? You are clever—you do nothing without an object. You must realise, that as for living with you, as I once lived with you, that I cannot do; not because I am angry with you, but because I have become a different man. I told you so the day after your return, and you yourself, at that moment, agreed with me in your heart. But you want to reinstate yourself in public opinion; it is not enough for you to live in my house, you want to live with me under the same roof—isn't that it?'

'I want your forgiveness,' pronounced Varvara Pavlovna, not raising her eyes.

'She wants your forgiveness,' repeated Marya Dmitrievna.

'And not for my own sake, but for Ada's,' murmured Varvara Pavlovna.

'And not for her own sake, but for your Ada's,' repeated Marya Dmitrievna.

'Very good. Is that what you want?' Lavretsky uttered with an effort. 'Certainly, I consent to that too.'

Varvara Pavlovna darted a swift glance at him, but Marya Dmitrievna cried: 'There, God be thanked!' and again drew Varvara Pavlovna forward by the arm. 'Take her now from my arms——'

'Stop a minute, I tell you,' Lavretsky interrupted her, 'I agree to live with you, Varvara Pavlovna,' he continued, 'that is to say, I will conduct you to Lavriky, and I will live there with you, as long as I can endure it, and then I will go away—and will come back again. You see, I do not want to deceive you; but do not demand anything more. You would laugh yourself if I were to carry out the desire of our respected cousin, were to press you to my breast, and to fall to assuring you that . . . that the past had not been; and the felled tree can bud again. But I see, I must submit. You will not understand these words . . . but that's no matter. I repeat, I will live with you . . . or no, I cannot promise that . . . I will be reconciled with you, I will regard you as my wife again.'

'Give her, at least, your hand on it,' observed Marya Dmitrievna, whose tears had long since dried up.

'I have never deceived Varvara Pavlovna hitherto,' returned Lavretsky; 'she will believe me without that. I will take her to Lavriky; and remember, Varvara Pavlovna, our treaty is to be reckoned as broken directly you go away from Lavriky. And now allow me to take leave.'

He bowed to both the ladies, and hurriedly went away.

'Are you not going to take her with you!' Marya Dmitrievna cried after him. . . . 'Leave him alone,' Varvara Pavlovna whispered to her. And at once she embraced her, and began thanking her, kissing her hands and calling her her saviour.

Marya Dmitrievna received her caresses indulgently; but at heart she was discontented with Lavretsky, with Varvara Pavlovna, and with the whole scene she had prepared. Very little sentimentality had come of it; Varvara Pavlovna, in her opinion, ought to have flung herself at her husband's feet.

'How was it you didn't understand me?' she commented: 'I kept saying "down."'

'It is better as it was, dear auntie; do not be uneasy—it was all for the best,' Varvara Pavlovna assured her.

'Well, any way, he's as cold as ice,' observed Marya Dmitrievna. 'You didn't weep, it is true, but I was in floods of tears before his eyes. He wants to shut you up at Lavriky. Why, won't you even be able to come and see me? All men are unfeeling,' she concluded, with a significant shake of the head.

'But then women can appreciate goodness and noble-heartedness,' said Varvara Pavlovna, and gently dropping on her knees before Marya Dmitrievna, she flung her arms about her round person, and pressed her face against it. That face wore a sly smile, but Marya Dmitrievna's tears began to flow again.

When Lavretsky returned home, he locked himself in his valet's room, and flung himself on a sofa; he lay like that till morning.

CHAPTER XLIV

THE following day was Sunday. The sound of bells ringing for early mass did not wake Lavretsky—he had not closed his eyes all night—but it reminded him of another Sunday, when at Lisa's desire he had gone to church. He got up hastily; some secret voice told him that he would see her there to-day. He went noiselessly out of the house, leaving a message for Varvara Pavlovna that he would be back to dinner, and with long strides he made his way in the direction in which the monotonously mournful bells were calling him. He arrived early; there was scarcely any one in the church; a deacon was reading the service in the chair; the measured drone of his voice—sometimes broken by a cough—fell and rose at even intervals. Lavretsky placed himself not far from the entrance. Worshippers came in one by one, stopped, crossed themselves, and bowed in all directions; their steps rang out in the empty, silent church, echoing back distinctly under the arched roof. An infirm poor little old woman in a worn-out cloak with a hood was on her knees near Lavretsky, praying assiduously; her toothless, yellow, wrinkled face expressed intense emotion; her red eyes were gazing fixedly upwards at the holy figures on the iconostasis; her bony hand was constantly coming out from under her cloak, and slowly and earnestly making a great sign of the cross. A peasant with a bushy beard and a surly face, dishevelled and unkempt, came into the church, and at once fell on both knees, and began directly crossing himself in haste, bending back his head with a shake after each prostration. Such bitter grief was expressed in his face, and in all his actions, that Lavretsky made up his mind to go up to him and ask him what was wrong. The peasant timidly and morosely started back, looked at him. . . . 'My son is dead,' he articulated quickly, and again fell to bowing to the earth. 'What could replace the consolations of the Church to them?' thought Lavretsky; and he tried himself to pray, but his heart was hard and heavy, and his thoughts were far away. He kept expecting Lisa, but Lisa did not come. The church began to be full of people; but still she was not there. The service commenced, the deacon had already read the gospel, they began ringing for the last prayer; Lavretsky moved a little forward—and suddenly caught sight of Lisa. She had come before him, but he had not seen her; she was hidden in a recess between the wall and the choir, and neither moved nor looked round. Lavretsky did not take his eyes off her till the very end of the service; he was saying farewell to her. The people began to disperse, but she still remained; it seemed as though she were waiting for Lavretsky to go out. At last she crossed herself for the last time and went out—there was only a maid with her—not turning round. Lavretsky went out of the church after her and overtook her in the street; she was walking very quickly, with downcast head, and a veil over her face.

'Good-morning, Lisaveta Mihalovna,' he said aloud with assumed carelessness: 'may I accompany you?'

She made no reply; he walked beside her.

'Are you content with me?' he asked her, dropping his voice. 'Have you heard what happened yesterday?'

'Yes, yes,' she replied in a whisper, 'that was well.' And she went still more quickly.

'Are you content?'

Lisa only bent her head in assent.

'Fedor Ivanitch,' she began in a calm but faint voice, 'I wanted to beg you not to come to see us any more; go away as soon as possible, we may see each other again later—sometime—in a year. But now, do this for my sake; fulfil my request, for God's sake.'

'I am ready to obey you in everything, Lisaveta Mihalovna; but are we really to part like this? will you not say one word to me?'

'Fedor Ivanitch, you are walking near me now. . . . But already you are so far from me. And not only you, but——'

'Speak out, I entreat you!' cried Lavretsky, 'what do you mean?'

'You will hear, perhaps . . . but whatever it may be, forget . . . no, do not forget; remember me.'

'Me forget you——'

'That's enough, good-bye. Do not come after me.'

'Lisa!' Lavretsky was beginning.

'Good-bye, good-bye!' she repeated, pulling her veil still lower and almost running forward. Lavretsky looked after her, and with bowed head, turned back along the street. He stumbled up against Lemm, who was also walking along with his eyes on the ground, and his hat pulled down to his nose.

They looked at one another without speaking.

'Well, what have you to say?' Lavretsky brought out at last.

'What have I to say?' returned Lemm, grimly. 'I have nothing to say. All is dead, and we are dead (*Alles ist todt, und wir sind todt*). So you're going to the right, are you?'

'Yes.'

'And I go to the left. Good-bye.'

The following morning Fedor Ivanitch set off with his wife for Lavriky. She drove in front in the carriage with Ada and Justine; he behind, in the coach. The pretty little girl did not move away from the window the whole journey; she was astonished at everything: the peasants, the women, the wells, the yokes over the horses' heads, the bells and the flocks of crows. Justine shared her wonder. Varvara Pavlovna laughed at their remarks and exclamations. She was in excellent spirits; before leaving town, she had come to an explanation with her husband.

'I understand your position,' she said to him, and from the look in her subtle eyes, he was able to infer that she understood his position fully, 'but you must do me, at least, this justice, that I am easy to live with; I will not fetter you or hinder you: I wanted to secure Ada's future, I want nothing more.'

'Well, you have obtained your object,' observed Fedor Ivanitch.

'I only dream of one thing now: to hide myself for ever in obscurity. I shall remember your goodness always.'

'Enough of that,' he interrupted.

'And I shall know how to respect your independence and tranquillity,' she went on, completing the phrases she had prepared.

Lavretsky made her a low bow. Varvara Pavlovna then believed her husband was thanking her in his heart.

On the evening of the next day they reached Lavriky; a week later, Lavretsky set off for Moscow, leaving his wife five thousand roubles for her household expenses; and the day after Lavretsky's departure, Panshin made his appearance. Varvara Pavlovna had begged him not to forget her in her solitude. She gave him the best possible reception, and, till a late hour of the night, the lofty apartments of the house and even the garden re-echoed with the sound of music, singing, and lively French talk. For three days Varvara Pavlovna entertained Panshin; when he took leave of her, warmly pressing her lovely hands, he promised to come back very soon—and he kept his word.

CHAPTER XLV

LISA had a room to herself on the second story of her mother's house, a clean bright little room with a little white bed, with pots of flowers in the corners and before the windows, a small writing-table, a book-stand, and a crucifix on the wall. It was always called the nursery; Lisa had been born in it. When she returned from the church where she had seen Lavretsky she set everything in her room in order more carefully than usual, dusted it everywhere, looked through and tied up with ribbon all her copy-books, and the letters of her girl-friends, shut up all the drawers, watered the flowers and caressed every blossom with her hand. All this she did without haste, noiselessly, with a kind of rapt and gentle solicitude on her face. She stopped at last in the middle of the room, slowly looked around, and going up to the table above which the crucifix was hanging, she fell on her knees, dropped her head on to her clasped hands and remained motionless.

Marfa Timofyevna came in and found her in this position. Lisa did not observe her entrance. The old lady stepped out on tip-toe and coughed loudly several times outside the door. Lisa rose quickly and wiped her eyes, which were bright with unshed tears.

'Ah! I see, you have been setting your cell to rights again,' observed Marfa Timofyevna, and she bent low over a young rose-tree in a pot; 'how nice it smells!'

Lisa looked thoughtfully at her aunt.

'How strange you should use that word!' she murmured.

'What word, eh?' the old lady returned quickly. 'What do you mean? This is horrible,' she began, suddenly flinging off her cap and sitting down on Lisa's little bed: 'it is more than I can bear! this is the fourth day now that I have been boiling over inside; I can't pretend not to notice any longer; I can't see you getting pale, and fading away, and weeping, I can't, I can't!'

'Why, what is the matter, auntie?' said Lisa, 'it's nothing.'

'Nothing!' cried Marfa Timofyevna; 'you may tell that to others but not to me. Nothing, who was on her knees just this minute? and whose eyelashes are still wet with tears? Nothing, indeed! why, look at yourself, what have you done with your face, what has become of your eyes?—Nothing! do you suppose I don't know all?

'It will pass off, auntie; give me time.'

'It will pass off, but when? Good God! Merciful Saviour! can you have loved him like this? why, he's an old man, Lisa, darling. There, I don't dispute he's a good fellow, no harm in him; but what of that? we are all good people, the world is not so small, there will be always plenty of that commodity.'

'I tell you, it will all pass away, it has all passed away already.'

'Listen, Lisa, darling, what I am going to say to you,' Marfa Timofyevna said suddenly, making Lisa sit beside her, and straightening her hair and her neckerchief. 'It seems to you now in the midst of the worst of it that nothing can ever heal your sorrow. Ah, my darling, the only thing that can't be cured is death. You only say to yourself now: "I won't give in to it—so there!" and you will be surprised yourself how soon, how easily it will pass off. Only have patience.'

'Auntie,' returned Lisa, 'it has passed off already, it is all over.'

'Passed! how has it passed? Why, your poor little nose has grown sharp already and you say it is over. A fine way of getting over it!'

'Yes, it is over, auntie, if you will only try to help me,' Lisa declared with sudden animation, and she flung herself on Marfa Timofyevna's neck. 'Dear auntie, be a friend to me, help me, don't be angry, understand me' . . .

'Why, what is it, what is it, my good girl? Don't terrify me, please; I shall scream directly; don't look at me like that; tell me quickly what is it?'

'I—I want,' Lisa hid her face on Marfa Timofyevna's bosom, 'I want to go into a convent,' she articulated faintly.

The old lady almost bounded off the bed.

'Cross yourself, my girl, Lisa, dear, think what you are saying; what are you thinking of? God have mercy on you!' she stammered at last. 'Lie down, my darling, sleep a little, all this comes from sleeplessness, my dearie.'

Lisa raised her head, her cheeks were glowing.

'No, auntie,' she said, 'don't speak like that; I have made up my mind, I prayed, I asked counsel of God; all is at an end, my life with you is at an end. Such a lesson was not for nothing; and it is not the first time that I have thought of it. Happiness was not for me; even when I had hopes of happiness, my heart was always heavy. I knew all my own sins and those of others, and how papa made our fortune; I know it all. For all that there must be expiation. I am sorry for you, sorry for mamma, for Lenotchka; but there is no help; I feel that there is no living here for me; I have taken leave of all, I have greeted everything in the house for the last time; something calls to me: I am sick at heart, I want to hide myself away for ever. Do not hinder me, do not dissuade me, help me, or else I must go away alone.'

Marfa Timofyevna listened to her niece with horror.

'She is ill, she is raving,' she thought: 'we must send for a doctor; but for which one? Gedeonovsky was praising one the other day; he always tells lies—but perhaps this time he spoke the truth.' But when she was convinced that Lisa was not ill, and was not raving, when she constantly made the same answer to all her expostulations, Marfa Timofyevna was alarmed and distressed in earnest. 'But you don't know, my darling,' she began to reason with her, 'what a life it is in those convents! Why, they would feed you, my own, on green hemp oil, and they would put you in the coarsest coarsest linen, and make you go about in the cold; you will never be able to bear all that, Lisa, darling. All this is Agafya's doing; she led you astray. But then you know she began by living and lived for her own pleasure; you must live too. At least, let me die in peace, and then do as you like. And who has ever heard of such a thing, for the sake of such a—for the sake of a goat's beard, God forgive us!—for the sake of a man—to go into a convent! Why, if you are so sick at heart, go on a pilgrimage, offer prayers to some saint, have a *Te Deum* sung, but don't put the black hood on your head, my dear creature, my good girl.'

And Marfa Timofyevna wept bitterly.

Lisa comforted her, wiped away her tears and wept herself, but remained unshaken. In her despair Marfa Timofyevna had recourse to threats: to tell her mother all about it . . . but that too was of no avail. Only at the old lady's most earnest entreaties Lisa agreed to put off carrying out her plan for six months. Marfa Timofyevna was obliged to promise in return that if, within six months, she did not change her mind, she would herself help her and would do all she could to gain Marya Dmitrievna's consent.

In spite of her promise to bury herself in seclusion, at the first approach of cold weather, Varvara Pavlovna, having provided herself with funds, removed to Petersburg, where she took a modest but charming set of apartments, found for her by Panshin, who had left the O—— district a little before. During the latter part of his residence in O—— he had completely lost Marya Dmitrievna's good graces; he had suddenly given up visiting her and scarcely stirred from Lavriky. Varvara Pavlovna had enslaved him, literally enslaved him, no other word can describe her boundless, irresistible, unquestioned sway over him.

Lavretsky spent the winter in Moscow; and in the spring of the following year the news reached him that Lisa had taken the veil in the B—— convent, in one of the remote parts of Russia.

EPILOGUE

EIGHT years had passed by. Once more the spring had come. . . . But we will say a few words first of the fate of Mihalevitch, Panshin, and Madame Lavretsky—and then take leave of them. Mihalevitch, after long wanderings, has at last fallen in with exactly the right work for him; he has received the position of senior superintendent of a government school. He is very well content with his lot; his pupils adore him, though they mimick him too. Panshin has gained great advancement in rank, and already has a directorship in view; he walks with a slight stoop, caused doubtless by the weight round his neck of the Vladimir cross which has been conferred on him. The official in him has finally gained the ascendency over the artist; his still youngish face has grown yellow, and his hair scanty; he now neither sings nor sketches, but applies himself in secret to literature; he has written a comedy, in the style of a 'proverb,' and as nowadays all writers have to draw a portrait of some one or something, he has drawn in it the portrait of a coquette, and he reads it privately to two or three ladies who look kindly upon him. He has, however, not entered upon matrimony, though many excellent opportunities of doing so have presented themselves. For this Varvara Pavlovna was responsible. As for her, she lives constantly at Paris, as in former days. Fedor Ivanitch has given her a promissory note for a large sum, and has so secured immunity from the possibility of her making a second sudden descent upon him. She has grown older and stouter, but is still charming and elegant. Every one has his ideal. Varvara Pavlovna found hers in the dramatic works of M. Dumas Fils. She diligently frequents the theatres, when consumptive and sentimental 'dames aux camélias' are brought on the stage; to be Madame Doche seems to her the height of human bliss; she once declared that she did not desire a better fate for her own daughter. It is to be hoped that fate will spare

Mademoiselle Ada from such happiness; from a rosy-cheeked, chubby child she has turned into a weak-chested, pale girl; her nerves are already deranged. The number of Varvara Pavlovna's adorers has diminished, but she still has some; a few she will probably retain to the end of her days. The most ardent of them in these later days is a certain Zakurdalo-Skubirnikov, a retired guardsman, a full-bearded man of thirty-eight, of exceptionally vigorous physique. The French *habitués* of Madame Lavretsky's salon call him *"le gros taureau de l'Ukrāine;"* Varvara Pavlovna never invites him to her fashionable evening reunions, but he is in the fullest enjoyment of her favours.

And so—eight years have passed by. Once more the breezes of spring breathed brightness and rejoicing from the heavens; once more spring was smiling upon the earth and upon men; once more under her caresses everything was turning to blossom, to love, to song. The town of O—— had undergone little change in the course of these eight years; but Marfa Dmitrievna's house seemed to have grown younger; its freshly-painted walls gave a bright welcome, and the panes of its open windows were crimson, shining in the setting sun; from these windows the light merry sound of ringing young voices and continual laughter floated into the street; the whole house seemed astir with life and brimming over with gaiety. The lady of the house herself had long been in her tomb; Marya Dmitrievna had died two years after Lisa took the veil, and Marfa Timofyevna had not long survived her niece; they lay side by side in the cemetery of the town. Nastasya Karpovna too was no more; for several years the faithful old woman had gone every week to say a prayer over her friend's ashes. . . . Her time had come, and now her bones too lay in the damp earth. But Marya Dmitrievna's house had not passed into strangers' hands, it had not gone out of her family, the home had not been broken up. Lenotchka, transformed into a slim, beautiful young girl, and her betrothed lover—a fair-haired officer of hussars; Marya Dmitrievna's son, who had just been married in Petersburg and had come with his young wife for the spring to O——; his wife's sister, a school-girl of sixteen, with glowing cheeks and bright eyes; Shurotchka, grown up and also pretty, made up the youthful household, whose laughter and talk set the walls of the Kalitins' house resounding. Everything in the house was changed, everything was in keeping with its new inhabitants. Beardless servant lads, grinning and full of fun, had replaced the sober old servants of former days. Two setter dogs dashed wildly about and gambolled over the sofas, where the fat Roska had at one time waddled in solemn dignity. The stables were filled with slender racers, spirited carriage horses, fiery out-riders with plaited manes, and riding horses from the Don. The breakfast, dinner, and supper-hours were all in confusion and disorder; in the words of the neighbours, 'unheard-of arrangements' were made.

On the evening of which we are speaking, the inhabitants of the Kalitins' house (the eldest of them, Lenotchka's betrothed, was only twenty-four) were engaged in a game, which, though not of a very complicated nature, was, to judge from their merry laughter, exceedingly entertaining to them; they were running about the rooms, chasing one another; the dogs, too, were running and barking, and the canaries, hanging in cages above the windows, were straining their throats in rivalry and adding to the general uproar by the shrill trilling of their piercing notes. At the very height of this deafening merry-making a mud-bespattered carriage stopped at the gate, and a man of five-and-forty, in a travelling dress, stepped out of it and stood still in amazement. He stood a little time without stirring, watching the house with attentive eyes; then went through the little gate in the courtyard, and slowly mounted the steps. In the hall he met no one; but the door of a room was suddenly flung open, and out of it rushed Shurotchka, flushed and hot, and instantly, with a ringing shout, all the young party in pursuit of her. They stopped short at once and were quiet at the sight of a stranger; but their clear eyes fixed on him wore the same friendly expression, and their fresh faces were still smiling as Marya Dmitrievna's son went up to the visitor and asked him cordially what he could do for him.

'I am Lavretsky,' replied the visitor.

He was answered by a shout in chorus—and not because these young people were greatly delighted at the arrival of a distant, almost forgotten relation, but simply because they were ready to be delighted and make a noise at every opportunity. They surrounded Lavretsky at once; Lenotchka, as an old acquaintance, was the first to mention her own name, and assured him that in a little while she would have certainly recognised him. She presented him to the rest of the party, calling each, even her betrothed, by their pet names. They all trooped through the dining-room into the drawing-room. The walls of both rooms had been repapered; but the furniture remained the same. Lavretsky recognised the piano; even the embroidery-frame in the window was just the same, and in the same position, and it seemed with the same unfinished embroidery on it, as eight years ago. They made him sit down in a comfortable arm-chair; all sat down politely in a circle round him. Questions, exclamations, and anecdotes followed.

'It's a long time since we have seen you,' observed Lenotchka simply, 'and Varvara Pavlovna we have seen nothing of either.'

'Well, no wonder!' her brother hastened to interpose. 'I carried you off to Petersburg, and Fedor Ivanitch has been living all the time in the country.'

'Yes, and mamma died soon after then.'

'And Marfa Timofyevna,' observed Shurotchka.

'And Nastasya Karpovna,' added Lenotchka, 'and Monsieur Lemm.'

'What? is Lemm dead?' inquired Lavretsky.

'Yes,' replied young Kalitin, 'he left here for Odessa; they say some one enticed him there; and there he died.'

'You don't happen to know, . . . did he leave any music?'

'I don't know; not very likely.'

All were silent and looked about them. A slight cloud of melancholy flitted over all the young faces.

'But Matross is alive,' said Lenotchka suddenly.

'And Gedeonovsky,' added her brother.

At Gedeonovsky's name a merry laugh broke out at once.

'Yes, he is alive, and as great a liar as ever,' Marya Dmitrievna's son continued; 'and only fancy, yesterday this madcap'—pointing to the school-girl, his wife's sister—'put some pepper in his snuff-box.'

'How he did sneeze!' cried Lenotchka, and again there was a burst of unrestrained laughter.

'We have had news of Lisa lately,' observed young Kalitin, and again a hush fell upon all; 'there was good news of her; she is recovering her health a little now.'

'She is still in the same convent?' Lavretsky asked, not without some effort.

'Yes, still in the same.'

'Does she write to you?'

'No, never; but we get news through other people.'

A sudden and profound silence followed. 'A good angel is passing over,' all were thinking.

'Wouldn't you like to go into the garden?' said Kalitin, turning to Lavretsky; 'it is very nice now, though we have let it run wild a little.'

Lavretsky went out into the garden, and the first thing that met his eyes was the very garden seat on which he had once spent with Lisa those few blissful moments, never repeated; it had grown black and warped; but he recognised it, and his soul was filled with that emotion, unequalled for sweetness and for bitterness—the emotion of keen sorrow for vanished youth, for the happiness which has once been possessed.

He walked along the avenues with the young people; the lime-trees looked hardly older or taller in the eight years, but their shade was thicker; on the other hand, all the bushes had sprung up, the raspberry bushes had grown strong, the hazels were tangled thicket, and from all sides rose the fresh scent of the trees and grass and lilac.

'This would be a nice place for Puss-in-the-Corner,' cried Lenotchka suddenly, as they came upon a small green lawn, surrounded by lime-trees, 'and we are just five, too.'

'Have you forgotten Fedor Ivanitch?' replied her brother, . . . 'or didn't you count yourself?'

Lenotchka blushed slightly.

'But would Fedor Ivanitch, at his age——' she began.

'Please, play your games,' Lavretsky hastened to interpose; 'don't pay attention to me. I shall be happier myself, when I am sure I am not in your way. And there's no need for you to entertain me; we old fellows have an occupation which you know nothing of yet, and which no amusement can replace—our memories.'

The young people listened to Lavretsky with polite, but rather ironical respect—as though a teacher were giving them a lesson—and suddenly they all dispersed, and ran to the lawn; four stood near trees, one in the middle, and the game began.

And Lavretsky went back into the house, went into the dining-room, drew near the piano and touched one of the keys; it gave out a faint but clear sound; on that note had begun the inspired melody with which long ago on that same happy night Lemm, the dead Lemm, had thrown him into such transports. Then Lavretsky went into the drawing-room, and for a long time he did not leave it; in that room where he had so often seen Lisa, her image rose most vividly before him; he seemed to feel the traces of her presence round him; but his grief for her was crushing, not easy to bear; it had none of the peace which comes with death. Lisa still lived somewhere, hidden and afar; he thought of her as of the living, but he did not recognise the girl he had once loved in that dim pale shadow, cloaked in a nun's dress and encircled in misty clouds of incense. Lavretsky would not have recognised himself, could he have looked at himself, as mentally he looked at Lisa. In the course of these eight years he had passed that turning-point in life, which many never pass, but without which no one can be a good man to the end; he had really ceased to think of his own happiness, of his personal aims. He had grown calm, and—why hide the truth?—he had grown old not only in face and in body, he had grown old in heart; to keep a young heart up to old age, as some say, is not only difficult, but almost ridiculous; he may well be content who has not lost his belief in goodness, his steadfast will, and his zeal for work. Lavretsky had good reason to be content; he had become actually an excellent farmer, he had really learnt to cultivate the land, and his labours were not only for himself; he had, to the best of his powers, secured on a firm basis the welfare of his peasants.

Lavretsky went out of the house into the garden, and sat down on the familiar garden seat. And on this loved spot, facing the house where for the last time he had vainly stretched out his hand for the enchanted cup which frothed and sparkled with the golden wine of delight, he, a solitary homeless wanderer, looked back upon his life, while the joyous shouts of the younger generation who were already filling his place floated across the garden to him. His heart was sad, but not weighed down, nor bitter; much there was to regret, nothing to be ashamed of.

'Play away, be gay, grow strong, vigorous youth!' he thought, and there was no bitterness in his meditations; 'your life is before you, and for you life will be easier; you have not, as we had, to find out a path for yourselves, to struggle, to fall, and to rise again in the dark; we had enough to do to last out—and how many of us did not last out?—but you need only do your duty, work away, and the blessing of an old man be with you. For me, after to-day, after these emotions, there remains to take my leave at last,—and though sadly, without envy, without any dark feelings, to say, in sight of the end, in sight of God who awaits me: "Welcome, lonely old age! burn out, useless life!"'

Lavretsky quietly rose and quietly went away; no one noticed him, no one detained him; the joyous cries sounded more loudly in the garden behind the thick green wall of high lime-trees. He took his seat in the carriage and bade the coachman drive home and not hurry the horses.

'And the end?' perhaps the dissatisfied reader will inquire. 'What became of Lavretsky afterwards, and of Lisa?' But what is there to tell of people who, though still alive, have withdrawn from the battlefield of life? They say, Lavretsky visited that remote convent where Lisa had hidden herself—that he saw her. Crossing over from choir to choir, she walked close past him, moving with the even, hurried, but meek walk of a nun; and she did not glance at him; only the eyelashes on the side towards him quivered a little, only she bent her emaciated face lower, and the fingers of her clasped hands, entwined with her rosary, were pressed still closer to one another. What were they both thinking, what were they feeling? Who can know? who can say? There are such moments in life, there are such feelings . . . One can but point to them—and pass them by.

FATHERS AND CHILDREN

A NOVEL

CONTENTS

FATHERS AND CHILDREN

		PAGE
LIST OF CHARACTERS	. . . .	196
CHAPTER I	. . . .	197
CHAPTER II	. . . .	201
CHAPTER III	. . . .	203
CHAPTER IV	. . . .	209
CHAPTER V	. . . .	214
CHAPTER VI	. . . .	221
CHAPTER VII	. . . .	225
CHAPTER VIII	. . . .	231
CHAPTER IX	. . . .	238
CHAPTER X	. . . .	242
CHAPTER XI	. . . .	254
CHAPTER XII	. . . .	258
CHAPTER XIII	. . . .	263
CHAPTER XIV	. . . .	269
CHAPTER XV	. . . .	274
CHAPTER XVI	. . . .	279
CHAPTER XVII	. . . .	289
CHAPTER XVIII	. . . .	300
CHAPTER XIX	. . . .	305
CHAPTER XX	. . . .	313
CHAPTER XXI	. . . .	323
CHAPTER XXII	. . . .	339
CHAPTER XXIII	. . . .	345
CHAPTER XXIV	. . . .	352
CHAPTER XXV	. . . .	369
CHAPTER XXVI	. . . .	379
CHAPTER XXVII	. . . .	387
CHAPTER XXVIII	. . . .	402

LIST OF CHARACTERS

NIKOLAI PETROVITCH KIRSANOV, a landowner.

PAVEL PETROVITCH KIRSANOV, his brother.

ARKADY (ARKASHA) NIKOLAEVITCH (*or* NIKOLAITCH), son of Nikolai.

YEVGENY (ENYUSHA) VASSILYEVITCH (*or* VASSILYITCH) BAZAROV, friend of Arkady.

VASSILY IVANOVITCH (*or* IVANITCH), father of Bazarov.

ARINA VLASYEVNA, mother of Bazarov.

FEDOSYA (FENITCHKA) NIKOLAEVNA, second wife of Nikolai.

ANNA SERGYEVNA ODINTSOV, a wealthy widow.

KATYA SERGYEVNA, her sister.

PORFIRY PLATONITCH, her neighbor.

MATVY ILYITCH KOLYAZIN, government commissioner.

EVDOKSYA (*or* AVDOTYA) NIKITISHNA KUKSHIN, an emancipated lady.

VIKTOR SITNIKOV, a would-be liberal.

PIOTR (*pron. P-yotr*), servant to Nikolai.

PROKOFITCH, head servant to Nikolai.

DUNYASHA, a maid servant.

MITYA, infant of Fedosya.

TIMOFEITCH, manager for Vassily.

FATHERS AND CHILDREN

A NOVEL

CHAPTER I

'WELL, Piotr, not in sight yet?' was the question asked on May the 20th, 1859, by a gentleman of a little over forty, in a dusty coat and checked trousers, who came out without his hat on to the low steps of the posting station at S——. He was addressing his servant, a chubby young fellow, with whitish down on his chin, and little, lack-lustre eyes.

The servant, in whom everything—the turquoise ring in his ear, the streaky hair plastered with grease, and the civility of his movements—indicated a man of the new, improved generation, glanced with an air of indulgence along the road, and made answer:

'No, sir; not in sight.'

'Not in sight?' repeated his master.

'No, sir,' responded the man a second time.

His master sighed, and sat down on a little bench. We will introduce him to the reader while he sits, his feet tucked under him, gazing thoughtfully round.

His name was Nikolai Petrovitch Kirsanov. He had, twelve miles from the posting station, a fine property of two hundred souls, or, as he expressed it—since he had arranged the division of his land with the peasants, and started 'a farm'—of nearly five thousand acres. His father, a general in the army, who served in 1812, a coarse, half-educated, but not ill-natured man, a typical Russian, had been in harness all his life, first in command of a brigade, and then of a division, and lived constantly in the provinces, where, by virtue of his rank, he played a fairly important part.

Nikolai Petrovitch was born in the south of Russia like his elder brother, Pavel, of whom more hereafter. He was educated at home till he was fourteen, surrounded by cheap tutors, free-and-easy but toadying adjutants, and all the usual regimental and staff set. His mother, one of the Kolyazin family, as a girl called Agathe, but as a general's wife Agathokleya Kuzminishna Kirsanov, was one of those military ladies who take their full share of the duties and dignities of office. She wore gorgeous caps and rustling silk dresses; in church she was the first to advance to the cross; she talked a great deal in a loud voice, let her children kiss her hand in the morning, and gave them her blessing at night—in fact, she got everything out of life she could. Nikolai Petrovitch, as a general's son—though so far from being distinguished by courage that he even deserved to be called 'a funk'—was intended, like his brother Pavel, to enter the army; but he broke his leg on the very day when the news of his commission came, and, after being two months in bed, retained a slight limp to the end of his days. His father gave him up as a bad job, and let him go into the civil service. He took him to Petersburg directly he was eighteen, and placed him in the university. His brother happened about the same time to be made an officer in the Guards. The young men started living together in one set of rooms, under the remote supervision of a cousin on their mother's side, Ilya Kolyazin, an official of high rank. Their father returned to his division and his wife, and only rarely sent his sons large sheets of grey paper, scrawled over in a bold clerkly hand. At the bottom of these sheets stood in letters, enclosed carefully in scroll-work, the words, 'Piotr Kirsanov, General-Major.' In 1835 Nikolai Petrovitch left the university, a graduate, and in the same year General Kirsanov was put on to the retired list after an unsuccessful review, and came to Petersburg with his wife to live. He was about to take a house in the Tavrichesky Gardens, and had joined the English club, but he died suddenly of an apoplectic fit. Agathokleya Kuzminishna soon followed him; she could not accustom herself to a dull life in the capital; she was consumed by the ennui of existence away from the regiment. Meanwhile Nikolai Petrovitch had already, in his

parents' lifetime and to their no slight chagrin, had time to
fall in love with the daughter of his landlord, a petty official,
Prepolovensky. She was a pretty and, as it is called, 'advanced' girl; she used to read the serious articles in the
'Science' column of the journals. He married her directly
the term of mourning was over; and leaving the civil service
in which his father had by favour procured him a post, was
perfectly blissful with his Masha, first in a country villa
near the Lyesny Institute, afterwards in town in a pretty
little flat with a clean staircase and a draughty drawing-
room, and then in the country, where he settled finally, and
where in a short time a son, Arkady, was born to him. The
young couple lived very happily and peacefully; they were
scarcely ever apart; they read together, sang and played
duets together on the piano; she tended her flowers and
looked after the poultry-yard; he sometimes went hunting,
and busied himself with the estate, while Arkady grew and
grew in the same happy and peaceful way. Ten years passed
like a dream. In 1847 Kirsanov's wife died. He almost
succumbed to this blow; in a few weeks his hair was grey;
he was getting ready to go abroad, if possible to distract his
mind . . . but then came the year 1848. He returned unwillingly to the country, and, after a rather prolonged period
of inactivity, began to take an interest in improvements in
the management of his land. In 1855 he brought his son to
the university; he spent three winters with him in Petersburg, hardly going out anywhere, and trying to make acquaintance with Arkady's young companions. The last
winter he had not been able to go, and here we have seen
him in the May of 1859, already quite grey, stoutish, and
rather bent, waiting for his son, who had just taken his
degree, as once he had taken it himself.

The servant, from a feeling of propriety, and perhaps,
too, not anxious to remain under the master's eye, had gone
to the gate, and was smoking a pipe. Nikolai Petrovitch
bent his head, and began staring at the crumbling steps; a
big mottled fowl walked sedately towards him, treading
firmly with its great yellow legs; a muddy cat gave him an
unfriendly look, twisting herself coyly round the railing.
The sun was scorching; from the half-dark passage of the

posting station came an odour of hot rye-bread. Nikolai Petrovitch fell to dreaming. 'My son . . . a graduate . . . Arkasha . . .' were the ideas that continually came round again and again in his head; he tried to think of something else, and again the same thoughts returned. He remembered his dead wife. . . . 'She did not live to see it!' he murmured sadly. A plump, dark-blue pigeon flew into the road, and hurriedly went to drink in a puddle near the well. Nikolai Petrovitch began looking at it, but his ear had already caught the sound of approaching wheels.

'It sounds as if they're coming, sir,' announced the servant, popping in from the gateway.

Nikolai Petrovitch jumped up, and bent his eyes on the road. A carriage appeared with three posting-horses harnessed abreast; in the carriage he caught a glimpse of the blue band of a student's cap, the familiar outline of a dear face.

'Arkasha! Arkasha!' cried Kirsanov, and he ran waving his hands. . . . A few instants later, his lips were pressed to the beardless, dusty, sunburnt-cheek of the youthful graduate.

CHAPTER II

'LET me shake myself first, daddy,' said Arkady, in a voice tired from travelling, but boyish and clear as a bell, as he gaily responded to his father's caresses; 'I am covering you with dust.'

'Never mind, never mind,' repeated Nikolai Petrovitch, smiling tenderly, and twice he struck the collar of his son's cloak and his own greatcoat with his hand. 'Let me have a look at you; let me have a look at you,' he added, moving back from him, but immediately he went with hurried steps towards the yard of the station, calling, 'This way, this way; and horses at once.'

Nikolai Petrovitch seemed far more excited than his son; he seemed a little confused, a little timid. Arkady stopped him.

'Daddy,' he said, 'let me introduce you to my great friend, Bazarov, about whom I have so often written to you. He has been so good as to promise to stay with us.'

Nikolai Petrovitch went back quickly, and going up to a tall man in a long, loose, rough coat with tassels, who had only just got out of the carriage, he warmly pressed the ungloved red hand, which the latter did not at once hold out to him.

'I am heartily glad,' he began, 'and very grateful for your kind intention of visiting us. . . . Let me know your name, and your father's.'

'Yevgeny Vassilyev,' answered Bazarov, in a lazy but manly voice; and turning back the collar of his rough coat, he showed Nikolai Petrovitch his whole face. It was long and lean, with a broad forehead, a nose flat at the base and sharper at the end, large greenish eyes, and drooping whiskers of a sandy colour; it was lighted up by a tranquil smile, and showed self-confidence and intelligence.

'I hope, dear Yevgeny Vassilyitch, you won't be dull with us,' continued Nikolai Petrovitch.

Bazarov's thin lips moved just perceptibly, though he made no reply, but merely took off his cap. His long, thick hair did not hide the prominent bumps on his head.

'Then, Arkady,' Nikolai Petrovitch began again, turning to his son, 'shall the horses be put to at once? or would you like to rest?'

'We will rest at home, daddy; tell them to harness the horses.'

'At once, at once,' his father assented. 'Hey, Piotr, do you hear? Get things ready, my good boy; look sharp.'

Piotr, who as a modernised servant had not kissed the young master's hand, but only bowed to him from a distance, again vanished through the gateway.

'I came here with the carriage, but there are three horses for your coach too,' said Nikolai Petrovitch fussily, while Arkady drank some water from an iron dipper brought him by the woman in charge of the station, and Bazarov began smoking a pipe and went up to the driver, who was taking out the horses; 'there are only two seats in the carriage, and I don't know how your friend' . . .

'He will go in the coach,' interposed Arkady in an under-tone. 'You must not stand on ceremony with him, please. He's a splendid fellow, so simple—you will see.'

Nikolai Petrovitch's coachman brought the horses round.

'Come, hurry up, bushy beard!' said Bazarov, addressing the driver.

'Do you hear, Mityuha,' put in another driver, standing by with his hands thrust behind him into the opening of his sheepskin coat, 'what the gentleman called you? It's a bushy beard you are too.'

Mityuha only gave a jog to his hat and pulled the reins off the heated shaft-horse.

'Look sharp, look sharp, lads, lend a hand,' cried Nikolai Petrovitch; 'there'll be something to drink our health with!'

In a few minutes the horses were harnessed; the father and son were installed in the carriage; Piotr climbed up on to the box; Bazarov jumped into the coach, and nestled his head down into the leather cushion; and both the vehicles rolled away.

CHAPTER III

'SO here you are, a graduate at last, and come home again,' said Nikolai Petrovitch, touching Arkady now on the shoulder, now on the knee. 'At last!'

'And how is uncle? quite well?' asked Arkady, who, in spite of the genuine, almost childish delight filling his heart, wanted as soon as possible to turn the conversation from the emotional into a commonplace channel.

'Quite well. He was thinking of coming with me to meet you, but for some reason or other he gave up the idea.'

'And how long have you been waiting for me?' inquired Arkady.

'Oh, about five hours.'

'Dear old dad!'

Arkady turned round quickly to his father, and gave him a sounding kiss on the cheek. Nikolai Petrovitch gave vent to a low chuckle.

'I have got such a capital horse for you!' he began. 'You will see. And your room has been fresh papered.'

'And is there a room for Bazarov?'

'We will find one for him too.'

'Please, dad, make much of him. I can't tell you how I prize his friendship.'

'Have you made friends with him lately?'

'Yes, quite lately.'

'Ah, that's how it is I did not see him last winter. What does he study?'

'His chief subject is natural science. But he knows everything. Next year he wants to take his doctor's degree.'

'Ah! he's in the medical faculty,' observed Nikolai Petrovitch, and he was silent for a little. 'Piotr,' he went on, stretching out his hand, 'aren't those our peasants driving along?'

Piotr looked where his master was pointing. Some carts harnessed with unbridled horses were moving rapidly along a narrow by-road. In each cart there were one or two peasants in sheepskin coats, unbuttoned.

'Yes, sir,' replied Piotr.

'Where are they going.—to the town?'

'To the town, I suppose. To the gin-shop,' he added contemptuously, turning slightly towards the coachman, as though he would appeal to him. But the latter did not stir a muscle; he was a man of the old stamp, and did not share the modern views of the younger generation.

'I have had a lot of bother with the peasants this year,' pursued Nikolai Petrovitch, turning to his son. 'They won't pay their rent. What is one to do?'

'But do you like your hired labourers?'

'Yes,' said Nikolai Petrovitch between his teeth. 'They're being set against me, that's the mischief; and they don't do their best. They spoil the tools. But they have tilled the land pretty fairly. When things have settled down a bit, it will be all right. Do you take an interest in farming now?'

'You've no shade; that's a pity,' remarked Arkady, without answering the last question.

'I have had a great awning put up on the north side over the balcony,' observed Nikolai Petrovitch; 'now we can have dinner even in the open air.'

'It'll be rather too like a summer villa. . . . Still, that's all nonsense. What air though here! How delicious it smells! Really I fancy there's nowhere such fragrance in the world as in the meadows here! And the sky too.'

Arkady suddenly stopped short, cast a stealthy look behind him, and said no more.

'Of course,' observed Nikolai Petrovitch, 'you were born here, and so everything is bound to strike you in a special——'

'Come, dad, that makes no difference where a man is born.'

'Still——'

'No; it makes absolutely no difference.'

Nikolai Petrovitch gave a sidelong glance at his son, and the carriage went on a half-a-mile further before the conversation was renewed between them.

'I don't recollect whether I wrote to you,' began Nikolai Petrovitch, 'your old nurse, Yegorovna, is dead.'

'Really? Poor thing! Is Prokofitch still living?'

'Yes, and not a bit changed As grumbling as ever. In fact, you won't find many changes at Maryino.'

'Have you still the same bailiff?'

'Well, to be sure there is a change there. I decided not to keep about me any freed serfs, who have been house servants, or, at least, not to intrust them with duties of any responsibility.' (Arkady glanced towards Piotr.) *Il est libre, en effet,*' observed Nikolai Petrovitch in an undertone; 'but, you see, he's only a valet. Now I have a bailiff, a townsman; he seems a practical fellow. I pay him two hundred and fifty roubles a year. But,' added Nikolai Petrovitch, rubbing his forehead and eyebrows with his hand, which was always an indication with him of inward embarrassment, 'I told you just now that you would not find changes at Maryino. . . . That's not quite correct. I think it my duty to prepare you, though. . . .'

He hesitated for an instant, and then went on in French.

'A severe moralist would regard my openness as improper; but, in the first place, it can't be concealed, and secondly, you are aware I have always had peculiar ideas as regards the relation of father and son. Though, of course, you would be right in blaming me. At my age. . . . In short . . . that . . . that girl, about whom you have probably heard already . . .'

'Fenitchka?' asked Arkady easily.

Nikolai Petrovitch blushed. 'Don't mention her name aloud, please. . . . Well . . . she is living with me now. I have installed her in the house . . . there were two little rooms there. But that can all be changed.'

'Goodness, daddy, what for?'

'Your friend is going to stay with us . . . it would be awkward . . .'

'Please don't be uneasy on Bazarov's account. He's above all that.'

'Well, but you too,' added Nikolai Petrovitch. 'The little lodge is so horrid—that's the worst of it.'

'Goodness, dad,' interposed Arkady, 'it's as if you were apologising; I wonder you're not ashamed.'

'Of course, I ought to be ashamed,' answered Nikolai Petrovitch, flushing more and more.

'Nonsense, dad, nonsense; please don't!' Arkady smiled affectionately. 'What a thing to apologise for!' he thought to himself, and his heart was filled with a feeling of condescending tenderness for his kind, soft-hearted father, mixed with a sense of secret superiority. 'Please, stop,' he repeated once more, instinctively revelling in a consciousness of his own advanced and emancipated condition.

Nikolai Petrovitch glanced at him from under the fingers of the hand with which he was still rubbing his forehead, and there was a pang in his heart. . . . But at once he blamed himself for it.

'Here are our meadows at last,' he said after a long silence.

'And that in front is our forest, isn't it?' asked Arkady.

'Yes. Only I have sold the timber. This year they will cut it down.

'Why did you sell it?'

'The money was needed; besides, that land is to go to the peasants.'

'Who don't pay you their rent?'

'That's their affair; besides, they will pay it some day.'

'I am sorry about the forest,' observed Arkady, and he began to look about him.

The country through which they were driving could not be called picturesque. Fields upon fields stretched all along to the very horizon, now sloping gently upwards, then dropping down again; in some places woods were to be seen, and winding ravines, planted with low, scanty bushes, recalling vividly the representation of them on the old-fashioned maps of the times of Catherine. They came upon little streams too with hollow banks; and tiny lakes with narrow dykes; and little villages, with low hovels under dark and often tumble-down roofs, and slanting barns with walls woven of brushwood and gaping doorways beside neglected threshing-floors; and churches, some brick-built, with stucco peeling off in patches, others wooden, with crosses fallen askew, and overgrown grave-yards. Slowly Arkady's heart sunk. To complete the picture, the peasants they met were all in tatters and on the sorriest little nags; the willows, with their trunks stripped of bark, and broken branches, stood like ragged beggars along the roadside; cows lean and shaggy and looking pinched up by hunger, were greedily tearing at the grass along the ditches. They looked as though they had just been snatched out of the murderous clutches of some threatening monster; and the piteous state of the weak, starved beasts in the midst of the lovely spring day, called up, like a white phantom, the endless, comfortless winter with its storms, and frosts, and snows. . . . 'No,' thought Arkady, 'this is not a rich country; it does not impress one by plenty or industry; it can't, it can't go on like this, reforms are absolutely necessary . . . but how is one to carry them out, how is one to begin?'

Such were Arkady's reflections; . . . but even as he reflected, the spring regained its sway. All around was golden green, all—trees, bushes, grass—shone and stirred gently in wide waves under the soft breath of the warm wind; from all sides flooded the endless trilling music of the larks; the peewits were calling as they hovered over the low-lying meadows, or noiselessly ran over the tussocks of grass; the rooks strutted among the half-grown short spring-corn, standing out black against its tender green; they disappeared in the already whitening rye, only from time to time their heads peeped out amid its grey waves. Arkady gazed and gazed, and his reflections grew slowly fainter and passed away. . . . He flung off his cloak and turned to his father, with a face so bright and boyish, that the latter gave him another hug.

'We're not far off now,' remarked Nikolai Petrovitch; 'we have only to get up this hill, and the house will be in sight. We shall get on together splendidly, Arkasha; you shall help me in farming the estate, if only it isn't a bore to you. We must draw close to one another now, and learn to know each other thoroughly, mustn't we!'

'Of course,' said Arkady; 'but what an exquisite day it is to-day!'

'To welcome you, my dear boy. Yes, it's spring in its full loveliness. Though I agree with Pushkin—do you remember in Yevgeny Onyegin—

> 'To me how sad thy coming is,
> Spring, spring, sweet time of love!
> What . . .'

'Arkady!' called Bazarov's voice from the coach, 'send me a match; I've nothing to light my pipe with.'

Nikolai Petrovitch stopped, while Arkady, who had begun listening to him with some surprise, though with sympathy too, made haste to pull a silver matchbox out of his pocket, and sent it to Bazarov by Piotr.

'Will you have a cigar?' shouted Bazarov again.

'Thanks,' answered Arkady.

Piotr returned to the carriage, and handed him with the match-box a thick black cigar, which Arkady began to smoke promptly, diffusing about him such a strong and pungent odour of cheap tobacco, that Nikolai Petrovitch, who had never been a smoker from his youth up, was forced to turn away his head, as imperceptibly as he could for fear of wounding his son.

A quarter of an hour later, the two carriages drew up before the steps of a new wooden house, painted grey, with a red iron roof. This was Maryino, also known as New-Wick, or, as the peasants had nicknamed it, Poverty Farm.

CHAPTER IV

NO crowd of house-serfs ran out on to the steps to meet the gentlemen; a little girl of twelve years old made her appearance alone. After her there came out of the house a young lad, very like Piotr, dressed in a coat of grey livery, with white armorial buttons, the servant of Pavel Petrovitch Kirsanov. Without speaking, he opened the door of the carriage, and unbuttoned the apron of the coach. Nikolai Petrovitch with his son and Bazarov walked through a dark and almost empty hall, from behind the door of which they caught a glimpse of a young woman's face, into a drawing room furnished in the most modern style.

'Here we are at home,' said Nikolai Petrovitch, taking off his cap, and shaking back his hair. 'That's the great thing; now we must have supper and rest.'

'A meal would not come amiss, certainly,' observed Bazarov, stretching, and he dropped on to a sofa.

'Yes, yes, let us have supper, supper directly.' Nikolai Petrovitch with no apparent reason stamped his foot. 'And here just at the right moment comes Prokofitch.'

A man about sixty entered, white-haired, thin, and swarthy, in a cinnamon-coloured dress-coat with brass buttons, and a pink neckerchief. He smirked, went up to kiss Arkady's hand, and bowing to the guest retreated to the door, and put his hands behind him.

'Here he is, Prokofitch,' began Nikolai Petrovitch; 'he's come back to us at last. . . . Well, how do you think him looking?'

'As well as could be,' said the old man, and was grinning again, but he quickly knitted his bushy brows. 'You wish supper to be served?' he said impressively.

'Yes, yes, please. But won't you like to go to your room first, Yevgeny Vassilyitch?'

'No, thanks; I don't care about it. Only give orders for

my little box to be taken there, and this garment, too,' he added, taking off his frieze overcoat.

'Certainly. Prokofitch, take the gentleman's coat.' (Prokofitch, with an air of perplexity, picked up Bazarov's 'garment' in both hands, and holding it high above his head, retreated on tiptoe.) 'And you, Arkady, are you going to your room for a minute?'

'Yes, I must wash,' answered Arkady, and was just moving towards the door, but at that instant there came into the drawing-room a man of medium height, dressed in a dark English suit, a fashionable low cravat, and kid shoes, Pavel Petrovitch Kirsanov. He looked about forty-five: his close-cropped, grey hair shone with a dark lustre, like new silver; his face, yellow but free from wrinkles, was exceptionally regular and pure in line, as though carved by a light and delicate chisel, and showed traces of remarkable beauty; specially fine were his clear, black, almond-shaped eyes. The whole person of Arkady's uncle, with its aristocratic elegance, had preserved the gracefulness of youth and that air of striving upwards, away from earth, which for the most part is lost after the twenties are past.

Pavel Petrovitch took out of his trouser pocket his exquisite hand with its long tapering pink nails, a hand which seemed still more exquisite from the snowy whiteness of the cuff, buttoned with a single, big opal, and gave it to his nephew. After a preliminary handshake in the European style, he kissed him thrice after the Russian fashion, that is to say, he touched his cheek three times with his perfumed moustaches, and said, 'Welcome.'

Nikolai Petrovitch presented him to Bazarov; Pavel Petrovitch greeted him with a slight inclination of his supple figure, and a slight smile, but he did not give him his hand, and even put it back into his pocket.

'I had begun to think you were not coming to-day,' he began in a musical voice, with a genial swing and shrug of the shoulders, as he showed his splendid white teeth. 'Did anything happen on the road,'

'Nothing happened?' answered Arkady; 'we were rather slow. But we're as hungry as wolves now. Hurry up Prokofitch, dad; and I'll be back directly.'

'Stay, I'm coming with you,' cried Bazarov, pulling himself up suddenly from the sofa. Both the young men went out.

'Who is he?' asked Pavel Petrovitch.

'A friend of Arkasha's; according to him, a very clever fellow.'

'Is he going to stay with us?'

'Yes.'

'That unkempt creature?'

'Why, yes.'

Pavel Petrovitch drummed with his finger tips on the table. 'I fancy Arkady *s'est dégourdi,*' he remarked. 'I'm glad he has come back.'

At supper there was little conversation. Bazarov especially said nothing, but he ate a great deal. Nikolai Petrovitch related various incidents in what he called his career as a farmer, talked about the impending government measures, about committees, deputations, the necessity of introducing machinery, etc. Pavel Petrovitch paced slowly up and down the dining-room (he never ate supper), sometimes sipping at a wineglass of red wine, and less often uttering some remark or rather exclamation, of the nature of 'Ah! aha! hm!' Arkady told some news from Petersburg, but he was conscious of a little awkwardness, that awkwardness, which usually overtakes a youth when he has just ceased to be a child, and has come back to a place where they are accustomed to regard him and treat him as a child. He made his sentences quite unnecessarily long, avoided the word 'daddy,' and even sometimes replaced it by the word 'father,' mumbled, it is true, between his teeth; with an exaggerated carelessness he poured into his glass far more wine than he really wanted, and drank it all off. Prokofitch did not take his eyes off him, and kept chewing his lips. After supper they all separated at once.

'Your uncle's a queer fish,' Bazarov said to Arkady, as he sat in his dressing-gown by his bedside, smoking a short pipe. 'Only fancy such style in the country! His nails, his nails—you ought to send them to an exhibition!'

'Why of course, you don't know,' replied Arkady. 'He was a great swell in his own day, you know. I will tell you his story one day. He was very handsome, you know, used to turn all the women's heads.'

'Oh, that's it, is it? So he keeps it up in memory of the past. It's a pity there's no one for him to fascinate here though. I kept staring at his exquisite collars. They're like marble, and his chin's shaved simply to perfection. Come, Arkady Nikolaitch, isn't that ridiculous?'

'Perhaps it is; but he's a splendid man, really.'

'An antique survival! But your father's a capital fellow. He wastes his time reading poetry, and doesn't know much about farming, but he's a good-hearted fellow.'

'My father's a man in a thousand.'

'Did you notice how shy and nervous he is?'

Arkady shook his head as though he himself were not shy and nervous.

'It's something astonishing,' pursued Bazarov, 'these old idealists, they develop their nervous systems till they break down . . . so balance is lost. But good-night. In my room there's an English washstand, but the door won't fasten. Anyway that ought to be encouraged—an English wash-stand stands for progress!'

Bazarov went away, and a sense of great happiness came over Arkady. Sweet it is to fall asleep in one's own home, in the familiar bed, under the quilt worked by loving hands, perhaps a dear nurse's hands, those kind, tender, untiring hands. Arkady remembered Yegorovna, and sighed and wished her peace in heaven. . . . For himself he made no prayer.

Both he and Bazarov were soon asleep, but others in the house were awake long after. His son's return had agitated Nikolai Petrovitch. He lay down in bed, but did not put out the candles, and his head propped on his hand, he fell into long reveries. His brother was sitting long after midnight in his study, in a wide armchair before the fireplace, on which there smouldered some faintly glowing embers. Pavel Petrovitch was not undressed, only some red Chinese slippers had replaced the kid shoes on his feet. He held in his hand the last number of *Galignani*, but he was not reading; he gazed fixedly into the grate, where a bluish flame flickered, dying down, then flaring up again. . . . God knows where his thoughts were rambling, but they were not rambling in the past only; the expression of his face was concentrated and surly, which is not the way when a man is absorbed solely in recollections. In a small back room there sat, on a large chest, a young woman in a blue dressing jacket with a white kerchief thrown over her dark hair, Fenitchka. She was half listening, half dozing, and often looked across towards the open door through which a child's cradle was visible, and the regular breathing of a sleeping baby could be heard.

CHAPTER V

THE next morning Bazarov woke up earlier than any one and went out of the house. 'Oh, my!' he thought, looking about him, 'the little place isn't much to boast of!' When Nikolai Petrovitch had divided the land with his peasants, he had had to build his new manor-house on four acres of perfectly flat and barren land. He had built a house, offices, and farm buildings, laid out a garden, dug a pond, and sunk two wells; but the young trees had not done well, very little water had collected in the pond, and that in the wells tasted brackish. Only one arbour of lilac and acacia had grown fairly well; they sometimes had tea and dinner in it. In a few minutes Bazarov had traversed all the little paths of the garden; he went into the cattle-yard and the stable, routed out two farm-boys, with whom he made friends at once, and set off with them to a small swamp about a mile from the house to look for frogs.

'What do you want frogs for, sir?' one of the boys asked him.

'I'll tell you what for,' answered Bazarov, who possessed the special faculty of inspiring confidence in people of a lower class, though he never tried to win them, and behaved very casually with them; 'I shall cut the frog open, and see what's going on in his inside, and then, as you and I are much the same as frogs, only that we walk on legs, I shall know what's going on inside us too.'

'And what do you want to know that for?'

'So as not to make a mistake, if you're taken ill, and I have to cure you.'

'Are you a doctor then?'

'Yes.'

'Vaska, do you hear, the gentleman says you and I are the same as frogs, that's funny!'

'I'm afraid of frogs,' observed Vaska, a boy of seven, with a head as white as flax, and bare feet, dressed in a grey smock with a stand-up collar.

'What is there to be afraid of? Do they bite?'

'There, paddle into the water, philosophers,' said Bazorov.

Meanwhile Nikolai Petrovitch too had waked up, and gone in to see Arkady, whom he found dressed. The father and son went out on to the terrace under the shelter of the awning; near the balustrade, on the table, among great bunches of lilacs, the samovar was already boiling. A little girl came up, the same who had been the first to meet them at the steps on their arrival the evening before. In a shrill voice she said—

'Fedosya Nikolaevna is not quite well, she cannot come; she gave orders to ask you, will you please to pour out tea yourself, or should she send Dunyasha?'

'I will pour out myself, myself,' interposed Nikolai Petrovitch hurriedly. 'Arkady, how do you take your tea, with cream, or with lemon?'

'With cream,' answered Arkady; and after a brief silence, he uttered interrogatively, 'Daddy?'

Nikolai Petrovitch in confusion looked at his son.

'Well?' he said.

Arkady dropped his eyes.

'Forgive me, dad, if my question seems unsuitable to you,' he began, 'but you yourself, by your openness yesterday, encourage me to be open . . . you will not be angry . . . ?'

'Go on.'

'You give me confidence to ask you. . . . Isn't the reason, Fen . . . isn't the reason she will not come here to pour out tea, because I'm here?'

Nikolai Petrovitch turned slightly away.

'Perhaps,' he said, at last, 'she supposes . . . she is ashamed.'

Arkady turned a rapid glance on his father.

'She has no need to be ashamed. In the first place, you are aware of my views' (it was very sweet to Arkady to utter that word); 'and secondly, could I be willing to hamper your life, your habits in the least thing? Besides, I am sure you could not make a bad choice; if you have allowed her to live under the same roof with you, she must be worthy of it; in any case, a son cannot judge his father,—

least of all, I, and least of all such a father who, like you, has never hampered my liberty in anything.'

Arkady's voice had been shaky at the beginning; he felt himself magnanimous, though at the same time he realised he was delivering something of the nature of a lecture to his father; but the sound of one's own voice has a powerful effect on any man, and Arkady brought out his last words resolutely, even with emphasis.

'Thanks, Arkasha,' said Nikolai Petrovitch thickly, and his fingers again strayed over his eyebrows and forehead. 'Your suppositions are just in fact. Of course, if this girl had not deserved. . . . It is not a frivolous caprice. It's not easy for me to talk to you about this; but you will understand that it is difficult for her to come here, in your presence, especially the first day of your return.'

'In that case I will go to her,' cried Arkady, with a fresh rush of magnanimous feeling, and he jumped up from his seat. 'I will explain to her that she has no need to be ashamed before me.'

Nikolai Petrovitch too got up.

'Arkady,' he began, 'be so good . . . how can . . . there . . . I have not told you yet . . .'

But Arkady did not listen to him, and ran off the terrace. Nikolai Petrovitch looked after him, and sank into his chair overcome by confusion. His heart began to throb. Did he at that moment realise the inevitable strangeness of the future relations between him and his son? Was he conscious that Arkady would perhaps have shown him more respect if he had never touched on this subject at all? Did he reproach himself for weakness?—it is hard to say; all these feelings were within him, but in the state of sensations —and vague sensations—while the flush did not leave his face, and his heart throbbed.

There was the sound of hurrying footsteps, and Arkady came on to the terrace. 'We have made friends, dad!' he cried, with an expression of a kind of affectionate and good-natured triumph on his face. 'Fedosya Nikolaevna is not quite well to-day really, and she will come a little later. But why didn't you tell me I had a brother? I should have kissed him last night, as I have kissed him just now.'

Nikolai Petrovitch tried to articulate something, tried to get up and open his arms. Arkady flung himself on his neck.

'What's this? embracing again?' sounded the voice of Pavel Petrovitch behind them.

Father and son were equally rejoiced at his appearance at that instant; there are positions, genuinely affecting, from which one longs to escape as soon as possible.

'Why should you be surprised at that?' said Nikolai Petrovitch gaily. 'Think what ages I have been waiting for Arkasha. I've not had time to get a good look at him since yesterday.'

'I'm not at all surprised,' observed Pavel Petrovitch; 'I feel not indisposed to be embracing him myself.'

Arkady went up to his uncle, and again felt his cheeks caressed by his perfumed moustache. Pavel Petrovitch sat down to the table. He wore an elegant morning suit in the English style, and a gay little fez on his head. This fez and the carelessly tied little cravat carried a suggestion of the freedom of country life, but the stiff collars of his shirt —not white, it is true, but striped, as is correct in morning dress—stood up as inexorably as ever against his well-shaved chin.

'Where's your new friend?' he asked Arkady.

'He's not in the house; he usually gets up early and goes off somewhere. The great thing is, we mustn't pay any attention to him; he doesn't like ceremony.'

'Yes, that's obvious.' Pavel Petrovitch began deliberately spreading butter on his bread. 'Is he going to stay long with us?'

'Perhaps. He came here on the way to his father's.'

'And where does his father live?'

'In our province, sixty-four miles from here. He has a small property there. He was formerly an army doctor.'

'Tut, tut, tut! To be sure, I kept asking myself, "Where have I heard that name, Bazarov?" Nikolai, do you remember, in our father's division there was a surgeon Bazarov?'

'I believe there was.'

'Yes, yes, to be sure. So that surgeon was his father. Hm!' Pavel Petrovitch pulled his moustaches. 'Well, and what is Mr. Bazarov himself?' he asked, deliberately.

'What is Bazarov?' Arkady smiled. 'Would you like me, uncle, to tell you what he really is?'

'If you will be so good, nephew.'

'He's a nihilist.'

'Eh?' inquired Nikolai Petrovitch, while Pavel Petrovitch lifted a knife in the air with a small piece of butter on its tip, and remained motionless.

'He's a nihilist,' repeated Arkady.

'A nihilist,' said Nikolai Petrovitch. 'That's from the Latin, *nihil, nothing*, as far as I can judge; the word must mean a man who . . . who accepts nothing?'

'Say, "who respects nothing,"' put in Pavel Petrovitch, and he set to work on the butter again.

'Who regards everything from the critical point of view,' observed Arkady.

'Isn't that just the same thing?' inquired Pavel Petrovitch.

'No, it's not the same thing. A nihilist is a man who does not bow down before any authority, who does not take any principle on faith, whatever reverence that principle may be enshrined in.'

'Well, and is that good?' interrupted Pavel Petrovitch.

'That depends, uncle. Some people it will do good to, but some people will suffer for it.'

'Indeed. Well, I see it's not in our line. We are old-fashioned people; we imagine that without principles, taken as you say on faith, there's no taking a step, no breathing. *Vous avez changé tout cela.* God give you good health and the rank of a general, while we will be content to look on and admire, worthy . . . what was it?'

'Nihilists,' Arkady said, speaking very distinctly.

'Yes. There used to be Hegelists, and now there are nihilists. We shall see how you will exist in void, in vacuum; and now ring, please, brother Nikolai Petrovitch; it's time I had my cocoa.'

Nikolai Petrovitch rang the bell and called, 'Dunyasha!' But instead of Dunyasha, Fenitchka herself came on to the terrace. She was a young woman about three-and-twenty, with a white soft skin, dark hair and eyes, red, childishly-pouting lips, and little delicate hands. She wore a neat print dress; a new blue kerchief lay lightly on her plump shoulders. She carried a large cup of cocoa, and setting it down before Pavel Petrovitch, she was overwhelmed with confusion; the hot blood rushed in a wave of crimson over the delicate skin of her pretty face. She dropped her eyes, and stood at the table, leaning a little on the very tips of her fingers. It seemed as though she were ashamed of having come in, and at the same time felt that she had a right to come.

Pavel Petrovitch knitted his brows severely, while Nikolai Petrovitch looked embarrassed.

'Good morning, Fenitchka,' he muttered through his teeth.

'Good morning,' she replied in a voice not loud but resonant, and with a sidelong glance at Arkady, who gave her a friendly smile, she went gently away. She walked with a slightly rolling gait, but even that suited her.

For some minutes silence reigned on the terrace. Pavel Petrovitch sipped his cocoa; suddenly he raised his head. 'Here is Sir Nihilist coming towards us,' he said in an undertone.

Bazarov was in fact approaching through the garden, stepping over the flower-beds. His linen coat and trousers were besmeared with mud; clinging marsh weed was twined round the crown of his old round hat; in his right hand he held a small bag; in the bag something alive was moving. He quickly drew near the terrace, and said with a nod, 'Good morning, gentlemen; sorry I was late for tea; I'll be back directly; I must just put these captives away.'

'What have you there—leeches?' asked Pavel Petrovitch.

'No, frogs.'

'Do you eat them—or keep them?'

'For experiment,' said Bazarov indifferently, and he went off into the house.

'So he's going to cut them up,' observed Pavel Petrovitch 'He has no faith in principles, but he has faith in frogs.'

Arkady looked compassionately at his uncle; Nikolai

Petrovitch shrugged his shoulders stealthily. Pavel Petrovitch himself felt that his epigram was unsuccessful, and
began to talk about husbandry and the new bailiff, who had
come to him the evening before to complain that a labourer,
Foma, 'was deboshed,' and quite unmanageable. 'He's such
an Æsop,' he said among other things; 'in all places he has
protested himself a worthless fellow; he's not a man to keep
his place; he'll walk off in a huff like a fool.'

CHAPTER VI

BAZAROV came back, sat down to the table, and began hastily drinking tea. The two brothers looked at him in silence, while Arkady stealthily watched first his father and then his uncle.

'Did you walk far from here?' Nikolai Petrovitch asked at last.

'Where you've a little swamp near the aspen wood. I started some half-dozen snipe; you might slaughter them; Arkady.'

'Aren't you a sportsman then?'

'No.'

'Is your special study physics?' Pavel Petrovitch in his turn inquired.

'Physics, yes; and natural science in general.'

'They say the Teutons of late have had great success in that line.'

'Yes; the Germans are our teachers in it,' Bazarov answered carelessly.

The word Teutons instead of Germans, Pavel Petrovitch had used with ironical intention; none noticed it however.

'Have you such a high opinion of the Germans?' said Pavel Petrovitch, with exaggerated courtesy. He was beginning to feel a secret irritation. His aristocratic nature was revolted by Bazarov's absolute nonchalance. This surgeon's son was not only not overawed, he even gave abrupt and indifferent answers, and in the tone of his voice there was something churlish, almost insolent.

'The scientific men there are a clever lot.'

'Ah, ah. To be sure, of Russian scientific men you have not such a flattering opinion, I dare say?'

'That is very likely.'

'That's very praiseworthy self-abnegation,' Pavel Petrovitch declared, drawing himself up, and throwing his head back. 'But how is this? Arkady Nikolaitch was telling us just now that you accept no authorities? Don't you believe in *them?*'

'And how am I accepting them? And what am I to believe in? They tell me the truth, I agree, that's all.'

'And do all Germans tell the truth?' said Pavel Petrovitch, and his face assumed an expression as unsympathetic, as remote, as if he had withdrawn to some cloudy height.

'Not all,' replied Bazarov, with a short yawn. He obviously did not care to continue the discussion.

Pavel Petrovitch glanced at Arkady, as though he would say to him, 'Your friend's polite, I must say.' 'For my own part,' he began again, not without some effort, 'I am so unregenerate as not to like Germans. Russian Germans I am not speaking of now; we all know what sort of creatures they are. But even German Germans are not to my liking. In former days there were some here and there; they had —well, Schiller, to be sure, Goethe . . my brother—he takes a particularly favourable view of them. . . . But now they have all turned chemists and materialists . . .'

'A good chemist is twenty times as useful as any poet,' broke in Bazarov.

'Oh, indeed,' commented Pavel Petrovitch, and, as though falling asleep, he faintly raised his eyebrows. 'You don't acknowledge art then, I suppose?'

'The art of making money or of advertising pills!' cried Bazarov, with a contemptuous laugh.

'Ah, ah. You are pleased to jest, I see. You reject all that, no doubt? Granted. Then you believe in science only?'

'I have already explained to you that I don't believe in anything; and what is science—science in the abstract? There are sciences, as there are trades and crafts; but abstract science doesn't exist at all.'

'Very good. Well, and in regard to the other traditions accepted in human conduct, do you maintain the same negative attitude?'

'What's this, an examination?' asked Bazarov.

Pavel Petrovitch turned slightly pale. . . Nikolai Petrovitch thought it his duty to interpose in the conversation.

'We will converse on this subject with you more in detail some day, dear Yevgeny Vassilyitch; we will hear your views, and express our own. For my part, I am heartily glad you are studying the natural sciences. I have heard that Liebig has made some wonderful discoveries in the amelioration of soils. You can be of assistance to me in my agricultural labours; you can give me some useful advice.'

'I am at your service, Nikolai Petrovitch; but Liebig's miles over our heads! One has first to learn the a b c, and then begin to read, and we haven't set eyes on the alphabet yet.'

'You are certainly a nihilist, I see that,' thought Nikolai Petrovitch. 'Still, you will allow me to apply to you on occasion,' he added aloud. 'And now I fancy, brother, it's time for us to be going to have a talk with the bailiff.'

Pavel Petrovitch got up from his seat.

'Yes,' he said, without looking at any one; 'it's a misfortune to live five years in the country like this, far from mighty intellects! You turn into a fool directly. You may try not to forget what you've been taught, but—in a snap!— they'll prove all that's rubbish, and tell you that sensible men have nothing more to do with such foolishness, and that you, if you please, are an antiquated old fogey. What's to be done? Young people, of course, are cleverer than we are!'

Pavel Petrovitch turned slowly on his heels, and slowly walked away; Nikolai Petrovitch went after him.

'Is he always like that?' Bazarov coolly inquired of Arkady directly the door had closed behind the two brothers.

'I must say, Yevgeny, you weren't nice to him,' remarked Arkady. 'You have hurt his feelings.'

'Well, am I going to consider them, these provincial aristocrats! Why, it's all vanity, dandy habits, fatuity. He should have continued his career in Petersburg, if that's his bent. But there, enough of him! I've found a rather rare species of a water-beetle, *Dytiscus marginatus;* do you know it? I will show you.'

'I promised to tell you his story,' began Arkady.

'The story of the beetle?'

'Come, don't, Yevgeny. The story of my uncle. You will see he's not the sort of man you fancy. He deserves pity rather than ridicule.'

'I don't dispute it; but why are you worrying over him?'
'One ought to be just, Yevgeny.'
'How does that follow?'
'No; listen . . .'

And Arkady told him his uncle's story. The reader will
find it in the following chapter.

CHAPTER VII

PAVEL PETROVITCH KIRSANOV was educated first at home, like his younger brother, and afterwards in the Corps of Pages. From childhood he was distinguished by remarkable beauty; moreover he was self-confident, somewhat ironical, and had a rather biting humour; he could not fail to please. He began to be seen everywhere, directly he had received his commission as an officer. He was much admired in society, and he indulged every whim, even every caprice and every folly, and gave himself airs, but that too was attractive in him. Women went out of their senses over him; men called him a coxcomb, and were secretly jealous of him. He lived, as has been related already, in the same apartments as his brother, whom he loved sincerely, though he was not at all like him. Nikolai Petrovitch was a little lame, he had small, pleasing features of a rather melancholy cast, small, black eyes, and thin, soft hair; he liked being lazy, but he also liked reading, and was timid in society.

Pavel Petrovitch did not spend a single evening at home, prided himself on his ease and audacity (he was just bringing gymnastics into fashion among young men in society), and had read in all some five or six French books. At twenty-eight he was already a captain; a brilliant career awaited him. Suddenly everything was changed.

At that time, there was sometimes seen in Petersburg society a woman who has even yet not been forgotten. Princess R——. She had a well-educated, well-bred, but rather stupid husband, and no children. She used suddenly to go abroad, and suddenly return to Russia, and led an eccentric life in general. She had the reputation of being a frivolous coquette, abandoned herself eagerly to every sort of pleasure, danced to exhaustion, laughed and jested with young men, whom she received in the dim light of her drawing-room before dinner; while at night she wept and prayed, found no peace in anything, and often paced her room till morning, wringing her hands in anguish, or sat, pale and chill, over a psalter. Day came, and she was transformed again into a grand lady; again she went out, laughed, chattered, and simply flung herself headlong into anything which could afford her the slightest distraction. She was marvellously well-proportioned, her hair coloured like gold and heavy as gold hung below her knees, but no one would have called her a beauty; in her whole face the only good point was her eyes, and even her eyes were not good—they were grey, and not large—but their glance was swift and deep, unconcerned to the point of audacity, and thoughtful to the point of melancholy—an enigmatic glance. There was a light of something extraordinary in them, even while her tongue was lisping the emptiest of inanities. She dressed with elaborate care. Pavel Petrovitch met her at a ball, danced a mazurka with her, in the course of which she did not utter a single rational word, and fell passionately in love with her. Being accustomed to make conquests, in this instance, too, he soon attained his object, but his easy success did not damp his ardour. On the contrary, he was in still more torturing, still closer bondage to this woman, in whom, even at the very moment when she surrendered herself utterly, there seemed always something still mysterious and unattainable, to which none could penetrate. What was hidden in that soul—God knows! It seemed as though she were in the power of mysterious forces, incomprehensible even to herself; they seemed to play on her at will; her intellect was not powerful enough to master their caprices. Her whole behaviour presented a series of inconsistencies; the only letters which could have awakened her husband's just suspicions, she wrote to a man who was almost a stranger to her, whilst her love had always an element of melancholy; with a man she had chosen as a lover, she ceased to laugh and to jest, she listened to him, and gazed at him with a look of bewilderment. Sometimes, for the most part suddenly, this bewilderment passed into chill horror; her face took a wild, death-like expression; she locked herself up in her bedroom, and her maid, putting her ear to the keyhole, could hear her smothered sobs. More than once, as he went home after a tender interview, Kirsanov felt within him that heartrending, bitter vexation which follows on a total failure.

'What more do I want?' he asked himself, while his heart was heavy. He once gave her a ring with a sphinx engraved on the stone.

'What's that?' she asked; 'a sphinx?'

'Yes,' he answered, 'and that sphinx is you.'

'I?' she queried, and slowly raising her enigmatical glance upon him. 'Do you know that's awfully flattering?' she added with a meaningless smile, while her eyes still kept the same strange look.

Pavel Petrovitch suffered even while Princess R—— loved him; but when she grew cold to him, and that happened rather quickly, he almost went out of his mind. He was on the rack, and he was jealous; he gave her no peace, followed her about everywhere; she grew sick of his pursuit of her, and she went abroad. He resigned his commission in spite of the entreaties of his friends and the exhortations of his superiors, and followed the princess; four years he spent in foreign countries, at one time pursuing her, at another time intentionally losing sight of her. He was ashamed of himself, he was disgusted with his own lack of spirit . . . but nothing availed. Her image, that incomprehensible, almost meaningless, but bewitching image, was deeply rooted in his heart. At Baden he once more regained his old footing with her; it seemed as though she had never loved him so passionately . . . but in a month it was all at an end: the flame flickered up for the last time and went out for ever. Foreseeing inevitable separation, he wanted at least to remain her friend, as though friendship with such a woman was possible. . . . She secretly left Baden, and from that time steadily avoided Kirsanov. He returned to Russia, and tried to live his former life again; but he could not get back into the old groove. He wandered from place to place like a man possessed; he still went into society; he still retained the habits of a man of the world; he could boast of two or three fresh conquests; but he no longer expected anything much of himself or of others, and he undertook nothing. He grew old and grey; spending all his evenings at the club, jaundiced and bored, and arguing in bachelor society became a necessity for him—a bad sign, as we all know. Marriage, of course, he did not even think of. Ten years passed in this way; they passed by colourless and fruitless—and quickly, fearfully quickly. Nowhere does time fly past as in Russia; in prison they say it flies even faster. One day at dinner at the club, Pavel Petrovitch heard of the death of the Princess R——. She had died at Paris in a state bordering on insanity.

He got up from the table, and a long time he paced about the rooms of the club, or stood stockstill near the card-players, but he did not go home earlier than usual. Some time later he received a packet addressed to him; in it was the ring he had given the princess. She had drawn lines in the shape of a cross over the sphinx and sent him word that the solution of the enigma—was the cross.

This happened at the beginning of the year 1848, at the very time when Nikolai Petrovitch came to Petersburg, after the loss of his wife. Pavel Petrovitch had scarcely seen his brother since the latter had settled in the country; the marriage of Nikolai Petrovitch had coincided with the very first days of Pavel Petrovitch's acquaintance with the princess. When he came back from abroad, he had gone to him with the intention of staying a couple of months with him, in sympathetic enjoyment of his happiness, but he had only succeeded in standing a week of it. The difference in the positions of the two brothers was too great. In 1848, this difference had grown less; Nikolai Petrovitch had lost his wife, Pavel Petrovitch had lost his memories; after the death of the princess he tried not to think of her. But to Nikolai, there remained the sense of a well-spent life, his son was growing up under his eyes; Pavel, on the contrary, a solitary bachelor, was entering upon that indefinite twilight period of regrets that are akin to hopes, and hopes that are akin to regrets, when youth is over, while old age has not yet come.

This time was harder for Pavel Petrovitch than for another man; in losing his past, he lost everything.

'I will not invite you to Maryino now,' Nikolai Petrovitch said to him one day, (he had called his property by that name in honour of his wife); 'you were dull there in

my dear wife's time, and now I think you would be bored
to death.'

'I was stupid and fidgety then,' answered Pavel Petrovitch; 'since then I have grown quieter, if not wiser. On
the contrary, now, if you will let me, I am ready to settle
with you for good.'

For all answer Nikolai Petrovitch embraced him; but a
year and a half passed after this conversation, before Pavel
Petrovitch made up his mind to carry out his intention.
When he was once settled in the country, however, he did
not leave it, even during the three winters which Nikolai
Petrovitch spent in Petersburg with his son. He began
to read, chiefly English; he arranged his whole life, roughly
speaking, in the English style, rarely saw the neighbours,
and only went out to the election of marshals, where he
was generally silent, only occasionally annoying and alarm-
ing land-owners of the old school by his liberal sallies, and
not associating with the representatives of the younger
generation. Both the latter and the former considered him
'stuck up'; and both parties respected him for his fine aristocratic manners; for his reputation for successes in love;
for the fact that he was very well dressed and always
stayed in the best room in the best hotel; for the fact that
he generally dined well, and had once even dined with Well-
ington at Louis Philippe's table; for the fact that he always
took everywhere with him a real silver dressing-case and
a portable bath; for the fact that he always smelt of some
exceptionally 'good form' scent; for the fact that he played
whist in masterly fashion, and always lost; and lastly, they
respected him also for his incorruptible honesty. Ladies
considered him enchantingly romantic, but he did not cultivate ladies' acquaintance. . . .

'So you see, Yevgeny,' observed Arkady, as he finished
his story, 'how unjustly you judge of my uncle! To say
nothing of his having more than once helped my father
out of difficulties, given him all his money—the property,
perhaps you don't know, wasn't divided—he's glad to help
any one, among other things he always sticks up for the
peasants; it's true, when he talks to them he frowns and
sniffs eau de cologne.' . . .

'His nerves, no doubt,' put in Bazarov.

'Perhaps; but his heart is very good. And he's far from being stupid. What useful advice he has given me especially . . . especially in regard to relations with women.'

'Aha! a scalded dog fears cold water, we know that!'

'In short,' continued Arkady, 'he's profoundly unhappy, believe me; it's a sin to despise him.'

'And who does despise him?' retorted Bazarov. 'Still, I must say that a fellow who stakes his whole life on one card —a woman's love—and when that card fails, turns sour, and lets himself go till he's fit for nothing, is not a man, but a male. You say he's unhappy; you ought to know best; to be sure, he's not got rid of all his fads. I'm convinced that he solemnly imagines himself a superior creature because he reads that wretched *Galignani,* and once a month saves a peasant from a flogging.'

'But remember his education, the age in which he grew up,' observed Arkady.

'Education?' broke in Bazarov. 'Every man must educate himself, just as I've done, for instance. . . . And as for the age, why should I depend on it? Let it rather depend on me. No, my dear fellow, that's all shallowness, want of backbone! And what stuff it all is, about these mysterious relations between a man and woman? We physiologists know what these relations are. You study the anatomy of the eye; where does the enigmatical glance you talk about come in there? That's all romantic, nonsensical, æsthetic rot. We had much better go and look at the beetle.'

And the two friends went off to Bazarov's room, which was already pervaded by a sort of medico-surgical odour, mingled with the smell of cheap tobacco.

CHAPTER VIII

PAVEL PETROVITCH did not long remain present at his brother's interview with his bailiff, a tall, thin man with a sweet consumptive voice and knavish eyes, who to all Nikolai Petrovitch's remarks answered, 'Certainly, sir,' and tried to make the peasants out to be thieves and drunkards. The estate had only recently been put on to the new reformed system, and the new mechanism worked, creaking like an ungreased wheel, warping and cracking like home-made furniture of unseasoned wood. Nikolai Petrovitch did not lose heart, but often he sighed, and was gloomy; he felt that the thing could not go on without money, and his money was almost all spent. Arkady had spoken the truth; Pavel Petrovitch had more than once helped his brother; more than once, seeing him struggling and cudgelling his brains, at a loss which way to turn, Pavel Petrovitch moved deliberately to the window, and with his hands thrust into his pockets, muttered between his teeth, '*mais je puis vous de l'argent*,' and gave him money; but to-day he had none himself, and he preferred to go away. The petty details of agricultural management worried him; besides, it constantly struck him that Nikolai Petrovitch, for all his zeal and industry, did not set about things in the right way, though he would not have been able to point out precisely where Nikolai Petrovitch's mistake lay. 'My brother's not practical enough,' he reasoned to himself; 'they impose upon him.' Nikolai Petrovitch, on the other hand, had the highest opinion of Pavel Petrovitch's practical ability, and always asked his advice. 'I'm a soft, weak fellow, I've spent my life in the wilds,' he used to say; 'while you haven't seen so much of the world for nothing, you see through people; you have an eagle eye.' In answer to which Pavel Petrovitch only turned away, but did not contradict his brother.

Leaving Nikolai Petrovitch in his study, he walked along the corridor, which separated the front part of the house from the back; when he had reached a low door, he stopped in hesitation, then pulling his moustaches, he knocked at it.

'Who's there? Come in,' sounded Fenitchka's voice.

'It's I,' said Pavel Petrovitch, and he opened the door.

Fenitchka jumped up from the chair on which she was sitting with her baby, and giving him into the arms of a girl, who at once carried him out of the room, she put straight her kerchief hastily.

'Pardon me, if I disturb you,' began Pavel Petrovitch, not looking at her; 'I only wanted to ask you . . . they are sending into the town to-day, I think . . . please let them buy me some green tea.'

'Certainly,' answered Fenitchka; 'how much do you desire them to buy?'

'Oh, half a pound will be enough, I imagine. You have made a change here, I see,' he added, with a rapid glance round him, which glided over Fenitchka's face too. 'The curtains here,' he explained, seeing she did not understand him.

'Oh, yes, the curtains; Nikolai Petrovitch was so good as to make me a present of them; but they have been put up a long while now.'

'Yes, and it's a long while since I have been to see you. Now it is very nice here.'

'Thanks to Nikolai Petrovitch's kindness,' murmured Fenitchka.

'You are more comfortable here than in the little lodge you used to have?' inquired Pavel Petrovitch urbanely, but without the slightest smile.

'Certainly, it's more comfortable.'

'Who has been put in your place now?'

'The laundry-maids are there now.'

'Ah!'

Pavel Petrovitch was silent. 'Now he is going,' thought Fenitchka; but he did not go, and she stood before him motionless.

'What did you send your little one away for?' said Pavel Petrovitch at last. 'I love children; let me see him.'

Fenitchka blushed all over with confusion and delight.

She was afraid of Pavel Petrovitch; he had scarcely ever spoken to her.

'Dunyasha,' she called; 'will you bring Mitya, please.' (Fenitchka did not treat any one in the house familiarly.) 'But wait a minute, he must have a frock on,' Fenitchka was going towards the door.

'That doesn't matter,' remarked Pavel Petrovitch.

'I will be back directly,' answered Fenitchka, and she went out quickly.

Pavel Petrovitch was left alone, and he looked round this time with special attention. The small low-pitched room in which he found himself was very clean and snug. It smelt of the freshly painted floor and of camomile. Along the walls stood chairs with lyre-shaped backs, bought by the late general on his campaign in Poland; in one corner was a little bedstead under a muslin canopy beside an iron-clamped chest with a convex lid. In the opposite corner a little lamp was burning before a big dark picture of St. Nikolai the wonder-worker; a tiny porcelain egg hung by a red ribbon from the protruding gold halo down to the saint's breast; by the windows greenish glass jars of last year's jam carefully tied down could be seen; on their paper covers Fenitchka herself had written in big letters 'Gooseberry'; Nikolai Petrovitch was particularly fond of that preserve. On a long cord from the ceiling a cage hung with a short-tailed siskin in it; he was constantly chirping and hopping about, the cage was constantly shaking and swinging, while hempseeds fell with a light tap on to the floor. On the wall just above a small chest of drawers hung some rather bad photographs of Nikolai Petrovitch in various attitudes, taken by an itinerant photographer; there too hung a photograph of Fenitchka herself, which was an absolute failure; it was an eyeless face wearing a forced smile, in a dingy frame, nothing more could be made out; while above Fenitchka, General Yermolov, in a Circassian cloak, scowled menacingly upon the Caucasian mountains in the distance, from beneath a little silk shoe for pins which fell right on to his brows.

Five minutes passed; bustling and whispering could be heard in the next room. Pavel Petrovitch took up from the chest of drawers a greasy book, an odd volume of Masalsky's

Musketeer, and turned over a few pages. . . . The door opened, and Fenitchka came in with Mitya in her arms. She had put on him a little red smock with embroidery on the collar, had combed his hair and washed his face; he was breathing heavily, his whole body working, and his little hands waving in the air, as is the way with all healthy babies; but his smart smock obviously impressed him, an expression of delight was reflected in every part of his little fat person. Fenitchka had put her own hair too in order, and had arranged her kerchief; but she might well have remained as she was. And really is there anything in the world more captivating than a beautiful young mother with a healthy baby in her arms?

'What a chubby fellow!' said Pavel Petrovitch graciously, and he tickled Mitya's little double chin with the tapering nail of his forefinger. The baby stared at the siskin, and chuckled.

'That's uncle,' said Fenitchka, bending her face down to him and slightly rocking him, while Dunyasha quietly set in the window a smouldering perfumed stick, putting a half-penny under it.

'How many months old is he?' asked Pavel Petrovitch.

'Six months; it will soon be seven, on the eleventh.'

'Isn't it eight, Fedosya Nikolaevna?' put in Dunyasha, with some timidity.

'No, seven; what an idea!' The baby chuckled again, stared at the chest, and suddenly caught hold of his mother's nose and mouth with all his five little fingers. 'Saucy mite,' said Fenitchka, not drawing her face away.

'He's like my brother,' observed Pavel Petrovitch.

'Who else should he be like?' thought Fenitchka.

'Yes,' continued Pavel Petrovitch, as though speaking to himself; 'there's an unmistakable likeness.' He looked attentively, almost mournfully, at Fenitchka.

'That's uncle,' she repeated, in a whisper this time.

'Ah! Pavel! so you're here!' was heard suddenly the voice of Nikolai Petrovitch.

Pavel Petrovitch turned hurriedly round, frowning; but his brother looked at him with such delight, such gratitude, that **he could not** help responding to his smile.

'You've a splendid little cherub,' he said, and looking at his watch. 'I came in here to speak about some tea.'

And, assuming an expression of indifference, Pavel Petrovitch at once went out of the room.

'Did he come of himself?' Nikolai Petrovitch asked Fenitchka.

'Yes; he knocked and came in.'

'Well, and has Arkasha been in to see you again?'

'No. Hadn't I better move into the lodge, Nikolai Petrovitch?'

'Why so?'

'I wonder whether it wouldn't be best just for the first.'

'N . . . no,' Nikolai Petrovitch brought out hesitatingly, rubbing his forehead. 'We ought to have done it before. . . . How are you, fatty?' he said, suddenly brightening, and going up to the baby, he kissed him on the cheek; then he bent a little and pressed his lips to Fenitchka's hand, which lay white as milk upon Mitya's little red smock.

'Nikolai Petrovitch! what are you doing?' she whispered, dropping her eyes, then slowly raising them. Very charming was the expression of her eyes when she peeped, as it were, from under her lids, and smiled tenderly and a little foolishly.

Nikolai Petrovitch had made Fenitchka's acquaintance in the following manner. He had once happened three years before to stay a night at an inn in a remote district town. He was agreeably struck by the cleanness of the room assigned to him, the freshness of the bed-linen. Surely the woman of the house must be a German? was the idea that occurred to him; but she proved to be a Russian, a woman of about fifty, neatly dressed, of a good-looking, sensible countenance and discreet speech. He entered into conversation with her at tea; he liked her very much. Nikolai Petrovitch had at that time only just moved into his new home, and not wishing to keep serfs in the house, he was on the look-out for wage-servants; the woman of the inn on her side complained of the small number of visitors to the town, and the hard times; he proposed to her to come into his house in the capacity of housekeeper; she consented. Her husband had long been dead, leaving her an only daughter, Fenitchka.

Within a fortnight Arina Savishna (that was the new house-keeper's name) arrived with her daughter at Maryino and in-stalled herself in the little lodge. Nikolai Petrovitch's choice proved a successful one. Arina brought order into the house-hold. As for Fenitchka, who was at that time seventeen, no one spoke of her, and scarcely any one saw her; she lived quietly and sedately, and only on Sundays Nikolai Petrovitch noticed in the church somewhere in a side place the deli-cate profile of her white face. More than a year passed thus.

One morning, Arina came into his study, and bowing low as usual, she asked him if he could do anything for her daughter, who had got a spark from the stove in her eye. Nikolai Petrovitch, like all stay-at-home people, had studied doctoring and even compiled a homœopathic guide. He at once told Arina to bring the patient to him. Fenitchka was much frightened when she heard the master had sent for her; however, she followed her mother. Nikolai Petrovitch led her to the window and took her head in his two hands. After thoroughly examining her red and swollen eye, he prescribed a fomentation, which he made up himself at once, and tearing his handkerchief in pieces, he showed her how it ought to be applied. Fenitchka listened to all he had to say, and then was going. 'Kiss the master's hand, silly girl,' said Arina. Nikolai Petrovitch did not give her his hand, and in confusion himself kissed her bent head on the parting of her hair. Fenitchka's eye was soon well again, but the impression she had made on Nikolai Petro-vitch did not pass away so quickly. He was for ever haunted by that pure, delicate, timidly raised face; he felt on the palms of his hands that soft hair, and saw those innocent, slightly parted lips, through which pearly teeth gleamed with moist brilliance in the sunshine. He began to watch her with great attention in church, and tried to get into conversation with her. At first she was shy of him, and one day meeting him at the approach of evening in a narrow footpath through a field of rye, she ran into the tall thick rye, overgrown with cornflowers and wormwood, so as not to meet him face to face. He caught sight of her little head through a golden network of ears of rye, from which she was peeping out like a little animal, and called affectionately to her—

'Good-evening, Fenitchka! I don't bite.'

'Good-evening,' she whispered, not coming out of her ambush.

By degrees she began to be more at home with him, but was still shy in his presence, when suddenly her mother, Arina, died of cholera. What was to become of Fenitchka? She inherited from her mother a love for order, regularity, and respectability; but she was so young, so alone. Nikolai Petrovitch was himself so good and considerate. . . . It's needless to relate the rest. . . .

'So my brother came in to see you?' Nikolai Petrovitch questioned her. 'He knocked and came in?'

'Yes.'

'Well, that's a good thing. Let me give Mitya a swing.'

And Nikolai Petrovitch began tossing him almost up to the ceiling, to the huge delight of the baby, and to the considerable uneasiness of the mother, who every time he flew up stretched her arms up towards his little bare legs.

Pavel Petrovitch went back to his artistic study, with its walls covered with handsome bluish-grey hangings, with weapons hanging upon a variegated Persian rug nailed to the wall; with walnut furniture, upholstered in dark green velveteen, with a *renaissance* bookcase of old black oak, with bronze statuettes on the magnificent writing-table, with an open hearth. He threw himself on the sofa, clasped his hands behind his head, and remained without moving, looking with a face almost of despair at the ceiling. Whether he wanted to hide from the very walls that which was reflected in his face, or for some other reason, he got up, drew the heavy window curtains, and again threw himself on the sofa.

CHAPTER IX

ON the same day Bazarov made acquaintance with Fenitchka. He was walking with Arkady in the garden, and explaining to him why some of the trees, especially the oaks, had not done well.

'You ought to have planted silver poplars here by preference, and spruce firs, and perhaps limes, giving them some loam. The arbour there has done well,' he added, 'because it's acacia and lilac; they're accommodating good fellows, those trees, they don't want much care. But there's some one in here.'

In the arbour was sitting Fenitchka, with Dunyasha and Mitya. Bazarov stood still, while Arkady nodded to Fenitchka like an old friend.

'Who's that?' Bazarov asked him directly they had passed by. 'What a pretty girl!'

'Whom are you speaking of?'

'You know; only one of them was pretty.'

Arkady, not without embarrassment, explained to him briefly who Fenitchka was.

'Aha!' commented Bazarov; 'your father's got good taste, one can see. I like him, your father, ay, ay! He's a jolly fellow. We must make friends though,' he added, and turned back towards the arbour.

'Yevgeny!' Arkady cried after him in dismay; 'mind what you are about, for mercy's sake.'

'Don't worry yourself,' said Bazarov; 'I know how to behave myself—I'm not a booby.'

Going up to Fenitchka, he took off his cap.

'Allow me to introduce myself,' he began, with a polite bow. 'I'm a harmless person, and a friend of Arkady Nikolaevitch's.'

Fenitchka got up from the garden seat and looked at him without speaking.

'What a splendid baby!' continued Bazarov; 'don't be

uneasy, my praises have never brought ill-luck yet. Why is it his cheeks are so flushed? Is he cutting his teeth?'

'Yes,' said Fenitchka; 'he has cut four teeth already, and now the gums are swollen again.'

'Show me, and don't be afraid, I'm a doctor.'

Bazarov took the baby up in his arms, and to the great astonishment both of Fenitchka and Dunyasha the child made no resistance, and was not frightened.

'I see, I see. . . . It's nothing, everything's as it should be; he will have a good set of teeth. If anything goes wrong, tell me. And are you quite well yourself?'

'Quite, thank God.'

'Thank God, indeed—that's the great thing. And you?' he added, turning to Dunyasha.

Dunyasha, a girl very prim in the master's house, and a romp outside the gates, only giggled in answer.

'Well, that's all right. Here's your gallant fellow.'

Fenitchka received the baby in her arms.

'How good he was with you!' she commented in an under-tone.

'Children are always good with me,' answered Bazarov; 'I have a way with them.'

'Children know who loves them,' remarked Dunyasha.

'Yes, they certainly do,' Fenitchka said. 'Why, Mitya will not go to some people for anything.'

'Will he come to me?' asked Arkady, who, after standing in the distance for some time, had gone up to the arbour.

He tried to entice Mitya to come to him, but Mitya threw his head back and screamed, to Fenitchka's great confusion.

'Another day, when he's had time to get used to me,' said Arkady indulgently, and the two friends walked away.

'What's her name?' asked Bazarov.

'Fenitchka . . . Fedosya,' answered Arkady.

'And her father's name? One must know that too.'

'Nikolaevna.'

'Bene. What I like in her is that she's not too embarrassed. Some people, I suppose, would think ill of her for it. What nonsense! What is there to embarrass her? She's a mother—she's all right.'

'She's all right,' observed Arkady,—'but my father.'

'And he's right too,' put in Bazarov.

'Well, no, I don't think so.'

'I suppose an extra heir's not to your liking?'

'I wonder you're not ashamed to attribute such ideas to me!' retorted Arkady hotly; 'I don't consider my father wrong from that point of view; I think he ought to marry her.'

'Hoity-toity!' responded Bazarov tranquilly. 'What magnanimous fellows we are! You still attach significance to marriage; I did not expect that of you.'

The friends walked a few paces in silence.

'I have looked at all your father's establishment,' Bazarov began again. 'The cattle are inferior, the horses are broken down; the buildings aren't up to much, and the workmen look confirmed loafers; while the superintendent is either a fool, or a knave, I haven't quite found out which yet.'

'You are rather hard on everything to-day, Yevgeny Vassilyevitch.'

'And the dear good peasants are taking your father in to a dead certainty. You know the Russian proverb, "The Russian peasant will cheat God Himself."'

'I begin to agree with my uncle,' remarked Arkady; 'you certainly have a poor opinion of Russians.'

'As though that mattered! The only good point in a Russian is his having the lowest possible opinion of himself. What does matter is that two and two make four, and the rest is all foolery.'

'And is nature foolery?' said Arkady, looking pensively at the bright-coloured fields in the distance, in the beautiful soft light of the sun, which was not yet high up in the sky.

'Nature, too, is foolery in the sense you understand it. Nature's not a temple, but a workshop, and man's the workman in it.'

At that instant, the long drawn notes of a violoncello floated out to them from the house. Some one was playing Schubert's *Expectation* with much feeling, though with an untrained hand, and the melody flowed with honey sweetness through the air.

'What's that?' cried Bazarov in amazement.

'It's my father.'

'Your father plays the violoncello?'

'Yes.'

'And how old is your father?'

'Forty-four.'

Bazarov suddenly burst into a roar of laughter.

'What are you laughing at?'

'Upon my word, a man of forty-four, a *paterfamilias* in this out-of-the-way district, playing on the violoncello!'

Bazarov went on laughing; but much as he revered his master, this time Arkady did not even smile.

CHAPTER X

ABOUT a fortnight passed by. Life at Maryino went on
its accustomed course, while Arkady was lazy and
enjoyed himself, and Bazarov worked. Every one in
the house had grown used to him, to his careless manners,
and his curt and abrupt speeches. Fenitchka, in particular,
was so far at home with him that one night she sent to
wake him up; Mitya had had convulsions; and he had gone,
and, half joking, half-yawning as usual, he stayed two hours
with her and relieved the child. On the other hand Pavel
Petrovitch had grown to detest Bazarov with all the strength
of his soul; he regarded him as stuck-up, impudent, cynical,
and vulgar; he suspected that Bazarov had no respect for
him, that he had all but a contempt for him—him, Pavel
Kirsanov!

Nikolai Petrovitch was rather afraid of the young
'nihilist,' and was doubtful whether his influence over
Arkady was for the good; but he was glad to listen to him,
and was glad to be present at his scientific and chemical
experiments. Bazarov had brought with him a microscope,
and busied himself for hours together with it. The servants,
too, took to him, though he made fun of them; they felt, all
the same, that he was one of themselves, not a master.
Dunyasha was always ready to giggle with him, and used to
cast significant and stealthy glances at him when she skipped
by like a rabbit; Piotr, a man vain and stupid to the last
degree, for ever wearing an affected frown on his brow, a
man whose whole merit consisted in the fact that he looked
civil, could spell out a page of reading, and was diligent in
brushing his coat—even he smirked and brightened up
directly Bazarov paid him any attention; the boys on the
farm simply ran after the 'doctor' like puppies. The old
man Prokofitch was the only one who did not like him; he
handed him the dishes at table with a surly face, called him
a 'butcher' and 'an upstart,' and declared that with his great

whiskers he looked like a pig in a stye. Prokofitch in his own way was quite as much of an aristocrat as Pavel Petrovitch.

The best days of the year had come—the first days of June. The weather kept splendidly fine; in the distance, it is true, the cholera was threatening, but the inhabitants of that province had had time to get used to its visits. Bazarov used to get up very early and go out for two or three miles, not for a walk—he couldn't bear walking without an object— but to collect specimens of plants and insects. Sometimes he took Arkady with him.

On the way home an argument usually sprang up, and Arkady was usually vanquished in it, though he said more than his companion.

One day they had lingered rather late; Nikolai Petrovitch went to meet them in the garden, and as he reached the arbour he suddenly heard the quick steps and voices of the two young men. They were walking on the other side of the arbour, and could not see him.

'You don't know my father well enough,' said Arkady.

'Your father's a nice chap,' said Bazarov, 'but he's behind the times; his day is done.'

Nikolai Petrovitch listened intently. . . . Arkady made no answer.

The man whose day was done remained two minutes motionless, and stole slowly home.

'The day before yesterday I saw him reading Pushkin,' Bazarov was continuing meanwhile. 'Explain to him, please, that that's no earthly use. He's not a boy, you know; it's time to throw up that rubbish. And what an idea to be a romantic at this time of day! Give him something sensible to read.'

'What ought I to give him?' asked Arkady.

'Oh, I think Büchner's *Stoff und Kraft* to begin with.'

'I think so too,' observed Arkady approving, '*Stoff und Kraft* is written in popular language. . . .'

'So it seems,' Nikolai Petrovitch said the same day after dinner to his brother, as he sat in his study, 'you and I are behind the times, our day's over. Well, well. Perhaps Bazarov is right; but one thing I confess, makes me feel sore; I did so hope, precisely now, to get on to such close intimate terms with Arkady, and it turns out I'm left behind, and he has gone forward, and we can't understand one another.'

'How has he gone forward? And in what way is he so superior to us already?' cried Pavel Petrovitch impatiently. 'It's that high and mighty gentleman, that nihilist, who's knocked all that into his head. I hate that doctor fellow; in my opinion, he's simply a quack; I'm convinced, for all his tadpoles, he's not got very far even in medicine.'

'No, brother, you musn't say that; Bazarov is clever, and knows his subject.'

'And his conceit's something revolting,' Pavel Petrovitch broke in again.

'Yes,' observed Nikolai Petrovitch, 'he is conceited. But there's no doing without that, it seems; only that's what I did not take into account. I thought I was doing everything to keep up with the times; I have started a model farm; I have done well by the peasants, so that I am positively called a "Red Radical" all over the province; I read, I study, I try in every way to keep abreast with the requirements of the day—and they say my day's over. And, brother, I begin to think that it is.'

'Why so?'

'I'll tell you why. This morning I was sitting reading Pushkin. . . . I remember, it happened to be *The Gipsies* . . . all of a sudden Arkady came up to me, and, without speaking, with such a kindly compassion on his face, as gently as if I were a baby, took the book away from me, and laid another before me—a German book . . . smiled, and went away, carrying Pushkin off with him.'

'Upon my word! What book did he give you?'

'This one here.'

And Nikolai Petrovitch pulled the famous treatise of Büchner, in the ninth edition, out of his coat-tail pocket.

Pavel Petrovitch turned it over in his hands. 'Hm!' he growled. 'Arkady Nikolaevitch is taking your education in hand. Well, did you try reading it?'

'Yes, I tried it.

'Well, what did you think of it?'

'Either I'm stupid, or it's all—nonsense. I must be stupid, I suppose.'

'Haven't you forgotten your German?' queried Pavel Petrovitch.

'Oh, I understand the German.'

Pavel Petrovitch again turned the book over in his hands, and glanced from under his brows at his brother. Both were silent.

'Oh, by the way,' began Nikolai Petrovitch, obviously wishing to change the subject, 'I've got a letter from Kolyazin.'

'Matvy Ilyitch?'

'Yes. He has come to——to inspect the province. He's quite a bigwig now; and writes to me that, as a relation, he should like to see us again, and invites you and me and Arkady to the town.'

'Are you going?' asked Pavel Petrovitch.

'No; are you?'

'No, I shan't go either. Much object there would be in dragging oneself over forty miles on a wild-goose chase. *Mathieu* wants to show himself in all his glory. Damn him! he will have the whole province doing him homage; he can get on without the likes of us. A grand dignity, indeed, a privy councillor! If I had stayed in the service, if I had drudged on in official harness, I should have been a general-adjutant by now. Besides, you and I are behind the times, you know.'

'Yes, brother; it's time, it seems, to order a coffin and cross one's arms on one's breast,' remarked Nikolai Petrovitch, with a sigh.

'Well, I'm not going to give in quite so soon,' muttered his brother. 'I've got a tussle with that doctor fellow before me, I feel sure of that.'

A tussle came off that same day at evening tea. Pavel Petrovitch came into the drawing-room, all ready for the fray, irritable and determined. He was only waiting for an excuse to fall upon the enemy; but for a long while an excuse did not present itself. As a rule, Bazarov said little in the presence of the 'old Kirsanovs' (that was how he spoke of the brothers), and that evening he felt out of humour, and drank off cup after cup of tea without a word. Pavel Petrovitch was all aflame with impatience; his wishes were fulfilled at last.

The conversation turned on one of the neighbouring landowners. 'Rotten aristocratic snob,' observed Bazarov indifferently. He had met him in Petersburg.

'Allow me to ask you,' began Pavel Petrovitch, and his lips were trembling, 'according to your ideas, have the words "rotten" and "aristocrat" the same meaning?'

'I said "aristocratic snob," ' replied Bazarov, lazily swallowing a sip of tea.

'Precisely so; but I imagine you have the same opinion of aristocrats as of aristocratic snobs. I think it my duty to inform you that I do not share that opinion. I venture to assert that every one knows me for a man of liberal ideas and devoted to progress; but, exactly for that reason, I respect aristocrats—real aristocrats. Kindly remember, sir' (at these words Bazarov lifted his eyes and looked at Pavel Petrovitch), 'kindly remember, sir,' he repeated, with acrimony—'the English aristocracy. They do not abate one iota of their rights, and for that reason they respect the rights of others; they demand the performance of what is due to them, and for that reason they perform their own duties. The aristocracy has given freedom to England, and maintains it for her.'

'We've heard that story a good many times,' replied Bazarov; 'but what are you trying to prove by that?'

'I am tryin' to prove by that, sir' (when Pavel Petrovitch was angry he intentionally clipped his words in this way, though, of course, he knew very well that such forms are not strictly grammatical. In this fashionable whim could be discerned a survival of the habits of the times of Alexander. The exquisites of those days, on the rare occasions when they spoke their own language, made use of such slipshod forms; as much as to say, 'We, of course, are born Russians, at the same time we are great swells, who are at liberty to neglect the rules of scholars') ; 'I am tryin' to prove by that, sir, that without the sense of personal dignity, without self-respect—and these two sentiments are well developed in the aristocrat—there is no secure foundation for the social . . . *bien public* . . . the social fabric. Personal character, sir—that is the chief thing; a man's personal character must be firm as a rock, since everything is built on it. I am very well aware, for instance, that you are pleased to consider my habits, my dress, my refinements, in fact, ridiculous; but all that proceeds from a sense of self-respect, from a sense of duty—yes, indeed, of duty. I live in the country, in the wilds, but I will not lower myself. I respect the dignity of man in myself.'

'Let me ask you, Pavel Petrovitch,' commented Bazarov; 'you respect yourself, and sit with your hands folded; what sort of benefit does that do to the *bien public?* If you didn't respect yourself, you'd do just the same.'

Pavel Petrovitch turned white. 'That's a different question. Its absolutely unnecessary for me to explain to you now why I sit with folded hands, as you are pleased to express yourself. I wish only to tell you that aristocracy is a principle, and in our days none but immoral or silly people can live without principles. I said that to Arkady the day after he came home, and I repeat it now. Isn't it so, Nikolai?'

Nikolai Petrovitch nodded his head.

'Aristocracy, Liberalism, progress, principles,' Bazarov was saying meanwhile; 'if you think of it, what a lot of foreign . . . and useless words! To a Russian they're good for nothing.'

'What is good for something according to you? If we listen to you, we shall find ourselves outside humanity, outside its laws. Come—the logic of history demands . . .'

'But what's that logic to us? We can get on without that too.'

'How do you mean?'

'Why, this. You don't need logic, I hope, to put a bit of bread in your mouth when you're hungry. What's the object of these abstractions to us?'

Pavel Petrovitch raised his hands in horror.

'I don't understand you, after that. You insult the Russian people. I don't understand how it's possible not to acknowledge principles, rules! By virtue of what do you act then?'

'I've told you already, uncle, that we don't accept any authorities,' put in Arkady.

'We act by virtue of what we recognise as beneficial,' observed Bazarov. 'At the present time, negation is the most beneficial of all—and we deny——'

'Everything?'

'Everything!'

'What? not only art and poetry . . . but even . . . horrible to say . . .'

'Everything,' repeated Bazarov, with indescribable composure.

Pavel Petrovitch stared at him. He had not expected this; while Arkady fairly blushed with delight.

'Allow me, though,' began Nikolai Petrovitch. 'You deny everything; or, speaking more precisely, you destroy everything. . . . But one must construct too, you know.'

'That's not our business now. . . . The ground wants clearing first.'

'The present condition of the people requires it,' added Arkady, with dignity; 'we are bound to carry out these requirements, we have no right to yield to the satisfaction of our personal egoism.'

This last phrase obviously displeased Bazarov; there was a flavour of philosophy, that is to say, romanticism about it, for Bazarov called philosophy, too, romanticism, but he did not think it necessary to correct his young disciple.

'No, no!' cried Pavel Petrovitch, with sudden energy. 'I'm not willing to believe that you, young men, know the Russian people really, that you are the representatives of their requirements, their efforts! No; the Russian people is not what you imagine it. Tradition it holds sacred; it is a patriarchal people; it cannot live without faith . . .'

'I'm not going to dispute that,' Bazarov interrupted. 'I'm even ready to agree that in that you're right.'

'But if I am right . . .'

'And, all the same, that proves nothing.'

'It just proves nothing,' repeated Arkady, with the confidence of a practised chess-player, who has foreseen an apparently dangerous move on the part of his adversary, and so is not at all taken aback by it.

'How does it prove nothing?' muttered Pavel Petrovitch, astounded. 'You must be going against the people then?'

'And what if we are?' shouted Bazarov. 'The people imagine that, when it thunders, the prophet Ilya's riding across the sky in his chariot. What then? Are we to agree with them? Besides, the people's Russian; but am I not Russian too?'

'No, you are not Russian, after all you have just been saying! I can't acknowledge you as Russian.'

'My grandfather ploughed the land,' answered Bazarov with haughty pride. 'Ask any one of your peasants which of us—you or me—he'd more readily acknowledge as a fellow-countryman. You don't even know how to talk to them.'

'While you talk to him and despise him at the same time.'

'Well, suppose he deserves contempt. You find fault with my attitude, but how do you know that I have got it by chance, that it's not a product of that very national spirit, in the name of which you wage war on it?'

'What an idea! Much use in nihilists!'

'Whether they're of use or not, is not for us to decide. Why, even you suppose you're not a useless person.'

'Gentlemen, gentlemen, no personalities, please!' cried Nikolai Petrovitch, getting up.

Pavel Petrovitch smiled, and laying his hand on his brother's shoulder, forced him to sit down again.

'Don't be uneasy,' he said; 'I shall not forget myself, just through that sense of dignity which is made fun of so mercilessly by our friend—our friend, the doctor. Let me ask,' he resumed, turning again to Bazarov; 'you suppose, possibly, that your doctrine is a novelty? That is quite a mistake. The materialism you advocate has been more than once in vogue already, and has always proved insufficient . . .'

'A foreign word again!' broke in Bazarov. He was beginning to feel vicious, and his face assumed a peculiar coarse coppery hue. 'In the first place, we advocate nothing; that's not our way.'

'What do you do, then?'

'I'll tell you what we do. Not long ago we used to say that our officials took bribes, that we had no roads, no commerce, no real justice . . .'

'Oh, I see, you are reformers—that's what that's called, I fancy. I too should agree to many of your reforms, but . . .'

'Then we suspected that talk, perpetual talk, and nothing but talk, about our social diseases, was not worth while, that it all led to nothing but superficiality and pedantry; we saw that our leading men, so-called advanced people and reformers, are no good; that we busy ourselves over foolery, talk rubbish about art, unconscious creativeness, parliamentarism, trial by jury, and the deuce knows what all; while, all the while, it's a question of getting bread to eat, while we're stifling under the grossest superstition, while all our enterprises come to grief, simply because there aren't honest men enough to carry them on, while the very emancipation our Government's busy upon will hardly come to any good, because peasants are glad to rob even themselves to get drunk at the gin-shop.'

'Yes,' interposed Pavel Petrovitch, 'yes; you were convinced of all this, and decided not to undertake anything seriously, yourselves.'

'We decided not to undertake anything,' repeated Bazarov grimly. He suddenly felt vexed with himself for having, without reason, been so expansive before this gentleman.

'But to confine yourselves to abuse?'

'To confine ourselves to abuse.'

'And that is called nihilism?'

'And that's called nihilism,' Bazarov repeated again, this time with peculiar rudeness.

Pavel Petrovitch puckered up his face a little. 'So that's it!' he observed in a strangely composed voice. 'Nihilism is to cure all our woes, and you, you are our heroes and saviours. But why do you abuse others, those reformers even? Don't you do as much talking as every one else?'

'Whatever faults we have, we do not err in that way,' Bazarov muttered between his teeth.

'What, then? Do you act, or what? Are you preparing for action?'

Bazarov made no answer. Something like a tremor passed over Pavel Petrovitch, but he at once regained control of himself.

'Hm! . . . Action, destruction . . .' he went on. 'But how destroy without even knowing why?'

'We shall destroy, because we are a force,' observed Arkady.

Pavel Petrovitch looked at his nephew and laughed.

'Yes, a force is not to be called to account,' said Arkady, drawing himself up.

'Unhappy boy!' wailed Pavel Petrovitch, he was positively incapable of maintaining his firm demeanour any longer. 'If you could only realise what it is you are doing for your country. No; it's enough to try the patience of an angel! Force! There's force in the savage Kalmuck, in the Mongolian; but what is it to us? What is precious to us is civilisation; yes, yes, sir, its fruits are precious to us. And don't tell me those fruits are worthless; the poorest dauber, *un barbouilleur,* the man who plays dance music for five farthings an evening, is of more use than you, because they are the representatives of civilisation, and not of brute Mongolian force! You fancy yourselves advanced people, and all the while you are only fit for the Kalmuck's hovel! Force! And recollect, you forcible gentlemen, that you're only four men and a half, and the others are millions, who won't let you trample their sacred traditions under foot, who will crush you and walk over you!'

'If we're crushed, serve us right,' observed Bazarov. 'But that's an open question. We are not so few as you suppose.'

'What? You seriously suppose you will come to terms with a whole people?'

'All Moscow was burnt down, you know, by a farthing dip,' answered Bazarov.

'Yes, yes. First a pride almost Satanic, then ridicule— that, that's what it is attracts the young, that's what gains an ascendancy over the inexperienced hearts of boys! Here's one of them sitting beside you, ready to worship the ground under your feet. Look at him! (Arkady turned away and frowned.) And this plague has spread far already. I have been told that in Rome our artists never set foot in the Vatican. Raphael they regard as almost a fool, because, if you please, he's an authority; while they're all the while most disgustingly sterile and unsuccessful, men whose imagination does not soar beyond 'Girls at a Fountain,' however they try! And the girls even out of drawing. They are fine fellows to your mind, are they not?'

'To my mind,' retorted Bazarov, 'Raphael's not worth a brass farthing; and they're no better than he.'

'Bravo! bravo! Listen, Arkady . . . that's how young men of to-day ought to express themselves! And if you come to think of it, how could they fail to follow you! In old days, young men had to study; they didn't want to be called dunces, so they had to work hard whether they liked it or not. But now, they need only say, "Everything in the world is foolery!" and the trick's done. Young men are delighted. And, to be sure, they were simply geese before, and now they have suddenly turned nihilists.'

'Your praiseworthy sense of personal dignity has given way,' remarked Bazarov phlegmatically, while Arkady was hot all over, and his eyes were flashing. 'Our argument has gone too far; it's better to cut it short, I think. I shall be quite ready to agree with you,' he added, getting up, 'when you bring forward a single institution in our present mode of life, in family or in social life, which does not call for complete and unqualified destruction.'

'I will bring forward millions of such institutions,' cried Pavel Petrovitch—'millions! Well—the Mir, for instance.'

A cold smile curved Bazarov's lips. 'Well, as regards the Mir,' he commented; 'you had better talk to your brother. He has seen by now, I should fancy, what sort of thing the Mir is in fact—its common guarantee, its sobriety, and other features of the kind.'

'The family, then, the family as it exists among our peasants!' cried Pavel Petrovitch.

'And that subject, too, I imagine, it will be better for yourselves not to go into in detail. Don't you realise all the advantages of the head of the family choosing his daughters-in-law? Take my advice, Pavel Petrovitch, allow yourself two days to think about it; you're not likely to find anything on the spot. Go through all our classes, and think well over each, while I and Arkady will . . .'

'Will go on turning everything into ridicule,' broke in Pavel Petrovitch.

'No, will go on dissecting frogs. Come, Arkady; goodbye for the present, gentlemen!'

The two friends walked off. The brothers were left alone, and at first they only looked at one another.

'So that,' began Pavel Petrovitch, 'so that's what our young men of this generation are! They are like that—our successors!'

'Our successors!' repeated Nikolai Petrovitch, with a dejected smile. He had been sitting on thorns, all through the argument, and had done nothing but glance stealthily, with a sore heart, at Arkady. 'Do you know what I was reminded of, brother? I once had a dispute with our poor mother; she stormed, and wouldn't listen to me. At last I said to her, "Of course, you can't understand me; we belong," I said, "to two different generations." She was dreadfully offended, while I thought, "There's no help for it. It's a bitter pill, but she has to swallow it." You see, now, our turn has come, and our successors can say to us, "You are not of our generation; swallow your pill." '

'You are beyond everything in your generosity and modesty,' replied Pavel Petrovitch. 'I'm convinced, on the contrary, that you and I are far more in the right than these young gentlemen, though we do perhaps express ourselves in old-fashioned language, *vieilli*, and have not the same insolent conceit. . . . And the swagger of the young men nowadays! You ask one, "Do you take red wine or white?" "It is my custom to prefer red!" he answers in a deep bass, with a face as solemn as if the whole universe had its eyes on him at that instant. . . .'

'Do you care for any more tea?' asked Fenitchka, putting her head in at the door; she had not been able to make up her mind to come into the drawing-room while there was the sound of voices in dispute there.

'No, you can tell them to take the samovar,' answered Nikolai Petrovitch, and he got up to meet her. Pavel Petrovitch said *'bon soir'* to him abruptly, and went away to his study.

CHAPTER XI

HALF an hour later Nikolai Petrovitch went into the garden to his favourite arbour. He was overtaken by melancholy thoughts. For the first time he realised clearly the distance between him and his son; he foresaw that every day it would grow wider and wider. In vain, then, had he spent whole days sometimes in the winter at Petersburg over the newest books; in vain had he listened to the talk of the young men; in vain had he rejoiced when he succeeded in putting in his word too in their heated discussions. 'My brother says we are right,' he thought, 'and apart from all vanity, I do think myself that they are further from the truth than we are, though at the same time I feel there is something behind them we have not got, some superiority over us. . . . Is it youth? No; not only youth. Doesn't their superiority consist in there being fewer traces of the slaveowner in them than in us?'

Nikolai Petrovitch's head sank despondently, and he passed his hand over his face.

'But to renounce poetry?' he thought again; 'to have no feeling for art, for nature . . .'

And he looked round, as though trying to understand how it was possible to have no feeling for nature. It was already evening; the sun was hidden behind a small copse of aspens which lay a quarter of a mile from the garden; its shadow stretched indefinitely across the still fields. A peasant on a white nag went at a trot along the dark, narrow path close beside the copse; his whole figure was clearly visible even to the patch on his shoulder, in spite of his being in the shade; the horse's hoofs flew along bravely. The sun's rays from the farther side fell full on the copse, and piercing through its thickets, threw such a warm light on the aspen trunks that they looked like pines, and their leaves were almost a dark blue, while above them rose a pale blue sky, faintly tinged by the glow of sunset. The swallows flew high; the wind had quite died away, belated bees hummed slowly and drowsily among the lilac blossom; a swarm of midges hung like a cloud over a solitary branch which stood out against the sky. 'How beautiful, my God!' thought Nikolai Petrovitch, and his favourite verses were almost on his lips; he remembered Arkady's *Stoff und Kraft* —and was silent, but still he sat there, still he gave himself up to the sorrowful consolation of solitary thought. He was fond of dreaming; his country life had developed the tendency in him. How short a time ago, he had been dreaming like this, waiting for his son at the posting station, and what a change already since that day; their relations that were then undefined, were defined now—and how defined! Again his dead wife came back to his imagination, but not as he had known her for many years, not as the good domestic housewife, but as a young girl with a slim figure, innocently inquiring eyes, and a tight twist of hair on her childish neck. He remembered how he had seen her for the first time. He was still a student then. He had met her on the staircase of his lodgings, and, jostling by accident against her, he tried to apologise, and could only mutter, '*Pardon, monsieur,*' while she bowed, smiled, and suddenly seemed frightened, and ran away, though at the bend of the staircase she had glanced rapidly at him, assumed a serious air, and blushed. Afterwards, the first timid visits, the half-words, the half-smiles, and embarrassment; and melancholy, and yearnings, and at last that breathing rapture. . . . Where had it all vanished? She had been his wife, he had been happy as few on earth are happy. . . . 'But,' he mused, 'these sweet first moments, why could one not live an eternal, undying life in them?'

He did not try to make his thought clear to himself; but he felt that he longed to keep that blissful time by something stronger than memory; he longed to feel his Marya near him again to have the sense of her warmth and breathing, and already he could fancy that over him. . . .

'Nikolai Petrovitch,' came the sound of Fenitchka's voice close by him; 'where are you?'

He started. He felt no pang, no shame. He never even admitted the possibility of comparison between his wife and

Fenitchka, but he was sorry she had thought of coming to look for him. Her voice had brought back to him at once his grey hairs, his age, his reality. . . .

The enchanted world into which he was just stepping, which was just rising out of the dim mists of the past, was shaken—and vanished.

'I'm here,' he answered; 'I'm coming, run along.' 'There it is, the traces of the slave owner,' flashed through his mind. Fenitchka peeped into the arbour at him without speaking, and disappeared; while he noticed with astonishment that the night had come on while he had been dreaming. Everything around was dark and hushed. Fenitchka's face had glimmered so pale and slight before him. He got up, and was about to go home; but the emotion stirred in his heart could not be soothed at once, and he began slowly walking about the garden, sometimes looking at the ground at his feet, and then raising his eyes towards the sky where swarms of stars were twinkling. He walked a great deal, till he was almost tired out, while the restlessness within him, a kind of yearning, vague, melancholy restlessness, still was not appeased. Oh, how Bazarov would have laughed at him, if he had known what was passing within him then! Arkady himself would have condemned him. He, a man forty-four years old, an agriculturist and a farmer, was shedding tears, causeless tears; this was a hundred times worse than the violoncello.

Nikolai Petrovitch continued walking, and could not make up his mind to go into the house, into the snug peaceful nest, which looked out at him so hospitably from all its lighted windows; he had not the force to tear himself away from the darkness, the garden, the sense of the fresh air in his face, from that melancholy, that restless craving.

At a turn in the path, he was met by Pavel Petrovitch. 'What's the matter with you?' he asked Nikolai Petrovitch; 'you are as white as a ghost; you are not well; why don't you go to bed?'

Nikolai Petrovitch explained to him briefly his state of feeling and moved away. Pavel Petrovitch went to the end of the garden, and he too grew thoughtful, and he too raised his eyes toward the heavens. But in his beautiful dark eyes, nothing was reflected but the light of the stars. He was not born an idealist, and his fastidiously dry and sensuous soul, with its French tinge of cynicism was not capable of dreaming. . . .

'Do you know what?' Bazarov was saying to Arkady the same night. 'I've got a splendid idea. Your father was saying to-day that he'd had an invitation from your illustrious relative. Your father's not going; let us be off to X——; you know the worthy man invites you too. You see what fine weather it is; we'll stroll about and look at the town. We'll have five or six days' outing, and enjoy ourselves.'

'And you'll come back here again?'

'No; I must go to my father's. You know, he lives about twenty-five miles from X——. I've not seen him for a long while, and my mother too; I must cheer the old people up. They've been good to me, especially my father; he's awfully funny. I'm their only one too.'

'And will you be long with them?'

'I don't suppose so. It will be dull, of course.'

'And you'll come to us on your way back?'

'I don't know . . . I'll see. Well, what do you say? Shall we go?'

'If you like,' observed Arkady languidly.

In his heart he was highly delighted with his friend's suggestion, but he thought it a duty to conceal his feeling. He was not a nihilist for nothing!

The next day he set off with Bazarov to X——. The younger part of the household at Maryino were sorry at their going; Dunyasha even cried . . . but the old folks breathed more easily.

CHAPTER XII

THE town of X—— to which our friends set off was in the jurisdiction of a governor who was a young man, and at once a progressive and a despot, as often happens with Russians. Before the end of the first year of his government, he had managed to quarrel not only with the marshal of nobility, a retired officer of the guards, who kept open house and a stud of horses, but even with his own subordinates. The feuds arising from this cause assumed at last such proportions that the ministry in Petersburg had found it necessary to send down a trusted personage with a commission to investigate it all on the spot. The choice of the authorities fell upon Matvy Ilyitch Kolyazin, the son of the Kolyazin, under whose protection the brothers Kirsanov had once found themselves. He, too, was a 'young man'; that is to say, he had not long passed forty, but he was already on the high road to becoming a statesman, and wore a star on each side of his breast—one, to be sure, a foreign star, not of the first magnitude. Like the governor, whom he had come down to pass judgment upon, he was reckoned a progressive; and though he was already a bigwig, he was not like the majority of bigwigs. He had the highest opinion of himself; his vanity knew no bounds, but he behaved simply, looked affable, listened condescendingly, and laughed so good-naturedly, that on a first acquaintance he might even be taken for 'a jolly good fellow.' On important occasions, however, he knew, as the saying is, how to make his authority felt. 'Energy is essential,' he used to say then, *l'énergie est la première qualité d'un homme d'état;* and for all that, he was usually taken in, and any moderately experienced official could turn him round his finger. Matvy Ilyitch used to speak with great respect of Guizot, and tried to impress every one with the idea that he did not belong to the class of *routiniers* and high-and-dry bureaucrats, that not a single phenomenon of social life passed unnoticed by him. . . . All such phrases were very familiar to him. He even followed, with dignified indifference, it is true, the development of contemporary literature; so a grown-up man who meets a procession of small boys in the street will sometimes walk after it. In reality, Matvy Ilyitch had not got much beyond those political men of the days of Alexander, who used to prepare for an evening party at Madame Svyetchin's by reading a page of Condillac; only his methods were different, more modern. He was an adroit courtier, a great hypocrite, and nothing more; he had no special aptitude for affairs, and no intellect, but he knew how to manage his own business successfully; no one could get the better of him there, and, to be sure, that's the principal thing.

Matvy Ilyitch received Arkady with the good-nature, we might even call it playfulness, characteristic of the enlightened higher official. He was astonished, however, when he heard that the cousins he had invited had remained at home in the country. 'Your father was always a queer fellow,' he remarked, playing with the tassels of his magnificent velvet dressing-gown, and suddenly turning to a young official in a discreetly buttoned-up uniform, he cried, with an air of concentrated attention, 'What?' The young man, whose lips were glued together from prolonged silence, got up and looked in perplexity at his chief. But, having nonplussed his subordinate, Matvy Ilyitch paid him no further attention. Our higher officials are fond as a rule of nonplussing their subordinates; the methods to which they have recourse to attain that end are rather various. The following means, among others, is in great vogue, '*is quite a favourite,*' as the English say; a high official suddenly ceases to understand the simplest words, assuming total deafness. He will ask, for instance, 'What's to-day?'

He is respectfully informed, 'To-day's Friday, your Ex-s-s-s-lency.'

'Eh? What? What's that? What do you say?' the great man repeats with intense attention.

'To-day's Friday, your Ex—s—s—lency.'

'Eh? What? What's Friday? What Friday?'

'Friday, your Ex—s—s—s—lency, the day of the week.'

'What, do you pretend to teach me, eh?'

Matvy Ilyitch was a higher official all the same, though he was reckoned a liberal.

'I advise you, my dear boy, to go and call on the Governor,' he said to Arkady; 'you understand, I don't advise you to do so because I adhere to old-fashioned ideas of the necessity of paying respect to authorities, but simply because the Governor's a very decent fellow; besides, you probably want to make acquaintance with the society here. . . . You're not a bear, I hope? And he's giving a great ball the day after to-morrow.'

'Will you be at the ball?' inquired Arkady.

'He gives it in my honour,' answered Matvy Ilyitch, almost pityingly. 'Do you dance?'

'Yes; I dance, but not well.'

'That's a pity! There are pretty girls here, and it's a disgrace for a young man not to dance. Again, I don't say that through any old-fashioned ideas; I don't in the least imagine that a man's wit lies in his feet, but Byronism is ridiculous, *il a fait son temps.*'

'But, uncle, it's not through Byronism, I . . .'

'I will introduce you to the ladies here; I will take you under my wing,' interrupted Matvy Ilyitch, and he laughed complacently. 'You'll find it warm, eh?'

A servant entered and announced the arrival of the superintendent of the Crown domains, a mild-eyed old man, with deep creases round his mouth, who was excessively fond of nature, especially on a summer day, when, in his words, 'every little busy bee takes a little bribe from every little flower.' Arkady withdrew.

He found Bazarov at the tavern where they were staying, and was a long while persuading him to go with him to the Governor's. 'Well, there's no help for it,' said Bazarov at last. 'It's no good doing things by halves. We came to look at the gentry; let's look at them!'

The Governor received the young men affably, but he did not ask them to sit down, nor did he sit down himself. He was in an everlasting fuss and hurry; in the morning he used to put on a tight uniform and an excessively stiff cravat; he never ate or drank enough; he was for ever making arrangements. He invited Kirsanov and Bazarov to his ball, and within a few minutes invited them a second time, regarding them as brothers, and calling them Kisarov.

They were on their way home from the Governor's, when suddenly a short man, in a Slavophil national dress, leaped out of a trap that was passing them, and crying, 'Yevgeny Vassilyitch!' dashed up to Bazarov.

'Ah! it's you, Herr Sitnikov,' observed Bazarov, still stepping along on the pavement; 'by what chance did you come here?'

'Fancy, absolutely by chance,' he replied, and returning to the trap, he waved his hand several times, and shouted, 'Follow, follow us! My father had business here,' he went on, hopping across the gutter, 'and so he asked me. . . . I heard to-day of your arrival, and have already been to see you. . . . (The friends did, in fact, on returning to their room, find there a card, with the corners turned down, bearing the name of Sitnikov, on one side in French, on the other in Slavonic characters.) 'I hope you are not coming from the Governor's?'

'It's no use to hope; we come straight from him.'

'Ah! in that case I will call on him too. . . . Yevgeny Vassilyitch, introduce me to your . . . to the . . .'

'Sitnikov, Kirsanov,' mumbled Bazarov, not stopping.

'I am greatly flattered,' began Sitnikov, walking sidewise, smirking, and hurriedly pulling off his really over-elegant gloves. 'I have heard so much. . . . I am an old acquaintance of Yevgeny Vassilyitch, and, I may say—his disciple. I am indebted to him for my regeneration. . . .'

Arkady looked at Bazarov's disciple. There was an expression of excitement and dulness imprinted on the small but pleasant features of his well-groomed face; his small eyes, that seemed squeezed in, had a fixed and uneasy look, and his laugh, too, was uneasy—a sort of short, wooden laugh.

'Would you believe it,' he pursued, 'when Yevgeny Vassilyitch for the first time said before me that it was not right to accept any authorities, I felt such enthusiasm . . . as though my eyes were opened! Here, I thought, at last I have found a man! By the way, Yevgeny Vassilyitch, you positively must come to know a lady here, who is really capable of understanding you, and for whom your visit would be a real festival; you have heard of her, I suppose?'

'Who is it?' Bazarov brought out unwillingly.

'Kukshina, *Eudoxie, Evdoksya* Kukshin. She's a remarkable nature, *émancipée* in the true sense of the word, an advanced woman. Do you know what? We'll all go together to see her now. She lives only two steps from here. We will have lunch there. I suppose you have not lunched yet?'

'No; not yet.'

'Well, that's capital. She has separated, you understand, from her husband; she is not dependent on any one.'

'Is she pretty?' Bazarov cut in.

'N-no, one couldn't say that.'

'Then, what the devil are you asking us to see her for?'

'Fie; you must have your joke. . . . She will give us a bottle of champagne.'

'Oh, that's it. One can see the practical man at once. By the way, is your father still in the gin business?'

'Yes,' said Sitnikov, hurriedly, and he gave a shrill spasmodic laugh. 'Well? Will you come?'

'I don't really know.'

'You wanted to see people, go along,' said Arkady in an undertone.

'And what do you say to it, Mr. Kirsanov?' Sitnikov put in. 'You must come too; we can't go without you.'

'But how can we burst in upon her all at once?'

'That's no matter. Kukshina's a brick!'

'There will be a bottle of champagne?' asked Bazarov.

'Three!' cried Sitnikov; 'that I answer for.'

'What with?'

'My own head.'

'Your father's purse would be better. However, we are coming.'

CHAPTER XIII

THE small gentleman's house in the Moscow style, in which Avdotya Nikitishna, otherwise Evdoksya, Kukshin, lived, was in one of the streets of X——, which had been lately burnt down; it is well known that our provincial towns are burnt down every five years. At the door, above a visiting card nailed on all askew, there was a bell-handle to be seen, and in the hall the visitors were met by some one, not exactly a servant, nor exactly a companion, in a cap—unmistakable tokens of the progressive tendencies of the lady of the house. Sitnikov inquired whether Avdotya Nikitishna was at home.

'Is that you, *Victor?*' sounded a shrill voice from the adjoining room. 'Come in.'

The woman in the cap disappeared at once.

'I'm not alone,' observed Sitnikov, with a sharp look at Arkady and Bazarov as he briskly pulled off his overcoat, beneath which appeared something of the nature of a coachman's velvet jacket.

'No matter,' answered the voice. *'Entrez.'*

The young men went in. The room into which they walked was more like a working study than a drawing-room. Papers, letters, fat numbers of Russian journals, for the most part uncut, lay at random on the dusty tables; white cigarette ends lay scattered in every direction. On a leather-covered sofa, a lady, still young, was half reclining. Her fair hair was rather dishevelled; she wore a silk gown, not perfectly tidy, heavy bracelets on her short arms, and a lace handkerchief on her head. She got up from the sofa, and carelessly drawing a velvet cape trimmed with yellowish ermine over her shoulders, she said languidly, 'Good-morning, *Victor,*' and pressed Sitnikov's hand.

'Bazarov, Kirsanov,' he announced abruptly in imitation of Bazarov.

'Delighted,' answered Madame Kukshin, and fixing on Bazarov a pair of round eyes, between which was a forlorn little turned-up red nose, 'I know you,' she added, and pressed his hand too.

Bazarov scowled. There was nothing repulsive in the little plain person of the emancipated woman; but the expression of her face produced a disagreeable effect on the spectator. One felt impelled to ask her, 'What's the matter; are you hungry? Or bored? Or shy? What are you in a fidget about?' Both she and Sitnikov had always the same uneasy air. She was extremely unconstrained, and at the same time awkward; she obviously regarded herself as a good-natured, simple creature, and all the while, whatever she did, it always struck one that it was not just what she wanted to do; everything with her seemed, as children say, done on purpose, that's to say, not simply, not naturally.

'Yes, yes, I know you, Bazarov,' she repeated. (She had the habit—peculiar to many provincial and Moscow ladies—of calling men by their surnames from the first day of acquaintance with them.) 'Will you have a cigar?'

'A cigar's all very well,' put in Sitnikov, who by now was lolling in an armchair, his legs in the air; 'but give us some lunch. We're awfully hungry; and tell them to bring us up a little bottle of champagne.'

'Sybarite,' commented Evdoksya, and she laughed. (When she laughed the gum showed above her upper teeth.) 'Isn't it true, Bazarov; he's a Sybarite?'

'I like comfort in life,' Sitnikov brought out, with dignity. 'That does not prevent my being a Liberal.'

'No, it does; it does prevent it!' cried Evdoksya. She gave directions, however, to her maid, both as regards the lunch and the champagne.

'What do you think about it?' she added, turning to Bazarov. 'I'm persuaded you share my opinion.'

'Well, no,' retorted Bazarov; 'a piece of meat's better than a piece of bread even from the chemical point of view.'

'You are studying chemistry? That is my passion. I've even invented a new sort of composition myself.'

'A composition? You?'

'Yes. And do you know for what purpose? To make dolls' heads so that they shouldn't break. I'm practical, too, you see. But everything's not quite ready yet. I've still to read Liebig. By the way, have you read Kislyakov's article on Female Labour, in the *Moscow Gazette?* Read it please. You're interested in the woman question, I suppose? And in the schools too? What does your friend do? What is his name?'

Madame Kukshin shed her questions one after another with affected negligence, not waiting for an answer; spoilt children talk so to their nurses.

'My name's Arkady Nikolaitch Kirsanov, said Arkady, 'and I'm doing nothing.'

Evdoksya giggled. 'How charming! What, don't you smoke? Victor, do you know, I'm very angry with you.'

'What for?'

'They tell me you've begun singing the praises of George Sand again. A retrograde woman, and nothing else! How can people compare her with Emerson! She hasn't an idea on education, nor physiology, nor anything. She'd never, I'm persuaded, heard of embryology, and in these days—what can be done without that?' (Evdoksya even threw up her hands.) 'Ah, what a wonderful article Elisye-vitch has written on that subject! He's a gentleman of genius.' (Evdoksya constantly made use of the word 'gentle-man' instead of the word 'man.') 'Bazarov, sit by me on the sofa. You don't know, perhaps, I'm awfully afraid of you.'

'Why so? Allow me to ask.'

'You're a dangerous gentleman; you're such a critic. Good God! yes! why, how absurd, I'm talking like some country lady. I really am a country lady, though. I manage my property myself; and only fancy, my bailiff Erofay's a won-derful type, quite like Cooper's Pathfinder; something in him so spontaneous! I've come to settle here finally; it's an intolerable town, isn't it? But what's one to do?'

'The town's like every town,' Bazarov remarked coolly.

'All its interests are so petty, that's what's so awful! I used to spend the winters in Moscow . . . but now my law-ful spouse, Monsieur Kukshin's residing there. And besides, Moscow nowadays . . . there, I don't know—it's not the same as it was. I'm thinking of going abroad; last year I was on the point of setting off.'

'To Paris, I suppose?' queried Bazarov.

S—10

'To Paris and to Heidelberg.'

'Why to Heidelberg?'

'How can you ask? Why, Bunsen's there!'

To this Bazarov could find no reply.

Pierre Sapozhnikov . . . do you know him?'

'No, I don't.'

'Not know *Pierre* Sapozhnikov . . . he's always at Lidia Hestatov's.'

'I don't know her either.'

'Well, it was he undertook to escort me. Thank God, I'm independent; I've no children. . . . What was that I said: *thank God!* It's no matter though.'

Evdoksya rolled a cigarette up between her fingers, which were brown with tobacco stains, put it to her tongue, licked it up, and began smoking. The maid came in with a tray.

'Ah, here's lunch! Will you have an appetiser first? Victor, open the bottle; that's in your line.'

'Yes, it's in my line,' muttered Sitnikov, and again he gave vent to the same convulsive laugh.

'Are there any pretty women here?' inquired Bazarov, as he drank off a third glass.

'Yes, there are,' answered Evdoksya; 'but they're all such empty-headed creatures. *Mon amie,* Odintsova, for instance, is nice-looking. It's a pity her reputation's rather doubtful. . . . That wouldn't matter, though, but she's no independence in her views, no width, nothing . . . of all that. The whole system of education wants changing. I've thought a great deal about it, our women are very badly educated.'

'There's no doing anything with them,' put in Sitnikov; 'one ought to despise them, and I do despise them fully and completely!' (The possibility of feeling and expressing contempt was the most agreeable sensation to Sitnikov; he used to attack women in especial, never suspecting that it was to be his fate a few months later to be cringing before his wife merely because she had been born a princess Durdoleosov.) 'Not a single one of them would be capable of understanding our conversation; not a single one deserves to be spoken of by serious men like us!'

'But there's not the least need for them to understand our conversation,' observed Bazarov.

'Whom do you mean?' put in Evdoksya.

'Pretty women.'

'What? Do you adopt Proudhon's ideas, then?'

Bazarov drew himself up haughtily. 'I don't adopt any one's ideas; I have my own.'

'Damn all authorities!' shouted Sitnikov, delighted to have a chance of expressing himself boldly before the man he slavishly admired.

'But even Macaulay,' Madame Kukshin was beginning . . .

'Damn Macaulay,' thundered Sitnikov. 'Are you going to stand up for the silly hussies?'

'For silly hussies, no, but for the rights of women, which I have sworn to defend to the last drop of my blood.'

'Damn!'—but here Sitnikov stopped. 'But I don't deny them,' he said.

'No, I see you're a Slavophil.'

'No, I'm not a Slavophil, though, of course . . .'

'No, no, no! You are a Slavophil. You're an advocate of patriarchal despotism. You want to have the whip in your hand!'

'A whip's an excellent thing,' remarked Bazarov; 'but we've got to the last drop.'

'Of what?' interrupted Evdoksya.

'Of champagne, most honoured Avdotya Nikitishna, of champagne—not of your blood.'

'I can never listen calmly when women are attacked,' pursued Evdoksya. 'It's awful, awful. Instead of attacking them, you'd better read Michelet's book, *De l'amour*. That's exquisite! Gentlemen, let us talk of love,' added Evdoksya, letting her arm fall languidly on the rumpled sofa cushion.

A sudden silence followed. 'No, why should we talk of love,' said Bazarov; 'but you mentioned just now a Madame Odintsov . . . That was what you called her, I think? Who is that lady?'

'She's charming, charming!' piped Sitnikov. 'I will introduce you. Clever, rich, a widow. It's a pity, she's not yet advanced enough; she ought to see more of our Evdoksya. I drink to your health, *Evdoxie!* Let us clink glasses! *Et toc, et toc, et tin-tin-tin! Et toc, et toc, et tin-tin-tin!!!*'

'Victor, you're a wretch.'

The lunch dragged on a long while. The first bottle of champagne was followed by another, a third, and even a fourth. . . . Evdoksya chattered without pause; Sitnikov seconded her. They had much discussion upon the question whether marriage was a prejudice or a crime, and whether men were born equal or not, and precisely what individuality consists in. Things came at last to Evdoksya, flushed from the wine she had drunk, tapping with her flat finger-tips on the keys of a discordant piano, and beginning to sing in a hoarse voice, first gipsy songs, and then Seymour Schiff's song, 'Granada lies slumbering'; while Sitnikov tied a scarf round his head, and represented the dying lover at the words—

> 'And thy lips to mine
> In burning kiss entwine.'

Arkady could not stand it at last. 'Gentlemen, it's getting something like Bedlam,' he remarked aloud. Bazarov, who had at rare intervals put in an ironical word in the conversation—he paid more attention to the champagne—gave a loud yawn, got up, and, without taking leave of their hostess, he walked off with Arkady. Sitnikov jumped up and followed them.

'Well, what do you think of her?' he inquired, skipping obsequiously from right to left of them. 'I told you, you see, a remarkable personality! If we only had more women like that! She is, in her own way, an expression of the highest morality.'

'And is that establishment of your governor's an expression of the highest morality too?' observed Bazarov, pointing to a ginshop which they were passing at that instant.

Sitnikov again went off into a shrill laugh. He was greatly ashamed of his origin, and did not know whether to feel flattered or offended at Bazarov's unexpected familiarity.

CHAPTER XIV

A FEW days later the ball at the Governor's took place. Matvy Ilyitch was the real 'hero of the occasion.' The marshal of nobility declared to all and each that he had come simply out of respect for him; while the Governor, even at the ball, even while he remained perfectly motionless, was still 'making arrangements.' The affability of Matvy Ilyitch's demeanour could only be equalled by its dignity. He was gracious to all, to some with a shade of disgust, to others with a shade of respect; he was all bows and smiles *'en vrai chevalier français'* before the ladies, and was continually giving vent to a hearty, sonorous, unshared laugh, such as befits a high official. He slapped Arkady on the back, and called him loudly 'nephew'; vouchsafed Bazarov—who was attired in a rather old evening coat—a sidelong glance in passing—absent but condescending—and an indistinct but affable grunt, in which nothing could be distinguished but 'I . . .' and 'very much'; gave Sitnikov a finger and a smile, though with his head already averted; even to Madame Kukshin, who made her appearance at the ball with dirty gloves, no crinoline, and a bird of Paradise in her hair, he said *'enchanté.* There were crowds of people, and no lack of dancing men; the civilians were for the most part standing close along the walls, but the officers danced assiduously, especialy one of them who had spent six weeks in Paris, where he had mastered various daring interjections of the kind of—*'zut,' 'Ah, fichtr-re,' 'pst, pst, mon bibi,'* and such. He pronounced them to perfection with genuine Parisian *chic,* and at the same time he said *'si j'aurais'* for *'si j'avais,' 'absolument'* in the sense of 'absolutely,' expressed himself, in fact, in that Great Russo-French jargon which the French ridicule so when they have no reason for assuring us that we speak French like angels, *'comme des anges.'*

Arkady, as we are aware, danced badly, while Bazarov did not dance at all; they both took up their position in a corner; Sitnikov joined himself on to them, with an expression of contemptuous scorn on his face, and giving vent to spiteful comments, he looked insolently about him, and seemed to be really enjoying himself. Suddenly his face changed, and turning to Arkady, he said, with some show of embarrassment it seemed, 'Odintsova is here!'

Arkady looked round, and saw a tall woman in a black dress standing at the door of the room. He was struck by the dignity of her carriage. Her bare arms lay gracefully beside her slender waist; gracefully some light sprays of fuchsia drooped from her shining hair on to her sloping shoulders; her clear eyes looked out from under a rather overhanging white brow, with a tranquil and intelligent expression—tranquil it was precisely, not pensive—and on her lips was a scarcely perceptible smile. There was a kind of gracious and gentle force about her face.

'Do you know her?' Arkady asked Sitnikov.

'Intimately. Would you like me to introduce you?'

'Please . . . after this quadrille.'

Bazarov's attention, too, was directed to Madame Odintsov.

'That's a striking figure,' he remarked. 'Not like the other females.'

After waiting till the end of the quadrille, Sitnikov led Arkady up to Madame Odintsov; but he hardly seemed to be intimately acquainted with her; he was embarrassed in his sentences, while she looked at him in some surprise. But her face assumed an expression of pleasure when she heard Arkady's surname. She asked him whether he was not the son of Nikolai Petrovitch.

'Yes.'

'I have seen your father twice, and have heard a great deal about him,' she went on; 'I am glad to make your acquaintance.'

At that instant some adjutant flew up to her and begged for a quadrille. She consented.

'Do you dance then?' asked Arkady respectfully.

'Yes, I dance. Why do you suppose I don't dance? Do you think I am too old?'

'Really, how could I possibly. . . . But in that case, let me ask you for a mazurka.'

Madame Odintsov smiled graciously. 'Certainly,' she said, and she looked at Arkady not exactly with an air of superiority, but as married sisters look at very young brothers. Madame Odintsov was a little older than Arkady —she was twenty-nine—but in her presence he felt himself a schoolboy, a little student, so that the difference in age between them seemed of more consequence. Matvy Ilyitch approached her with a majestic air and ingratiating speeches. Arkady moved away, but he still watched her; he could not take his eyes off her even during the quadrille. She talked with equal ease to her partner and to the grand official, softly turned her head and eyes, and twice laughed softly. Her nose—like almost all Russian noses—was a little thick; and her complexion was not perfectly clear; Arkady made up his mind, for all that, that he had never before met such an attractive woman. He could not get the sound of her voice out of his ears; the very folds of her dress seemed to hang upon her differently from all the rest—more gracefully and amply—and her movements were distinguished by a peculiar smoothness and naturalness.

Arkady felt some timidity in his heart when at the first sounds of the mazurka he began to sit it out beside his partner; he had prepared to enter into a conversation with her, but he only passed his hand through his hair, and could not find a single word to say. But his timidity and agitation did not last long; Madame Odintsov's tranquillity gained upon him too; before a quarter of an hour had passed he was telling her freely about his father, his uncle, his life in Petersburg and in the country. Madame Odintsov listened to him with courteous sympathy, slightly opening and closing her fan; his talk was broken off when partners came for her; Sitnikov, among others, twice asked her. She came back, sat down again, took up her fan, and her bosom did not even heave more rapidly, while Arkady fell to chattering again, filled through and through by the happiness of being near her, talking to her, looking at her eyes, her lovely brow, all her sweet, dignified, clever face. She said little, but her words showed a knowledge of life; from some of her observations Arkady gathered that this young woman had already felt and thought much. . . .

'Who is that you were standing with?' she asked him,
'when Mr. Sitnikov brought you to me?'

'Did you notice him?' Arkady asked in his turn. 'He has
a splendid face, hasn't he? That's Bazarov, my friend.'

Arkady fell to discussing 'his friend.' He spoke of him
in such detail, and with such enthusiasm, that Madame
Odintsov turned towards him and looked attentively at him.
Meanwhile, the mazurka was drawing to a close. Arkady
felt sorry to part from his partner; he had spent nearly an
hour so happily with her! He had, it is true, during the
whole time continually felt as though she were condescending to him, as though he ought to be grateful to her . . .
but young hearts are not weighed down by that feeling.

The music stopped. '*Merci*,' said Madame Odintsov, getting up. 'You promised to come and see me; bring your
friend with you. I shall be very curious to see the man who
has the courage to believe in nothing.'

The Governor came up to Madame Odintsov, announced
that supper was ready, and, with a careworn face, offered
her his arm. As she went away, she turned to give a last
smile and bow to Arkady. He bowed low, looked after her
(how graceful her figure seemed to him, draped in the greyish lustre of the black silk!), and thinking, 'This minute she
has forgotten my existence,' was conscious of an exquisite
humility in his soul.

'Well?' Bazarov questioned him, directly he had gone back
to him in the corner. 'Did you have a good time? A gentleman has just been talking to me about that lady; he said,
"She's—oh, fie! fie!" but I fancy the fellow was a fool.
What do you think, what is she?—oh, fie! fie!'

'I don't quite understand that definition,' answered Arkady.

'Oh, my! What innocence!'

'In that case, I don't understand the gentleman you quote.
Madame Odintsov is very sweet, no doubt, but she behaves
so coldly and severely, that. . . .'

'Still waters . . . you know!' put in Bazarov. 'That's
just what gives it piquancy. You like ices, I expect?'

'Perhaps,' muttered Arkady. 'I can't give an opinion about
that. She wishes to make your acquaintance, and has asked
me to bring you to see her.'

'I can imagine how you've described me! But you did very well. Take me. Whatever she may be—whether she's simply a provincial lioness, or "advanced" after Kukshina's fashion—any way she's got a pair of shoulders such as I've not set eyes on for a long while.'

Arkady was wounded by Bazarov's cynicism, but—as often happens—he reproached his friend not precisely for what he did not like in him . . .

'Why are you unwilling to allow freethinking in women?' he said in a low voice.

'Because, my boy, as far as my observations go, the only freethinkers among women are frights.'

The conversation was cut short at this point. Both the young men went away immediately after supper. They were pursued by a nervously malicious, but somewhat faint-hearted laugh from Madame Kukshin; her vanity had been deeply wounded by neither of them having paid any attention to her. She stayed later than any one at the ball, and at four o'clock in the morning she was dancing a polka-mazurka with Sitnikov in the Parisian style. This edifying spectacle was the final event of the Governor's ball.

CHAPTER XV

'LET'S see what species of mammalia this specimen belongs to,' Bazarov said to Arkady the following day, as they mounted the staircase of the hotel in which Madame Odintsov was staying. 'I scent out something wrong here.'

'I'm surprised at you!' cried Arkady. 'What? You, you, Bazarov, clinging to the narrow morality, which . . .'

'What a funny fellow you are!' Bazarov cut him short, carelessly. 'Don't you know that "something wrong" means "something right" in my dialect and for me? It's an advantage for me, of course. Didn't you tell me yourself this morning that she made a strange marriage, though, to my mind, to marry a rich old man is by no means a strange thing to do, but, on the contrary, very sensible. I don't believe the gossip of the town; but I should like to think, as our cultivated Governor says, that it's well-grounded.'

Arkady made no answer, and knocked at the door of the apartments. A young servant in livery conducted the two friends in to a large room, badly furnished, like all rooms in Russian hotels, but filled with flowers. Soon Madame Odintsov herself appeared in a simple morning dress. She seemed still younger by the light of the spring sunshine. Arkady presented Bazarov, and noticed with secret amazement that he seemed embarrassed, while Madame Odintsov remained perfectly tranquil, as she had been the previous day. Bazarov himself was conscious of being embarrassed, and was irritated by it. 'Here's a go!—frightened of a petticoat!' he thought, and lolling, quite like Sitnikov, in an easy-chair, he began talking with an exaggerated appearance of ease, while Madame Odintsov kept her clear eyes fixed on him.

Anna Sergyevna Odintsov was the daughter of Sergay Nikolaevitch Loktev, notorious for his personal beauty, his speculations, and his gambling propensities, who after cutting a figure and making a sensation for fifteen years in Petersburg

274

and Moscow, finished by ruining himself completely at cards, and was forced to retire to the country, where, however, he soon after died, leaving a very small property to his two daughters—Anna, a girl of twenty, and Katya, a child of twelve. Their mother, who came of an impoverished line of princes—the H——s— had died at Petersburg when her husband was in his heydey. Anna's position after her father's death was very difficult. The brilliant education she had received in Petersburg had not fitted her for putting up with the cares of domestic life and economy,—for an obscure existence in the country. She knew positively no one in the whole neighbourhood, and there was no one she could consult. Her father had tried to avoid all contact with the neighbours; he despised them in his way, and they despised him in theirs. She did not lose her head, however, and promptly sent for a sister of her mother's, Princess Avdotya Stepanovna H——, a spiteful and arrogant old lady, who, on installing herself in her niece's house, appropriated all the best rooms for her own use, scolded and grumbled from morning till night, and would not go a walk even in the garden unattended by her one serf, a surly footman in a threadbare pea-green livery with light blue trimming and a three-cornered hat. Anna put up patiently with all her aunt's whims, gradually set to work on her sister's education, and was, it seemed, already getting reconciled to the idea of wasting her life in the wilds. . . . But destiny had decreed another fate for her. She chanced to be seen by Odintsov, a very wealthy man of forty-six, an eccentric hypochrondriac, stout, heavy, and sour, but not stupid, and not ill-natured; he fell in love with her, and offered her his hand. She consented to become his wife, and he lived six years with her, and on his death settled all his property upon her. Anna Sergyevna remained in the country for nearly a year after his death; then she went abroad with her sister, but only stopped in Germany; she got tired of it, and came back to live at her favourite Nikolskoe, which was nearly thirty miles from the town of X——. There she had a magnificent, splendidly furnished house and a beautiful garden, with conservatories; her late husband had spared no expense to gratify his fancies. Anna Sergyevna went very rarely to the town, generally only on business, and even then she did not stay long. She was not liked in the province; there had been a fearful outcry at her marriage with Odintsov, all sorts of fictions were told about her; it was asserted that she had helped her father in his cardsharping tricks, and even that she had gone abroad for excellent reasons, that it had been necessary to conceal the lamentable consequences . . . 'You understand?' the indignant gossips would wind up. 'She has gone through the fire,' was said of her; to which a noted provincial wit usually added: 'And through all the other elements?' All this talk reached her; but she turned a deaf ear to it; there was much independence and a good deal of determination in her character.

Madame Odintsov sat leaning back in her easy-chair, and listened with folded hands to Bazarov. He, contrary to his habit, was talking a good deal, and obviously trying to interest her—again a surprise for Arkady. He could not make up his mind whether Bazarov was attaining his object. It was difficult to conjecture from Anna Sergyevna's face what impression was being made on her; it retained the same expression, gracious and refined; her beautiful eyes were lighted up by attention, but by quiet attention. Bazarov's bad manners had impressed her unpleasantly for the first minutes of the visit like a bad smell or a discordant sound; but she saw at once that he was nervous, and that even flattered her. Nothing was repulsive to her but vulgarity, and no one could have accused Bazarov of vulgarity. Arkady was fated to meet with surprises that day. He had expected that Bazarov would talk to a clever woman like Madame Odintsov about his opinions and his views; she had herself expressed a desire to listen to the man 'who dares to have no belief in anything'; but, instead of that, Bazarov talked about medicine, about homœpathy, and about botany. It turned out that Madame Odintsov had not wasted her time in solitude; she had read a good many excellent books, and spoke herself in excellent Russian. She turned the conversation upon music; but noticing that Bazarov did not appreciate art, she quietly brought it back to botany, even though Arkady was just launching into a discourse upon the significance of national melodies. Madame Odintsov treated him as though he were a younger brother; she seemed to appreciate his good-nature and youthful simplicity—and that was all. For over three hours, a lively conversation was kept up, ranging freely over various subjects.

The friends at last got up and began to take leave. Anna Sergyevna looked cordially at them, held out her beautiful, white hand to both, and, after a moment's thought, said with a doubtful but delightful smile, 'If you are not afraid of being dull, gentlemen, come and see me at Nikolskoe.'

'Oh, Anna Sergyevna,' cried Arkady, 'I shall think it the greatest happiness . . .'

'And you, Monsieur Bazarov?'

Bazarov only bowed, and a last surprise was in store for Arkady; he noticed that his friend was blushing.

'Well?' he said to him in the street; 'are you still of the same opinion—that she's . . .'

'Who can tell? See how correct she is!' retorted Bazarov; and after a brief pause he added, 'She's a perfect grand-duchess, a royal personage. She only needs a train on behind, and a crown on her head.'

'Our grand-duchesses don't talk Russian like that,' remarked Arkady.

'She's seen ups and downs, my dear boy; she's known what it is to be hard up!'

'Any way, she's charming,' observed Arkady.

'What a magnificent body!' pursued Bazarov. 'Shouldn't I like to see it on the dissecting-table.'

'Hush, for mercy's sake, Yevgeny! that's beyond everything.'

'Well, don't get angry, you baby. I meant it's first-rate. We must go to stay with her.'

'When?'

'Well, why not the day after to-morrow. What is there to do here? Drink champagne with Kukshina. Listen to your cousin, the Liberal dignitary? . . . Let's be off the day after to-morrow. By the way, too—my father's little place is not far from there. This Nikolskoe's on the S—— road, isn't it?'

'Yes.'

'Optime, why hesitate? leave that to fools and prigs! I say, what a splendid body!'

Three days later the two friends were driving along the road to Nikolskoe. The day was bright, and not too hot, and the sleek posting-horses trotted smartly along, switching their tied and plaited tails. Arkady looked at the road, and not knowing why, he smiled.

'Congratulate me,' cried Bazarov suddenly, 'to-day's the 22nd of June, my guardian angel's day. Let's see how he will watch over me. To-day they expect me home,' he added, dropping his voice. . . . 'Well, they can go on expecting. . . . What does it matter!'

CHAPTER XVI

THE country-house in which Anna Sergyevna lived stood on an exposed hill at no great distance from a yellow stone church with a green roof, white columns, and a fresco over the principal entrance representing the 'Resurrection of Christ' in the 'Italian' style. Sprawling in the foreground of the picture was a swarthy warrior in a helmet, specially conspicuous for his rotund contours. Behind the church a long village stretched in two rows, with chimneys peeping out here and there above the thatched roofs. The manor-house was built in the same style as the church, the style known among us as that of Alexander; the house too was painted yellow, and had a green roof, and white columns, and a pediment with an escutcheon on it. The architect had designed both buildings with the approval of the deceased Odintsov, who could not endure—as he expressed it—idle and arbitrary innovations. The house was enclosed on both sides by the dark trees of an old garden; an avenue of lopped pines led up to the entrance.

Our friends were met in the hall by two tall footmen in livery; one of them at once ran for the steward. The steward, a stout man in a black dress coat, promptly appeared and led the visitors by a staircase covered with rugs to a special room, in which two bedsteads were already prepared for them with all necessaries for the toilet. It was clear that order reigned supreme in the house; everything was clean, everywhere there was a peculiar delicate fragrance, just as there is in the reception rooms of ministers.

'Anna Sergyevna asks you to come to her in half-an-hour,' the steward announced; 'will there be orders to give meanwhile?'

'No orders,' answered Bazarov; 'perhaps you will be so good as to trouble yourself to bring me a glass of vodka.'

'Yes, sir,' said the steward, looking in some perplexity, and he withdrew, his boots creaking as he walked.

'What *grand genre!*' remarked Bazarov. 'That's what it's called in your set, isn't it? She's a grand-duchess, and that's all about it.'

'A nice grand-duchess,' retorted Arkady, 'at the very first meeting she invited such great aristocrats as you and me to stay with her.'

'Especially me, a future doctor, and a doctor's son, and a village sexton's grandson. . . . You know, I suppose, I'm the grandson of a sexton? Like the great Speransky,' added Bazarov after a brief pause, contracting his lips. 'At any rate she likes to be comfortable; oh, doesn't she, this lady! Oughtn't we to put on evening dress?'

Arkady only shrugged his shoulders . . . but he too was conscious of a little nervousness.

Half-an-hour later Bazarov and Arkady went together into the drawing-room. It was a large lofty room, furnished rather luxuriously but without particularly good taste. Heavy expensive furniture stood in the ordinary stiff arrangement along the walls, which were covered with cinnamon-coloured paper with gold flowers on it; Odintsov had ordered the furniture from Moscow through a friend and agent of his, a spirit merchant. Over a sofa in the centre of one wall hung a portrait of a faded light-haired man—and it seemed to look with displeasure at the visitors. 'It must be the late lamented,' Bazarov whispered to Arkady, and turning up his nose, he added, 'Hadn't we better bolt . . . ?' But at that instant the lady of the house entered. She wore a light barège dress; her hair smoothly combed back behind her ears gave a girlish expression to her pure and fresh face.

'Thank you for keeping your promise,' she began. 'You must stay a little while with me; it's really not bad here. I will introduce you to my sister; she plays the piano well. That is a matter of indifference to you, Monsieur Bazarov; but you, I think, Monsieur Kirsanov, are fond of music. Besides my sister I have an old aunt living with me, and one of our neighbours comes in sometimes to play cards; that makes up all our circle. And now let us sit down.'

Madame Odintsov delivered all this little speech with peculiar precision, as though she had learned it by heart;

then she turned to Arkady. It appeared that her mother had known Arkady's mother, and had even been her confidante in her love for Nikolai Petrovitch. Arkady began talking with great warmth of his dead mother; while Bazarov fell to turning over albums. 'What a tame cat I'm getting!' he was thinking to himself.

A beautiful greyhound with a blue collar on, ran into the drawing-room, tapping on the floor with his paws, and after him entered a girl of eighteen, black-haired and dark-skinned, with a rather round but pleasing face, and small dark eyes. In her hands she held a basket filled with flowers.

'This is my Katya,' said Madame Odintsov, indicating her with a motion of her head. Katya made a slight curtsey, placed herself beside her sister, and began picking out flowers. The greyhound, whose name was Fifi, went up to both of the visitors, in turn wagging his tail, and thrusting his cold nose into their hands.

'Did you pick all that yourself?' asked Madame Odintsov.

'Yes,' answered Katya.

'Is auntie coming to tea?'

'Yes.'

When Katya spoke, she had a very charming smile, sweet, timid, and candid, and looked up from under her eyebrows with a sort of humorous severity. Everything about her was still young and undeveloped; the voice, and the bloom on her whole face, and the rosy hands, with white palms, and the rather narrow shoulders. . . . She was constantly blushing and getting out of breath.

Madame Odintsov turned to Bazarov. 'You are looking at pictures from politeness, Yevgeny Vassilyitch,' she began. 'That does not interest you. You had better come nearer to us, and let us have a discussion about something.'

Bazarov went closer. 'What subject have you decided upon for discussion?' he said.

'What you like. I warn you, I am dreadfully argumentative.'

'You?'

'Yes. That seems to surprise you. Why?'

'Because, as far as I can judge, you have a calm, cool character, and one must be impulsive to be argumentative.'

'How can you have had time to understand me so soon? In the first place, I am impatient and obstinate—you should ask Katya; and secondly, I am very easily carried away.'

Bazarov looked at Anna Sergyevna. 'Perhaps; you must know best. And so you are inclined for a discussion—by all means. I was looking through the views of the Saxon mountains in your album, and you remarked that that couldn't interest me. You said so, because you suppose me to have no feeling for art, and as a fact I haven't any; but these views might be interesting to me from a geological standpoint, for the formation of the mountains, for instance.'

'Excuse me; but as a geologist, you would sooner have recourse to a book, to a special work on the subject, and not to a drawing.'

'The drawing shows me at a glance what would be spread over ten pages in a book.'

Anna Sergyevna was silent for a little.

'And so you haven't the least artistic feeling?' she observed, putting her elbow on the table, and by that very action bringing her face nearer to Bazarov. 'How can you get on without it?'

'Why, what is it wanted for, may I ask?'

'Well, at least to enable one to study and understand men.'

Bazarov smiled. 'In the first place, experience of life does that; and in the second, I assure you, studying separate individuals is not worth the trouble. All people are like one another, in soul as in body; each of us has brain, spleen, heart, and lungs made alike; and the so-called moral qualities are the same in all; the slight variations are of no importance. A single human specimen is sufficient to judge of all by. People are like trees in a forest; no botanist would think of studying each individual birch-tree.'

Katya, who was arranging the flowers, one at a time in a leisurely fashion, lifted her eyes to Bazarov with a puzzled look, and meeting his rapid and careless glance, she crimsoned up to her ears. Anna Sergyevna shook her head.

'The trees in a forest,' she repeated. 'Then according to you there is no difference between the stupid and the clever person, between the good-natured and ill-natured?'

'No, there is a difference, just as between the sick and the healthy. The lungs of a consumptive patient are not in the same condition as yours and mine, though they are made on the same plan. We know approximately what physical diseases come from; moral diseases come from bad education, from all the nonsense people's heads are stuffed with from childhood up, from the defective state of society; in short, reform society, and there will be no diseases.'

Bazarov said all this with an air, as though he were all the while thinking to himself, 'Believe me or not, as you like, it's all one to me!' He slowly passed his fingers over his whiskers, while his eyes strayed about the room.

'And you conclude,' observed Anna Sergyevna, 'that when society is reformed, there will be no stupid nor wicked people?'

'At any rate, in a proper organisation of society, it will be absolutely the same whether a man is stupid or clever, wicked or good.'

'Yes, I understand; they will all have the same spleen.'

'Precisely so, madam.'

Madame Odintsov turned to Arkady. 'And what is your opinion, Arkady Nikolaevitch?'

'I agree with Yevgeny,' he answered.

Katya looked up at him from under her eyelids.

'You amaze me, gentlemen,' commented Madame Odintsov, 'but we will have more talk together. But now I hear my aunt coming to tea; we must spare her.'

Anna Sergyevna's aunt, Princess H——, a thin little woman with a pinched-up face, drawn together like a fist, and staring ill-natured-looking eyes under a grey front, came in, and, scarcely bowing to the guests, she dropped into a wide velvet covered arm-chair, upon which no one but herself was privileged to sit. Katya put a footstool under her feet; the old lady did not thank her, did not even look at her, only her hands shook under the yellow shawl, which almost covered her feeble body. The Princess liked yellow; her cap, too, had bright yellow ribbons.

'How have you slept, aunt?' inquired Madame Odintsov, raising her voice.

'That dog in here again,' the old lady muttered in reply, and noticing Fifi was making two hesitating steps in her direction, she cried, 'Ss——ss!'

Katya called Fifi and opened the door for him.

Fifi rushed out delighted, in the expectation of being taken out for a walk; but when he was left alone outside the door, he began scratching and whining. The princess scowled. Katya was about to go out. . . .

'I expect tea is ready,' said Madame Odintsov.

'Come gentlemen; aunt, will you go in to tea?'

The princess got up from her chair without speaking and led the way out of the drawing-room. They all followed her in to the dining-room. A little page in livery drew back, with a scraping sound, from the table, an arm-chair covered with cushions, devoted to the princess's use; she sank into it; Katya in pouring out the tea handed her first a cup emblazoned with a heraldic crest. The old lady put some honey in her cup (she considered it both sinful and extravagant to drink tea with sugar in it, though she never spent a farthing herself on anything), and suddenly asked in a hoarse voice, 'And what does Prince Ivan write?'

No one made her any reply. Bazarov and Arkady soon guessed that they paid no attention to her though they treated her respectfully.

'Because of her grand family,' thought Bazarov. . . .

After tea, Anna Sergyevna suggested they should go out for a walk; but it began to rain a little, and the whole party, with the exception of the princess, returned to the drawing-room. The neighbour, the devoted card-player, arrived; his name was Porfiry Platonitch, a stoutish, greyish man with short, spindly legs, very polite and ready to be amused. Anna Sergyevna, who still talked principally with Bazarov, asked him whether he'd like to try a contest with them in the old-fashioned way at preference? Bazarov assented, saying 'that he ought to prepare himself beforehand for the duties awaiting him as a country doctor.'

'You must be careful,' observed Anna Sergyevna; 'Porfiry Platonitch and I will beat you. And you, Katya,' she added, 'play something to Arkady Nikolaevitch; he is fond of music, and we can listen, too.'

Katya went unwillingly to the piano; and Arkady, though he certainly was fond of music, unwillingly followed her; it seemed to him that Madame Odintsov was sending him away, and already, like every young man at his age, he felt a vague and oppressive emotion surging up in his heart, like the forebodings of love. Katya raised the top of the piano, and not looking at Arkady, she said in a low voice—

'What am I to play you?'

'What you like,' answered Arkady indifferently.

'What sort of music do you like best?' repeated Katya, without changing her attitude.

'Classical,' Arkady answered in the same tone of voice.

'Do you like Mozart?'

'Yes, I like Mozart.'

Katya pulled out Mozart's Sonata-Fantasia in C minor. She played very well, though rather over correctly and precisely. She sat upright and immovable, her eyes fixed on the notes, and her lips tightly compressed, only at the end of the sonata her face glowed, her hair came loose, and a little lock fell on to her dark brow.

Arkady was particularly struck by the last part of the sonata, the part in which, in the midst of the bewitching gaiety of the careless melody, the pangs of such mournful, almost tragic suffering, suddenly break in. . . . But the ideas stirred in him by Mozart's music had no reference to Katya. Looking at her, he simply thought, 'Well, that young lady doesn't play badly, and she's not bad-looking either.'

When she had finished the sonata, Katya without taking her hands from the keys, asked, 'Is that enough?' Arkady declared that he could not venture to trouble her again, and began talking to her about Mozart; he asked her whether she had chosen that sonata herself, or some one had recommended it to her. But Katya answered him in monosyllables; she withdrew into herself, went back into her shell. When this happened to her, she did not very quickly come out again; her face even assumed at such times an obstinate, almost stupid expression. She was not exactly shy, but diffident, and rather overawed by her sister, who had educated her, and who had no suspicion of the fact. Arkady was reduced at last to calling Fifi to him, and with an affable smile patting him on the head to give himself an appearance of being at home.

Katya set to work again upon her flowers.

Bazarov meanwhile was losing and losing. Anna Sergyevna played cards in masterly fashion; Porfiry Platonitch, too, could hold his own in the game. Bazarov lost a sum which, though trifling in itself, was not altogether pleasant for him. At supper Anna Sergyevna again turned the conversation on botany.

'We will go for a walk to-morrow morning,' she said to him; 'I want you to teach me the Latin names of the wild flowers and their species.'

'What use are the Latin names to you?' asked Bazarov.

'Order is needed in everything,' she answered.

'What an exquisite woman Anna Sergyevna is!' cried Arkady, when he was alone with his friend in the room assigned to them.

'Yes,' answered Bazarov, 'a female with brains. Yes, and she's seen life too.'

'In what sense do you mean that, Yevgeny Vassilyitch?'

'In a good sense, a good sense, my dear friend, Arkady Nikolaevitch! I'm convinced she manages her estate capitally too. But what's splendid is not her, but her sister.'

'What, that little dark thing?'

'Yes, that little dark thing. She now is fresh and untouched, and shy and silent, and anything you like. She's worth educating and developing. You might make something fine out of her; but the other's—a stale loaf.'

Arkady made no reply to Bazarov, and each of them got into bed with rather singular thoughts in his head.

Anna Sergyevna, too, thought of her guests that evening. She liked Bazarov for the absence of gallantry in him, and even for his sharply defined views. She found in him something new, which she had not chanced to meet before, and she was curious.

Anna Sergyevna was a rather strange creature. Having no prejudices of any kind, having no strong convictions even, she never gave way or went out of her way for anything. She had seen many things very clearly; she had been interested in many things, but nothing had completely satisfied her; indeed, she hardly desired complete satisfaction. Her intellect was at the same time inquiring and indifferent; her doubts were never soothed to forgetfulness, and they never grew strong enough to distract her. Had she not been rich and independent, she would perhaps have thrown herself into the struggle, and have known passion. But life was easy for her, though she was bored at times, and she went on passing day after day with deliberation, never in a hurry, placid, and only rarely disturbed. Dreams sometimes danced in rainbow colours before her eyes even, but she breathed more freely when they died away, and did not regret them. Her imagination indeed overstepped the limits of what is reckoned permissible by conventional morality; but even then her blood flowed as quietly as ever in her fascinatingly graceful, tranquil body. Sometimes coming out of her fragrant bath all warm and enervated, she would fall to musing on the nothingness of life, the sorrow, the labour, the malice of it. . . . Her soul would be filled with sudden daring, and would flow with generous ardour, but a draught would blow from a half-closed window, and Anna Sergyevna would shrink into herself, and feel plaintive and almost angry, and there was only one thing she cared for at that instant—to get away from that horrid draught.

Like all women who have not succeeded in loving, she wanted something, without herself knowing what. Strictly speaking, she wanted nothing; but it seemed to her that she wanted everything. She could hardly endure the late Odintsov (she had married him from prudential motives, though probably she would not have consented to become his wife if she had not considered him a good sort of man), and had conceived a secret repugnance for all men, whom she could only figure to herself as slovenly, heavy, drowsy, and feebly importunate creatures. Once, somewhere abroad, she had met a handsome young Swede, with a chivalrous expression, with honest blue eyes under an open brow; he had made a powerful impression on her, but it had not prevented her from going back to Russia.

'A strange man this doctor!' she thought as she lay in her luxurious bed on lace pillows under a light silk coverlet. . . . Anna Sergyevna had inherited from her father a little of his inclination for splendour. She had fondly loved her sinful but good-natured father, and he had idolised her, used to joke with her in a friendly way as though she were an equal, and to confide in her fully, to ask her advice. Her mother she scarcely remembered.

'This doctor is a strange man!' she repeated to herself. She stretched, smiled, clasped her hands behind her head, then ran her eyes over two pages of a stupid French novel, dropped the book—and fell asleep, all pure and cold, in her pure and fragrant linen.

The following morning Anna Sergyevna went off botanising with Bazarov directly after lunch, and returned just before dinner; Arkady did not go off anywhere, and spent about an hour with Katya. He was not bored with her; she offered of herself to repeat the sonata of the day before; but when Madame Odintsov came back at last, when he caught sight of her, he felt an instantaneous pang at his heart. She came through the garden with a rather tired step; her cheeks were glowing and her eyes shining more brightly than usual under her round straw hat. She was twirling in her fingers the thin stalk of a wildflower, a light mantle had slipped down to her elbows, and the wide gray ribbons of her hat were clinging to her bosom. Bazarov walked behind her, self-confident and careless as usual, but the expression of his face, cheerful and even friendly as it was, did not please Arkady. Muttering between his teeth, 'Good-morning!' Bazarov went away to his room, while Madame Odintsov shook Arkady's hand abstractedly, and also walked past him.

'Good-morning!' thought Arkady . . . 'As though we had not seen each other already to-day!'

CHAPTER XVII

TIME, it is well known, sometimes flies like a bird, sometimes crawls like a worm; but man is wont to be particularly happy when he does not even notice whether it passes quickly or slowly. It was in that way Arkady and Bazarov spent a fortnight at Madame Odintsov's. The good order she had established in her house and in her life partly contributed to this result. She adhered strictly to this order herself, and forced others to submit to it. Everything during the day was done at a fixed time. In the morning, precisely at eight o'clock, all the party assembled for tea; from morning-tea till lunch-time every one did what he pleased, the hostess herself was engaged with her bailiff (the estate was on the rent-system), her steward, and her head housekeeper. Before dinner the party met again for conversation or reading; the evening was devoted to walking, cards, and music; at half-past ten Anna Sergyevna retired to her own room, gave her orders for the following day, and went to bed. Bazarov did not like this measured, somewhat ostentatious punctuality in daily life, 'like moving along rails,' he pronounced it to be; the footmen in livery, the decorous stewards, offended his democratic sentiments. He declared that if one went so far, one might as well dine in the English style at once—in tail-coats and white ties. He once spoke plainly upon the subject to Anna Sergyevna. Her attitude was such that no one hesitated to speak his mind freely before her. She heard him out; and then her comment was, 'From your point of view, you are right—and perhaps, in that respect, I am too much of a lady; but there's no living in the country without order, one would be devoured by ennui,' and she continued to go her own way. Bazarov grumbled, but the very reason life was so easy for him and Arkady at Madame Odintsov's was that everything in the house 'moved on rails.' For all that, a change had taken place in both the young men since the first days of their stay at

Nikolskoe. Bazarov, in whom Anna Sergyevna was obviously interested, though she seldom agreed with him, began to show signs of an unrest, unprecedented in him; he was easily put out of temper, and unwilling to talk, he looked irritated, and could not sit still in one place, just as though he were possessed by some secret longing; while Arkady, who had made up his mind conclusively that he was in love with Madame Odintsov, had begun to yield to a gentle melancholy. This melancholy did not, however, prevent him from becoming friendly with Katya; it even impelled him to get into friendly, affectionate terms with her. 'She does not appreciate me? So be it! . . . But here is a good creature, who does not repulse me,' he thought, and his heart again knew the sweetness of magnanimous emotions. Katya vaguely realised that he was seeking a sort of consolation in her company, and did not deny him or herself the innocent pleasure of a half-shy, half-confidential friendship. They did not talk to each other in Anna Sergyevna's presence; Katya always shrank into herself under her sister's sharp eyes; while Arkady, as befits a man in love, could pay attention to nothing else when near the object of his passion; but he was happy with Katya alone. He was conscious that he did not possess the power to interest Madame Odintsov; he was shy and at a loss when he was left alone with her, and she did not know what to say to him, he was too young for her. With Katya, on the other hand, Arkady felt at home; he treated her condescendingly, encouraged her to express the impressions made on her by music, reading novels, verses, and other such trifles, without noticing or realising that these trifles were what interested him too. Katya, on her side, did not try to drive away melancholy. Arkady was at his ease with Katya, Madame Odintsov with Bazarov, and thus it usually came to pass that the two couples, after being a little while together, went off on their separate ways, especially during the walks. Katya adored nature, and Arkady loved it, though he did not dare to acknowledge it; Madame Odintsov was, like Bazarov, rather indifferent to the beauties of nature. The almost continual separation of the two friends was not without its consequences; the relations between them began to change. Bazarov gave up talking to Arkady about Madame Odintsov, gave up even abusing her 'aristocratic ways'; Katya, it is true, he praised as before, and only advised him to restrain her sentimental tendencies, but his praises were hurried, his advice dry, and in general he talked less to Arkady than before . . . he seemed to avoid him, seemed ill at ease with him.

Arkady observed it all, but he kept his observations to himself.

The real cause of all this 'newness' was the feeling inspired in Bazarov by Madame Odintsov, a feeling which tortured and maddened him, and which he would at once have denied, with scornful laughter and cynical abuse, if any one had ever so remotely hinted at the possibility of what was taking place in him. Bazarov had a great love for women and for feminine beauty; but love in the ideal, or, as he expressed it, romantic sense, he called lunacy, unpardonable imbecility; he regarded chivalrous sentiments as something of the nature of deformity or disease, and had more than once expressed his wonder that Toggenburg and all the minnesingers and troubadours had not been put into a lunatic asylum. 'If a woman takes your fancy,' he used to say, 'try and gain your end; but if you can't—well, turn your back on her—there are lots of good fish in the sea.' Madame Odintsov had taken his fancy; the rumours about her, the freedom and independence of her ideas, her unmistakable liking for him, all seemed to be in his favour, but he soon saw that with her he would not 'gain his ends,' and to turn his back on her he found, to his own bewilderment, beyond his power. His blood was on fire directly if he merely thought of her; he could easily have mastered his blood, but something else was taking root in him, something he had never admitted, at which he had always jeered, at which all his pride revolted. In his conversations with Anna Sergyevna he expressed more strongly than ever his calm contempt for everything idealistic; but when he was alone, with indignation he recognised idealism in himself. Then he would set off to the forest and walk with long strides about it, smashing the twigs that came in his way, and cursing under his breath both her and himself; or he would get into the hay-loft in the barn, and, obstinately closing his eyes, try to force himself to sleep, in which, of course, he did not always succeed. Suddenly his fancy would bring before him those chaste hands twining one day about his neck, those proud lips responding to his kisses, those intellectual eyes dwelling with tenderness—yes, with tenderness—on his, and his head went round, and he forgot himself for an instant, till indignation boiled up in him again. He caught himself in all sorts of 'shameful' thoughts, as though he were driven on by a devil mocking him. Sometimes he fancied that there was a change taking place in Madame Odintsov too; that there were signs in the expression of her face of something special; that, perhaps . . . but at that point he would stamp, or grind his teeth, and clench his fists.

Meanwhile Bazarov was not altogether mistaken. He had struck Madame Odintsov's imagination; he interested her, she thought a great deal about him. In his absence, she was not dull, she was not impatient for his coming, but she always grew more lively on his appearance; she liked to be left alone with him, and she liked talking to him, even when he irritated her or offended her taste, her refined habits. She was, as it were, eager at once to sound him and to analyse herself.

One day walking in the garden with her, he suddenly announced, in a surly voice, that he intended going to his father's place very soon. . . . She turned white, as though something had given her a pang, and such a pang, that she wondered and pondered long after, what could be the meaning of it. Bazarov had spoken of his departure with no idea of putting her to the test, of seeing what would come of it; he never 'fabricated.' On the morning of that day he had an interview with his father's bailiff, who had taken care of him when he was a child, Timofeitch. This Timofeitch, a little old man of much experience and astuteness, with faded yellow hair, a weather-beaten red face, and tiny tear-drops in his shrunken eyes, unexpectedly appeared before Bazarov, in his shortish overcoat of stout greyish-blue cloth, girt with a strip of leather, and in tarred boots.

'Hullo, old man; how are you?' cried Bazarov.

'How do you do, Yevgeny Vassilyitch?' began the little old man, and he smiled with delight, so that his whole face was all at once covered with wrinkles.

'What have you come for? They sent for me, eh?'

'Upon my word, sir, how could we?' mumbled Timofeitch. (He remembered the strict injunctions he had received from his master on starting.) 'We were sent to the town on business, and we'd heard news of your honour, so here we turned off on our way, that's to say—to have a look at your honour . . . as if we could think of disturbing you!'

'Come, don't tell lies!' Bazarov cut him short. 'Is this the road to the town, do you mean to tell me?' Timofeitch hesitated, and made no answer. 'Is my father well?'

'Thank God, yes.'

'And my mother?'

'Anna Vlasyevna too, glory be to God.'

'They are expecting me, I suppose?'

The little old man held his tiny head on one side.

'Ah, Yevgeny Vassilyitch, it makes one's heart ache to see them; it does really.'

'Come, all right, all right! shut up! Tell them I'm coming soon.'

'Yes, sir,' answered Timofeitch, with a sigh.

As he went out of the house, he pulled his cap down on his head with both hands, clambered into a wretched-looking racing droshky, and went off at a trot, but not in the direction of the town.

On the evening of the same day, Madame Odintsov was sitting in her own room with Bazarov, while Arkady walked up and down the hall listening to Katya's playing. The princess had gone upstairs to her own room; she could not bear guests as a rule, and 'especially this new riff-raff lot,' as she called them. In the common rooms she only sulked; but she made up for it in her own room by breaking out into such abuse before her maid that the cap danced on her head, wig and all. Madame Odintsov was well aware of all this.

'How is it you are proposing to leave us?' she began; 'how about your promise?'

Bazarov started. 'What promise?'

'Have you forgotten? You meant to give me some lessons in chemistry.'

'It can't be helped! My father expects me; I can't loiter any longer. However, you can read Pelouse et Frémy, *No-*

tions générales de Chimie; it's a good book, and clearly written. You will find everything you need in it.'

'But do you remember; you assured me a book cannot take the place of . . . I've forgotten how you put it, but you know what I mean . . . do you remember?'

'It can't be helped!' repeated Bazarov.

'Why go away?' said Madame Odintsov, dropping her voice.

He glanced at her. Her head had fallen on to the back of her easy-chair, and her arms, bare to the elbow, were folded on her bosom. She seemed paler in the light of the single lamp covered with a perforated paper shade. An ample white gown hid her completely in its soft folds; even the tips of her feet, also crossed, were hardly seen.

'And why stay?' answered Bazarov.

Madame Odintsov turned her head slightly. 'You ask why. Have you not enjoyed yourself with me? Or do you suppose you will not be missed here?'

'I am sure of it.'

Madame Odintsov was silent a minute. 'You are wrong in thinking that. But I don't believe you. You could not say that seriously.' Bazarov still sat immovable. 'Yevgeny Vassilyitch, why don't you speak?'

'Why, what am I to say to you? People are not generally worth being missed, and I less than most.'

'Why so?'

'I'm a practical, uninteresting person. I don't know how to talk.'

'You are fishing, Yevgeny Vassilyitch.'

'That's not a habit of mine. Don't you know yourself that I've nothing in common with the elegant side of life, the side you prize so much?'

Madame Odintsov bit the corner of her handkerchief.

'You may think what you like, but I shall be dull when you go away.'

'Arkady will remain,' remarked Bazarov. Madame Odintsov shrugged her shoulders slightly. 'I shall be dull,' she repeated.

'Really? In any case you will not feel dull for long.'

'What makes you suppose that?'

'Because you told me yourself that you are only dull when your regular routine is broken in upon. You have ordered your existence with such unimpeachable regularity that there can be no place in it for dulness or sadness . . . for any unpleasant emotions.'

'And do you consider I am so unimpeachable . . . that's to say, that I have ordered my life with such regularity?'

'I should think so. Here's an example; in a few minutes it will strike ten, and I know beforehand that you will drive me away.'

'No; I'm not going to drive you away, Yevgeny Vassilyitch. You may stay. Open that window. . . . I feel half-stifled.'

Bazarov got up and gave a push to the window. It flew up with a loud crash. . . . He had not expected it to open so easily; besides, his hands were shaking. The soft, dark night looked in to the room with its almost black sky, its faintly rustling trees, and the fresh fragrance of the pure open air.

'Draw the blind and sit down,' said Madame Odintsov; 'I want to have a talk with you before you go away. Tell me something about yourself; you never talk about yourself.'

'I try to talk to you upon improving subjects, Anna Sergyevna.'

'You are very modest. . . . But I should like to know something about you, about your family, about your father, for whom you are forsaking us.'

'Why is she talking like that?' thought Bazarov.

'All that's not in the least interesting,' he uttered aloud, 'especially for you; we are obscure people. . . .'

'And you regard me as an aristocrat?'

Bazarov lifted his eyes to Madame Odintsov.

'Yes,' he said, with exaggerated sharpness.

She smiled. 'I see you know me very little, though you do maintain that all people are alike, and it's not worth while to study them. I will tell you my life some time or other . . . but first you tell me yours.'

'I know you very little,' repeated Bazarov. 'Perhaps you are right; perhaps, really, every one is a riddle. You, for instance; you avoid society, you are oppressed by it, and you have invited two students to stay with you. What makes you, with your intellect, with your beauty, live in the country?'

'What? What was it you said?' Madame Odintsov interposed eagerly. 'With my . . . beauty?'

Bazarov scowled. 'Never mind that,' he muttered; 'I meant to say that I don't exactly understand why you have settled in the country?'

'You don't understand it. . . . But you explain it to yourself in some way?'

'Yes . . . I assume that you remain continually in the same place because you indulge yourself, because you are very fond of comfort and ease, and very indifferent to everything else.'

Madame Odintsov smiled again. 'You would absolutely refuse to believe that I am capable of being carried away by anything?'

Bazarov glanced at her from under his brows.

'By curiosity, perhaps; but not otherwise.'

'Really? Well, now I understand why we are such friends; you are just like me, you see.'

'We are such friends . . .' Bazarov articulated in a choked voice.

'Yes! . . . Why, I'd forgotten you wanted to go away.'

Bazarov got up. The lamp burnt dimly in the middle of the dark, luxurious, isolated room; from time to time the blind was shaken, and there flowed in the freshness of the insidious night; there was heard its mysterious whisperings. Madame Odintsov did not move in a single limb; but she was gradually possessed by concealed emotion.

It communicated itself to Bazarov. He was suddenly conscious that he was alone with a young and lovely woman. . . .

'Where are you going?' she said slowly.

He answered nothing, and sank into a chair.

'And so you consider me a placid, pampered, spoiled creature,' she went on in the same voice, never taking her eyes off the window. 'While I know so much about myself, that I am unhappy.'

'You unhappy? What for? Surely you can't attach any importance to idle gossip?'

Madame Odintsov frowned. It annoyed her that he had given such a meaning to her words.

'Such gossip does not affect me, Yevgeny Vassilyitch, and I am too proud to allow it to disturb me. I am unhappy because . . . I have no desires, no passion for life. You look at me incredulously; you think that's said by an "aristocrat," who is all in lace, and sitting in a velvet armchair. I don't conceal the fact: I love what you call comfort, and at the same time I have little desire to live. Explain that contradiction as best you can. But all that's romanticism in your eyes.'

Bazarov shook his head. 'You are in good health, independent, rich; what more would you have? What do you want?'

'What do I want,' echoed Madame Odintsov, and she sighed, 'I am very tired, I am old, I feel as if I have had a very long life. Yes, I am old,' she added, softly drawing the ends of her lace over her bare arms. Her eyes met Bazarov's eyes, and she faintly blushed. 'Behind me I have already so many memories: my life in Petersburg, wealth, then poverty, then my father's death, marriage, then the inevitable tour in due order. . . . So many memories, and nothing to remember, and before me, before me—a long, long road, and no goal. . . . I have no wish to go on.'

'Are you so disillusioned?' queried Bazarov.

'No, but I am dissatisfied,' Madame Odintsov replied, dwelling on each syllable. 'I think if I could interest myself strongly in something. . . .'

'You want to fall in love,' Bazarov interrupted her, 'and you can't love; that's where your unhappiness lies.'

Madame Odintsov began to examine the sleeve of her lace.

'Is it true I can't love?' she said.

'I should say not! Only I was wrong in calling that an unhappiness. On the contrary, any one's more to be pitied when such a mischance befalls him.'

'Mischance, what?'

'Falling in love.'

'And how do you come to know that?'

'By hearsay,' answered Bazarov angrily.

S—11

'You're flirting,' he thought; 'you're bored, and teasing me for want of something to do, while I . . .' His heart really seemed as though it were being torn to pieces.

'Besides, you are perhaps too exacting,' he said, bending his whole frame forward and playing with the fringe of the chair.

'Perhaps. My idea is everything or nothing. A life for a life. Take mine, give up thine, and that without regret or turning back. Or else better have nothing.'

'Well?' observed Bazarov; 'that's fair terms, and I'm surprised that so far you . . . have not found what you wanted.'

'And do you think it would be easy to give oneself up wholly to anything whatever?'

'Not easy, if you begin reflecting, waiting and attaching value to yourself, prizing yourself, I mean; but to give oneself up without reflection is very easy.'

'How can one help prizing oneself? If I am of no value, who could need my devotion?'

'That's not my affair; that's the other's business to discover what is my value. The chief thing is to be able to devote oneself.'

Madame Odintsov bent forward from the back of her chair. 'You speak,' she began, 'as though you had experienced all that.'

'It happened to come up, Anna Sergyevna; all that, as you know, is not in my line.'

'But you could devote yourself?'

'I don't know. I shouldn't like to boast.'

Madame Odintsov said nothing, and Bazarov was mute. The sounds of the piano floated up to them from the drawing-room.

'How is it Katya is playing so late?' observed Madame Odintsov.

Bazarov got up. 'Yes, it is really late now; it's time for you to go to bed.'

'Wait a little; why are you in a hurry? . . . I want to say one word to you.'

'What is it?'

'Wait a little,' whispered Madame Odintsov. Her eyes

rested on Bazarov; it seemed as though she were examining him attentively.

He walked across the room, then suddenly went up to her, hurriedly said 'Good-bye,' squeezed her hand so that she almost screamed, and was gone. She raised her crushed fingers to her lips, breathed on them, and suddenly, impulsively getting up from her low chair, she moved with rapid steps towards the door, as though she wished to bring Bazarov back. . . . A maid came into the room with a decanter on a silver tray. Madame Odintsov stood still, told her she could go, and sat down again, and again sank into thought. Her hair slipped loose and fell in a dark coil down her shoulders. Long after the lamp was still burning in Anna Sergyevna's room, and for long she stayed without moving, only from time to time chafing her hands, which ached a little from the cold of the night.

Bazarov went back two hours later to his bed-room with his boots wet with dew, dishevelled and ill-humoured. He found Arkady at the writing-table with a book in his hands, his coat buttoned up to the throat.

'You're not in bed yet?' he said, in a tone, it seemed, of annoyance.

'You stopped a long while with Anna Sergyevna this evening,' remarked Arkady, not answering him.

'Yes, I stopped with her all the while you were playing the piano with Katya Sergyevna.'

'I did not play . . .' Arkady began, and he stopped. He felt the tears were coming into his eyes, and he did not like to cry before his sarcastic friend.

CHAPTER XVIII

THE following morning when Madame Odintsov came down to morning tea, Bazarov sat a long while bending over his cup, then suddenly he glanced up at her. . . . She turned to him as though he had struck her a blow, and he fancied that her face was a little paler since the night before. She quickly went off to her own room, and did not appear till lunch. It rained from early morning; there was no possibility of going for a walk. The whole company assembled in the drawing-room. Arkady took up the new number of a journal and began reading it aloud. The princess, as was her habit, tried to express her amazement in her face, as though he were doing something improper, then glared angrily at him; but he paid no attention to her.

'Yevgeny Vassilyitch' said Anna Sergyevna, 'come to my room. . . . I want to ask you. . . . You mentioned a text-book yesterday . . .'

She got up and went to the door. The princess looked round with an expression that seemed to say, 'Look at me; see how shocked I am!' and again glared at Arkady; but he raised his voice, and exchanging glances with Katya, near whom he was sitting, he went on reading.

Madame Odintsov went with rapid steps to her study. Bazarov followed her quickly, not raising his eyes, and only with his ears catching the delicate swish and rustle of her silk gown gliding before him. Madame Odintsov sank into the same easy-chair in which she had sat the previous evening, and Bazarov took up the same position as before.

'What was the name of that book?' she began, after a brief silence.

'Pelouse et Frémy, *Notions générales,*' answered Bazarov. 'I might though recommend you also Ganot, *Traité élémentaire de physique expérimentale*. In that book the illustrations are clearer, and in general it's a text-book.'

Madame Odintsov stretched out her hand. 'Yevgeny Vassilyitch, I beg your pardon, but I didn't invite you in here to discuss text-books. I wanted to continue our conversation of last night. You went away so suddenly. . . . It will not bore you . . .'

'I am at your service, Anna Sergyevna. But what were we talking about last night?'

Madame Odintsov flung a sidelong glance at Bazarov.

'We were talking of happiness, I believe. I told you about myself. By the way, I mentioned the word "happiness." Tell me why it is that even when we are enjoying music, for instance, or a fine evening, or a conversation with sympathetic people, it all seems an intimation of some measureless happiness existing apart somewhere rather than actual happiness—such, I mean, as we ourselves are in possession of? Why is it? Or perhaps you have no feeling like that?'

'You know the saying, "Happiness is where we are not,"' replied Bazarov; 'besides, you told me yesterday you are discontented. I certainly never have such ideas come into my head.'

'Perhaps they seem ridiculous to you?'

'No; but they don't come into my head.'

'Really? Do you know, I should very much like to know what you do think about?'

'What? I don't understand.'

'Listen; I have long wanted to speak openly to you. There's no need to tell you—you are conscious of it yourself —that you are not an ordinary man; you are still young— all life is before you. What are you preparing yourself for? What future is awaiting you? I mean to say—what object do you want to attain? What are you going forward to? What is in your heart? in short, who are you? What are you?'

'You surprise me, Anna Sergyevna. You are aware that I am studying natural science, and who I . . .'

'Well, who are you?'

'I have explained to you already that I am going to be a district doctor.'

Anna Sergyevna made a movement of impatience.

'What do you say that for? You don't believe it yourself. Arkady might answer me in that way, but not you.'

'Why, in what is Arkady . . .'

'Stop! Is it possible you could content yourself with such a humble career, and aren't you always maintaining yourself that you don't believe in medicine? You—with your ambition—a district doctor! You answer me like that to put me off, because you have no confidence in me. But, do you know, Yevgeny Vassilyitch, that I could understand you; I have been poor myself, and ambitious, like you; I have been perhaps through the same trials as you.'

'That is all very well, Anna Sergyevna, but you must pardon me for . . . I am not in the habit of talking freely about myself at any time as a rule, and between you and me there is such a gulf . . .'

'What sort of gulf? You mean to tell me again that I am an aristocrat? No more of that, Yevgeny Vassilyitch; I thought I had proved to you . . .'

'And even apart from that,' broke in Bazarov, 'what could induce one to talk and think about the future, which for the most part does not depend on us? If a chance turns up of doing something—so much the better; and if it doesn't turn up—at least one will be glad one didn't gossip idly about it beforehand.'

'You call a friendly conversation idle gossip? . . . Or perhaps you consider me as a woman unworthy of your confidence? I know you despise us all.'

'I don't despise you, Anna Sergyevna, and you know that.'

'No, I don't know anything . . . but let us suppose so. I understand your disinclination to talk of your future career; but as to what is taking place within you now . . .'

'Taking place!' repeated Bazarov, 'as though I were some sort of government or society! In any case, it is utterly uninteresting; and besides, can a man always speak of everything that "takes place" in him?'

'Why, I don't see why you can't speak freely of everything you have in your heart.'

'Can *you?*' asked Bazarov.

'Yes,' answered Anna Sergyevna, after a brief hesitation. Bazarov bowed his head. 'You are more fortunate than I am.'

Anna Sergyevna looked at him questioningly. 'As you please,' she went on. 'but still something tells me that we have

not come together for nothing; that we shall be great friends.
I am sure this—what should I say, constraint, reticence in
you will vanish at last.'

'So you have noticed reticence . . . as you expressed it
. . . constraint?'

'Yes.'

Bazarov got up and went to the window. 'And would you
like to know the reason of this reticence? Would you like
to know what is passing within me?'

'Yes,' repeated Madame Odintsov, with a sort of dread she
did not at the time understand.

'And you will not be angry?'

'No.'

'No?' Bazarov was standing with his back to her. 'Let
me tell you then that I love you like a fool, like a madman.
. . . There, you've forced it out of me.'

Madame Odintsov held both hands out before her; but
Bazarov was leaning with his forehead pressed against the
window pane. He breathed hard; his whole body was visibly
trembling. But it was not the tremor of youthful timidity,
not the sweet alarm of the first declaration that possessed
him; it was passion struggling in him, strong and painful—
passion not unlike hatred, and perhaps akin to it. . . . Madame Odintsov felt both afraid and sorry for him.

'Yevgeny Vassilyitch!' she said, and there was the ring
of unconscious tenderness in her voice.

He turned quickly, flung a searching look on her, and
snatching both her hands, he drew her suddenly to his breast.

She did not at once free herself from his embrace, but an
instant later, she was standing far away in a corner, and
looking from there at Bazarov. He rushed at her . . .

'You have misunderstood me,' she whispered hurriedly, in
alarm. It seemed if he had made another step she would
have screamed. . . . Bazarov bit his lips, and went out.

Half-an-hour after, a maid gave Anna Sergyevna a note
from Bazarov; it consisted simply of one line: 'Am I to go
to-day, or can I stop till to-morrow?'

'Why should you go? I did not understand you—you did
not understand me,' Anna Sergyevna answered him, but to
herself she thought: 'I did not understand myself either.'

She did not show herself till dinner-time, and kept walking
to and fro in her room, stopping sometimes at the window,
sometimes at the looking-glass, and slowly rubbing her handkerchief over her neck, on which she still seemed to feel a
burning spot. She asked herself what had induced her to
'force' Bazarov's words, his confidence, and whether she had
suspected nothing . . . 'I am to blame,' she decided aloud,
'but I could not have foreseen this.' She fell to musing, and
blushed crimson, remembering Bazarov's almost animal face
when he had rushed at her. . . .

'Oh?' she uttered suddenly aloud, and she stopped short and
shook back her curls. . . . She caught sight of herself in the
glass; her head thrown back, with a mysterious smile on the
half-closed, half-opened eyes and lips, told her, it seemed,
in a flash something at which she herself was confused. . . .

'No,' she made up her mind at last. 'God knows what it
would lead to; he couldn't be played with; peace is anyway
the best thing in the world.'

Her peace of mind was not shaken; but she felt gloomy,
and even shed a few tears once, though she could not have
said why—certainly not for the insult done her. She did not
feel insulted; she was more inclined to feel guilty. Under the
influence of various vague emotions, the sense of life passing
by, the desire of novelty, she had forced herself to go up
to a certain point, forced herself to look behind herself, and
had seen behind her not even an abyss, but what was empty
. . . or revolting.

CHAPTER XIX

GREAT as was Madame Odintsov's self-control, and superior as she was to every kind of prejudice, she felt awkward when she went into the dining-room to dinner. The meal went off fairly successfully, however. Porfiry Platonitch made his appearance and told various anecdotes; he had just come back from the town. Among other things, he informed them that the governor had ordered his secretaries on special commissions to wear spurs, in case he might send them off anywhere for greater speed on horseback. Arkady talked in an undertone to Katya, and diplomatically attended to the princess's wants. Bazarov maintained a grim and obstinate silence. Madame Odintsov looked at him twice, not stealthily, but straight in the face, which was bilious and forbidding, with downcast eyes, and contemptuous determination stamped on every feature, and thought: 'No . . . no . . . no.' . . . After dinner, she went with the whole company into the garden, and seeing that Bazarov wanted to speak to her, she took a few steps to one side and stopped. He went up to her, but even then did not raise his eyes, and said hoarsely—

'I have to apologise to you, Anna Sergyevna. You must be in a fury with me.'

'No, I'm not angry with you, Yevgeny Vassilyitch,' answered Madame Odintsov; 'but I am sorry.'

'So much the worse. Any way, I'm sufficiently punished. My position, you will certainly agree, is most foolish. You wrote to me, "Why go away?" But I cannot stay, and don't wish to. To-morrow I shall be gone.'

'Yevgeny Vassilyitch, why are you . . .'

'Why am I going away?'

'No; I didn't mean to say that.'

'There's no recalling the past, Anna Sergyevna . . . and this was bound to come about sooner or later. Consequently I must go. I can only conceive of one condition upon which

I could remain; but that condition will never be. Excuse my impertinence, but you don't love me, and you never will love me, I suppose?'

Bazarov's eyes glittered for an instant under their dark brows.

Anna Sergyevna did not answer him. 'I'm afraid of this man,' flashed through her brain.

'Good-bye, then,' said Bazarov, as though he guessed her thought, and he went back into the house.

Anna Sergyevna walked slowly after him, and calling Katya to her, she took her arm. She did not leave her side till quite evening. She did not play cards, and was constantly laughing, which did not at all accord with her pale and perplexed face. Arkady was bewildered, and looked on at her as all young people look on—that's to say, he was constantly asking himself, 'What is the meaning of that?' Bazarov shut himself up in his room; he came back to tea, however. Anna Sergyevna longed to say some friendly word to him, but she did not know how to address him. . . .

An unexpected incident relieved her from her embarrassment; a steward announced the arrival of Sitnikov.

It is difficult to do justice in words to the strange figure cut by the young apostle of progress as he fluttered into the room. Though, with his characteristic impudence, he had made up his mind to go into the country to visit a woman whom he hardly knew, who had never invited him; but with whom, according to information he had gathered, such talented and intimate friends were staying, he was nevertheless trembling to the marrow of his bones; and instead of bringing out the apologies and compliments he had learned by heart beforehand, he muttered some absurdity about Evdoksya Kukshin having sent him to inquire after Anna Sergyevna's health, and Arkady Nikolaevitch's too, having always spoken to him in the highest terms. . . . At this point he faltered and lost his presence of mind so completely that he sat down on his own hat. However, since no one turned him out, and Anna Sergyevna even presented him to her aunt and her sister, he soon recovered himself and began to chatter volubly. The introduction of the commonplace is often an advantage in life; it relieves over-strained tension, and sobers too self-confident or self-sacrificing emotions by recalling its close kinship with them. With Sitnikov's appearance everything became somehow duller and simpler; they all even ate a more solid supper, and retired to bed half-an-hour earlier than usual.

'I might now repeat to you,' said Arkady, as he lay down in bed, to Bazarov, who was also undressing, what you once said to me, 'Why are you so melancholy? One would think you had fulfilled some sacred duty.' For some time past a sort of pretence of free-and-easy banter had sprung up between the two young men, which is always an unmistakable sign of secret displeasure or unexpressed suspicions.

'I'm going to my father's to-morrow,' said Bazarov.

Arkady raised himself and leaned on his elbow. He felt both surprised, and for some reason or other pleased. 'Ah!' he commented, 'and is that why you're sad?'

Bazarov yawned. 'You'll get old if you know too much.'

'And Anna Sergyevna?' persisted Arkady.

'What about Anna Sergyevna?'

'I mean, will she let you go?'

'I'm not her paid man.'

Arkady grew thoughtful, while Bazarov lay down and turned with his face to the wall.

Some minutes went by in silence. 'Yevgeny?' cried Arkady suddenly.

'Well?'

'I will leave with you to-morrow too.'

Bazarov made no answer.

'Only I will go home,' continued Arkady. 'We will go together as far as Hohlovsky, and there you can get horses at Fedot's. I should be delighted to make the acquaintance of your people, but I'm afraid of being in their way and yours. You are coming to us again later, of course?'

'I've left all my things with you,' Bazarov said, without turning round.

'Why doesn't he ask me why I am going, and just as suddenly as he?' thought Arkady. 'In reality, why am I going, and why is he going?' he pursued his reflections. He could find no satisfactory answer to his own question, though his heart was filled with some bitter feeling. He felt it would be hard to part from this life to which he had grown so accustomed; but for him to remain alone would be rather odd. 'Something has passed between them,' he reasoned to himself; 'what good would it be for me to hang on after he's gone? She's utterly sick of me; I'm losing the last that remained to me.' He began to imagine Anna Sergyevna to himself, then other features gradually eclipsed the lovely image of the young widow.

'I'm sorry to lose Katya too!' Arkady whispered to his pillow, on which a tear had already fallen. . . . All at once he shook back his hair and said aloud—

'What the devil made that fool of a Sitnikov turn up here?'

Bazarov at first stirred a little in his bed, then he uttered the following rejoinder: 'You're still a fool, my boy, I see. Sitnikovs are indispensable to us. I—do you understand? I need dolts like him. It's not for the gods to bake bricks, in fact!' . . .

'Oho!' Arkady thought to himself, and then in a flash all the fathomless depths of Bazarov's conceit dawned upon him. 'Are you and I gods then? at least, you're a god; am not I a dolt then?'

'Yes,' repeated Bazarov; 'you're still a fool.'

Madame Odintsov expressed no special surprise when Arkady told her the next day that he was going with Bazarov; she seemed tired and absorbed. Katya looked at him silently and seriously; the princess went so far as to cross herself under her shawl so that he could not help noticing it. Sitnikov, on the other hand, was completely disconcerted. He had only just come in to lunch in a new and fashionable get-up, not on this occasion of a Slavophil cut; the evening before he had astonished the man told off to wait on him by the amount of linen he had brought with him, and now all of a sudden his comrades were deserting him! He took a few tiny steps, doubled back like a hunted hare at the edge of a copse, and abruptly, almost with dismay, almost with a wail, announced that he proposed going too. Madame Odintsov did not attempt to detain him.

'I have a very comfortable carriage,' added the luckless young man, turning to Arkady; 'I can take you, while Yevgeny Vassilyitch can take your coach, so it will be even more convenient.'

'But, really, it's not at all in your way, and it's a long way to my place.'

'That's nothing, nothing; I've plenty of time; besides, I have business in that direction.'

'Gin-selling?' asked Arkady, rather too contemptuously.

But Sitnikov was reduced to such desperation that he did not even laugh as usual. 'I assure you, my carriage is exceedingly comfortable,' he muttered; 'and there will be room for all.'

'Don't wound Monsieur Sitnikov by a refusal,' commented Anna Sergyevna.

Arkady glanced at her, and bowed his head significantly.

The visitors started off after lunch. As she said good-bye to Bazarov, Madame Odintsov held out her hand to him, and said, 'We shall meet again, shan't we?'

'As you command,' answered Bazarov.

'In that case, we shall.'

Arkady was the first to descend the steps; he got into Sitnikov's carriage. A steward tucked him in respectfully, but he could have killed him with pleasure, or have burst into tears.

Bazarov took his seat in the coach. When they reached Hohlovsky, Arkady waited till Fedot, the keeper of the posting-station, had put in the horses, and going up to the coach, he said, with his old smile, to Bazarov, 'Yevgeny, take me with you; I want to come to you.'

'Get in,' Bazarov brought out through his teeth.

Sitnikov, who had been walking to and fro round the wheels of his carriage, whistling briskly, could only gape when he heard these words; while Arkady coolly pulled his luggage out of the carriage, took his seat beside Bazarov, and bowing politely to his former fellow-traveller, he called, 'Whip up!' The coach rolled away, and was soon out of sight. . . . Sitnikov, utterly confused, looked at his coachman, but the latter was flicking his whip about the tail of the off horse. Then Sitnikov jumped into the carriage, and growling at two passing peasants, 'Put on your caps, idiots!' he drove to the town, where he arrived very late, and where,

next day, at Madame Kukshin's, he dealt very severely with
two 'disgusting stuck-up churls.'

When he was seated in the coach by Bazarov, Arkady
pressed his hand warmly, and for a long while he said nothing. It seemed as though Bazarov understood and appreci-
ated both the pressure and the silence. He had not slept all
the previous night, and had not smoked, and had eaten
scarcely anything for several days. His profile, already
thinner, stood out darkly and sharply under his cap, which
was pulled down to his eyebrows.

'Well, brother,' he said at last, 'give us a cigarette. But
look, I say, is my tongue yellow?'

'Yes, it is,' answered Arkady.

'Hm . . . and the cigarette's tasteless. The machine's out
of gear.'

'You look changed lately certainly,' observed Arkady.

'It's nothing! we shall soon be all right. One thing's a
bother—my mother's so tender-hearted; if you don't grow
as round as a tub, and eat ten times a day, she's quite upset.
My father's all right, he's known all sorts of ups and downs
himself. No, I can't smoke,' he added, and he flung the
cigarette into the dust of the road.

'Do you think it's twenty miles?' asked Arkady.

'Yes. But ask this sage here.' He indicated the peasant
sitting on the box, a labourer of Fedot's.

But the sage only answered, 'Who's to know—miles here-
about aren't measured,' and went on swearing in an undertone at the shaft horse for 'kicking with her head-piece,'
that is, shaking with her head down.

'Yes, yes,' began Bazarov; 'it's a lesson to you, my young
friend, an instructive example. God knows, what rot it is?
Every man hangs on a thread, the abyss may open under his
feet any minute, and yet he must go and invent all sorts of
discomforts for himself, and spoil his life.'

'What are you alluding to?' asked Arkady.

'I'm not alluding to anything; I'm saying straight out
that we've both behaved like fools. What's the use of
talking about it! Still, I've noticed in hospital practice,
the man who's furious at his illness—he's sure to get
over it.'

'I don't quite understand you,' observed Arkady; 'I should have thought you had nothing to complain of.'

'And since you don't quite understand me, I'll tell you this —to my mind, it's better to break stones on the highroad than to let a woman have the mastery of even the end of one's little finger. That's all . . .' Bazarov was on the point of uttering his favourite word, 'romanticism,' but he checked himself, and said, 'rubbish. You don't believe me now, but I tell you; you and I have been in feminine society, and very nice we found it; but to throw up society like that is for all the world like a dip in cold water on a hot day. A man hasn't time to attend to such trifles; a man ought not to be tame, says an excellent Spanish proverb. Now, you, I suppose, my sage friend,' he added, turning to the peasant sitting on the box—'you've a wife?'

The peasant showed both the friends his dull blear-eyed face.

'A wife? Yes. Every man has a wife.'

'Do you beat her?'

'My wife? Everything happens sometimes. We don't beat her without good reason!'

'That's excellent. Well, and does she beat you?'

The peasant gave a tug at the reins. 'That's a strange thing to say, sir. You like your joke.' . . . He was obviously offended.

'You hear, Arkady Nikolaevitch! But we have taken a beating . . . that's what comes of being educated people.'

Arkady gave a forced laugh, while Bazarov turned away, and did not open his mouth again the whole journey.

The twenty miles seemed to Arkady quite forty. But at last, on the slope of some rising ground, appeared the small hamlet where Bazarov's parents lived. Beside it, in a young birch copse, could be seen a small house with a thatched roof.

Two peasants stood with their hats on at the first hut, abusing each other. 'You're a great sow,' said one; 'and worse than a little sucking pig.'

'And your wife's a witch, retorted the other.

'From their unconstrained behaviour,' Bazarov remarked to Arkady, 'and the playfulness of their retorts, you can guess that my father's peasants are not too much oppressed. Why, there he is himself coming out on the steps of his house. They must have heard the bells. It's he; it's he—I know his figure. Ay, ay! how grey he's grown though, poor chap!'

CHAPTER XX

BAZAROV leaned out of the coach, while Arkady thrust his head out behind his companion's back, and caught sight on the steps of the little manor-house of a tall, thinnish man with dishevelled hair, and a thin hawk nose, dressed in an old military coat not buttoned up. He was standing, his legs wide apart, smoking a long pipe and screwing up his eyes to keep the sun out of them.

The horses stopped.

'Arrived at last,' said Bazarov's father, still going on smoking though the pipe was fairly dancing up and down between his fingers. 'Come, get out; get out; let me hug you.'

He began embracing his son . . . 'Enyusha, Enyusha,' was heard a trembling woman's voice. The door was flung open, and in the doorway was seen a plump, short, little old woman in a white cap and a short striped jacket. She moaned, staggered, and would certainly have fallen, had not Bazarov supported her. Her plump little hands were instantly twined round his neck, her head was pressed to his breast, and there was a complete hush. The only sound heard was her broken sobs.

Old Bazarov breathed hard and screwed his eyes up more than ever.

'There, that's enough, that's enough, Arisha! give over,' he said, exchanging a glance with Arkady, who remained motionless in the coach, while the peasant on the box even turned his head away; 'that's not at all necessary, please give over.'

'Ah, Vassily Ivanitch,' faltered the old woman, 'for what ages, my dear one, my darling, Enyusha,' . . . and, not unclasping her hands, she drew her wrinkled face, wet with tears and working with tenderness, a little away from Bazarov, and gazed at him with blissful and comic-looking eyes, and again fell on his neck.

'Well, well, to be sure, that's all in the nature of things,'

commented Vassily Ivanitch, 'only we'd better come indoors.
Here's a visitor come with Yevgeny. You must excuse it,'
he added, turning to Arkady, and scraping with his foot;
'you understand, a woman's weakness; and well, a mother's
heart . . .'

His lips and eyebrows too were twitching, and his beard
was quivering . . . but he was obviously trying to control
himself and appear almost indifferent.

'Let's come in, mother, really,' said Bazarov, and he led
the enfeebled old woman into the house. Putting her into
a comfortable armchair, he once more hurriedly embraced
his father and introduced Arkady to him.

'Heartily glad to make your acquaintance,' said Vassily
Ivanovitch, 'but you mustn't expect great things; everything
here in my house is done in a plain way, on a military footing. Arina Vlasyevna, calm yourself, pray; what weakness!
The gentleman our guest will think ill of you.'

'My dear sir,' said the old lady through her tears, 'your
name and your father's I haven't the honour of knowing. . . .'

'Arkady Nikolaitch,' put in Vassily Ivanitch solemnly, in
a low voice.

'You must excuse a silly old woman like me.' The old
woman blew her nose, and bending her head to right and to
left, carefully wiped one eye after the other. 'You must
excuse me. You see, I thought I should die, that I should
not live to see my da . . arling.'

'Well, here we have lived to see him, madam,' put in
Vassily Ivanovitch. 'Tanyushka,' he turned to a bare-legged
little girl of thirteen in a bright red cotton dress, who was
timidly peeping in at the door, 'bring your mistress a glass
of water—on a tray, do you hear?—and you, gentlemen,' he
added, with a kind of old-fashioned playfulness, 'let me ask
you into the study of a retired old veteran.'

'Just once more let me embrace you, Enyusha,' moaned
Arina Vlasyevna. Bazarov bent down to her. 'Why, what
a handsome fellow you have grown!'

'Well, I don't know about being handsome,' remarked
Vassily Ivanovitch, 'but he's a man, as the saying is,
ommfay. And now I hope, Arina Vlasyevna, that having
satisfied your maternal heart, you will turn your thoughts

to satisfying the appetites of our dear guests, because, as you're aware, even nightingales can't be fed on fairy tales.'

The old lady got up from her chair. 'This minute, Vassily Ivanovitch, the table shall be laid. I will run myself to the kitchen and order the samovar to be brought in; everything shall be ready, everything. Why, I have not seen him, not given him food or drink these three years; is that nothing?'

'There, mind, good mother, bustle about; don't put us to shame; while you, gentlemen, I beg you to follow me. Here's Timofeitch come to pay his respects to you, Yevgeny. He, too, I daresay, is delighted, the old dog. Eh, aren't you delighted, old dog? Be so good as to follow me.'

And Vassily Ivanovitch went bustling forward, scraping and flapping with his slippers trodden down at heel.

His whole house consisted of six tiny rooms. One of them—the one to which he led our friends—was called the study. A thick-legged table, littered over with papers black with the accumulation of ancient dust as though they had been smoked, occupied all the space between the two windows: on the walls hung Turkish firearms, whips, a sabre, two maps, some anatomical diagrams, a portrait of Hoffland, a monogram woven in hair in a blackened frame, and a diploma under glass; a leather sofa, torn and worn into hollows in parts, was placed between two huge cupboards of birchwood; on the shelves books, boxes, stuffed birds, jars, and phials were huddled together in confusion; in one corner stood a broken galvanic battery.

'I warned you, my dear Arkady Nikolaitch,' began Vassily Ivanitch, 'that we live, so to say, bivouacking. . . .'

'There, stop that, what are you apologising for?' Bazarov interrupted. 'Kirsanov knows very well we're not Crœsuses, and that you have no butler. Where are we going to put him, that's the question?'

'To be sure, Yevgeny; I have a capital room there in the little lodge; he will be very comfortable there.'

'Have you had a lodge put up then?'

'Why, where the bath-house is,' put in Timofeitch.

'That is next to the bathroom,' Vassily Ivanitch added hurriedly. 'It's summer now . . . I will run over there at once, and make arrangements; and you, Timofeitch, meanwhile bring in their things. You, Yevgeny, I shall of course offer my study. *Suum cuique.*'

'There you have him! A comical old chap, and very good-natured,' remarked Bazarov, directly Vassily Ivanitch had gone. 'Just such a queer fish as yours, only in another way. He chatters too much.'

'And your mother seems an awfully nice woman,' observed Arkady.

'Yes, there's no humbug about her. You'll see what a dinner she'll give us.'

'They didn't expect you to-day, sir; they've not brought any beef?' observed Timofeitch, who was just dragging in Bazarov's box.

'We shall get on very well without beef. It's no use crying for the moon. Poverty, they say, is no vice.'

'How many serfs has your father?' Arkady asked suddenly.

'The estate's not his, but mother's; there are fifteen serfs, if I remember.'

'Twenty-two in all,' Timofeitch added, with an air of displeasure.

The flapping of slippers was heard, and Vassily Ivanovitch reappeared. 'In a few minutes your room will be ready to receive you,' he cried triumphantly. Arkady . . . Nikolaitch? I think that is right? And here is your attendant,' he added, indicating a short-cropped boy, who had come in with him in a blue full-skirted coat with ragged elbows and a pair of boots which did not belong to him. 'His name is Fedka. Again, I repeat, even though my son tells me not to, you mustn't expect great things. He knows how to fill a pipe, though. You smoke, of course?'

'I generally smoke cigars,' answered Arkady.

'And you do very sensibly. I myself give the preference to cigars, but in these solitudes it is exceedingly difficult to obtain them.'

'There, that's enough humble pie,' Bazarov interrupted again. 'You'd much better sit here on the sofa and let us have a look at you.'

Vassily Ivanovitch laughed and sat down. He was very

like his son in face, only his brow was lower and narrower, and his mouth rather wider, and he was for ever restless, shrugging up his shoulder as though his coat cut him under the armpits, blinking, clearing his throat, and gesticulating with his fingers, while his son was distinguished by a kind of nonchalant immobility.

'Humble-pie!' repeated Vassily Ivanovitch. 'You must not imagine, Yevgeny, I want to appeal, so to speak, to our guest's sympathies by making out we live in such a wilderness. Quite the contrary, I maintain that for a thinking man nothing is a wilderness. At least, I try as far as possible not to get rusty, so to speak, not to fall behind the age.'

Vassily Ivanovitch drew out of his pocket a new yellow silk handkerchief, which he had had time to snatch up on the way to Arkady's room, and flourishing it in the air, he proceeded: 'I am not now alluding to the fact that, for example, at the cost of sacrifices not inconsiderable for me, I have put my peasants on the rent-system and given up my land to them on half profits. I regarded that as my duty; common sense itself enjoins such a proceeding, though other proprietors do not even dream of it; I am alluding to the sciences, to culture.'

'Yes; I see you have here *The Friend of Health* for 1855,' remarked Bazarov.

'It's sent me by an old comrade out of friendship,' Vassily Ivanovitch made haste to answer; 'but we have, for instance, some idea even of phrenology,' he added, addressing himself principally, however, to Arkady, and pointing to a small plaster head on the cupboard, divided into numbered squares; 'we are not unacquainted even with Schenlein and Rademacher.'

'Why do people still believe in Rademacher in this province?' asked Bazarov.

Vassily Ivanovitch cleared his throat. 'In this province. . . . Of course, gentlemen, you know best; how could we keep pace with you? You are here to take our places. In my day, too, there was some sort of a Humouralist school, Hoffmann, and Brown too with his vitalism—they seemed very ridiculous to us, but, of course, they too had been great men at one time or other. Some one new has taken the place of Rademacher with you; you bow down to him, but in another twenty years it will be his turn to be laughed at.'

'For your consolation I will tell you,' observed Bazarov, 'that nowadays we laugh at medicine altogether, and don't bow down to any one.'

'How's that? Why, you're going to be a doctor, aren't you?'

'Yes, but the one fact doesn't prevent the other.'

Vassily Ivanovitch poked his third finger into his pipe, where a little smouldering ash was still left. 'Well, perhaps, perhaps—I am not going to dispute. What am I? A retired army-doctor, *volla-too;* now fate has made me take to farming. I served in your grandfather's brigade,' he addressed himself again to Arkady; 'yes, yes, I have seen many sights in my day. And I was thrown into all kinds of society, brought into contact with all sorts of people! I myself, the man you see before you now, have felt the pulse of Prince Wittgenstein and of Zhukovsky! They were in the southern army, in the fourteenth, you understand' (and here Vassily Ivanovitch pursed his mouth up significantly). 'Well, well, but my business was on one side; stick to your lancet, and let everything else go hang! Your grandfather was a very honourable man, a real soldier.'

'Confess, now, he was rather a blockhead,' remarked Bazarov lazily.

'Ah, Yevgeny, how can you use such an expression! Do consider. . . . Of course, General Kirsanov was not one of the . . .'

'Come, drop him,' broke in Bazarov; 'I was pleased as I was driving along here to see your birch copse; it has shot up capitally.'

Vassily Ivanovitch brightened up. 'And you must see what a little garden I've got now! I planted every tree myself. I've fruit, and raspberries, and all kinds of medicinal herbs. However clever you young gentlemen may be, old Paracelsus spoke the holy truth: *in herbis verbis et lapidibus.* . . . I've retired from practice, you know, of course, but two or three times a week it will happen that I'm brought back to my old work. They come for advice—I can't drive them away. Sometimes the poor have recourse to me for help. And indeed there are no doctors here at all. There's one of the neighbours here, a retired major, only fancy, he doctors the people too. I asked the question, "Has he studied medicine?" And they told me, "No, he's not studied; he does it more from philanthropy." . . . Ha! ha! ha! from philanthropy! What do you think of that? Ha! ha! ha!'

'Fedka, fill me a pipe!' said Bazarov rudely.

'And there's another doctor here who just got to a patient,' Vassily Ivanovitch persisted in a kind of desperation, 'when the patient had gone *ad patres;* the servant didn't let the doctor speak; you're no longer wanted, he told him. He hadn't expected this, got confused, and asked, "Why, did your master hiccup before his death?" "Yes." "Did he hiccup much?" "Yes." "Ah, well, that's all right," and off he set back again. Ha! ha! ha!'

The old man was alone in his laughter; Arkady forced a smile on his face. Bazarov simply stretched. The conversation went on in this way for about an hour; Arkady had time to go to his room, which turned out to be the anteroom attached to the bathroom, but was very snug and clean. At last Tanyusha came in and announced that dinner was ready.

Vassily Ivanovitch was the first to get up. 'Come, gentlemen. You must be magnanimous and pardon me if I've bored you. I daresay my good wife will give you more satisfaction.'

The dinner, though prepared in haste, turned out to be very good, even abundant; only the wine was not quite up to the mark; it was almost black sherry, bought by Timofeitch in the town at a well-known merchant's, and had a faint coppery, resinous taste, and the flies were a great nuisance. On ordinary days a serf-boy used to keep driving them away with a large green branch; but on this occasion Vassily Ivanovitch had sent him away through dread of the criticism of the younger generation. Arina Vlasyevna had had time to dress: she had put on a high cap with silk ribbons and a pale blue flowered shawl. She broke down again directly she caught sight of her Enyusha, but her husband had no need to admonish her; she made haste to wipe away her tears herself, for fear of spotting her shawl. Only the young men ate anything; the master and mistress of the

house had dined long ago. Fedka waited at table, obviously
encumbered by having boots on for the first time; he was
assisted by a woman of a masculine cast of face and one
eye, by name Anfisushka, who performed the duties of housekeeper, poultry-woman, and laundress. Vassily Ivanovitch
walked up and down during the whole of dinner, and with a
perfectly happy, positively beatific countenance, talked about
the serious anxiety he felt at Napoleon's policy, and the in-
tricacy of the Italian question. Arina Vlasyevna took no
notice of Arkady. She did not press him to eat; leaning her
round face, to which the full cherry-coloured lips and the
little moles on the cheeks and over the eyebrows gave a very
simple good-natured expression, on her little closed fist, she
did not take her eyes off her son, and kept constantly sighing; she was dying to know for how long he had come, but
she was afraid to ask him.

'What if he says for two days,' she thought, and her heart
sank. After the roast Vassily Ivanovitch disappeared for
an instant, and returned with an opened half-bottle of champagne. 'Here,' he cried, 'though we do live in the wilds, we
have something to make merry with on festive occasions!'
He filled three champagne glasses and a little wineglass,
proposed the health of 'our inestimable guests,' and at once
tossed off his glass in military fashion; while he made Arina
Vlasyevna drink her wineglass to the last drop. When the
time came in due course for preserves, Arkady, who could
not bear anything sweet, thought it his duty, however, to
taste four different kinds which had been freshly made, all
the more as Bazarov flatly refused them and began at once
smoking a cigarette. Then tea came on the scene with
cream, butter, and cracknels; then Vassily Ivanovitch took
them all into the garden to admire the beauty of the evening. As they passed a garden seat he whispered to
Arkady—

'At this spot I love to meditate, as I watch the sunset; it
suits a recluse like me. And there, a little farther off, I
have planted some of the trees beloved of Horace.'

'What trees?' asked Bazarov, overhearing.

'Oh . . . acacias.'

Bazarov began to yawn.

'I imagine it's time our travellers were in the arms of Morpheus,' observed Vassily Ivanovitch.

'That is, it's time for bed,' Bazarov put in. 'That's a correct idea. It is time, certainly.'

As he said good-night to his mother, he kissed her on the forehead, while she embraced him, and stealthily behind his back she gave him her blessing three times. Vassily Ivanovitch conducted Arkady to his room, and wished him 'as refreshing repose as I enjoyed at your happy years.' And Arkady did as a fact sleep excellently in his bath-house; there was a smell of mint in it, and two crickets behind the stove rivalled each other in their drowsy chirping. Vassily Ivanovitch went from Arkady's room to his study, and perching on the sofa at his son's feet, he was looking forward to having a chat with him; but Bazarov at once sent him away, saying he was sleepy, and did not fall asleep till morning. With wide open eyes he stared vindictively into the darkness; the memories of childhood had no power over him; and besides, he had not yet had time to get rid of the impression of his recent bitter emotions. Arina Vlasyevna first prayed to her heart's content, then she had a long, long conversation with Anfisushka, who stood stock-still before her mistress, and fixing her solitary eye upon her, communicated in a mysterious whisper all her observations and conjectures in regard to Yevgeny Vassilyevitch. The old lady's head was giddy with happiness and wine and tobacco smoke: her husband tried to talk to her, but with a wave of his hand gave it up in despair.

Arina Vlasyevna was a genuine Russian gentlewoman of the olden times; she ought to have lived two centuries before, in the old Moscow days. She was very devout and emotional; she believed in fortune-telling, charms, dreams, and omens of every possible kind; she believed in the prophecies of crazy people, in house-spirits, in wood-spirits, in unlucky meetings, in the evil eye, in popular remedies, she ate specially prepared salt on Holy Thursday, and believed that the end of the world was at hand; she believed that if on Easter Sunday the lights did not go out at vespers, then there would be a good crop of buckwheat, and that a mushroom will not grow after it has been looked on by the

eye of man; she believed that the devil likes to be where
there is water, and that every Jew has a blood-stained patch
on his breast; she was afraid of mice, of snakes, of frogs,
of sparrows, of leeches, of thunder, of cold water, of
draughts, of horses, of goats, of red-haired people, and
black cats, and she regarded crickets and dogs as unclean
beasts; she never ate veal, doves, crayfishes, cheese,
asparagus, artichokes, hares, nor water-melons, because a
cut water-melon suggested the head of John the Baptist,
and of oysters she could not speak without a shudder; she
was fond of eating—and fasted rigidly; she slept ten hours
out of the twenty-four—and never went to bed at all if
Vassily Ivanovitch had so much as a headache; she had
never read a single book except *Alexis or the Cottage in the
Forest;* she wrote one, or at the most two letters in a year,
but was great in housewifery, preserving, and jam-making,
though with her own hands she never touched a thing, and
was generally disinclined to move from her place. Arina
Vlasyevna was very kindhearted, and in her way not at all
stupid. She knew that the world is divided into masters
whose duty it is to command, and simple folk whose duty
it is to serve them—and so she felt no repugnance to
servility and prostrations to the ground; but she treated
those in subjection to her kindly and gently, never let a
single beggar go away empty-handed, and never spoke ill of
any one, though she was fond of gossip. In her youth she
had been pretty, had played the clavichord, and spoken
French a little; but in the course of many years' wanderings with her husband, whom she had married against her
will, she had grown stout, and forgotten music and French.
Her son she loved and feared unutterably; she had given up
the management of the property to Vassily Ivanovitch—and
now did not interfere in anything; she used to groan, wave
her handkerchief, and raise her eyebrows higher and higher
with horror directly her old husband began to discuss the
impending government reforms and his own plans. She
was apprehensive, and constantly expecting some great misfortune, and began to weep directly she remembered anything sorrowful. . . . Such women are not common nowadays. God knows whether we ought to rejoice!

CHAPTER XXI

ON getting up Arkady opened the window, and the first object that met his view was Vassily Ivanovitch. In an Oriental dressing-gown girt round the waist with a pocket-handkerchief he was industriously digging in his garden. He perceived his young visitor, and leaning on his spade, he called, 'The best of health to you! How have you slept?'

'Capitally,' answered Arkady.

'Here am I, as you see, like some Cincinnatus, marking out a bed for late turnips. The time has come now—and thank God for it!—when every one ought to obtain his sustenance with his own hands; it's useless to reckon on others; one must labour oneself. And it turns out that Jean Jacques Rousseau is right. Half an hour ago, my dear young gentleman, you might have seen me in a totally different position. One peasant woman, who complained of looseness —that's how they express it, but in our language, dysentery —I . . . how can I express it best? I administered opium, and for another I extracted a tooth. I proposed an anæsthetic to her . . . but she would not consent. All that I do *gratis—anamatyer (en amateur)*. I'm used to it, though; you see, I'm a plebeian, *homo novus*—not one of the old stock, not like my spouse. . . . Wouldn't you like to come this way into the shade, to breathe the morning freshness a little before tea?'

Arkady went out to him.

'Welcome once again,' said Vassily Ivanovitch, raising his hand in a military salute to the greasy skull-cap which covered his head. 'You, I know, are accustomed to luxury, to amusements, but even the great ones of this world do not disdain to spend a brief space under a cottage roof.'

'Good heavens,' protested Arkady, 'as though I were one of the great ones of this world! And I'm not accustomed to luxury.'

'Pardon me, pardon me,' rejoined Vassily Ivanovitch with a polite simper. 'Though I am laid on the shelf now, I have knocked about the world too—I can tell a bird by its flight. I am something of a psychologist too in my own way, and a physiognomist. If I had not, I will venture to say, been endowed with that gift, I should have come to grief long ago; I should have stood no chance, a poor man like me. I tell you without flattery, I am sincerely delighted at the friendship I observe between you and my son. I have just seen him; he got up as he usually does—no doubt you are aware of it—very early, and went a ramble about the neighbourhood. Permit me to inquire—have you known my son long?'

'Since last winter.'

'Indeed. And permit me to question you further—but hadn't we better sit down? Permit me, as a father, to ask without reserve, What is your opinion of my Yevgeny?'

'Your son is one of the most remarkable men I have ever met,' Arkady answered emphatically.

Vassily Ivanovitch's eyes suddenly grew round, and his cheeks were suffused with a faint flush. The spade fell out of his hand.

'And so you expect,' he began . . .

'I'm convinced,' Arkady put in, 'that your son has a great future before him; that he will do honour to your name. I've been certain of that ever since I first met him.'

'How . . . how was that?' Vassily Ivanovitch articulated with an effort. His wide mouth was relaxed in a triumphant smile, which would not leave it.

'Would you like me to tell you how we met?'

'Yes . . . and altogether. . . .'

Arkady began to tell his tale, and to talk of Bazarov with even greater warmth, even greater enthusiasm than he had done on the evening when he danced a mazurka with Madame Odintsov.

Vassily Ivanovitch listened and listened, blinked, and rolled his handkerchief up into a ball in both his hands, cleared his throat, ruffled up his hair, and at last could stand it no longer; he bent down to Arkady and kissed him on his shoulder. 'You have made me perfectly happy,' he said, never ceasing to smile. 'I ought to tell you, I . . . idolise my son; my old wife I won't speak of—we all know what mothers are!—but I dare not show my feelings before him, because he doesn't like it. He is averse to every kind of demonstration of feeling; many people even find fault with him for such firmness of character, and regard it as a proof of pride or lack of feeling, but men like him ought not to be judged by the common standard, ought they? And here, for example, many another fellow in his place would have been a constant drag on his parents; but he, would you believe it? has never from the day he was born taken a farthing more than he could help, that's God's truth!'

'He is a disinterested, honest man,' observed Arkady.

'Exactly so; he is disinterested. And I don't only idolise him, Arkady Nikolaitch, I am proud of him, and the height of my ambition is that some day there will be the following lines in his biography: "The son of a simple army-doctor, who was, however, capable of divining his greatness betimes, and spared nothing for his education . . ."' The old man's voice broke.

Arkady pressed his hand.

'What do you think,' inquired Vassily Ivanovitch, after a short silence, 'will it be in the career of medicine that he will attain the celebrity you anticipate for him?'

'Of course, not in medicine, though even in that department he will be one of the leading scientific men.'

'In what then, Arkady Nikolaitch?'

'It would be hard to say now, but he will be famous.'

'He will be famous!' repeated the old man, and he sank into a reverie.

'Arina Vlasyevna sent me to call you in to tea,' announced Anfisushka, coming by with an immense dish of ripe raspberries.

Vassily Ivanovitch started. 'And will there be cooled cream for the raspberries?'

'Yes.'

'Cold now, mind! Don't stand on ceremony, Arkady Nikolaitch; take some more. How is it Yevgeny doesn't come?'

'I'm here,' was heard Bazarov's voice from Arkady's room.

Vassily Ivanovitch turned round quickly. 'Aha! you

wanted to pay a visit to your friend; but you were too late, *amice,* and we have already had a long conversation with him. Now we must go in to tea, mother summons us. By the way, I want to have a little talk with you.'

'What about?'

'There's a peasant here; he's suffering from icterus. . . .'

'You mean jaundice?'

'Yes, a chronic and very obstinate case of icterus. I have prescribed him centaury and St. John's wort, ordered him to eat carrots, given him soda; but all that's merely palliative measures; we want some more decided treatment. Though you do laugh at medicine, I am certain you can give me practical advice. But we will talk of that later. Now come in to tea.'

Vassily Ivanovitch jumped up briskly from the garden seat, and hummed from *Robert le Diable—*

> 'The rule, the rule we set ourselves,
> To live, to live for pleasure!'

'Singular vitality!' observed Bazarov, going away from the window.

It was midday. The sun was burning hot behind a thin veil of unbroken whitish clouds. Everything was hushed; there was no sound but the cocks crowing irritably at one another in the village, producing in every one who heard them a strange sense of drowsiness and ennui; and some-where, high up in a tree-top, the incessant plaintive cheep of a young hawk. Arkady and Bazarov lay in the shade of a small haystack, putting under themselves two armfuls of dry and rustling, but still greenish and fragrant grass.

'That aspen-tree,' began Bazarov, 'reminds me of my childhood; it grows at the edge of the clay-pits where the bricks were dug, and in those days I believed firmly that that clay-pit and aspen-tree possessed a peculiar talismanic power; I never felt dull near them. I did not understand then that I was not dull, because I was a child. Well, now I'm grown up, the talisman's lost its power.'

'How long did you live here altogether?' asked Arkady.

'Two years on end; then we travelled about. We led a roving life, wandering from town to town for the most part.'

'And has this house been standing long?'

'Yes. My grandfather built it—my mother's father.'

'Who was he—your grandfather?'

'Devil knows. Some second-major. He served with Suvorov, and was always telling stories about the crossing of the Alps—inventions probably.

'You have a portrait of Suvorov hanging in the drawing-room. I like these dear little houses like yours; they're so warm and old-fashioned; and there's always a special sort of scent about them.'

'A smell of lamp-oil and clover,' Bazarov remarked, yawning. 'And the flies in those dear little houses. . . . Faugh!'

'Tell me,' began Arkady, after a brief pause, 'were they strict with you when you were a child?'

'You can see what my parents are like. They're not a severe sort.'

'Are you fond of them, Yevgeny?'

'I am, Arkady.'

'How fond they are of you!'

Bazarov was silent for a little. 'Do you know what I'm thinking about?' he brought out at last, clasping his hands behind his head.

'No. What is it?'

'I'm thinking life is a happy thing for my parents. My father at sixty is fussing around, talking about "palliative" measures, doctoring people, playing the bountiful master with the peasants—having a festive time, in fact; and my mother's happy too; her day's so chockful of duties of all sorts, and sighs and groans that she's no time even to think of herself; while I . . .'

'While you?'

'I think; here I lie under a haystack. . . . The tiny space I occupy is so infinitely small in comparison with the rest of space, in which I am not, and which has nothing to do with me; and the period of time in which it is my lot to live is so petty beside the eternity in which I have not been, and shall not be. . . . And in this atom, this mathematical point, the blood is circulating, the brain is working and wanting something. . . . Isn't it loathsome? Isn't it petty?'

'Allow me to remark that what you're saying applies to men in general.'

'You are right,' Bazarov cut in. 'I was going to say that they now—my parents, I mean—are absorbed and don't trouble themselves about their own nothingness; it doesn't sicken them . . . while I . . . I feel nothing but weariness and anger.'

'Anger? why anger?'

'Why? How can you ask why? Have you forgotten?'

'I remember everything, but still I don't admit that you have any right to be angry. You're unlucky, I'll allow, but . . .'

'Pooh! then you, Arkady Nikolaevitch, I can see, regard love like all modern young men; cluck, cluck, cluck you call to the hen, but if the hen comes near you, you run away. I'm not like that. But that's enough of that. What can't be helped, it's shameful to talk about.' He turned over on his side. 'Aha! there goes a valiant ant dragging off a half-dead fly. Take her, brother, take her! Don't pay attention to her resistance; it's your privilege as an animal to be free from the sentiment of pity—make the most of it—not like us conscientious self-destructive animals!'

'You shouldn't say that, Yevgeny! When have you destroyed yourself?'

Bazarov raised his head. 'That's the only thing I pride myself on. I haven't crushed myself, so a woman can't crush me. Amen! It's all over! You shall not hear another word from me about it.'

Both the friends lay for some time in silence.

'Yes,' began Bazarov, 'man's a strange animal. When one gets a side view from a distance of the dead-alive life our "fathers" lead here, one thinks, What could be better? You eat and drink, and know you are acting in the most reasonable, most judicious manner. But if not, you're devoured by ennui. One wants to have to do with people if only to abuse them.'

'One ought so to order one's life that every moment in it should be of significance,' Arkady affirmed reflectively.

'I dare say! What's of significance is sweet, however mistaken; one could make up one's mind to what's insignificant even. But pettiness, pettiness, that's what's insufferable.'

'Pettiness doesn't exist for a man so long as he refuses to recognise it.'

'H'm . . . what you've just said is a common-place reversed.'

'What? What do you mean by that term?'

'I'll tell you; saying, for instance, that education is beneficial, that's a common-place; but to say that education is injurious, that's a common-place turned upside down. There's more style about it, so to say, but in reality it's one and the same.'

'And the truth is—where, which side?'

'Where? Like an echo I answer, Where?'

'You're in a melancholy mood to-day, Yevgeny.'

'Really? The sun must have softened my brain, I suppose, and I can't stand so many raspberries either.'

'In that case, a nap's not a bad thing,' observed Arkady.

'Certainly; only don't look at me; every man's face is stupid when he's asleep.'

'But isn't it all the same to you what people think of you?'

'I don't know what to say to you. A real man ought not to care; a real man is one whom it's no use thinking about, whom one must either obey or hate.'

'It's funny! I don't hate anybody,' observed Arkady, after a moment's thought.

'And I hate so many. You are a soft-hearted, mawkish creature; how could you hate any one? . . . You're timid; you don't rely on yourself much.'

'And you,' interrupted Arkady, 'do you expect much of yourself? Have you a high opinion of yourself?'

Bazarov paused. 'When I meet a man who can hold his own beside me,' he said, dwelling on every syllable, 'then I'll change my opinion of myself. Yes, hatred! You said, for instance, to-day as we passed our bailiff Philip's cottage—it's the one that's so nice and clean—well, you said, Russia will come to perfection when the poorest peasant has a house like that, and every one of us ought to work to bring it about. . . . And I felt such a hatred for this poorest peasant, this Philip or Sidor, for whom I'm to be ready to jump out of my skin,

S—12

and who won't even thank me for it . . . and why should he thank me? Why, suppose he does live in a clean house, while the nettles are growing out of me,—well what do I gain by it?'

'Hush, Yevgeny . . . if one listened to you to-day one would be driven to agreeing with those who reproach us for want of principles.'

'You talk like your uncle. There are no general principles —you've not made out that even yet! There are feelings. Everything depends on them.'

'How so?'

'Why, I, for instance, take up a negative attitude, by virtue of my sensations; I like to deny—my brain's made on that plan, and that's all about it! Why do I like chemistry? Why do you like apples?—by virtue of our sensations. It's all the same thing. Deeper than that men will never penetrate. Not every one will tell you that, and, in fact, I shan't tell you so another time.'

'What? and is honesty a matter of the senses?'

'I should rather think so.'

'Yevgeny!' Arkady was beginning in a dejected voice . . .

'Well? What? Isn't it to your taste?' broke in Bazarov. 'No, brother. If you've made up your mind to mow down everything, don't spare your own legs. But we've talked enough metaphysics. "Nature breathes the silence of sleep," said Pushkin.'

'He never said anything of the sort,' protested Arkady.

'Well, if he didn't, as a poet he might have—and ought to have said it. By the way, he must have been a military man.'

'Pushkin never was a military man!'

'Why, on every page of him there's, "To arms! to arms! for Russia's honour!"'

'Why, what stories you invent! I declare, it's positive calumny.'

'Calumny? That's a mighty matter! What a word he's found to frighten me with! Whatever charge you make against a man, you may be certain he deserves twenty times worse than that in reality.'

'We had better go to sleep,' said Arkady, in a tone of vexation.

'With the greatest pleasure,' answered Bazarov. But neither of them slept. A feeling almost of hostility had come over both the young men. Five minutes later, they opened their eyes and glanced at one another in silence.

'Look,' said Arkady suddenly, 'a dry maple leaf has come off and is falling to the earth; its movement is exactly like a butterfly's flight. Isn't it strange? Gloom and decay— like brightness and life.'

'Oh, my friend, Arkady Nikolaitch!' cried Bazarov, 'one thing I entreat of you; no fine talk.'

'I talk as best I can. . . . And, I declare, its perfect despotism. An idea came into my head; why shouldn't I utter it?'

'Yes; and why shouldn't I utter my ideas? I think that fine talk's positively indecent.'

'And what is decent? Abuse?'

'Ha! ha! you really do intend, I see, to walk in your uncle's footsteps. How pleased that worthy imbecile would have been if he had heard you!'

'What did you call Pavel Petrovitch?'

'I called him, very justly, an imbecile.'

'But this is unbearable!' cried Arkady.

'Aha! family feeling spoke there,' Bazarov commented coolly. 'I've noticed how obstinately it sticks to people. A man's ready to give up everything and break with every prejudice; but to admit that his brother, for instance, who steals handkerchiefs, is a thief—that's too much for him. And when one comes to think of it: my brother, mine—and no genius . . . that's an idea no one can swallow.'

'It was a simple sense of justice spoke in me and not in the least family feeling,' retorted Arkady passionately. 'But since that's a sense you don't understand, since you haven't that sensation, you can't judge of it.'

'In other words, Arkady Kirsanov is too exalted for my comprehension. I bow down before him and say no more.'

'Don't, please, Yevgeny; we shall really quarrel at last.'

'Ah, Arkady! do me a kindness. I entreat you, let us quarrel for once in earnest. . . .'

'But then perhaps we should end by . . .'

'Fighting?' put in Bazarov. 'Well? Here, on the hay, in these idyllic surroundings, far from the world and the eyes of men, it wouldn't matter. But you'd be no match for me. I'd have you by the throat in a minute.'

Bazarov spread out his long, cruel fingers. . . . Arkady turned round and prepared, as though in jest, to resist. . . . But his friend's face struck him as so vindictive—there was such menace in grim earnest in the smile that distorted his lips, and in his glittering eyes, that he felt instinctively afraid.

'Ah! so this is where you have got to!' the voice of Vassily Ivanovitch was heard saying at that instant, and the old army-doctor appeared before the young men, garbed in a home-made linen pea-jacket, with a straw hat, also home-made, on his head. 'I've been looking everywhere for you. . . . Well, you've picked out a capital place, and you're excellently employed. Lying on the "earth, gazing up to heaven." Do you know, there's a special significance in that?'

'I never gaze up to heaven except when I want to sneeze,' growled Bazarov, and turning to Arkady he added in an undertone. 'Pity he interrupted us.'

'Come, hush!' whispered Arkady, and he secretly squeezed his friend's hand. But no friendship can long stand such shocks.

'I look at you, my youthful friends,' Vassily Ivanovitch was saying meantime, shaking his head, and leaning his folded arms on a rather cunningly bent stick of his own carving, with a Turk's figure for a top,—'I look, and I cannot refrain from admiration. You have so much strength, such youth and bloom, such abilities, such talents! Positively, a Castor and Pollux!'

'Get along with you—going off into mythology!' commented Bazarov. 'You can see at once that he was a great Latinist in his day! Why, I seem to remember, you gained the silver medal for Latin prose—didn't you?'

'The Dioscuri, the Dioscuri!' repeated Vassily Ivanovitch.

'Come, shut up, father; don't show off.'

'Once in a way it's surely permissible,' murmured the old man. 'However, I have not been seeking for you, gentlemen, to pay you compliments; but with the object, in the first place, of announcing to you that we shall soon be dining; and secondly, I wanted to prepare you, Yevgeny. . . . You are a sensible man, you know the world, and you know what women are, and consequently you will excuse. . . . Your mother wished to have a Te Deum sung on the occasion of your arrival. You must not imagine that I am inviting you to attend this thanksgiving—it is over indeed now; but Father Alexey . . .'

'The village parson?'

'Well, yes, the priest; he . . . is to dine . . . with us. . . . I did not anticipate this, and did not even approve of it . . . but it somehow came about . . . he did not understand me. . . . And, well . . . Arina Vlasyevna . . . Besides, he's a worthy, reasonable man.'

'He won't eat my share at dinner, I suppose?' queried Bazarov.

Vassily Ivanovitch laughed. 'How you talk!'

'Well, that's all I ask. I'm ready to sit down to table with any man.'

Vassily Ivanovitch set his hat straight. 'I was certain before I spoke,' he said, 'that you were above any kind of prejudice. Here am I, an old man at sixty-two, and I have none.' (Vassily Ivanovitch did not dare to confess that he had himself desired the thanksgiving service. He was no less religious than his wife.) 'And Father Alexey very much wanted to make your acquaintance. You will like him, you'll see. He's no objection even to cards, and he sometimes— but this is between ourselves . . . positively smokes a pipe.'

'All right. We'll have a round of whist after dinner, and I'll clean him out.'

'He! he! he! We shall see! That remains to be seen.'

'I know you're an old hand,' said Bazarov, with a peculiar emphasis.

Vassily Ivanovitch's bronzed cheeks were suffused with an uneasy flush.

'For shame, Yevgeny. . . . Let bygones be bygones. Well, I'm ready to acknowledge before this gentleman I had that passion in my youth; and I have paid for it too! How hot it is, though! Let me sit down with you. I shan't be in your way, I hope?'

'Oh, not at all,' answered Arkady.

Vassily Ivanovitch lowered himself, sighing, into the hay.
'Your present quarters remind me, my dear sirs,' he began,
'of my military bivouacking existence, the ambulance halts,
somewhere like this under a haystack, and even for that we
were thankful.' He sighed. 'I had many, many experiences
in my life. For example, if you will allow me, I will tell
you a curious episode of the plague in Bessarabia.'

'For which you got the Vladimir cross?' put in Bazarov.
'We know, we know. . . . By the way, why is it you're not
wearing it?'

'Why, I told you that I have no prejudices,' muttered
Vassily Ivanovitch (he had only the evening before had
the red ribbon unpicked off his coat), and he proceeded to
relate the episode of the plague. 'Why, he's fallen asleep,'
he whispered all at once to Arkady, pointing to Yevgeny,
and winking good-naturedly. 'Yevgeny! get up,' he went on
aloud. 'Let's go in to dinner.'

Father Alexey, a good-looking stout man with thick, care-
fully-combed hair, with an embroidered girdle round his lilac
silk cassock, appeared to be a man of much tact and adapta-
bility. He made haste to be the first to offer his hand to
Arkady and Bazarov, as though understanding beforehand
that they did not want his blessing, and he behaved himself
in general without constraint. He neither derogated from
his own dignity, nor gave offence to others; he vouchsafed
a passing smile at the seminary Latin, and stood up for his
bishop; drank two small glasses of wine, but refused a third;
accepted a cigar from Arkady, but did not proceed to smoke
it, saying he would take it home with him. The only thing
not quite agreeable about him was a way he had of constantly
raising his hand with care and deliberation to catch the flies
on his face, sometimes succeeding in smashing them. He
took his seat at the green table, expressing his satisfaction at
so doing in measured terms, and ended by winning from
Bazarov two roubles and a half in paper money; they had
no idea of even reckoning in silver in the house of Arina
Vlasyevna. . . . She was sitting, as before, near her son
(she did not play cards), her cheek, as before, propped on
her little fist; she only got up to order some new dainty to be
served. She was afraid to caress Bazarov, and he gave her

no encouragement, he did not invite her caresses; and besides, Vassily Ivanovitch had advised her not to 'worry' him
too much. 'Young men are not fond of that sort of thing,'
he declared to her. (It's needless to say what the dinner
was like that day; Timofeitch in person had galloped off
at early dawn for beef; the bailiff had gone off in another
direction for turbot, gremille, and crayfish; for mushrooms
alone forty-two farthings had been paid the peasant women
in copper); but Arina Vlasyevna's eyes, bent steadfastly on
Bazarov, did not express only devotion and tenderness; in
them was to be seen sorrow also, mingled with awe and
curiosity; there was to be seen too a sort of humble reproachfulness.

Bazarov, however, was not in a humour to analyse the
exact expression of his mother's eyes; he seldom turned to
her, and then only with some short question. Once he asked
her for her hand 'for luck'; she gently laid her soft, little
hand on his rough, broad palm.

'Well,' she asked, after waiting a little, 'has it been any
use?'

'Worse luck than ever,' he answered, with a careless
laugh.

'He plays too rashly,' pronounced Father Alexey, as it
were compassionately, and he stroked his beard.

'Napoleon's rule, good Father, Napoleon's rule,' put in
Vassily Ivanovitch, leading an ace.

'It brought him to St. Helena, though,' observed Father
Alexey, as he trumped the ace.

'Wouldn't you like some currant tea, Enyusha?' inquired
Arina Vlasyevna.

Bazarov merely shrugged his shoulders.

'No!' he said to Arkady the next day, 'I'm off from here
to-morrow. I'm bored; I want to work, but I can't work
here. I will come to your place again; I've left all my ap-
paratus there too. In your house one can at any rate shut
oneself up. While here my father repeats to me, "My study
is at your disposal—nobody shall interfere with you," and
all the time he himself is never a yard away. And I'm
ashamed somehow to shut myself away from him. It's the
same thing too with mother. I hear her sighing the other

side of the wall, and if one goes in to her, one's nothing to say to her.'

'She will be very much grieved,' observed Arkady, 'and so will he.'

'I shall come back again to them.'

'When?'

'Why, when on my way to Petersburg.'

'I feel sorry for your mother particularly.'

'Why's that? Has she won your heart with strawberries, or what?'

Arkady dropped his eyes. 'You don't understand your mother, Yevgeny. She's not only a very good woman, she's very clever really. This morning she talked to me for half-an-hour, and so sensibly, interestingly.'

'I suppose she was expatiating upon me all the while?'

'We didn't talk only about you.'

'Perhaps; lookers-on see most. If a woman can keep up half-an-hour's conversation, it's always a hopeful sign. But I'm going, all the same.'

'It won't be very easy for you to break it to them. They are always making plans for what we are to do in a fortnight's time.'

'No; it won't be easy. Some demon drove me to tease my father to-day; he had one of his rent-paying peasants flogged the other day, and quite right too—yes, yes, you needn't look at me in such horror—he did quite right, because he's an awful thief and drunkard; only my father had no idea that I, as they say, was cognisant of the facts. He was greatly perturbed, and now I shall have to upset him more than ever. . . . Never mind! Never say die! He'll get over it!'

Bazarov said, 'Never mind'; but the whole day passed before he could make up his mind to inform Vassily Ivanovitch of his intentions. At last, when he was just saying good-night to him in the study, he observed, with a feigned yawn—

'Oh . . . I was almost forgetting to tell you. . . . Send to Fedot's for our horses to-morrow.'

Vassily Ivanovitch was dumbfounded. 'Is Mr. Kirsanov leaving us, then?'

'Yes; and I'm going with him.'

Vassily Ivanovitch positively reeled. 'You are going?'

'Yes . . . I must. Make the arrangements about the horses, please.'

'Very good. . . .' faltered the old man; 'to Fedot's . . . very good . . . only . . . only. . . . How is it?'

'I must go to stay with him for a little time. I will come back again later.'

'Ah! For a little time . . . very good.' Vassily Ivanovitch drew out his handkerchief, and, blowing his nose, doubled up almost to the ground. 'Well . . . everything shall be done. I had thought you were to be with us . . . a little longer. Three days. . . . After three years, it's rather little; rather little, Yevgeny!'

'But, I tell you, I'm coming back directly. It's necessary for me to go.'

'Necessary. . . . Well! Duty before everything. So the horses shall be in readiness. Very good. Arina and I, of course, did not anticipate this. She has just begged some flowers from a neighbour; she meant to decorate the room for you.' (Vassily Ivanovitch did not even mention that every morning almost at dawn he took counsel with Timofeitch, standing with his bare feet in his slippers, and pulling out with trembling fingers one dog's-eared rouble note after another, charged him with various purchases, with special reference to good things to eat, and to red wine, which, as far as he could observe, the young men liked extremely.) 'Liberty . . . is the great thing; that's my rule. . . . I don't want to hamper you . . . not . . .'

He suddenly ceased, and made for the door.

'We shall soon see each other again, father, really.'

But Vassily Ivanovitch, without turning round, merely waved his hand and was gone. When he got back to his bedroom he found his wife in bed, and began to say his prayers in a whisper, so as not to wake her up. She woke, however. 'Is that you, Vassily Ivanovitch?' she asked.

'Yes, mother.'

'Have you come from Enyusha? Do you know, I'm afraid of his not being comfortable on that sofa. I told Anfisushka to put him on your travelling mattress and the new pillows; I should have given him our feather-bed, but I seem to remember he doesn't like too soft a bed. . . .'

'Never mind, mother; don't worry yourself. He's all right.
Lord, have mercy on me, a sinner,' he went on with his
prayer in a low voice. Vassily Ivanovitch was sorry for his
old wife; he did not mean to tell her over night what a
sorrow there was in store for her.

Bazarov and Arkady set off the next day. From early
morning all was dejection in the house; Anfisushka let the
tray slip out of her hands; even Fedka was bewildered, and
was reduced to taking off his boots. Vassily Ivanitch was
more fussy than ever; he was obviously trying to put a good
face on it, talked loudly, and stamped with his feet, but his
face looked haggard, and his eyes were continually avoiding
his son. Arina Vlasyevna was crying quietly; she was utterly crushed, and could not have controlled herself at all
if her husband had not spent two whole hours early in the
morning exhorting her. When Bazarov, after repeated
promises to come back certainly not later than in a month's
time, tore himself at last from the embraces detaining him,
and took his seat in the coach; when the horses had started,
the bell was ringing, and the wheels were turning round,
and when it was no longer any good to look after them, and
the dust had settled, and Timofeitch, all bent and tottering
as he walked, had crept back to his little room; when the
old people were left alone in their little house, which seemed
suddenly to have grown shrunken and decrepit too, Vassily
Ivanovitch, after a few more moments of hearty waving of
his handkerchief on the steps, sank into a chair, and his head
dropped on to his breast. 'He has cast us off; he has forsaken us,' he faltered; 'forsaken us; he was dull with
us. Alone, alone!' he repeated several times. Then
Arina Vlasyevna went up to him, and, leaning her grey head
against his grey head, said, 'There's no help for it, Vasya!
A son is a separate piece cut off. He's like the falcon that
flies home and flies away at his pleasure; while you and I
are like funguses in the hollow of a tree, we sit side by side,
and don't move from our place. Only I am left you unchanged for ever, as you for me.'

Vassily Ivanovitch took his hands from his face and
clasped his wife, his friend, as warmly as he had never
clasped in youth; she comforted him in his grief.

CHAPTER XXII

IN silence, only rarely exchanging a few insignificant words, our friends travelled as far as Fedot's. Bazarov was not altogether pleased with himself. Arkady was displeased with him. He was feeling, too, that causeless melancholy which is only known to very young people. The coachman changed the horses, and getting up on to the box, inquired, 'To the right or to the left?'

Arkady started. The road to the right led to the town. and from there home; the road to the left led to Madame Odintsov's.

He looked at Bazarov.

'Yevgeny,' he queried; 'to the left?'

Bazarov turned away. 'What folly is this?' he muttered.

'I know it's folly,' answered Arkady. . . . 'But what does that matter? It's not the first time.'

Bazarov pulled his cap down over his brows. 'As you choose,' he said at last. 'Turn to the left,' shouted Arkady.

The coach rolled away in the direction of Nikolskoe. But having resolved on the folly, the friends were even more obstinately silent than before, and seemed positively ill-humoured.

Directly the steward met them on the steps of Madame Odintsov's house, the friends could perceive that they had acted injudiciously in giving way so suddenly to a passing impulse. They were obviously not expected. They sat rather a long while, looking rather foolish, in the drawing-room. Madame Odintsov came in to them at last. She greeted them with her customary politeness, but was surprised at their hasty return; and, so far as could be judged from the deliberation of her gestures and words, she was not over pleased at it. They made haste to announce that they had only called on their road, and must go on farther, to the town, within four hours. She confined herself to a slight exclamation, begged Arkady to remember her to his father, and sent for her aunt. The princess appeared very sleepy, which gave her wrinkled old face an even more ill-natured expression. Katya was not well; she did not leave her room. Arkady suddenly realised that he was at least as anxious to see Katya as Anna Sergyevna herself. The four hours were spent in insignificant discussion of one thing and another; Anna Sergyevna both listened and spoke without a smile. It was only quite at parting that her former friendliness seemed, as it were, to revive.

'I have an attack of spleen just now,' she said; 'but you must not pay attention to that, and come again—I say this to both of you—before long.'

Both Bazarov and Arkady responded with a silent bow, took their seats in the coach, and without stopping again anywhere, went straight home to Maryino, where they arrived safely on the evening of the following day. During the whole course of the journey neither one nor the other even mentioned the name of Madame Odintsov; Bazarov, in particular, scarcely opened his mouth, and kept staring in a side direction away from the road, with a kind of exasperated intensity.

At Maryino every one was exceedingly delighted to see them. The prolonged absence of his son had begun to make Nikolai Petrovitch uneasy; he uttered a cry of joy, and bounced about on the sofa, dangling his legs, when Fenitchka ran to him with sparkling eyes, and informed him of the arrival of the 'young gentlemen'; even Pavel Petrovitch was conscious of some degree of agreeable excitement, and smiled condescendingly as he shook hands with the returned wanderers. Talk, questions followed; Arkady talked most, especially at supper, which was prolonged long after midnight. Nikolai Petrovitch ordered up some bottles of porter which had only just been sent from Moscow, and partook of the festive beverage till his cheeks were crimson, and he kept laughing in a half-childish, half-nervous little chuckle. Even the servants were infected by the general gaiety. Dunyasha ran up and down like one possessed, and was continually slamming doors; while Piotr was, at three o'clock in the morning, still attempting to strum a Cossack waltz on the guitar. The strings gave forth a sweet and plaintive

sound in the still air; but with the exception of a small
preliminary flourish, nothing came of the cultured valet's
efforts; nature had given him no more musical talent than
all the rest of the world.

But meanwhile things were not going over harmoniously
at Maryino, and poor Nikolai Petrovitch was having a bad
time of it. Difficulties on the farm sprang up every day—
senseless, distressing difficulties. The troubles with the hired
labourers had become insupportable. Some asked for their
wages to be settled, or for an increase of wages, while
others made off with the wages they had received in advance;
the horses fell sick; the harness fell to pieces as though it
were burnt; the work was carelessly done; a threshing
machine that had been ordered from Moscow turned out to
be useless from its great weight, another was ruined the
first time it was used; half the cattle sheds were burnt down
through an old blind woman on the farm going in windy
weather with a burning brand to fumigate her cow . . . the
old woman, it is true, maintained that the whole mischief
could be traced to the master's plan of introducing new-
fangled cheeses and milk-products. The overseer suddenly
turned lazy, and began to grow fat, as every Russian grows
fat when he gets a snug berth. When he caught sight of
Nikolai Petrovitch in the distance, he would fling a stick at
a passing pig, or threaten a half-naked urchin, to show his
zeal, but the rest of the time he was generally asleep.
The peasants who had been put on the rent system did
not bring their money at the time due, and stole the forest-
timber; almost every night the keepers caught peasants'
horses in the meadows of the 'farm,' and sometimes forcibly
bore them off. Nikolai Petrovitch would fix a money fine for
damages, but the matter usually ended after the horses had
been kept a day or two on the master's forage by their
returning to their owners. To crown all, the peasants began
quarrelling among themselves; brothers asked for a division
of property, their wives could not get on together in one
house; all of a sudden the squabble, as though at a given
signal, came to a head, and at once the whole village came
running to the counting-house steps, crawling to the master
often drunken and with battered face, demanding justice and

judgment; then arose an uproar and clamour, the shrill wailing of the women mixed with the curses of the men. Then one had to examine the contending parties, and shout oneself hoarse, knowing all the while that one could never anyway arrive at a just decision. . . . There were not hands enough for the harvest; a neighbouring small owner, with the most benevolent countenance, contracted to supply him with reapers for a commission of two roubles an acre, and cheated him in the most shameless fashion; his peasant women demanded unheard-of sums, and the corn meanwhile went to waste; and here they were not getting on with the mowing, and there the Council of Guardians threatened and demanded prompt payment, in full, of interest due. . . .

'I can do nothing!' Nikolai Petrovitch cried more than once in despair. 'I can't flog them myself; and as for calling in the police captain, my principles don't allow of it, while you can do nothing with them without the fear of punishment!'

'*Du calme, du calme,*' Pavel Petrovitch would remark upon this, but even he hummed to himself, knitted his brows, and tugged at his moustache.

Bazarov held aloof from these matters, and indeed as a guest it was not for him to meddle in other people's business. The day after his arrival at Maryino, he set to work on his frogs, his infusoria, and his chemical experiments, and was for ever busy with them. Arkady, on the contrary, thought it his duty, if not to help his father, at least to make a show of being ready to help him. He gave him a patient hearing, and once offered him some advice, not with any idea of its being acted upon, but to show his interest. Farming details did not arouse any aversion in him; he used even to dream with pleasure of work on the land, but at this time his brain was swarming with other ideas. Arkady, to his own astonishment, thought incessantly of Nikolskoe; in former days he would simply have shrugged his shoulders if any one had told him that he could ever feel dull under the same roof as Bazarov—and that roof his father's! but he actually was dull and longed to get away. He tried going long walks till he was tired, but that was no use. In conversation with his father one day, he found out that Nikolai Petrovitch had in his possession rather interesting letters, written by Madame Odintsov's mother to his wife, and he gave him no rest till he got hold of the letters, for which Nikolai Petrovitch had to rummage in twenty drawers and boxes. Having gained possession of these half-crumbling papers, Arkady felt, as it were, soothed, just as though he had caught a glimpse of the goal towards which he ought now to go. 'I mean that for both of you,' he was constantly whispering—she had added that herself! 'I'll go, I'll go, hang it all!' But he recalled the last visit, the cold reception, and his former embarrassment, and timidity got the better of him. The 'go-ahead' feeling of youth, the secret desire to try his luck, to prove his powers in solitude, without the protection of any one whatever, gained the day at last. Before ten days had passed after his return to Maryino, on the pretext of studying the working of the Sunday schools, he galloped off to the town again, and from there to Nikolskoe. Urging the driver on without intermission, he flew along, like a young officer riding to battle; and he felt both frightened and light-hearted, and was breathless with impatience. 'The great thing is—one mustn't think,' he kept repeating to himself. His driver happened to be a lad of spirit; he halted before every public house, saying, 'A drink or not a drink?' but, to make up for it, when he had drunk he did not spare his horses. At last the lofty roof of the familiar house came in sight. . . . 'What am I to do?' flashed through Arkady's head. 'Well, there's no turning back now!' The three horses galloped in unison; the driver whooped and whistled at them. And now the bridge was groaning under the hoofs and wheels, and now the avenue of lopped pines seemed running to meet them. . . . There was a glimpse of a woman's pink dress against the dark green, a young face peeped out from under the light fringe of a parasol. . . . He recognised Katya, and she recognised him. Arkady told the driver to stop the galloping horses, leaped out of the carriage, and went up to her. 'It's you!' she cried, gradually flushing all over; 'let us go to my sister, she's here in the garden; she will be pleased to see you.'

Katya led Arkady into the garden. His meeting with her struck him as a particularly happy omen; he was delighted to see her, as though she were of his own kindred. Everything had happened so splendidly; no steward, no formal announcement. At a turn in the path he caught sight of Anna Sergyevna. She was standing with her back to him. Hearing footsteps, she turned slowly round.

Arkady felt confused again, but the first words she uttered soothed him at once. 'Welcome back, runaway!' she said in her even, caressing voice, and came to meet him, smiling and frowning to keep the sun and wind out of her eyes. 'Where did you pick him up, Katya?'

'I have brought you something, Anna Sergyevna,' he began, 'which you certainly don't expect.'

'You have brought yourself; that's better than anything.'

CHAPTER XXIII

HAVING seen Arkady off with ironical compassion, and given him to understand that he was not in the least deceived as to the real object of his journey, Bazarov shut himself up in complete solitude; he was overtaken by a fever for work. He did not dispute now with Pavel Petrovitch, especially as the latter assumed an excessively aristocratic demeanour in his presence, and expressed his opinions more in inarticulate sounds than in words. Only on one occasion Pavel Petrovitch fell into a controversy with the *nihilist* on the subject of the question then much discussed of the rights of the nobles of the Baltic province; but suddenly he stopped of his own accord, remarking with chilly politeness, 'However, we cannot understand one another; I, at least, have not the honour of understanding you.'

'I should think not!' cried Bazarov. 'A man's capable of understanding anything—how the æther vibrates, and what's going on in the sun—but how any other man can blow his nose differently from him, that he's incapable of understanding.

'What, is that an epigram?' observed Pavel Petrovitch inquiringly, and he walked away.

However, he sometimes asked permission to be present at Bazarov's experiments, and once even placed his perfumed face, washed with the very best soap, near the microscope to see how a transparent infusoria swallowed a green speck, and busily munched it with two very rapid sort of clappers which were in its throat. Nikolai Petrovitch visited Bazarov much oftener than his brother; he would have come every day, as he expressed it, to 'study,' if his worries on the farm had not taken off his attention. He did not hinder the young man in his scientific researches; he used to sit down somewhere in a corner of the room and look on attentively, occasionally permitting himself a discreet question. During dinner and supper-time he used to try to turn the

conversation upon physics, geology, or chemistry, seeing that
all other topics, even agriculture, to say nothing of politics,
might lead, if not to collisions, at least to mutual unpleas-
antness. Nikolai Petrovitch surmised that his brother's dislike for Bazarov was no less. An unimportant incident,
among many others, confirmed his surmises. The cholera
began to make its appearance in some places in the neighbourhood, and even 'carried off' two persons from Maryino
itself. In the night Pavel Petrovitch happened to have
rather severe symptoms. He was in pain till the morning,
but did not have recourse to Bazarov's skill. And when
he met him the following day, in reply to his question, 'Why
he had not sent for him?' answered, still quite pale, but
scrupulously brushed and shaved, 'Why, I seem to recollect
you said yourself you didn't believe in medicine.' So the
days went by. Bazarov went on obstinately and grimly
working . . . and meanwhile there was in Nikolai Petrovitch's house one creature to whom, if he did not open his
heart, he at least was glad to talk. . . . That creature was
Fenitchka.

He used to meet her for the most part early in the morning,
in the garden, or the farmyard; he never used to go to her
room to see her, and she had only once been to his door to
inquire—ought she to let Mitya have his bath or not? It
was not only that she confided in him, that she was not
afraid of him—she was positively freer and more at her
ease in her behaviour with him than with Nikolai Petrovitch
himself. It is hard to say how it came about; perhaps it
was because she unconsciously felt the absence in Bazarov
of all gentility, of all that superiority which at once attracts
and overawes. In her eyes he was both an excellent doctor
and a simple man. She looked after her baby without constraint in his presence; and once when she was suddenly
attacked with giddiness and headache—she took a spoonful
of medicine from his hand. Before Nikolai Petrovitch
she kept, as it were, at a distance from Bazarov; she acted
in this way not from hypocrisy, but from a kind of feeling
of propriety. Pavel Petrovitch she was more afraid of than
ever; for some time he had begun to watch her, and would
suddenly make his appearance, as though he sprang out of

the earth behind her back, in his English suit, with his
immovable vigilant face, and his hands in his pockets. 'It's
like a bucket of cold water on one,' Fenitchka complained
to Dunyasha, and the latter sighed in response, and thought
of another 'heartless' man. Bazarov, without the least suspicion of the fact, had become the *cruel tyrant* of her heart.

Fenitchka liked Bazarov; but he liked her too. His face
was positively transformed when he talked to her; it took
a bright, almost kind expression, and his habitual nonchalance was replaced by a sort of jesting attentiveness. Fenitchka was growing prettier every day. There is a time
in the life of young women when they suddenly begin to
expand and blossom like summer roses; this time had come
for Fenitchka. Dressed in a delicate white dress, she seemed
herself slighter and whiter; she was not tanned by the sun;
but the heat, from which she could not shield herself, spread
a slight flush over her cheeks and ears, and, shedding a soft
indolence over her whole body, was reflected in a dreamy
languor in her pretty eyes. She was almost unable to work;
her hands seem to fall naturally into her lap. She scarcely
walked at all, and was constantly sighing and complaining
with comic helplessness.

'You should go oftener to bathe, Nikolai Petrovitch told
her. He had made a large bath covered in with an awning
in one of his ponds which had not yet quite disappeared.

'Oh, Nikolai Petrovitch! But by the time one gets to the
pond, one's utterly dead, and, coming back, one's dead again.
You see, there's no shade in the garden.'

'That's true, there's no shade,' replied Nikolai Petrovitch,
rubbing his forehead.

One day at seven o'clock in the morning Bazarov, returning from a walk, came upon Fenitchka in the lilac arbour,
which was long past flowering, but was still thick and green.
She was sitting on the garden seat, and had as usual thrown
a white kerchief over her head; near her lay a whole heap
of red and white roses still wet with dew. He said good
morning to her.

'Ah! Yevgeny Vassilyitch!' she said, and lifted the edge
of her kerchief a little to look at him, in doing which her
arm was left bare to the elbow.

'What are you doing here?' said Bazarov, sitting down beside her. 'Are you making a nosegay?'

'Yes, for the table at lunch. Nikolai Petrovitch likes it.'

'But it's a long while yet to lunch time. What a heap of flowers!'

'I gathered them now, for it will be hot then, and one can't go out. One can only just breathe now. I feel quite weak with the heat. I'm really afraid whether I'm not going to be ill.'

'What an idea! Let me feel your pulse.' Bazarov took her hand, felt for the evenly-beating pulse, but did not even begin to count its throbs. 'You'll live a hundred years!' he said, dropping her hand.

'Ah, God forbid!' she cried.

'Why? Don't you want a long life?'

'Well, but a hundred years! There was an old woman near us eighty-five years old—and what a martyr she was! Dirty and deaf and bent and coughing all the time; nothing but a burden to herself. That's a dreadful life!'

'So it's better to be young?'

'Well, isn't it?'

'But why is it better? Tell me!'

'How can you ask why? Why, here I now, while I'm young, I can do everything—go and come and carry, and needn't ask any one for anything. . . . What can be better?'

'And to me it's all the same whether I'm young or old.'

'How do you mean—it's all the same? It's not possible what you say.'

'Well, judge for yourself, Fedosya Nikolaevna, what good is my youth to me. I live alone, a poor lonely creature . . .'

'That always depends on you.'

'It doesn't at all depend on me! At least, some one ought to take pity on me.'

Fenitchka gave a sidelong look at Bazarov, but said nothing. 'What's this book you have?' she asked after a short pause.

'That? That's a scientific book, very difficult.'

'And are you still studying? And don't you find it dull? You know everything already I should say.'

'It seems not everything. You try to read a little.'

'But I don't understand anything here. Is it Russian?' asked Fenitchka, taking the heavily bound book in both hands. 'How thick it is!'

'Yes, it's Russian.'

'All the same, I shan't understand anything.'

'Well, I didn't give it you for you to understand it. I wanted to look at you while you were reading. When you read, the end of your little nose moves so nicely.'

Fenitchka, who had set to work to spell out in a low voice the article on 'Creosote' she had chanced upon, laughed and threw down the book . . . it slipped from the seat on to the ground.

'Nonsense!'

'I like it too when you laugh,' observed Bazarov.

'I like it when you talk. It's just like a little brook babbling.'

Fenitchka turned her head away. 'What a person you are to talk!' she commented, picking the flowers over with her finger. 'And how can you care to listen to me? You have talked with such clever ladies.'

'Ah, Fedosya Nikolaevna! believe me; all the clever ladies in the world are not worth your little elbow.'

'Come, there's another invention!' murmured Fenitchka, clasping her hands.

Bazarov picked the book up from the ground.

'That's a medical book; why do you throw it away?'

'Medical?' repeated Fenitchka, and she turned to him again. 'Do you know, ever since you gave me those drops— do you remember?—Mitya has slept so well! I really can't think how to thank you; you are so good, really.'

'But you have to pay doctors,' observed Bazarov with a smile. 'Doctors, you know yourself, are grasping people.'

Fenitchka raised her eyes, which seemed still darker from the whitish reflection cast on the upper part of her face, and looked at Bazarov. She did not know whether he was joking or not.

'If you please, we shall be delighted. . . . I must ask Nikolai Petrovitch . . .'

'Why, do you think I want money?' Bazarov interposed. 'No; I don't want money from you.'

'What then?' asked Fenitchka.

'What?' repeated Bazarov. 'Guess!'

'A likely person I am to guess!'

'Well, I will tell you; I want . . . one of those roses.'

Fenitchka laughed again, and even clapped her hands, so amusing Bazarov's request seemed to her. She laughed, and at the same time felt flattered. Bazarov was looking intently at her.

'By all means,' she said at last; and, bending down to the seat, she began picking over the roses. 'Which will you have —a red one or a white one?'

'Red, and not too large.'

She sat up again. 'Here, take it,' she said, but at once drew back her outstretched hand, and, biting her lips, looked towards the entrance of the arbour, then listened.

'What is it?' asked Bazarov. 'Nikolai Petrovitch?'

'No . . . Mr. Kirsanov has gone to the fields . . . besides, I'm not afraid of him . . . but Pavel Petrovitch . . .I fancied . . .'

'What?'

'I fancied he was coming here. No . . . it was no one. Take it.' Fenitchka gave Bazarov the rose.

'On what grounds are you afraid of Pavel Petrovitch?'

'He always scares me. And I know you don't like him. Do you remember, you always used to quarrel with him? I don't know what your quarrel was about, but I can see you turn him about like this and like that.'

Fenitchka showed with her hands how in her opinion Bazarov turned Pavel Petrovitch about.

Bazarov smiled. 'But if he gave me a beating,' he asked, 'would you stand up for me?'

'How could I stand up for you? but no, no one will get the better of you.'

'Do you think so? But I know a hand which could overcome me if it liked.'

'What hand?'

'Why, don't you know, really? Smell, how delicious this rose smells you gave me.'

Fenitchka stretched her little neck forward, and put her face close to the flower. . . . The kerchief slipped from her head on to her shoulders; her soft mass of dark, shining, slightly ruffled hair was visible.

'Wait a minute; I want to smell it with you,' said Bazarov. He bent down and kissed her vigorously on her parted lips.

She started, pushed him back with both her hands on his breast, but pushed feebly, and he was able to renew and prolong his kiss.

A dry cough was heard behind the lilac bushes. Fenitchka instantly moved away to the other end of the seat. Pavel Petrovitch showed himself, made a slight bow, and saying with a sort of malicious mournfulness, 'You are here,' he retreated. Fenitchka at once gathered up all her roses and went out of the arbour. 'It was wrong of you, Yevgeny Vassilyevitch,' she whispered as she went. There was a note of genuine reproach in her whisper.

Bazarov remembered another recent scene, and he felt both shame and contemptuous annoyance. But he shook his head directly, ironically congratulated himself 'on his final assumption of the part of the gay Lothario,' and went off to his own room.

Pavel Petrovitch went out of the garden, and made his way with deliberate steps to the copse. He stayed there rather a long while; and when he returned to lunch, Nikolai Petrovitch inquired anxiously whether he were quite well— his face looked so gloomy.

'You know, I sometimes suffer with my liver,' Pavel Petrovitch answered tranquilly.

CHAPTER XXIV

TWO hours later he knocked at Bazarov's door.

'I must apologise for hindering you in your scientific pursuits,' he began, seating himself on a chair in the window, and leaning with both hands on a handsome walking-stick with an ivory knob (he usually walked without a stick), 'but I am constrained to beg you to spare me five minutes of your time . . . no more.'

'All my time is at your disposal,' answered Bazarov, over whose face there passed a quick change of expression directly Pavel Petrovitch crossed the threshold.

'Five minutes will be enough for me. I have come to put a single question to you.'

'A question? What is it about?'

'I will tell you, if you will kindly hear me out. At the commencement of your stay in my brother's house, before I had renounced the pleasure of conversing with you, it was my fortune to hear your opinions on many subjects; but so far as my memory serves, neither between us, nor in my presence, was the subject of single combats and duelling in general broached. Allow me to hear what are your views on that subject?'

Bazarov, who had risen to meet Pavel Petrovitch, sat down on the edge of the table and folded his arms.

'My view is,' he said, 'that from the theoretical standpoint, duelling is absurd; from the practical standpoint, now—it's quite a different matter.'

'That is, you mean to say, if I understand you right, that whatever your theoretical views on duelling, you would not in practice allow yourself to be insulted without demanding satisfaction?'

'You have guessed my meaning absolutely.'

'Very good. I am very glad to hear you say so. Your words relieve me from a state of incertitude.'

'Of uncertainty, you mean to say.'

'That is all the same! I express myself so as to be understood; I . . . am not a seminary rat. Your words save me from a rather deplorable necessity. I have made up my mind to fight you.'

Bazarov opened his eyes wide. 'Me?'

'Undoubtedly.'

'But what for, pray?'

'I could explain the reason to you,' began Pavel Petrovitch, 'but I prefer to be silent about it. To my idea your presence here is superfluous; I cannot endure you; I despise you; and if that is not enough for you . . .'

Pavel Petrovitch's eyes glittered . . . Bazarov's too were flashing.

'Very good,' he assented. 'No need of further explanations. You've a whim to try your chivalrous spirit upon me. I might refuse you this pleasure, but—so be it!'

'I am sensible of my obligation to you,' replied Pavel Petrovitch; 'and may reckon then on your accepting my challenge without compelling me to resort to violent measures.'

'That means, speaking without metaphor, to that stick?' Bazarov remarked coolly. 'That is precisely correct. It's quite unnecessary for you to insult me. Indeed, it would not be a perfectly safe proceeding. You can remain a gentleman. . . . I accept your challenge, too, like a gentleman.'

'That is excellent,' observed Pavel Petrovitch, putting his stick in the corner. 'We will say a few words directly about the conditions of our duel; but I should like first to know whether you think it necessary to resort to the formality of a trifling dispute, which might serve as a pretext for my challenge?'

'No; it's better without formalities.'

'I think so myself. I presume it is also out of place to go into the real grounds of our difference. We cannot endure one another. What more is necessary?'

'What more, indeed?' repeated Bazarov ironically.

'As regards the conditions of the meeting itself, seeing that we shall have no seconds—for where could we get them?'

'Exactly so; where could we get them?'

'Then I have the honour to lay the following proposition before you: The combat to take place early to-morrow, at six, let us say, behind the copse, with pistols, at a distance of ten paces. . . .'

'At ten paces? that will do; we hate one another at that distance.'

'We might have it eight,' remarked Pavel Petrovitch.

'We might.'

'To fire twice; and, to be ready for any result, let each put a letter in his pocket, in which he accuses himself of his end.'

'Now, that I don't approve of at all,' observed Bazarov. 'There's a slight flavour of the French novel about it, something not very plausible.'

'Perhaps. You will agree, however, that it would be unpleasant to incur a suspicion of murder?'

'I agree as to that. But there is a means of avoiding that painful reproach. We shall have no seconds, but we can have a witness.'

'And whom, allow me to inquire?'

'Why, Piotr.'

'What Piotr?'

'Your brother's valet. He's a man who has attained to the acme of contemporary culture, and he will perform his part with all the *comilfo (comme il faut)* necessary in such cases.'

'I think you are joking, sir.'

'Not at all. If you think over my suggestion, you will be convinced that it's full of common-sense and simplicity. You can't hide a candle under a bushel; but I'll undertake to prepare Piotr in a fitting manner, and bring him on to the field of battle.'

'You persist in jesting still,' Pavel Petrovitch declared, getting up from his chair. 'But after the courteous readiness you have shown me, I have no right to pretend to lay down. . . . And so, everything is arranged. . . . By the way, perhaps you have no pistols?'

'How should I have pistols, Pavel Petrovitch? I'm not in the army.'

'In that case, I offer you mine. You may rest assured that it's five years now since I shot with them.'

'That's a very consoling piece of news.'

Pavel Petrovitch took up his stick. . . . 'And now, my dear sir, it only remains for me to thank you and to leave you to your studies. I have the honour to take leave of you.'

'Till we have the pleasure of meeting again, my dear sir,' said Bazarov, conducting his visitor to the door.

Pavel Petrovitch went out, while Bazarov remained standing a minute before the door, and suddenly exclaimed, 'Pish, well, I'm dashed! how fine, and how foolish! A pretty farce we've been through! Like trained dogs dancing on their hind-paws. But to decline was out of the question; why, I do believe he'd have struck me, and then . . .' (Bazarov turned white at the very thought; all his pride was up in arms at once)—'then it might have come to my strangling him like a cat.' He went back to his microscope, but his heart was beating, and the composure necessary for taking observations had disappeared. 'He caught sight of us to-day,' he thought; 'but would he really act like this on his brother's account? And what a mighty matter is it—a kiss? There must be something else in it. Bah! isn't he perhaps in love with her himself? To be sure, he's in love; it's as clear as day. What a complication! It's a nuisance!' he decided at last; 'it's a bad job, look at it which way you will. In the first place, to risk a bullet through one's brains, and in any case to go away; and then Arkady . . . and that dear innocent pussy, Nikolai Petrovitch. It's a bad job, an awfully bad job.'

The day passed in a kind of peculiar stillness and languor. Fenitchka gave no sign of her existence; she sat in her little room like a mouse in its hole. Nikolai Petrovitch had a careworn air. He had just heard that blight had begun to appear in his wheat, upon which he had in particular rested his hopes. Pavel Petrovitch overwhelmed every one, even Prokofitch, with his icy courtesy. Bazarov began a letter to his father, but tore it up, and threw it under the table.

'If I die,' he thought,' 'they will find it out; but I'm not going to die. No, I shall struggle along in this world a good while yet.' He gave Piotr orders to come to him on

important business the next morning directly it was light.
Piotr imagined that he wanted to take him to Petersburg
with him. Bazarov went late to bed, and all night long he
was harassed by disordered dreams. . . Madame Odintsov
kept appearing in them, now she was his mother, and she
was followed by a kitten with black whiskers, and this kitten
seemed to be Fenitchka; then Pavel Petrovitch took the
shape of a great wood, with which he had yet to fight. Piotr
waked him up at four o'clock; he dressed at once, and went
out with him.

It was a lovely, fresh morning; tiny flecked clouds hovered
overhead in little curls of foam on the pale clear blue; a fine
dew lay in drops on the leaves and grass, and sparkled like
silver on the spiders' webs; the damp, dark earth seemed still
to keep traces of the rosy dawn; from the whole sky the
songs of larks came pouring in showers. Bazarov walked
as far as the copse, sat down in the shade at its edge, and
only then disclosed to Piotr the nature of the service he
expected of him. The refined valet was mortally alarmed;
but Bazarov soothed him by the assurance that he would
have nothing to do but stand at a distance and look on, and
that he would not incur any sort of responsibility. 'And
meantime,' he added, 'only think what an important part you
have to play!' Piotr threw up his hands, looked down, and
leaned against a birch-tree, looking green with terror.

The road from Maryino skirted the copse; a light dust lay
on it, untouched by wheel or foot since the previous day.
Bazarov unconsciously stared along this road, picked and
gnawed a blade of grass, while he kept repeating to himself,
'What a piece of foolery!' The chill of the early morning
made him shiver twice. . . . Piotr looked at him dejectedly,
but Bazarov only smiled; he was not afraid.

The tramp of horses' hoofs was heard along the road. . . .
A peasant came into sight from behind the trees. He was
driving before him two horses hobbled together, and as he
passed Bazarov he looked at him rather strangely, without
touching his cap, which it was easy to see disturbed Piotr,
as an unlucky omen. 'There's some one else up early too,'
thought Bazarov; 'but he at least has got up for work, while
we . . .'

'Fancy the gentleman's coming,' Piotr faltered suddenly.

Bazarov raised his head and saw Pavel Petrovitch. Dressed in a light check jacket and snow-white trousers, he was walking rapidly along the road; under his arm he carried a box wrapped up in green cloth.

'I beg your pardon, I believe I have kept you waiting,' he observed, bowing first to Bazarov, then to Piotr, whom he treated respectfully at that instant, as representing something in the nature of a second. 'I was unwilling to wake my man.'

'It doesn't matter,' answered Bazarov; 'we've only just arrived ourselves.'

'Ah! so much the better!' Pavel Petrovitch took a look round. 'There's no one in sight; no one hinders us. We can proceed?'

'Let us proceed.'

'You do not, I presume, desire any fresh explanations?'

'No, I don't.'

'Would you like to load?' inquired Pavel Petrovitch, taking the pistols out of the box.

'No; you load, and I will measure out the paces. My legs are longer,' added Bazarov with a smile. 'One, two, three.'

'Yevgeny Vassilyevitch,' Piotr faltered with an effort (he was shaking as though he were in a fever), 'say what you like, I am going farther off.'

'Four . . . five. . . . Good. Move away, my good fellow, move away; you may get behind a tree even, and stop up your ears, only don't shut your eyes; and if any one falls, run and pick him up. Six . . . seven . . . eight. . . .' Bazarov stopped. 'Is that enough?' he said, turning to Pavel Petrovitch; 'or shall I add two paces more?'

'As you like,' replied the latter, pressing down the second bullet.

'Well, we'll make it two paces more.' Bazarov drew a line on the ground with the toe of his boot. 'There's the barrier then. By the way, how many paces may each of us go back from the barrier? That's an important question too. That point was not discussed yesterday.'

'I imagine, ten,' replied Pavel Petrovitch, handing Bazarov both pistols. 'Will you be so good as to choose?'

'I will be so good. But, Pavel Petrovitch, you must admit our combat is singular to the point of absurdity. Only look at the countenance of our second.'

'You are disposed to laugh at everything,' answered Pavel Petrovitch. 'I acknowledge the strangeness of our duel, but I think it my duty to warn you that I intend to fight seriously. *A bon entendeur, salut!*'

'Oh! I don't doubt that we've made up our minds to make away with each other; but why not laugh too and unite *utile dulci?* You talk to me in French, while I talk to you in Latin.'

'I am going to fight in earnest,' repeated Pavel Petrovitch, and he walked off to his place. Bazarov on his side counted off ten paces from the barrier, and stood still.

'Are you ready?' asked Pavel Petrovitch.

'Perfectly.'

'We can approach one another.'

Bazarov moved slowly forward, and Pavel Petrovitch, his left hand thrust in his pocket, walked towards him, gradually raising the muzzle of his pistol. . . . 'He's aiming straight at my nose,' thought Bazarov, 'and doesn't he blink down it carefully, the ruffian! Not an agreeable sensation though. I'm going to look at his watch chain.'

Something whizzed sharply by his very ear, and at the same instant there was the sound of a shot. 'I heard it, so it must be all right,' had time to flash through Bazarov's brain. He took one more step, and without taking aim, pressed the spring.

Pavel Petrovitch gave a slight start, and clutched at his thigh. A stream of blood began to trickle down his white trousers.

Bazarov flung aside the pistol, and went up to his antagonist. 'Are you wounded?' he said.

'You had the right to call me up to the barrier,' said Pavel Petrovitch, 'but that's of no consequence. According to our agreement, each of us has the right to one more shot.'

'All right, but, excuse me, that'll do another time," answered Bazarov, catching hold of Pavel Petrovitch, who was beginning to turn pale. 'Now, I'm not a duellist, but a doctor, and I must have a look at your wound before anything else. Piotr! come here, Piotr! where have you got to?'

'That's all nonsense. . . . I need no one's aid,' Pavel Petrovitch declared jerkily, 'and . . . we must . . . again . . .' He tried to pull at his moustaches, but his hand failed him, his eyes grew dim, and he lost consciousness.

'Here's a pretty pass! A fainting fit! What next!' Bazarov cried unconsciously, as he laid Pavel Petrovitch on the grass. 'Let's have a look what's wrong.' He pulled out a handkerchief, wiped away the blood, and began feeling round the wound. . . . 'The bone's not touched,' he muttered through his teeth; 'the ball didn't go deep; one muscle, *vastus externus*, grazed. He'll be dancing about in three weeks! . . . And to faint! Oh, these nervous people, how I hate them! My word, what a delicate skin!'

'Is he killed?' the quaking voice of Piotr came rustling behind his back.

Bazarov looked round. 'Go for some water as quick as you can, my good fellow, and he'll outlive us yet.'

But the modern servant seemed not to understand his words, and he did not stir. Pavel Petrovitch slowly opened his eyes. 'He will die!' whispered Piotr, and he began crossing himself.

'You are right . . . What an imbecile countenance!' remarked the wounded gentleman with a forced smile.

'Well, go for the water, damn you!' shouted Bazarov.

'No need. . . . It was a momentary *vertigo*. . . . Help me to sit up . . . there, that's right. . . . I only need something to bind up this scratch, and I can reach home on foot, or else you can send a droshky for me. The duel, if you are willing, shall not be renewed. You have behaved honourably . . . to-day, to-day—observe.'

'There's no need to recall the past,' rejoined Bazarov; 'and as regards the future, it's not worth while for you to trouble your head about that either, for I intend being off without delay. Let me bind up your leg now; your wound's not serious, but it's always best to stop bleeding. But first I must bring this corpse to his senses.'

Bazarov shook Piotr by the collar, and sent him for a droshky.

'Mind you don't frighten my brother,' Pavel Petrovitch said to him; 'don't dream of informing him.'

Piotr flew off; and while he was running for a droshky, the two antagonists sat on the ground and said nothing. Pavel Petrovitch tried not to look at Bazarov; he did not want to be reconciled to him in any case; he was ashamed of his own haughtiness, of his failure; he was ashamed of the whole position he had brought about, even while he felt it could not have ended in a more favourable manner. 'At any rate, there will be no scandal,' he consoled himself by reflecting, 'and for that I am thankful.' The silence was prolonged, a silence distressing and awkward. Both of them were ill at ease. Each was conscious that the other understood him. That is pleasant to friends, and always very unpleasant to those who are not friends, especially when it is impossible either to have things out or to separate.

'Haven't I bound up your leg too tight?' inquired Bazarov at last.

'No, not at all; it's capital,' answered Pavel Petrovitch; and after a brief pause, he added, 'There's no deceiving my brother; we shall have to tell him we quarrelled over politics.'

'Very good,' assented Bazarov. 'You can say I insulted all anglomaniacs.'

'That will do capitally. What do you imagine that man thinks of us now?' continued Pavel Petrovitch, pointing to the same peasant, who had driven the hobbled horses past Bazarov a few minutes before the duel, and going back again along the road, took off his cap at the sight of the 'gentlefolk.'

'Who can tell!' answered Bazarov; 'it's quite likely he thinks nothing. The Russian peasant is that mysterious unknown about whom Mrs. Radcliffe used to talk so much. Who is to understand him! He doesn't understand himself!'

'Ah! so that's your idea!' Pavel Petrovitch began; and suddenly he cried, 'Look what your fool of a Piotr has done! Here's my brother galloping up to us!'

Bazarov turned round and saw the pale face of Nikolai Petrovitch, who was sitting in the droshky. He jumped out of it before it had stopped, and rushed up to his brother.

'What does this mean?' he said in an agitated voice. 'Yevgeny Vassilyitch, pray, what is this?'

'Nothing,' answered Pavel Petrovitch; 'they have alarmed you for nothing. I had a little dispute with Mr. Bazarov, and I have had to pay for it a little.'

'But what was it all about, mercy on us!'

'How can I tell you? Mr. Bazarov alluded disrespectfully to Sir Robert Peel. I must hasten to add that I am the only person to blame in all this, while Mr. Bazarov has behaved most honourably. I called him out.'

'But you're covered with blood, good Heavens!'

'Well, did you suppose I had water in my veins? But this blood-letting is positively beneficial to me. Isn't that so, doctor? Help me to get into the droshky, and don't give way to melancholy. I shall be quite well to-morrow. That's it; capital. Drive on, coachman.'

Nikolai Petrovitch walked after the droshky; Bazarov was remaining where he was. . . .

'I must ask you to look after my brother,' Nikolai Petrovitch said to him, 'till we get another doctor from the town.'

Bazarov nodded his head without speaking. In an hour's time Pavel Petrovitch was already lying in bed with a skilfully bandaged leg. The whole house was alarmed; Fenitchka fainted. Nikolai Petrovitch kept stealthily wringing his hands, while Pavel Petrovitch laughed and joked, especially with Bazarov; he had put on a fine cambric night-shirt, an elegant morning wrapper, and a fez, did not allow the blinds to be drawn down, and humorously complained of the necessity of being kept from food.

Towards night, however, he began to be feverish; his head ached. The doctor arrived from the town. (Nikolai Petrovitch would not listen to his brother, and indeed Bazarov himself did not wish him to; he sat the whole day in his room, looking yellow and vindictive, and only went in to the invalid for as brief a time as possible; twice he happened to meet Fenitchka, but she shrank away from him with horror.) The new doctor advised a cooling diet; he confirmed, however, Bazarov's assertion that there was no danger. Nikolai Petrovitch told him his brother had wounded himself by accident, to which the doctor responded,

S—13

'Hm!' but having twenty-five silver roubles slipped into his hand on the spot, he observed, 'You don't say so! Well, it's a thing that often happens, to be sure.'

No one in the house went to bed or undressed. Nikolai Petrovitch kept going in to his brother on tiptoe, retreating on tiptoe again; the latter dozed, moaned a little, told him in French, *Couchez-vous,* and asked for drink. Nikolai Petrovitch sent Fenitchka twice to take him a glass of lemonade; Pavel Petrovitch gazed at her intently, and drank off the glass to the last drop. Towards morning the fever had increased a little; there was slight delirium. At first Pavel Petrovitch uttered incoherent words; then suddenly he opened his eyes, and seeing his brother near his bed bending anxiously over him, he said, 'Don't you think, Nikolai, Fenitchka has something in common with Nellie?'

'What Nellie, Pavel dear?'

'How can you ask? Princess R——. Especially in the upper part of the face. *C'est de la même famille.*'

Nikolai Petrovitch made no answer, while inwardly he marvelled at the persistence of old passions in man. 'It's like this when it comes to the surface,' he thought.

'Ah, how I love that light-headed creature!' moaned Pavel Petrovitch, clasping his hands mournfully behind his head. 'I can't bear any insolent upstart to dare to touch . . . he whispered a few minutes later.

Nikolai Petrovitch only sighed; he did not even suspect to whom these words referred.

Bazarov presented himself before him at eight o'clock the next day. He had already had time to pack, and to set free all his frogs, insects, and birds.

'You have come to say good-bye to me?' said Nikolai Petrovitch, getting up to meet him.

'Yes.'

'I understand you, and approve of you fully. My poor brother, of course, is to blame; and he is punished for it. He told me himself that he made it impossible for you to act otherwise. I believe that you could not avoid this duel, which . . . which to some extent is explained by the almost constant antagonism of your respective views.' (Nikolai Petrovitch began to get a little mixed up in his words.) 'My brother is a man of the old school, hot-tempered and obstinate. . . . Thank God that it has ended as it has. I have taken every precaution to avoid publicity.'

'I'm leaving you my address, in case there's any fuss,' Bazarov remarked casually.

'I hope there will be no fuss, Yevgeny Vassilyitch. . . . I am very sorry your stay in my house should have such a . . . such an end. It is the more distressing to me through Arkady's . . .'

'I shall be seeing him, I expect,' replied Bazarov, in whom 'explanations' and 'protestations' of every sort always aroused a feeling of impatience; 'in case I don't, I beg you to say good-bye to him for me, and accept the expression of my regret.'

'And I beg . . .' answered Nikolai Petrovitch. But Bazarov went off without waiting for the end of his sentence.

When he heard of Bazarov's going, Pavel Petrovitch expressed a desire to see him, and shook his hand. But even then he remained as cold as ice; he realised that Pavel Petrovitch wanted to play the magnanimous. He did not succeed in saying good-bye to Fenitchka; he only exchanged glances with her at the window. Her face struck him as looking dejected. 'She'll come to grief, perhaps,' he said to himself. . . . 'But who knows? she'll pull through somehow, I dare say!' Piotr, however, was so overcome that he wept on his shoulder, till Bazarov damped him by asking if he'd a constant supply laid on in his eyes; while Dunyasha was obliged to run away into the wood to hide her emotion. The originator of all this woe got into a light cart, smoked a cigar, and when at the third mile, at the bend in the road, the Kirsanovs' farm, with its new house, could be seen in a long line, he merely spat, and muttering, 'Cursed snobs!' wrapped himself closer in his cloak.

Pavel Petrovitch was soon better; but he had to keep his bed about a week. He bore his captivity, as he called it, pretty patiently, though he took great pains over his toilette, and had everything scented with eau-de-cologne. Nikolai Petrovitch used to read him the journals; Fenitchka waited on him as before, brought him lemonade, soup, boiled eggs, and tea; but she was overcome with secret dread whenever she went into his room. Pavel Petrovitch's unexpected action had alarmed every one in the house, and her more than any one; Prokofitch was the only person not agitated by it; he discoursed upon how gentlemen in his day used to fight, but only with real gentlemen; low curs like that they used to order a horsewhipping in the stable for their insolence.

Fenitchka's conscience scarcely reproached her; but she was tormented at times by the thought of the real cause of the quarrel; and Pavel Petrovitch too looked at her so strangely . . . that even when her back was turned, she felt his eyes upon her. She grew thinner from constant inward agitation, and, as is always the way, became still more charming.

One day—the incident took place in the morning—Pavel Petrovitch felt better and moved from his bed to the sofa, while Nikolai Petrovitch, having satisfied himself he was better, went off to the threshing-floor. Fenitchka brought him a cup of tea, and setting it down on a little table, was about to withdraw. Pavel Petrovitch detained her.

'Where are you going in such a hurry, Fedosya Niko-laevna?' he began; 'are you busy?'

' . . . I have to pour out tea.'

'Dunyasha will do that without you; sit a little while with a poor invalid. By the way, I must have a little talk with you.'

Fenitchka sat down on the edge of an easy-chair, without speaking.

'Listen,' said Pavel Petrovitch, tugging at his moustaches; 'I have long wanted to ask you something; you seem somehow afraid of me?'

'I?'

'Yes, you. You never look at me, as though your conscience were not at rest.'

Fenitchka crimsoned, but looked at Pavel Petrovitch. He impressed her as looking strange, and her heart began throbbing slowly.

'Is your conscience at rest?' he questioned her.

'Why should it not be at rest?' she faltered.

'Goodness knows why! Besides, whom can you have wronged? Me? That is not likely. Any other people in the house here? That, too, is something incredible. Can it be my brother? But you love him, don't you?'

'I love him.'

'With your whole soul, with your whole heart?'

'I love Nikolai Petrovitch with my whole heart.'

'Truly? Look at me, Fenitchka.' (It was the first time he had called her that name.) 'You know, it's a great sin telling lies!'

'I am not telling lies, Pavel Petrovitch. Not love Nikolai Petrovitch—I shouldn't care to live after that.'

'And will you never give him up for any one?'

'For whom could I give him up?'

'For whom indeed! Well, how about that gentleman who has just gone away from here?'

Fenitchka got up. 'My God, Pavel Petrovitch, what are you torturing me for? What have I done to you? How can such things be said?' . .

'Fenitchka,' said Pavel Petrovitch, in a sorrowful voice, 'you know I saw . . .'

'What did you see?'

'Well, there . . . in the arbour.'

Fenitchka crimsoned to her hair and to her ears. 'How was I to blame for that?' she articulated with an effort.

Pavel Petrovitch raised himself up. 'You were not to blame? No? Not at all?'

'I love Nikolai Petrovitch, and no one else in the world, and I shall always love him!' cried Fenitchka with sudden force, while her throat seemed fairly breaking with sobs. 'As for what you saw, at the dreadful day of judgment I will say I'm not to blame, and wasn't to blame for it, and I would rather die at once if people can suspect me of such a thing against my benefactor, Nikolai Petrovitch.'

But here her voice broke, and at the same time she felt that Pavel Petrovitch was snatching and pressing her hand. . . She looked at him, and was fairly petrified. He had turned even paler than before; his eyes were shining, and what was most marvellous of all, one large solitary tear was rolling down his cheek.

'Fenitchka!' he was saying in a strange whisper; 'love him, love my brother! Don't give him up for any one in the world; don't listen to any one else! Think what can be more terrible than to love and not be loved! Never leave my poor Nikolai!'

Fenitchka's eyes were dry, and her terror had passed away, so great was her amazement. But what were her feelings when Pavel Petrovitch, Pavel Petrovitch himself, put her hand to his lips and seemed to pierce into it without kissing it, and only heaving convulsive sighs from time to time. . . .

'Goodness,' she thought, 'isn't it some attack coming on him?' . . .

At that instant his whole ruined life was stirred up within him.

The staircase creaked under rapidly approaching footsteps. . . . He pushed her away from him, and let his head drop back on the pillow. The door opened, and Nikolai Petrovitch entered, cheerful, fresh, and ruddy. Mitya, as fresh and ruddy as his father, in nothing but his little shirt, was frisking on his shoulder, catching the big buttons of his rough country coat with his little bare toes.

Fenitchka simply flung herself upon him, and clasping him and her son together in her arms, dropped her head on his shoulder. Nikolai Petrovitch was surprised; Fenitchka, the reserved and staid Fenitchka, had never given him a caress in the presence of a third person.

'What's the matter?' he said, and, glancing at his brother, he gave her Mitya. 'You don't feel worse?' he inquired, going up to Pavel Petrovitch.

He buried his face in a cambric handkerchief. 'No . . . not at all . . . on the contrary, I am much better.'

'You were in too great a hurry to move on to the sofa. Where are you going?' added Nikolai Petrovitch, turning round to Fenitchka; but she had already closed the door behind her. 'I was bringing in my young hero to show you, he's been crying for his uncle. Why has she carried him off? What's wrong with you, though? Has anything passed between you, eh?'

'Brother!' said Pavel Petrovitch solemnly.

Nikolai Petrovitch started. He felt dismayed, he could not have said why himself.

'Brother,' repeated Pavel Petrovitch, 'give me your word that you will carry out my one request.'

'What request? Tell me.'

'It is very important; the whole happiness of your life, to my idea, depends on it. I have been thinking a great deal all this time over what I want to say to you now. . . . Brother, do your duty, the duty of an honest and generous man; put an end to the scandal and bad example you are setting—you, the best of men!'

'What do you mean, Pavel?'

'Marry Fenitchka. . . . She loves you; she is the mother of your son.'

Nikolai Petrovitch stepped back a pace, and flung up his hands. 'Do you say that, Pavel? you whom I have always regarded as the most determined opponent of such marriages! You say that? Don't you know that it has simply been out of respect for you that I have not done what you so rightly call my duty?'

'You were wrong to respect me in that case,' Pavel Petrovitch responded, with a weary smile. 'I begin to think Bazarov was right in accusing me of snobbishness. No, dear brother, don't let us worry ourselves about appearances and the world's opinion any more; we are old folks and humble now; it's time we laid aside vanity of all kinds. Let us, just as you say, do our duty; and mind, we shall get happiness that way into the bargain.'

Nikolai Petrovitch rushed to embrace his brother.

'You have opened my eyes completely!' he cried. 'I was right in always declaring you the wisest and kindest-hearted fellow in the world, and now I see you are just as reasonable as you are noble-hearted.'

'Quietly, quietly,' Pavel Petrovitch interrupted him; 'don't hurt the leg of your reasonable brother, who at close upon fifty has been fighting a duel like an ensign. So, then, it's a settled matter; Fenitchka is to be my . . . *belle sœur.*'

'My dearest Pavel! But what will Arkady say?'

'Arkady? he'll be in ecstasies, you may depend upon it! Marriage is against his principles, but then the sentiment of equality in him will be gratified. And, after all, what sense have class distinctions *au dix-neuvième siècle?'*

'Ah, Pavel, Pavel! let me kiss you once more! Don't be afraid, I'll be careful.'

The brothers embraced each other.

'What do you think, should you not inform her of your intention now?' queried Pavel Petrovitch.

'Why be in a hurry?' responded Nikolai Petrovitch. 'Has there been any conversation between you?'

'Conversation between us? *Quelle idée!'*

'Well, that is all right then. First of all, you must get well, and meanwhile there's plenty of time. We must think it over well, and consider . . .'

'But your mind is made up, I suppose?'

'Of course, my mind is made up, and I thank you from the bottom of my heart. I will leave you now; you must rest; any excitement is bad for you. . . . But we will talk it over again. Sleep well, dear heart, and God bless you!'

'What is he thanking me like that for?' thought Pavel Petrovitch, when he was left alone. 'As though it did not depend on him! I will go away directly he is married, somewhere a long way off—to Dresden or Florence, and will live there till I——'

Pavel Petrovitch moistened his forehead with eau de cologne, and closed his eyes. His beautiful, emaciated head, the glaring daylight shining full upon it, lay on the white pillow like the head of a dead man. . . . And indeed he was a dead man.

CHAPTER XXV

AT Nikolskoe Katya and Arkady were sitting in the garden on a turf seat in the shade of a tall ash tree; Fifi had placed himself on the ground near them, giving his slender body that graceful curve, which is known among dog-fanciers as 'the hare bend.' Both Arkady and Katya were silent; he was holding a half-open book in his hands, while she was picking out of a basket the few crumbs of bread left in it, and throwing them to a small family of sparrows, who with the frightened impudence peculiar to them were hopping and chirping at her very feet. A faint breeze stirring in the ash leaves kept slowly moving pale-gold flecks of sunlight up and down over the path and Fifi's tawny back; a patch of unbroken shade fell upon Arkady and Katya; only from time to time a bright streak gleamed on her hair. Both were silent, but the very way in which they were silent, in which they were sitting together, was expressive of confidential intimacy; each of them seemed not even to be thinking of his companion, while secretly rejoicing in his presence. Their faces, too, had changed since we saw them last; Arkady looked more tranquil, Katya brighter and more daring.

'Don't you think,' began Arkady, 'that the ash has been very well named in Russian *yasen;* no other tree is so lightly and brightly transparent *(yasno)* against the air as it is.'

Katya raised her eyes to look upward, and assented, 'Yes'; while Arkady thought, 'Well, she does not reproach me for *talking finely.*'

'I don't like Heine,' said Katya, glancing towards the book which Arkady was holding in his hands, 'either when he laughs or when he weeps; I like him when he's thoughtful and melancholy.'

'And I like him when he laughs,' remarked Arkady.

'That's the relics left in you of your old satirical tendencies.' ('Relics!' thought Arkady—'if Bazarov had heard that?') 'Wait a little; we shall transform you.'

'Who will transform me? You?'

'Who?—my sister; Porfiry Platonovitch, whom you've given up quarrelling with; auntie, whom you escorted to church the day before yesterday.'

'Well, I couldn't refuse! And as for Anna Sergyevna, she agreed with Yevgeny in a great many things, you remember?'

'My sister was under his influence then, just as you were.'

'As I was? Do you discover, may I ask, that I've shaken off his influence now?'

Katya did not speak.

'I know,' pursued Arkady, 'you never liked him.'

'I can have no opinion about him.'

'Do you know, Katerina Sergyevna, every time I hear that answer I disbelieve it. . . . There is no man that every one of us could not have an opinion about! That's simply a way of getting out of it.'

'Well, I'll say, then, I don't. . . . It's not exactly that I don't like him, but I feel that he's of a different order from me, and I am different from him . . . and you too are different from him.'

'How's that?'

'How can I tell you. . . . He's a wild animal, and you and I are tame.'

'Am I tame too?'

Katya nodded.

Arkady scratched his ear. 'Let me tell you, Katerina Sergyevna, do you know, that's really an insult?'

'Why, would you like to be a wild——'

'Not wild, but strong, full of force.'

'It's no good wishing for that. . . . Your friend, you see, doesn't wish for it, but he has it.'

'Hm! So you imagine he had a great influence on Anna Sergyevna?'

'Yes. But no one can keep the upper hand of her for long,' added Katya in a low voice.

'Why do you think that?'

'She's very proud. . . I didn't mean that . . . she values her independence a great deal.'

'Who doesn't value it?' asked Arkady, and the thought flashed through his mind, 'What good is it?' 'What good is it?' it occurred to Katya to wonder too. When young people are often together on friendly terms, they are constantly stumbling on the same ideas.

Arkady smiled, and, coming slightly closer to Katya, he said in a whisper, 'Confess that you are a little afraid of her.'

'Of whom?'

'Her,' repeated Arkady significantly.

'And how about you?' Katya asked in her turn.

'I am too, observe I said, I am *too.*'

Katya threatened him with her finger. 'I wonder at that,' she began; 'my sister has never felt so friendly to you as just now; much more so than when you first came.'

'Really!'

'Why, haven't you noticed it? Aren't you glad of it?'

Arkady grew thoughtful.

'How have I succeeded in gaining Anna Sergyevna's good opinion? Wasn't it because I brought her your mother's letters?'

'Both that and other causes, which I shan't tell you.'

'Why?'

'I shan't say.'

'Oh! I know; you're very obstinate.'

'Yes, I am.'

'And observant.'

Katya gave Arkady a sidelong look. 'Perhaps so; does that irritate you? What are you thinking of?'

'I am wondering how you have come to be as observant as in fact you are. You are so shy, so reserved; you keep every one at a distance.'

'I have lived a great deal alone; that drives one to reflection. But do I really keep every one at a distance?'

Arkady flung a grateful glance at Katya.

'That's all very well,' he pursued; 'but people in your position—I mean in your circumstances—don't often have that faculty; it is hard for them, as it is for sovereigns, to get at the truth.'

'But, you see, I am not rich.'

Arkady was taken aback, and did not at once understand Katya. 'Why, of course, the property's all her sister's!'

struck him suddenly; the thought was not unpleasing to him.
'How nicely you said that!' he commented.

'What?'

'You said it nicely, simply, without being ashamed or
making a boast of it. By the way, I imagine there must
always be something special, a kind of pride of a sort in the
feeling of any man, who knows and says he is poor.'

'I have never experienced anything of that sort, thanks
to my sister. I only referred to my position just now because
it happened to come up.'

'Well; but you must own you have a share of that pride
I spoke of just now.'

'For instance?'

'For instance, you—forgive the question—you wouldn't
marry a rich man, I fancy, would you?'

'If I loved him very much. . . . No, I think even then I
wouldn't marry him.'

'There! you see!' cried Arkady, and after a short pause he
added, 'And why wouldn't you marry him?'

'Because even in the ballads unequal matches are always
unlucky.'

'You want to rule, perhaps, or . . .'

'Oh, no! why should I? On the contrary, I am ready to
obey; only inequality is intolerable. To respect one's self
and obey, that I can understand, that's happiness; but a subordinate existence . . . No, I've had enough of that as it is.'

'Enough of that as it is,' Arkady repeated after Katya.
'Yes, yes,' he went on, 'you're not Anna Sergyevna's sister
for nothing; you're just as independent as she is; but you're
more reserved. I'm certain you wouldn't be the first to give
expression to your feeling, however strong and holy it
might be . . .'

'Well, what would you expect?' asked Katya.

'You're equally clever; and you've as much, if not more,
character than she.'

'Don't compare me with my sister, please,' interposed
Katya hurriedly; 'that's too much to my disadvantage. You
seem to forget my sister's beautiful and clever, and . . . you
in particular, Arkady Nikolaevitch, ought not to say such
things, and with such a serious face too.'

'What do you mean by "you in particular"—and what makes you suppose I am joking?'

'Of course, you are joking.'

'You think so? But what if I'm persuaded of what I say? If I believe I have not put it strongly enough even?'

'I don't understand you.'

'Really? Well, now I see; I certainly took you to be more observant than you are.'

'How?'

Arkady made no answer, and turned away, while Katya looked for a few more crumbs in the basket, and began throwing them to the sparrows; but she moved her arm too vigorously, and they flew away, without stopping to pick them up.

'Katerina Sergyevna!' began Arkady suddenly; 'it's of no consequence to you, probably; but, let me tell you, I put you not only above your sister, but above every one in the world.'

He got up and went quickly away, as though he were frightened at the words that had fallen from his lips.

Katya let her two hands drop together with the basket on to her lap, and with bent head she stared a long while after Arkady. Gradually a crimson flush came faintly out upon her cheeks; but her lips did not smile and her dark eyes had a look of perplexity and some other, as yet undefined, feeling.

'Are you alone?' she heard the voice of Anna Sergyevna near her; 'I thought you came into the garden with Arkady.'

Katya slowly raised her eyes to her sister (elegantly, even elaborately dressed, she was standing in the path and tickling Fifi's ears with the tip of her open parasol), and slowly replied. 'Yes, I'm alone.'

'So I see,' she answered with a smile; 'I suppose he has gone to his room.'

'Yes.'

'Have you been reading together?'

'Yes.'

Anna Sergyevna took Katya by the chin and lifted her face up.

'You have not been quarrelling, I hope?'

'No,' said Katya, and she quietly removed her sister's hand.

'How solemnly you answer! I expected to find him here, and meant to suggest his coming a walk with me. That's what he is always asking for. They have sent you some shoes from the town; go and try them on; I noticed only yesterday your old ones are quite shabby. You never think enough about it, and you have such charming little feet! Your hands are nice too . . . though they're large; so you must make the most of your little feet. But you're not vain.'

Anna Sergyevna went farther along the path with a light rustle of her beautiful gown; Katya got up from the grass, and, taking Heine with her, went away too—but not to try on her shoes.

'Charming little feet!' she thought, as she slowly and lightly mounted the stone steps of the terrace, which were burning with the heat of the sun; 'charming little feet you call them. . . . Well, he shall be at them.'

But all at once a feeling of shame came upon her, and she ran swiftly upstairs.

Arkady had gone along the corridor to his room; a steward had overtaken him, and announced that Mr. Bazarov was in his room.

'Yevgeny!' murmured Arkady, almost with dismay; 'has he been here long?'

'Mr. Bazarov arrived this minute, sir, and gave orders not to announce him to Anna Sergyevna, but to show him straight up to you.'

'Can any misfortune have happened at home?' thought Arkady, and running hurriedly up the stairs, he at once opened the door. The sight of Bazarov at once reassured him, though a more experienced eye might very probably have discerned signs of inward agitation in the sunken, though still energetic face of the unexpected visitor. With a dusty cloak over his shoulders, with a cap on his head, he was sitting at the window; he did not even get up when Arkady flung himself with noisy exclamations on his neck.

'This is unexpected! What good luck brought you?' he kept repeating, bustling about the room like one who both imagines himself and wishes to show himself delighted. 'I suppose everything's all right at home; every one's well, eh?'

'Everything's all right, but not every one's well,' said

Bazarov. 'Don't be a chatterbox, but send for some kvass for me, sit down, and listen while I tell you all about it in a few, but, I hope, pretty vigorous sentences.'

Arkady was quiet while Bazarov described his duel with Pavel Petrovitch. Arkady was very much surprised, and even grieved, but he did not think it necessary to show this; he only asked whether his uncle's wound was really not serious; and on receiving the reply that it was most interesting, but not from a medical point of view, he gave a forced smile, but at heart he felt both wounded and as it were ashamed. Bazarov seemed to understand him.

'Yes, my dear fellow,' he commented, 'you see what comes of living with feudal personages. You turn a feudal personage yourself, and find yourself taking part in knightly tournaments. Well, so I set off for my father's,' Bazarov wound up, 'and I've turned in here on the way . . . to tell you all this, I should say, if I didn't think a useless lie a piece of foolery. No, I turned in here—the devil only knows why. You see, it's sometimes a good thing for a man to take himself by the scruff of the neck and pull himself up, like a radish out of its bed; that's what I've been doing of late. . . . But I wanted to have one more look at what I'm giving up, at the bed where I've been planted.'

'I hope those words don't refer to me,' responded Arkady with some emotion; 'I hope you don't think of giving me up?'

Bazarov turned an intent, almost piercing look upon him.

'Would that be such a grief to you? It strikes me *you* have given me up already, you look so fresh and smart. . . . Your affair with Anna Sergyevna must be getting on successfully.'

'What do you mean by my affair with Anna Sergyevna?'

'Why, didn't you come here from the town on her account, chicken? By the way, how are those Sunday schools getting on? Do you mean to tell me you're not in love with her? Or have you already reached the stage of discretion?'

'Yevgeny, you know I have always been open with you; I can assure you, I will swear to you, you're making a mistake.'

'Hm! That's another story,' remarked Bazarov in an undertone. 'But you needn't be in a taking, it's a matter of absolute indifference to me. A sentimentalist would say,

"I feel that our paths are beginning to part," but I will simply say that we're tired of each other.'

'Yevgeny . . .'

'My dear soul, there's no great harm in that. One gets tired of much more than that in this life. And now I suppose we'd better say good-bye, hadn't we? Ever since I've been here I've had such a loathsome feeling, just as if I'd been reading Gogol's effusions to the governor of Kalouga's wife. By the way, I didn't tell them to take the horses out.'

'Upon my word, this is too much!'

'Why?'

'I'll say nothing of myself; but that would be discourteous to the last degree to Anna Sergyevna, who will certainly wish to see you.'

'Oh, you're mistaken there.'

'On the contrary, I am certain I'm right,' retorted Arkady. 'And what are you pretending for? If it comes to that, haven't you come here on her account yourself?'

'That may be so, but you're mistaken any way.'

But Arkady was right. Anna Sergyevna desired to see Bazarov, and sent a summons to him by a steward. Bazarov changed his clothes before going to her; it turned out that he had packed his new suit so as to be able to get it out easily.

Madame Odintsov received him not in the room where he had so unexpectedly declared his love to her, but in the draw-ing-room. She held her finger tips out to him cordially, but her face betrayed an involuntary sense of tension.

'Anna Sergyevna,' Bazarov hastened to say, 'before every-thing else I must set your mind at rest. Before you is a poor mortal, who has come to his senses long ago, and hopes other people too have forgotten his follies. I am going away for a long while; and though, as you will allow, I'm by no means a very soft creature, it would be anything but cheerful for me to carry away with me the idea that you remember me with repugnance.'

Anna Sergyevna gave a deep sigh like one who has just climbed up a high mountain, and her face was lighted up by a smile. She held out her hand a second time to Bazarov, and responded to his pressure.

'Let bygones be bygones,' she said. 'I am all the readier

to do so because, speaking from my conscience, I was to blame then too for flirting or something. In a word, let us be friends as before. That was a dream, wasn't it? And who remembers dreams?'

'Who remembers them? And besides, love . . . you know, is a purely imaginary feeling.'

'Really? I am very glad to hear that.'

So Anna Sergyevna spoke, and so spoke Bazarov; they both supposed they were speaking the truth. Was the truth, the whole truth, to be found in their words? They could not themselves have said, and much less could the author. But a conversation followed between them precisely as though they completely believed one another.

Anna Sergyevna asked Bazarov, among other things, what he had been doing at the Kirsanovs'. He was on the point of telling her about his duel with Pavel Petrovitch, but he checked himself with the thought that she might imagine he was trying to make himself interesting, and answered that he had been at work all the time.

'And I,' observed Anna Sergyevna, 'had a fit of depression at first, goodness knows why; I even made plans for going abroad, fancy! . . . Then it passed off, your friend Arkady Nikolaitch came, and I fell back into my old routine, and took up my real part again.'

'What part is that, may I ask?'

'The character of aunt, guardian, mother—call it what you like. By the way, do you know I used not quite to understand your close friendship with Arkady Nikolaitch; I thought him rather insignificant. But now I have come to know him better, and to see that he is clever. . . . And he's young, he's young . . . that's the great thing . . . not like you and me, Yevgeny Vassilyitch.'

'Is he still as shy in your company?' queried Bazarov.

'Why, was he?' . . . Anna Sergyevna began, and after a brief pause she went on: 'He has grown more confiding now; he talks to me. He used to avoid me before. Though, indeed, I didn't seek his society either. He's more friends with Katya.'

Bazarov felt irritated. 'A woman can't help humbugging, of course!' he thought. 'You say he used to avoid you,' he said aloud, with a chilly smile; 'but it is probably no secret to you that he was in love with you?'

'What! he too?' fell from Anna Sergyevna's lips.

'He too,' repeated Bazarov, with a submissive bow. 'Can it be you didn't know it, and I've told you something new?'

Anna Sergyevna dropped her eyes. 'You are mistaken, Yevgeny Vassilyitch.'

'I don't think so. But perhaps I ought not to have mentioned it.' 'And don't you try telling me lies again for the future,' he added to himself.

'Why not? But I imagine that in this too you are attributing too much importance to a passing impression. I begin to suspect you are inclined to exaggeration.'

'We had better not talk about it, Anna Sergyevna.'

'Oh, why?' she retorted; but she herself led the conversation into another channel. She was still ill at ease with Bazarov, though she had told him, and assured herself that everything was forgotten. While she was exchanging the simplest sentences with him, even while she was jesting with him, she was conscious of a faint spasm of dread. So people on a steamer at sea talk and laugh carelessly, for all the world as though they were on dry land; but let only the slightest hitch occur, let the least sign be seen of anything out of the common, and at once on every face there comes out an expression of peculiar alarm, betraying the constant consciousness of constant danger.

Anna Sergyevna's conversation with Bazarov did not last long. She began to seem absorbed in thought, answered abstractedly, and suggested at last that they should go into the hall, where they found the princess and Katya. 'But where is Arkady Nikolaitch?' inquired the lady of the house; and on hearing that he had not shown himself for more than an hour, she sent for him. He was not very quickly found; he had hidden himself in the very thickest part of the garden, and with his chin propped on his folded hands, he was sitting lost in meditation. They were deep and serious meditations, but not mournful. He knew Anna Sergyevna was sitting alone with Bazarov, and he felt no jealousy, as once he had; on the contrary, his face slowly brightened; he seemed to be at once wondering and rejoicing, and resolving on something.

CHAPTER XXVI

THE deceased Odintsov had not liked innovations, but he had tolerated 'the fine arts within a certain sphere,' and had in consequence put up in his garden, between the hothouse and the lake, an erection after the fashion of a Greek temple, made of Russian brick. Along the dark wall at the back of this temple or gallery were placed six niches for statues, which Odintsov had proceeded to order from abroad. These statues were to represent Solitude, Silence, Meditation, Melancholy, Modesty, and Sensibility. One of them, the goddess of Silence, with her finger on her lip, had been sent and put up; but on the very same day some boys on the farm had broken her nose; and though a plasterer of the neighbourhood undertook to make her a new nose 'twice as good as the old one,' Odintsov ordered her to be taken away, and she was still to be seen in the corner of the threshing barn, where she had stood many long years, a source of superstitious terror to the peasant women. The front part of the temple had long ago been overgrown with thick bushes; only the pediments of the columns could be seen above the dense green. In the temple itself it was cool even at mid-day. Anna Sergyevna had not liked visiting this place ever since she had seen a snake there; but Katya often came and sat on the wide stone seat under one of the niches. Here, in the midst of the shade and coolness, she used to read and work, or to give herself up to that sensation of perfect peace, known, doubtless, to each of us, the charm of which consists in the half-unconscious, silent listening to the vast current of life that flows for ever both around us and within us.

The day after Bazarov's arrival Katya was sitting on her favourite stone seat, and beside her again was sitting Arkady. He had besought her to come with him to the 'temple.'

There was about an hour still to lunch-time; the dewy morning had already given place to a sultry day. Arkady's face retained the expression of the preceding day; Katya had a preoccupied look. Her sister had, directly after their morning tea, called her into her room, and after some preliminary caresses, which always scared Katya a little, she had advised her to be more guarded in her behaviour with Arkady, and especially to avoid solitary talks with him, as likely to attract the notice of her aunt and all the household. Besides this, even the previous evening Anna Sergyevna had not been herself; and Katya herself had felt ill at ease, as though she were conscious of some fault in herself. As she yielded to Arkady's entreaties, she said to herself that it was for the last time.

'Katerina Sergyevna,' he began with a sort of bashful easiness, 'since I've had the happiness of living in the same house with you, I have discussed a great many things with you; but meanwhile there is one, very important . . . for me . . . one question, which I have not touched upon up till now. You remarked yesterday that I have been changed here,' he went on, at once catching and avoiding the questioning glance Katya was turning upon him. 'I have changed certainly a great deal, and you know that better than any one else—you to whom I really owe this change.'

'I? . . . Me? . . . ' said Katya.

'I am not now the conceited boy I was when I came here,' Arkady went on. 'I've not reached twenty-three for nothing; as before, I want to be useful, I want to devote all my powers to the truth; but I no longer look for my ideals where I did; they present themselves to me . . . much closer to hand. Up till now I did not understand myself; I set myself tasks which were beyond my powers. . . . My eyes have been opened lately, thanks to one feeling. . . . I'm not expressing myself quite clearly, but I hope you understand me.'

Katya made no reply, but she ceased looking at Arkady.

'I suppose,' he began again, this time in a more agitated voice, while above his head a chaffinch sang its song unheeding among the leaves of the birch—'I suppose it's the duty of every one to be open with those . . . with those people who . . . in fact, with those who are near to him, and so I . . . I resolved . . .'

But here Arkady's eloquence deserted him; he lost the thread, stammered, and was forced to be silent for a moment. Katya still did not raise her eyes. She seemed not to understand what he was leading up to in all this, and to be waiting for something.

'I foresee I shall surprise you,' began Arkady, pulling himself together again with an effort, 'especially since this feeling relates in a way . . . in a way, notice . . . to you. You reproached me, if you remember, yesterday with a want of seriousness,' Arkady went on, with the air of a man who has got into a bog, feels that he is sinking further and further in at every step, and yet hurries onwards in the hope of crossing it as soon as possible; 'that reproach is often aimed . . . often falls . . . on young men even when they cease to deserve it; and if I had more self-confidence . . .' ('Come, help me, do help me!' Arkady was thinking, in desperation; but, as before, Katya did not turn her head.) 'If I could hope . . .'

'If I could feel sure of what you say,' was heard at that instant the clear voice of Anna Sergyevna.

Arkady was still at once, while Katya turned pale. Close by the bushes that screened the temple ran a little path. Anna Sergyevna was walking along it escorted by Bazarov. Katya and Arkady could not see them, but they heard every word, the rustle of their clothes, their very breathing. They walked on a few steps, and, as though on purpose, stood still just opposite the temple.

'You see,' pursued Anna Sergyevna, 'you and I made a mistake; we are both past our first youth, I especially so; we have seen life, we are tired; we are both—why affect not to know it?—clever; at first we interested each other, curiosity was aroused . . . and then . . .'

'And then I grew stale,' put in Bazarov.

'You know that was not the cause of our misunderstanding. But, however, it was to be, we had no need of one another, that's the chief point; there was too much . . . what shall I say? . . . that was alike in us. We did not realise it all at once. Now, Arkady . . .'

'So you need him?' queried Bazarov.

'Hush, Yevgeny Vassilyitch. You tell me he is not indifferent to me, and it always seemed to me he liked me. I know that I might well be his aunt, but I don't wish to conceal from you that I have come to think more often of him. In such youthful, fresh feeling there is a special charm . . .'

'The word *fascination* is most usual in such cases,' Bazarov interrupted; the effervescence of his spleen could be heard in his choked though steady voice. 'Arkady was mysterious over something with me yesterday, and didn't talk either of you or your sister. . . . That's a serious symptom.'

'He is just like a brother with Katya,' commented Anna Sergyevna, 'and I like that in him, though, perhaps, I ought not to have allowed such intimacy between them.'

'That idea is prompted by . . . your feelings as a sister?' Bazarov brought out, drawling.

'Of course . . . but why are we standing still? Let us go on. What a strange talk we are having, aren't we? I could never have believed I should talk to you like this. You know, I am afraid of you . . . and at the same time I trust you, because in reality you are so good.'

'In the first place, I am not in the least good; and in the second place, I have lost all significance for you, and you tell me I am good. . . . It's like a laying a wreath of flowers on the head of a corpse.'

'Yevgeny Vassilyitch, we are not responsible . . .' Anna Sergyevna began; but a gust of wind blew across, set the leaves rustling, and carried away her words. 'Of course, you are free . . .' Bazarov declared after a brief pause. Nothing more could be distinguished; the steps retreated . . . everything was still.

Arkady turned to Katya. She was sitting in the same position, but her head was bent still lower. 'Katerina Sergyevna,' he said with a shaking voice, and clasping his hands tightly together, 'I love you for ever and irrevocably, and I love no one but you. I wanted to tell you this, to find out your opinion of me, and to ask for your hand, since I am not rich, and I feel ready for any sacrifice. . . . You don't answer me? You don't believe me? Do you think I speak lightly? But remember these last days! Surely for a long time past you must have known that everything—understand me—everything else has vanished long ago and left no trace?

Look at me, say one word to me . . . I love . . . I love you . . . believe me!'

Katya glanced at Arkady with a bright and serious look, and after long hesitation, with the faintest smile, she said, 'Yes.'

Arkady leapt up from the stone seat. 'Yes! You said Yes, Katerina Sergyevna! What does that word mean? Only that I do love you, that you believe me . . . or . . . or . . . I daren't go on . . .'

'Yes,' repeated Katya, and this time he understood her. He snatched her large beautiful hands, and, breathless with rapture, pressed them to his heart. He could scarcely stand on his feet, and could only repeat, 'Katya, Katya . . .' while she began weeping in a guileless way, smiling gently at her own tears. No one who has not seen those tears in the eyes of the beloved, knows yet to what a point, faint with shame and gratitude, a man may be happy on earth.

The next day, early in the morning, Anna Sergyevna sent to summon Bazarov to her boudoir, and with a forced laugh handed him a folded sheet of notepaper. It was a letter from Arkady; in it he asked for her sister's hand.

Bazarov quickly scanned the letter, and made an effort to control himself, that he might not show the malignant feeling which was instantaneously aflame in his breast.

'So that's how it is,' he commented; 'and you, I fancy, only yesterday imagined he loved Katerina Sergyevna as a brother. What are you intending to do now?'

'What do you advise me?' asked Anna Sergyevna, still laughing.

'Well, I suppose,' answered Bazarov, also with a laugh, though he felt anything but cheerful, and had no more inclination to laugh than she had; 'I suppose you ought to give the young people your blessing. It's a good match in every respect; Kirsanov's position is passable, he's the only son, and his father's a good-natured fellow, he won't try to thwart him.'

Madame Odintsov walked up and down the room. By turns her face flushed and grew pale. 'You think so,' she said. 'Well, I see no obstacles . . . I am glad for Katya. . . . and for Arkady Nikolaevitch too. Of course, I will wait for his father's answer. I will send him in person to him. But it turns out, you see, that I was right yesterday when I told you we were both old people. . . . How was it I saw nothing? That's what amazes me!' Anna Sergyevna laughed again, and quickly turned her head away.

'The younger generation have grown awfully sly,' remarked Bazarov, and he too laughed. 'Good-bye,' he began again after a short silence. 'I hope you will bring the matter to the most satisfactory conclusion; and I will rejoice from a distance.'

Madame Odintsov turned quickly to him. 'You are not going away? Why should you not stay *now?* Stay . . . it's exciting talking to you . . . one seems walking on the edge of a precipice. At first one feels timid, but one gains courage as one goes on. Do stay.'

'Thanks for the suggestion, Anna Sergyevna, and for your flattering opinion of my conversational talents. But I think I have already been moving too long in a sphere which is not my own. Flying fishes can hold out for a time in the air; but soon they must splash back into the water; allow me, too, to paddle in my own element.'

Madame Odintsov looked at Bazarov. His pale face was twitching with a bitter smile. 'This man did love me!' she thought, and she felt pity for him, and held out her hand to him with sympathy.

But he too understood her. 'No!' he said, stepping back a pace. 'I'm a poor man, but I've never taken charity so far. Good-bye, and good luck to you.'

'I am certain we are not seeing each other for the last time,' Anna Sergyevna declared with an unconscious gesture.

'Anything may happen!' answered Bazarov, and he bowed and went away.

'So you are thinking of making yourself a nest?' he said the same day to Arkady, as he packed his box, crouching on the floor. 'Well, it's a capital thing. But you needn't have been such a humbug. I expected something from you in quite another quarter. Perhaps, though, it took you by surprise yourself?'

'I certainly didn't expect this when I parted from you,' answered Arkady; 'but why are you a humbug yourself, call-

'You explain to me what your *mir* is,' Bazarov interrupted;
'and is it the same *mir* that is said to rest on three fishes?'

'That, little father, is the earth that rests on three fishes,'
the peasant would declare soothingly, in a kind of patriarchal, simple-hearted sing-song; 'and over against ours,
that's to say, the *mir,* we know there's the master's will;
wherefore you are our fathers. And the stricter the master's rule, the better for the peasant.'

After listening to such a reply one day, Bazarov shrugged
his shoulders contemptuously and turned away, while the
peasant sauntered slowly homewards.

'What was he talking about?' inquired another peasant of
middle age and surly aspect, who at a distance from the
door of his hut had been following his conversation with
Bazarov.—'Arrears? eh?'

'Arrears, no indeed, mate!' answered the first peasant, and
now there was no trace of patriarchal singsong in his voice;
on the contrary, there was a certain scornful gruffness to
be heard in it: 'Oh, he clacked away about something or
other; wanted to stretch his tongue a bit. Of course, he's
a gentleman; what does he understand?'

'What should he understand!' answered the other peasant,
and jerking back their caps and pushing down their belts,
they proceeded to deliberate upon their work and their wants.
Alas! Bazarov, shrugging his shoulders contemptuously,
Bazarov, who knew how to talk to peasants (as he had
boasted in his dispute with Pavel Petrovitch), did not in his
self-confidence even suspect that in their eyes he was all the
while something of the nature of a buffooning clown.

He found employment for himself at last, however. One
day Vassily Ivanovitch bound up a peasant's wounded leg
before him, but the old man's hands trembled, and he could
not manage the bandages; his son helped him, and from
time to time began to take a share in his practice, though at
the same time he was constantly sneering both at the remedies he himself advised and at his father, who hastened to
make use of them. But Bazarov's jeers did not in the least
perturb Vassily Ivanovitch; they were positively a comfort
to him. Holding his greasy dressing-gown across his
stomach with two fingers, and smoking his pipe, he used to

listen with enjoyment to Bazarov; and the more malicious
his sallies, the more good-humouredly did his delighted
father chuckle, showing every one of his black teeth. He
used even to repeat these sometimes flat or pointless retorts,
and would, for instance, for several days constantly without
rhyme or reason, reiterate, 'Not a matter of the first importance!' simply because his son, on hearing he was going
to matins, had made use of that expression. 'Thank God!
he has got over his melancholy!' he whispered to his wife;
'how he gave it to me to-day, it was splendid!' Moreover,
the idea of having such an assistant excited him to ecstasy,
filled him with pride. 'Yes, yes,' he would say to some peasant woman in a man's cloak, and a cap shaped like a horn,
as he handed her a bottle of Goulard's extract or a box of
white ointment, 'you ought to be thanking God, my good
woman, every minute that my son is staying with me; you
will be treated now by the most scientific, most modern
method. Do you know what that means? The Emperor
of the French, Napoleon, even, has no better doctor.' And
the peasant woman, who had come to complain that she felt
so sort of queer all over (the exact meaning of these words
she was not able, however, herself to explain), merely
bowed low and rummaged in her bosom, where four eggs
lay tied up in the corner of a towel.

Bazarov once even pulled out a tooth for a passing pedlar
of cloth; and though this tooth was an average specimen,
Vassily Ivanovitch preserved it as a curiosity, and incessantly repeated, as he showed it to Father Alexey, 'Just look,
what a fang! The force Yevgeny has! The pedlar seemed
to leap into the air. If it had been an oak, he'd have rooted
it up!'

'Most promising!' Father Alexey would comment at last,
not knowing what answer to make, and how to get rid of the
ecstatic old man.

One day a peasant from a neighbouring village brought his
brother to Vassily Ivanovitch, ill with typhus. The unhappy
man, lying flat on a truss of straw, was dying; his body was
covered with dark patches, he had long ago lost consciousness. Vassily Ivanovitch expressed his regret that no one
had taken steps to procure medical aid sooner, and declared

there was no hope. And, in fact, the peasant did not get his brother home again; he died in the cart.

Three days later Bazarov came into his father's room and asked him if he had any caustic.

'Yes; what do you want it for?'

'I must have some . . . to burn a cut.'

'For whom?'

'For myself.'

'What, yourself? Why is that? What sort of a cut? Where is it?'

'Look here, on my finger. I went to-day to the village, you know, where they brought that peasant with typhus fever. They were just going to open the body for some reason or other, and I've had no practice of that sort for a long while.'

'Well?'

'Well, so I asked the district doctor about it; and so I dissected it.'

Vassily Ivanovitch all at once turned quite white, and, without uttering a word, rushed to his study, from which he returned at once with a bit of caustic in his hand. Bazarov was about to take it and go away.

'For mercy's sake,' said Vassily Ivanovitch, 'let me do it myself.'

Bazarov smiled. 'What a devoted practitioner!'

'Don't laugh, please. Show me your finger. The cut is not a large one. Do I hurt?'

'Press harder; don't be afraid.'

Vassily Ivanovitch stopped. 'What do you think, Yevgeny; wouldn't it be better to burn it with hot iron?'

'That ought to have been done sooner; the caustic even is useless, really, now. If I've taken the infection, it's too late now.'

'How . . . too late . . .' Vassily Ivanovitch could scarcely articulate the words.

'I should think so! It's more than four hours ago.'

Vassily Ivanovitch burnt the cut a little more. 'But had the district doctor no caustic?'

'No.'

'How was that, good Heavens? A doctor not have such an indispensable thing as that!'

'You should have seen his lancets,' observed Bazarov as he walked away.

Up till late that evening, and all the following day, Vassily Ivanovitch kept catching at every possible excuse to go into his son's room; and though far from referring to the cut—he even tried to talk about the most irrelevant subjects —he looked so persistently into his face, and watched him in such trepidation, that Bazarov lost patience and threatened to go away. Vassily Ivanovitch gave him a promise not to bother him, the more readily as Arina Vlasyevna, from whom, of course, he kept it all secret, was beginning to worry him as to why he did not sleep, and what had come over him. For two whole days he held himself in, though he did not at all like the look of his son, whom he kept watching stealthily, . . . but on the third day, at dinner, he could bear it no longer. Bazarov sat with downcast looks, and had not touched a single dish.

'Why don't you eat, Yevgeny?' he inquired, putting on an expression of the most perfect carelessness. 'The food, I think, is very nicely cooked.'

'I don't want anything, so I don't eat.'

'Have you no appetite? And your head?' he added timidly; 'does it ache?'

'Yes. Of course, it aches.'

Arina Vlasyevna sat up and was all alert.

'Don't be angry, please, Yevgeny,' continued Vassily Ivanovitch; 'won't you let me feel your pulse?'

Bazarov got up. 'I can tell you without feeling my pulse; I'm feverish.'

'Has there been any shivering?'

'Yes, there has been shivering too. I'll go and lie down, and you can send me some lime-flower tea. I must have caught cold.'

'To be sure, I heard you coughing last night,' observed Arina Vlasyevna.

'I've caught cold,' repeated Bazarov, and he went away.

Arina Vlasyevna busied herself about the preparation of the decoction of lime-flowers, while Vassily Ivanovitch went into the next room and clutched at his hair in silent desperation.

Bazarov did not get up again that day, and passed the whole night in heavy, half-unconscious torpor. At one o'clock in the morning, opening his eyes with an effort, he saw by the light of a lamp his father's pale face bending over him, and told him to go away. The old man begged his pardon, but he quickly came back on tiptoe, and half-hidden by the cupboard door, he gazed persistently at his son. Arina Vlasyevna did not go to bed either, and leaving the study door just open a very little, she kept coming up to it to listen 'how Enyusha was breathing,' and to look at Vassily Ivanovitch. She could see nothing but his motion-less bent back, but even that afforded her some faint con-solation. In the morning Bazarov tried to get up; he was seized with giddiness, his nose began to bleed; he lay down again. Vassily Ivanovitch waited on him in silence; Arina Vlasyevna went in to him and asked him how he was feeling. He answered, 'Better,' and turned to the wall. Vassily Ivanovitch gesticulated at his wife with both hands; she bit her lips so as not to cry, and went away. The whole house seemed suddenly darkened; every one looked gloomy; there was a strange hush; a shrill cock was carried away from the yard to the village, unable to comprehend why he should be treated so. Bazarov still lay, turned to the wall. Vassily Ivanovitch tried to address him with various questions, but they fatigued Bazarov, and the old man sank into his arm-chair, motionless, only cracking his finger-joints now and then. He went for a few minutes into the garden, stood there like a statue, as though overwhelmed with unutterable bewilderment (the expression of amazement never left his face all through), and went back again to his son, trying to avoid his wife's questions. She caught him by the arm at last, and passionately, almost menacingly, said, 'What is wrong with him?' Then he came to himself, and forced himself to smile at her in reply; but to his own horror, instead of a smile, he found himself taken somehow by a fit of laughter. He had sent at daybreak for a doctor. He thought it necessary to inform his son of this, for fear he should be angry. Bazarov suddenly turned over on the ' sofa, bent a fixed dull look on his father, and asked for drink.

S—14

Vassily Ivanovitch gave him some water, and as he did so felt his forehead. It seemed on fire.

'Governor,' began Bazarov, in a slow, drowsy voice; 'I'm in a bad way; I've got the infection, and in a few days you'll have to bury me.

Vassily Ivanovitch staggered back, as though some one had aimed a blow at his legs.

'Yevgeny!' he faltered; 'what do you mean! . . . God have mercy on you! You've caught cold!'

'Hush!' Bazarov interposed deliberately. 'A doctor can't be allowed to talk like that. There's every symptom of infection; you know yourself.'

'Where are the symptoms . . . of infection Yevgeny? . . . Good Heavens!'

'What's this?' said Bazarov, and, pulling up his shirt-sleeve, he showed his father the ominous red patches coming out on his arm.

Vassily Ivanovitch was shaking and chill with terror.

'Supposing,' he said at last, 'even supposing . . . if even there's something like . . . infection . . .'

'Pyæmia,' put in his son.

'Well, well . . . something of the epidemic . . .'

'Pyæmia,' Bazarov repeated sharply and distinctly; 'have you forgotten your text-books?'

'Well, well—as you like. . . . Anyway, we will cure you!'

'Come, that's humbug. But that's not the point. I didn't expect to die so soon; it's a most unpleasant incident, to tell the truth. You and mother ought to make the most of your strong religious belief; now's the time to put it to the test.' He drank off a little water. 'I want to ask you about one thing . . . while my head is still under my control. To-morrow or next day my brain, you know, will send in its resignation. I'm not quite certain even now whether I'm expressing myself clearly. While I've been lying here, I've kept fancying red dogs were running round me, while you were making them point at me, as if I were a woodcock. Just as if I were drunk. Do you understand me all right?'

'I assure you, Yevgeny, you are talking perfectly correctly.'

'All the better. You told me you'd sent for the doctor. You did that to comfort yourself . . . comfort me too; send a messenger . . .'

'To Arkady Nikolaitch?' put in the old man.

'Who's Arkady Nikolaitch?' said Bazarov, as though in doubt. . . . 'Oh, yes! that chicken! No, let him alone; he's turned jackdaw now. Don't be surprised; that's not delirium yet. You send a messenger to Madame Odintsov, Anna Sergyevna; she's a lady with an estate. . . . Do you know?' (Vassily Ivanovitch nodded.) 'Yevgeny Bazarov, say, sends his greetings, and sends word he is dying. Will you do that?'

'Yes, I will do it. . . . But is it a possible thing for you to die, Yevgeny? . . . Think only! Where would divine justice be after that?'

'I know nothing about that; only you send the messenger.'

'I'll send this minute, and I'll write a letter myself.'

'No, why? Say I sent greetings; nothing more is necessary. And now I'll go back to my dogs. Strange! I want to fix my thoughts on death, and nothing comes of it. I see a kind of blur . . . and nothing more.'

He turned painfully back to the wall again; while Vassily Ivanovitch went out of the study, and struggling as far as his wife's bedroom, simply dropped down on to his knees before the holy pictures.

'Pray, Arina, pray for us!' he moaned; 'our son is dying.'

The doctor, the same district doctor who had had no caustic, arrived, and after looking at the patient, advised them to persevere with a cooling treatment, and at that point said a few words of the chance of recovery.

'Have you ever chanced to see people in my state *not* set off for Elysium?' asked Bazarov, and suddenly snatching the leg of a heavy table that stood near his sofa, he swung it round, and pushed it away. 'There's strength, there's strength,' he murmured; 'everything's here still, and I must die! . . . An old man at least has time to be weaned from life, but I . . . Well, go and try to disprove death. Death will disprove you, and that's all! Who's crying there?' he added, after a short pause.—'Mother? Poor thing! Whom will she feed now with her exquisite beetroot-soup? You,

Vassily Ivanovitch, whimpering too, I do believe! Why, if Christianity's no help to you, be a philosopher, a Stoic, or what not! Why, didn't you boast you were a philosopher?'

'Me a philosopher!' wailed Vassily Ivanovitch, while the tears fairly streamed down his cheeks.

Bazarov got worse every hour; the progress of the disease was rapid, as is usually the way in cases of surgical poisoning. He still had not lost consciousness, and understood what was said to him; he was still struggling. 'I don't want to lose my wits,' he muttered, clenching his fists; 'what rot it all is!' And at once he would say, 'Come, take ten from eight, what remains?' Vassily Ivanovitch wandered about like one possessed, proposed first one remedy, then another, and ended by doing nothing but cover up his son's feet. 'Try cold pack . . . emetic . . . mustard plasters on the stomach . . . bleeding,' he would murmur with an effort. The doctor, whom he had entreated to remain, agreed with him, ordered the patient lemonade to drink, and for himself asked for a pipe and something 'warming and strengthening'—that's to say, brandy. Arina Vlasyevna sat on a low stool near the door, and only went out from time to time to pray. A few days before, a looking-glass had slipped out of her hands and been broken, and this she had always considered an omen of evil; even Anfisushka could say nothing to her. Timofeitch had gone off to Madame Odintsov's.

The night passed badly for Bazarov. . . . He was in the agonies of high fever. Towards morning he was a little easier. He asked for Arina Vlasyevna to comb his hair, kissed her hand, and swallowed two gulps of tea. Vassily Ivanovitch revived a little.

'Thank God!' he kept declaring; 'the crisis is coming, the crisis is at hand!'

'There, to think now!' murmured Bazarov; 'what a word can do! He's found it; he's said "crisis," and is comforted. It's an astounding thing how man believes in words. If he's told he's a fool, for instance, though he's not thrashed, he'll be wretched; call him a clever fellow, and he'll be delighted if you go off without paying him.'

This little speech of Bazarov's, recalling his old retorts, moved Vassily Ivanovitch greatly.

'Bravo! well said, very good!' he cried, making as though he were clapping his hands.

Bazarov smiled mournfully.

'So what do you think,' he said; 'is the crisis over, or coming?'

'You are better, that's what I see, that's what rejoices me,' answered Vassily Ivanovitch.

'Well, that's good; rejoicings never come amiss. And to her, do you remember? did you send?'

'To be sure I did.'

The change for the better did not last long. The disease resumed its onslaughts. Vassily Ivanovitch was sitting by Bazarov. It seemed as though the old man were tormented by some special anguish. He was several times on the point of speaking—and could not.

'Yevgeny!' he brought out at last; 'my son, my one, dear son!'

This unfamiliar mode of address produced an effect on Bazarov. He turned his head a little, and, obviously trying to fight against the load of oblivion weighing upon him, he articulated: 'What is it, father?'

'Yevgeny,' Vassil Ivanovitch went on, and he fell on his knees before Bazarov, though the latter had closed his eyes and could not see him. 'Yevgeny, you are better now; please God, you will get well, but make use of this time, comfort your mother and me, perform the duty of a Christian! What it means for me to say this to you, it's awful; but still more awful . . . for ever and ever, Yevgeny . . . think a little, what . . .'

The old man's voice broke, and a strange look passed over his son's face, though he still lay with closed eyes.

'I won't refuse, if that can be any comfort to you,' he brought out at last; 'but it seems to me there's no need to be in a hurry. You say yourself I am better.'

'Oh, yes, Yevgeny, better certainly; but who knows, it is all in God's hands, and in doing the duty . . .'

'No, I will wait a bit,' broke in Bazarov. 'I agree with you that the crisis has come. And if we're mistaken, well! they give the sacrament to men who're unconscious, you know.'

'Yevgeny, I beg.'

'I'll wait a little. And now I want to go to sleep. Don't disturb me.' And he laid his head back on the pillow.

The old man rose from his knees, sat down in the arm-chair, and, clutching his beard, began biting his own fingers . . .

The sound of a light carriage on springs, that sound which is peculiarly impressive in the wilds of the country, suddenly struck upon his hearing. Nearer and nearer rolled the light wheels; now even the neighing of the horses could be heard. . . . Vassily Ivanovitch jumped up and ran to the little window. There drove into the courtyard of his little house a carriage with seats for two, with four horses harnessed abreast. Without stopping to consider what it could mean, with a rush of a sort of senseless joy, he ran out on to the steps. . . . A groom in livery was opening the carriage doors; a lady in a black veil and a black mantle was getting out of it . . .

'I am Madame Odintsov,' she said. 'Yevgeny Vassilvitch is still living? You are his father? I have a doctor with me.'

'Benefactress!' cried Vassily Ivanovitch, and snatching her hand, he pressed it convulsively to his lips, while the doctor brought by Anna Sergyevna, a little man in spectacles, of German physiognomy, stepped very deliberately out of the carriage. 'Still living, my Yevgeny is living, and now he will be saved! Wife! wife! . . . An angel from heaven has come to us. . . .'

'What does it mean, good Lord!' faltered the old woman, running out of the drawing-room; and, comprehending nothing, she fell on the spot in the passage at Anna Sergyevna's feet, and began kissing her garments like a mad woman.

'What are you doing!' protested Anna Sergyevna; but Arina Vlasyevna did not heed her, while Vassily Ivanovitch could only repeat, 'An angel! an angel!'

'*Wo ist der Kranke?* and where is the patient?' said the doctor at last, with some impatience.

Vassily Ivanovitch recovered himself. 'Here, here, follow me, würdigster Herr Collega,' he added through old associations.

'Ah!' articulated the German, grinning sourly.

Vassily Ivanovitch led him into the study. 'The doctor

from Anna Sergyevna Odintsov,' he said, bending down quite
to his son's ear, 'and she herself is here.'

Bazarov suddenly opened his eyes. 'What did you say?'

'I say that Anna Sergyevna is here, and has brought this
gentleman, a doctor, to you.'

Bazarov moved his eyes about him. 'She is here. . . .
I want to see her.'

'You shall see her, Yevgeny; but first we must have a little
talk with the doctor. I will tell him the whole history of
your illness since Sidor Sidoritch' (this was the name of the
district doctor) 'has gone, and we will have a little consultation.'

Bazarov glanced at the German. 'Well, talk away quickly,
only not in Latin; you see, I know the meaning of *jam
moritur.*'

'*Der Herr scheint des Deutschen mächtig zu sein,*' began
the new follower of Æsculapius, turning to Vassily Ivanovitch.

'*Ich . . . gabe . . .* We had better speak Russian,' said
the old man.

'Ah, ah! so that's how it is. . . . To be sure . . .' And
the consultation began.

Half-an-hour later Anna Sergyevna, conducted by Vassily
Ivanovitch, came into the study. The doctor had had time
to whisper to her that it was hopeless even to think of the
patient's recovery.

She looked at Bazarov . . . and stood still in the doorway,
so greatly was she impressed by the inflamed, and at the
same time deathly face, with its dim eyes fastened upon her.
She felt simply dismayed, with a sort of cold and suffocating
dismay; the thought that she would not have felt like that
if she had really loved him flashed instantaneously through
her brain.

'Thanks,' he said painfully, 'I did not expect this. It's a
deed of mercy. So we have seen each other again, as you
promised.'

'Anna Sergyevna has been so kind,' began Vassily Ivanovitch . . .

'Father, leave us alone. Anna Sergyevna, you will allow
it, I fancy, now?'

With a motion of his head, he indicated his prostrate help-
less frame.

Vassily Ivanovitch went out.

'Well, thanks,' repeated Bazarov. 'This is royally done.
Monarchs, they say, visit the dying too.'

'Yevgeny Vassilyitch, I hope——'

'Ah, Anna Sergyevna, let us speak the truth. It's all over
with me. I'm under the wheel. So it turns out that it was
useless to think of the future. Death's an old joke, but it
comes fresh to every one. So far I'm not afraid . . . but
there, senselessness is coming, and then it's all up!——' he
waved his hand feebly. 'Well, what had I to say to you . . .
I loved you! there was no sense in that even before, and less
than ever now. Love is a form, and my own form is already
breaking up. Better say how lovely you are! And now
here you stand, so beautiful . . .'

Anna Sergyevna gave an involuntary shudder.

'Never mind, don't be uneasy. . . . Sit down there. . . .
Don't come close to me; you know, my illness is catching.'

Anna Sergyevna swiftly crossed the room, and sat down
in the armchair near the sofa on which Bazarov was lying.

'Noble-hearted!' he whispered. 'Oh, how near, and how
young, and fresh, and pure . . . in this loathsome room!
. . . Well, good-bye! live long, that's the best of all, and
make the most of it while there is time. You see what a
hideous spectacle; the worm half-crushed, but writhing still.
And, you see, I thought too: I'd break down so many things,
I wouldn't die, why should I! there were problems to solve,
and I was a giant! And now all the problem for the giant
is how to die decently, though that makes no difference to
any one either. . . . Never mind; I'm not going to turn tail.'

Bazarov was silent, and began feeling with his hand for
the glass. Anna Sergyevna gave him some drink, not taking
off her glove, and drawing her breath timorously.

'You will forget me,' he began again; 'the dead's no companion for the living. My father will tell you what a man
Russia is losing. . . . That's nonsense, but don't contradict
the old man. Whatever toy will comfort the child . . .
you know. And be kind to mother. People like them
aren't to be found in your great world if you look by daylight

with a candle. . . . I was needed by Russia. . . . No, it's
clear, I wasn't needed. And who is needed? The shoemaker's needed, the tailor's needed, the butcher . . . gives
us meat . . . the butcher . . . wait a little, I'm getting mixed.
. . . There's a forest here . . .'

Bazarov put his hand to his brow.

Anna Sergyevna bent down to him. 'Yevgeny Vassilyitch,
I am here . . .'

He at once took his hand away, and raised himself.

'Good-bye,' he said with sudden force, and his eyes gleamed
with their last light. 'Good-bye. . . . Listen . . . you know
I didn't kiss you then. . . . Breathe on the dying lamp, and
let it go out . . .'

Anna Sergyevna put her lips to his forehead.

'Enough!' he murmured, and dropped back on to the pillow.
'Now . . . darkness . . .'

Anna Sergyevna went softly out. 'Well?' Vassily Ivanovitch asked her in a whisper.

'He has fallen asleep,' she answered, hardly audibly.
Bazarov was not fated to awaken. Towards evening he
sank into complete unconsciousness, and the following day
he died. Father Alexey performed the last rites of religion
over him. When they anointed him with the last unction,
when the holy oil touched his breast, one eye opened, and it
seemed as though at the sight of the priest in his vestments,
the smoking censers, the light before the image, something
like a shudder of horror passed over the death-stricken face.
When at last he had breathed his last, and there arose a universal lamentation in the house, Vassily Ivanovitch was
seized by a sudden frenzy. 'I said I should rebel,' he
shrieked hoarsely, with his face inflamed and distorted, shaking his fist in the air, as though threatening some one; 'and
I rebel, I rebel!' But Arina Vlasyevna, all in tears, hung
upon his neck, and both fell on their faces together. 'Side
by side,' Anfisushka related afterwards in the servants' room,
'they dropped their poor heads like lambs at noonday . . .'

But the heat of noonday passes, and evening comes and
night, and then, too, the return to the kindly refuge, where
sleep is sweet for the weary and heavy laden. . . .

CHAPTER XXVIII

SIX months had passed by. White winter had come with the cruel stillness of unclouded frosts, the thick-lying, crunching snow, the rosy rime on the trees, the pale emerald sky, the wreaths of smoke above the chimneys, the clouds of steam rushing out of the doors when they are opened for an instant, with the fresh faces, that look stung by the cold, and the hurrying trot of the chilled horses. A January day was drawing to its close; the cold evening was more keen than ever in the motionless air, and a lurid sunset was rapidly dying away. There were lights burning in the windows of the house at Maryino; Prokofitch in a black frockcoat and white gloves, with a special solemnity, laid the table for seven. A week before in the small parish church two weddings had taken place quietly, and almost without witnesses—Arkady and Katya's, and Nikolai Petrovitch and Fenitchka's; and on this day Nikolai Petrovitch was giving a farewell dinner to his brother, who was going away to Moscow on business. Anna Sergyevna had gone there also directly after the ceremony was over, after making very handsome presents to the young people.

Precisely at three o'clock they all gathered about the table. Mitya was placed there too; with him appeared a nurse in a cap of glazed brocade. Pavel Petrovitch took his seat between Katya and Fenitchka; the 'husbands' took their places beside their wives. Our friends had changed of late; they all seemed to have grown stronger and better looking; only Pavel Petrovitch was thinner, which gave even more of an elegant and 'grand seigneur' air to his expressive features. . . . And Fenitchka too was different. In a fresh silk gown, with a wide velvet head-dress on her hair, with a gold chain round her neck, she sat with deprecating immobility, respectful towards herself and everything surrounding her, and smiled as though she would say, 'I beg your pardon; I'm not to blame.' And not she alone—all the others smiled, and also seemed apologetic; they were all a little awkward, a little sorry, and in reality very happy. They all helped one another with humorous attentiveness, as though they had all agreed to rehearse a sort of artless farce. Katya was the most composed of all; she looked confidently about her, and it could be seen that Nikolai Petrovitch was already devotedly fond of her. At the end of dinner he got up, and, his glass in his hand, turned to Pavel Petrovitch.

'You are leaving us . . . you are leaving us, dear brother,' he began; 'not for long, to be sure; but still, I cannot help expressing what I . . . what we . . . how much I . . . how much we. . . . There, the worst of it is, we don't know how to make speeches. Arkady, you speak.'

'No, daddy, I've not prepared anything.'

'As though I were so well prepared! Well, brother, I will simply say, let us embrace you, wish you all good luck, and come back to us as quickly as you can!'

Pavel Petrovitch exchanged kisses with every one, of course not excluding Mitya; in Fenitchka's case, he kissed also her hand, which she had not yet learned to offer properly, and drinking off the glass which had been filled again, he said with a deep sigh, 'May you be happy, my friends! *Farewell!*' This English finale passed unnoticed; but all were touched.

'To the memory of Bazarov,' Katya whispered in her husband's ear, as she clinked glasses with him. Arkady pressed her hand warmly in response, but he did not venture to propose this toast aloud.

The end, would it seem? But perhaps some one of our readers would care to know what each of the characters we have introduced is doing in the present, the actual present. We are ready to satisfy him.

Anna Sergyevna has recently made a marriage, not of love but of good sense, with one of the future leaders of Russia, a very clever man, a lawyer, possessed of vigorous practical sense, a strong will, and remarkable fluency—still young, good-natured, and cold as ice. They live in the greatest harmony together, and will live perhaps to attain complete happiness . . . perhaps love. The Princess K—— is dead, forgotten the day of her death. The Kirsanovs, father

and son, live at Maryino; their fortunes are beginning to
mend. Arkady has become zealous in the management of the
estate, and the 'farm' now yields a fairly good income. Nikolai Petrovitch has been made one of the mediators appointed
to carry out the emancipation reforms, and works with all
his energies; he is for ever driving about over his district;
delivers long speeches (he maintains the opinion that the
peasants ought to be 'brought to comprehend things,' that is
to say, they ought to be reduced to a state of quiescence by
the constant repetition of the same words); and yet, to tell
the truth, he does not give complete satisfaction either to the
refined gentry, who talk with *chic,* or depression of the
emancipation (pronouncing it as though it were French),
nor of the uncultivated gentry, who unceremoniously curse
'the damned *'mancipation.'* He is too soft-hearted for both
sets. Katerina Sergyevna has a son, little Nikolai, while
Mitya runs about merrily and talks fluently. Fenitchka,
Fedosya Nikolaevna, after her husband and Mitya, adores
no one so much as her daughter-in-law, and when the latter
is at the piano, she would gladly spend the whole day at her
side.

A passing word of Piotr. He has grown perfectly
rigid with stupidity and dignity, but he too is married, and
received a respectable dowry with his bride, the daughter
of a market-gardener of the town, who had refused two excellent suitors, only because they had no watch; while Piotr
had not only a watch—he had a pair of kid shoes.

In the Brühl Terrace in Dresden, between two and four
o'clock—the most fashionable time for walking—you may
meet a man about fifty, quite grey, and looking as though he
suffered from gout, but still handsome, elegantly dressed,
and with that special stamp, which is only gained by moving
a long time in the higher strata of society. That is Pavel
Petrovitch. From Moscow he went abroad for the sake of his
health, and has settled for good at Dresden, where he associates most with English and Russian visitors. With English
people he behaves simply, almost modestly, but with dignity;
they find him rather a bore, but respect him for being, as
they say, *'a perfect gentleman.'* With Russians he is more
free and easy, gives vent to his spleen, and makes fun of

himself and them, but that is done by him with great amiability, negligence, and propriety. He holds Slavophil views; it is well known that in the highest society this is regarded as *très distingué!* He reads nothing in Russian, but on his writing table there is a silver ashpan in the shape of a peasant's plaited shoe. He is much run after by our tourists. Matvy Ilyitch Kolyazin, happening to be in temporary opposition, paid him a majestic visit; while the natives, with whom, however, he is very little seen, positively grovel before him. No one can so readily and quickly obtain a ticket for the court chapel, for the theatre, and such things as *der Herr Baron von Kirsanoff*. He does everything good-naturedly that he can; he still makes some little noise in the world; it is not for nothing that he was once a great society lion;— but life is a burden to him . . . a heavier burden than he suspects himself. One need but glance at him in the Russian church, when, leaning against the wall on one side, he sinks into thought, and remains long without stirring, bitterly compressing his lips, then suddenly recollects himself, and begins almost imperceptibly crossing himself. . . .

Madame Kukshin, too, went abroad. She is in Heidelberg, and is now studying not natural science, but architecture, in which, according to her own account, she has discovered new laws. She still fraternises with students, especially with the young Russians studying natural science and chemistry, with whom Heidelberg is crowded, and who, astounding the naïve German professors at first by the soundness of their views of things, astound the same professors no less in the sequel by their complete inefficiency and absolute idleness. In company with two or three such young chemists, who don't know oxygen from nitrogen, but are filled with scepticism and self-conceit, and, too, with the great Elisyevitch, Sitnikov roams about Petersburg, also getting ready to be great, and in his own conviction continues the 'work' of Bazarov. There is a story that some one recently gave him a beating; but he was avenged upon him; in an obscure little article, hidden in an obscure little journal, he has hinted that the man who beat him was a coward. He calls this irony. His father bullies him as before, while his wife regards him as a fool . . . and a literary man.

There is a small village graveyard in one of the remote corners of Russia. Like almost all our graveyards, it presents a wretched appearance; the ditches surrounding it have long been overgrown; the grey wooden crosses lie fallen and rotting under their once painted gables; the stone slabs are all displaced, as though some one were pushing them up from behind; two or three bare trees give a scanty shade; the sheep wander unchecked among the tombs. . . . But among them is one untouched by man, untrampled by beast, only the birds perch upon it and sing at daybreak. An iron railing runs round it; two young fir-trees have been planted, one at each end. Yevgeny Bazarov is buried in this tomb. Often from the little village not far off, two quite feeble old people come to visit it—a husband and wife. Supporting one another, they move to it with heavy steps; they go up to the railing, fall down, and remain on their knees, and long and bitterly they weep, and yearn and intently gaze at the dumb stone, under which their son is lying; they exchange some brief word, wipe away the dust from the stone, set straight a branch of a fir-tree, and pray again, and cannot tear themselves from this place, where they seem to be nearer to their son, to their memories of him. . . . Can it be that their prayers, their tears are fruitless? Can it be that love, sacred, devoted love, is not all-powerful? Oh, no! However passionate, sinning, and rebellious the heart hidden in the tomb, the flowers growing over it peep serenely at us with their innocent eyes; they tell us not of eternal peace alone, of that great peace of 'indifferent' nature; tell us too of eternal reconciliation and of life without end.